Praise for In the Moors:

"A truly spooky story set in the Somerset Levels, which had me on the edge of my seat."

—Ali Bacon, author of _A Kettle of Fish_

"_In the Moors_ has a cracking pace, evocative landscapes, and a shocking twist at the end. I've rarely read depictions of shamanic journeying that have felt so authentic."

—Ronald Hutton, author of _The Triumph of the Moon_

IN THE MOORS

NINA MILTON

IN THE MOORS

A SHAMAN MYSTERY

MIDNIGHT INK
WOODBURY, MINNESOTA

FIRST EDITION
First Printing, 2013

Book format by Bob Gaul
Cover design by Ellen Lawson
Cover art © iStockphoto.com/3325683/biffspandex
Editing by Nicole Nugent

Midnight Ink, an imprint of Llewellyn Worldwide Ltd.

Library of Congress Cataloging-in-Publication Data
Milton, Nina.
  In the Moors: a shaman mystery/Nina Milton.—First edition.
    pages cm
  ISBN 978-0-7387-3836-9
1. Shamans—Fiction. 2. Mystery fiction. I. Title.
  PS3613.I59198I5 2013
  813'.6—dc23
                                    2013012266

Midnight Ink
Llewellyn Worldwide Ltd.
2143 Wooddale Drive
Woodbury, MN 55125-2989
www.midnightinkbooks.com

Printed in the United States of America

For the endurance of Jim.

PRELUDE

THE DETECTIVE SERGEANT ARRIVED on a squad bike, riding behind a rookie female officer. Not the coolest way to travel, or the safest—for the final remnants of the rough track, she cut the engine and let the bike roll forward until it came to a natural halt. He slid off the back and tested the squelching ground with his heel.

"Sir?" Gary Abbott, the detective constable that DS Buckley now worked with, loomed out of mist and darkness. The younger man had not zipped his coat, but his hands were rammed into the pockets, pulling it closed against the bitterness. Abbott was a new DC, just out of uniform, and Buckley hadn't jelled with him. Not entirely.

"What's up?"

"Not sure sir. White male out there, alone, suspicious behaviour."

"Where, for God's sake?"

They were miles from the the nearest village. The wetlands were blacked out by the night. Charcoal clouds scuttled across the sky, playing hide and seek with a waning moon. Then he saw it. The swing of a flashlight beam, swaying wildly.

"Got him."

Abbott handed him a pair of night-vision binoculars. Buckley slotted them to his eyes. It was hard to judge distance through the ghostly green glow. There was nothing but the vastness of the Somerset Moors, where gales blew so hard and long that the leafless trees grew at low angles. Reeds and rushes were the natural uprights in this world, unlike the metal spikes holding the police tape, which were sinking into the peat. The blue and white tape flapped in the wind like alien birds; even at this distance Buckley could hear it crack.

He made a steady scan of the cordoned area until he had a sharp picture. A figure loomed, swathed in scarves, bog water halfway to the tops of his rubber boots. He was standing within the forest of bulrushes thick as a man's thumb and as tall as a man's thigh. Through the binoculars, Buckley could clearly see the man was stroking the suede-like top of a bulrush as he stared at the shallow grave.

"He hasn't responded to our presence," said Abbott. "Not a flicker."

"What in hell is he doing, middle of the night?" murmured Buckley. "There's nothing out there now the body's been moved."

"Just a ghoul?" suggested the rookie officer, wrinkling her pretty nose.

"Eh?" said Abbott. There was a touch of fear at the back of the sound.

"Ghoul, Abbott." Buckley didn't lower the glasses as he spoke. "Misery tourist. Hangs round traffic incidents hoping to get a photo of gore on their phone. But this is no ghoul. Ghouls don't come after dark." Buckley felt, rather than saw, a movement in the taped area. The suspect was scrabbling in a pocket. A blade caught a glimmering of moonlight. "Ghouls don't carry knives."

"Knife?" came Abbott's voice. "Okay, he has a weapon. I say let Reece go straight in."

"Who is Reece?" asked Buckley, but before he received an answer he saw the German shepherd leap upon the man, fastening wolf-teeth through the layers of his sleeve. Buckley heard the snarl and the following cry, high with fright. Man and beast toppled into the reed bed. Mud oozed around them, sucking them down.

The rookie hefted her bike around and turned on the headlight, illuminating the scene.

Buckley snatched the glasses from his eyes. "Who said you could bring a fucking dog? What're you playing at?"

"He could be dangerous, boss."

"He's drowning in fucking shit, at the moment."

The handler had whistled his dog away by the time Buckley reached the man. The three officers dragged the suspect free, but it took long seconds to clear his airways. The thin man was babbling incoherently as they brought him to firmer ground. He clung to the bulrush like a talisman.

"Can you tell me your name, sir?" Abbott managed to give an emphasis to the word *sir* that fell just short of derision. Buckley let it go.

The man took a bubbling breath. "Cliff … Houghton."

"Okay. Mr. Houghton, you are under arrest." By the time Abbott had finished intoning the caution, they had levered him into the car that stood waiting, up track. Abbott, who could never resist the big gesture, leaned in and snatched the bulrush. "Bloody poof," he said.

Buckley watched the reed sail through the night like a lance. He swallowed the urge to tell their suspect that Abbott called everyone a poof.

The guy had seemed sublime for a moment when Buckley first saw him, walking on the water in this bitter place. Close up, covered in mire and eyes layered with terror, Cliff Houghton only looked sad.

Just a ghoul, probably.

ONE

I DIDN'T KNOW IT, but Cliff Houghton was already in police custody when I woke with a dreadful sensation at the back of my dry throat. It was too early on Saturday morning, and I had the hangover to prove it.

Ivan was curled into his own hollow, back towards me, head deep in the pillow. I wrapped my body around him like peel round fruit. It had been a deliciously late night, and I was too heavy-eyed to prevent the warm waves pulling me down.

You'll dream, Sabbie, girl, you know you will, I warned myself. *You always dream of the most horrid things when you slip back into sleep.*

I dreamt of the snarl of canine teeth, the fast flapping of wings, of being dragged, face down, through mud.

When I woke again, a cold but determined dawn was edging its way through closed curtains. I scribbled down a hazy account of my dream before it was gone forever. Then I pulled on the cosy, stretchy garments that are my garden clothes—the ones that get washed only when they walk to the washing machine on their own—and went out to collect the eggs.

At the henhouse door I dropped my empty basket and cried out in raw distress. Slaughter lay at my feet. Saffron, the biggest of my hens, was gone, and Pettitgrain, my favourite, lay in the run, dead from a clean bite to the neck.

The henhouse smelt of gore. Sickness swelled in my stomach, an expansion of loathing for the fox, no doubt now slumbering, replete. My brave cockerel, Cocky Bastard, who must have defended his harem to the last, lay on his side twitching steadily. I picked him up. His body was bloodied and broken. His eyes stared deep into mine. Quickly I broke his neck. The three remaining birds huddled in a corner making low, tense cluckings, as if they were discussing their traumatic night in hushed whispers.

"Sabbie! What's wrong?" Ivan teetered on the bit of paving outside my back door as if there was an invisible line that prevented him entering the working part of the garden. He'd pulled on my dressing gown, a shabby navy towelling affair, and stuffed his bare feet into his shoes. A layer of fresh-grown beard gave his face a dishevelled appeal. His unbrushed hair was the colour, length, and softness of a golden retriever's coat. I could see what had enticed me the previous night, which made for a change; I have this dreadful habit of going off the men I find in my bed.

"Fox damage."

"What damage?"

"I had a dream," I said. "But Mr. Reynard was long gone by then."

"These hens belong to you?"

"Ivan, would you stop asking brainless questions?"

"We're in the middle of a town. Whatever is the point in keeping hens?"

I gave him a watery smile. "If the fox hadn't come, you'd've eaten eggs for breakfast and been enchanted with their clucking."

"This takes some beating." He picked his way along the clipped grass path. "Can't remember the last time I saw a chicken … or a fox."

"Stick around until tonight, then. He'll be back for second helpings, no doubt. He thinks he's created a larder here. They're not as wasteful or barbaric as they're painted."

"Sabbie …" Ivan pretended to inspect the damage, while slipping an arm around my waist and nuzzling at my neck. "Come back to bed, huh?"

I liked the nuzzling, but it was the sensation round the waist that turned me into marshmallow. I suppose in times gone by, it was the closest the Victorian maiden was ever going to get to an orgasm. A delicious quiver ran through me. It was so tempting, the thought of my squashy duvet and Ivan, with his rough blond chin, tucked beneath it.

"I can't. I must fox-proof this housing before my eleven o'clock client arrives." I started chivvying Juniper, Ginger, and Melissa to the far end of their run, blocking their return with whatever came to hand. They looked terrified out of what were already very tiny minds. "You poor things," I told them over the barricade. "You're not going to be giving me eggs for a while, are you?"

"You *talk* to them?"

I pecked a kiss onto his neck. "Could you give me a hand?"

"You want me to get rid of that fox?"

"What're you talking about?"

"I've got an old air rifle in my attic." His mouth stretched into a smirk, clearly interpreting my perplexed look as admiration. "I could pop over and pick it up."

"Why would you need an air gun?"

"You said it yourself. He might fancy a return trip tonight. I'd be waiting for him."

"Oh, Ivan." I doubted that Mr. Reynard realized how much hate he engendered. "All he's doing is getting on with living. Just popping into Pizza Hut."

"You don't want him taken out?"

"What's this 'taken out' stuff? This is Somerset, not the hood!" I didn't tell him that I already had a plan in my head, to leave Pettitgrain's body by the back hedge. I hoped this would stop him coming closer and scaring my remaining flock. Even more secretly, I thought of it as the animal's due; he'd made his killing, fair and square, thanks to my negligence. He deserved at least one more trip to the take-away. "You're an investment consultant. You shouldn't be touting a gun." I grinned. "Might scare the punters."

Ivan raised his arms, wide of his body, as if in defence, and shrugged. "Okay, forget I mentioned it. I'd be way out of practice, anyway. No, forget it."

I'd met Ivan a week ago, in a bar so crowded that all I had to do to become acquainted was turn around on the spot and join in his mates' conversation. I'm good at bloke chat; I held my own against big, bad boys most of my childhood. We swapped mobile numbers, and he rang a couple of days ago. We met at Surf, the only club in Bridgwater that comes near to being cool. After an hour of trying to hear what the other was saying, we both admitted there was no point tiptoeing around the central issue. Fussy as ever, I'd worked harder on getting to know how good he was in bed than probing his personality.

Don't think for one moment that I'm after a permanent man in my life. I'm not even after a steady flow of temporary men. And don't worry, I'm careful, in all the various ways you want to imagine. I've been partying most nights since the age of fourteen—that's half my entire life filled with parties—until I gave it up for self-sufficiency a couple of years ago. But I don't want to forget how to do it altogether.

I worked at the hen house solidly until past ten. The hens were exploring their upgraded accommodation as I left them. I hoped Ivan would be making me breakfast, but he was sound asleep in my bed, curled into his previous rounded heap, clutching my polar bear hot water bottle.

I didn't know whether to be amused or irritated.

I took a shower, dried, smeared a single drop of rose oil between my breasts, and spent a few minutes brushing out the tangles where my hair curls and kinks as it falls to my waist. I pulled a black dress over my body. I wear no underwear when working—it's too constricting—and nothing on my feet. I do wear earrings, though, usually long, complicated structures. In my opinion, this is what earlobes are for. I hitched a belt around my waist, from which dangled the tools of my trade ... the buckskin bag of talismans, a bean rattle, and my wand of yew.

I went downstairs into the therapy room, where I conduct my business. I moved around it, setting everything in order and giving the surface areas a damp-dust. I lit the church candle on the low circle of table at the centre of the room and watched the flame flicker and strengthen. The wall candles I would light later. I put the same match to the fragile underside of a small sprig of dried sage. The misty smoke rose up from the incense dish. I carried the dish around the room, wafting the curl of smoke with a blackbird feather, making sure each corner was cleansed. I could feel the heavy hem of my dress brush my bare ankles as I moved, and this strengthened my mood, making me feel empowered and calm. I took a deep inhalation of the smoke just for the joy of it and left the sage on the table to burn itself out.

At each corner of the room, where the north, south, east, and west of the outside world converged with this inner one, I stood to ask the spirits for their blessing. Then I settled on a floor cushion for a few moments, centring my thoughts, clearing my head. My other preoccupations—Ivan in my bed, the sorry huddle of hens in the garden—were not important now. The only relevance was my client, and how I could be of help to him.

The door bell sang its gentle wind-chime call. As I passed the clock in the hall, I registered that it was indeed on the dot of eleven. I hadn't put Cliff Houghton down as a good timekeeper—he'd been fifteen minutes late his first time.

Except, the man who stood on my doorstep was not Cliff. This chap was tall, but without the lankiness that characterized my client. He carried a considerable amount of weight, but mostly, I suspected, in hard muscle. His hair was mousy brown, chopped short over his head, a centimetre or so longer than the bog-standard crew—probably just coming up to his next clipping. He had a few years on my client; he wasn't thirty-something anymore. His suit had the crumpled appearance of quality wool worn day after day—a suit for the job. His face was uneven and battered, with the hint of a previously broken nose.

"Miss Dare?"

"You have her."

He raised his hand as if to wave at me. I almost waved back, until I realized he was showing me ID. "Detective Sergeant Buckley. I wonder if I could take a moment or two of your time?"

I gave him a polite smile. "I'm sorry. I'm about to see someone with an appointment." I gazed along my side path, looking towards the street in the hope that said appointee would appear and prove me right.

"Would the client in question be Clifford Houghton?"

Now the man had my full attention. I thought for a few seconds before I answered with a stiff nod.

"Mr. Houghton is helping us with our enquiries at the moment. He'll have to remake his appointment."

I don't know much about the workings of our great British police force, and what I do know is mostly gleaned from watching telly, but I presumed detective sergeants don't pop round just to let you know your client will be late.

I stepped back from the door and the man slid past me. His body language was deferential but assertive at the same time, no mean feat.

The therapy room was primed for work and its appearance has been known to faze unexpected guests, so I guided him to the far end of the kitchen and offered him a seat on my sofa. After the briefest of pauses, he took it.

"Tea? Coffee? Herbal? Water?"

"That would be kind. Coffee, black, one sugar, please. It's been a long morning."

I put the kettle on the stove. "Is Mr. Houghton a witness to something?"

I thought my question showed a pertinent understanding of police procedure, but it got short shrift.

"I'm afraid I can't go into that."

"He's not in some sort of trouble, is he?"

"I can't answer that, either."

"What can you tell me, then?"

"Nothing, I'm afraid, Miss Dare. I'm not here to answer your questions, I'm here to ask my own."

I made one mug of instant coffee with sugar and one mug of Barleycup tea and set them down before pulling a high stool from under my breakfast bar and leaning against it. I liked this arrangement—I was now looking down at DS Buckley. "Don't worry, I can guess. You want me to help with your enquiries too."

"I hope you'll be able to fill in some details about Mr. Houghton. And possibly do us a small favour."

"Why don't I like the sound of that?"

"I don't know, Miss Dare, bearing in mind that the police endeavour at all times to uphold the rule of law and defend the innocent."

"Cliff Houghton looked pretty innocent to me."

"How well do you know him?"

"This would have been his second session. I saw him last Saturday for a ground-working consultation, and today we were planning to start work properly."

"Uh-huh." DS Buckley gave a minimal nod and sipped his coffee. "That would be … psychotherapy sessions?"

"Is that what Cliff told you?" I waited for the almost imperceptible nod of the head before adding, "That's about it, yes."

"Let me just restate that, Miss Dare. He was coming to you for psychotherapy."

"Listen, could you cut down on the 'Miss Dares'? I don't recognise myself. Call me Sabbie, everyone does."

For the first time, I spotted a whisper of a genuine smile. "Pleased to meet you, Sabbie," said DS Buckley. He held out a hand, empty of ID, and I slid off my stool and shook it. "I'm Reynard."

"*What?*"

A charming tinge of pink emerged over his cheekbones. "My friends call me Rey."

"No, no," I protested. "I wasn't mocking your name! It's just I was visited by a fox during the night, and your name is so ... *foxy*." I realized right then that I'd never be able to think of him as anything but Rey from that moment on.

"You were visited by a fox?"

"My hens were."

I hadn't, until that second, noticed we were still touching, the handshake frozen in time. But I did notice it, clearly, as Ivan, finally shaved and dressed in last night's clothes—white jeans and a dashing shirt of crushed bilberry silk—walked into the kitchen. Foolishly, I pulled my hand away as if this Rey/ray was capable of dispensing electric shocks.

"Ivan," I said, "this is Detective Sergeant Buckley." My voice squeaked at the edges.

"Your eleven o'clock client?"

"I'm afraid not," said Rey. "I'm here on official business."

"Don't you chaps usually turn up in pairs?" said Ivan.

"This is a straightforward, informal interview."

"Informal official business," I said, trying to get a secret smile to Ivan.

It didn't work. He turned away, as if bored by the whole thing—hens, dead or alive, detectives, informal or official.

"Give me a ring!" I threw after him, but he'd already disappeared into the hallway. I heard the front door slam.

"I'm sorry," Rey began.

"Don't be."

"Your partner?" he queried.

I gave him a big, sunny smile. "My lover. Ex, probably."

TWO

After Ivan left, the detective sergeant became all professional and distant. He didn't actually put his palms out and say "whoa!" but I could see he was mentally reassessing his approach.

"Miss Dare," he began, "I'd be grateful if you could tell me anything you know about Mr. Houghton."

"That should be easy. I can't tell you anything. I'm bound by an agreement of confidentiality."

"We're investigating a serious matter, Miss Dare, and we'd appreciate your cooperation."

I took a couple of swallows of Barleycup while my head reeled. "How serious is serious?"

"Very. Homicide."

"Murder?" I yelped. "My client?"

"We're working on several leads. The more information we have, the sooner we can drop the ones that go nowhere."

I nodded once. I could feel the blood pumping under my temples. Was that because a murderer had been in my therapy room, or because the police were here now? "Even if I told you everything I knew, I don't think you'd be any the wiser. My sessions don't work like that."

"In about half an hour," said Rey, suddenly chatty, "Mr. Houghton will be released from an extended interview, free to go. I think he will immediately phone you to apologise for missing the appointment. He will not be told of my visit. I'm hoping he'll ask for a new appointment."

"Sounds as if he'll need it."

"As do we, Miss Dare. His next appointment may tell us whether this man is involved in the crime we're investigating."

It was like stepping into a sudden draught of cold air. I swallowed hard on the Barleycup in my mouth, almost choking. "You want me to pass things he tells me over to you? That's immoral."

"Not when lives are at risk."

"I couldn't do that if my *own* life was at risk."

"Your life is not at risk. I wouldn't ask you to do this if I thought it was."

It was the *I* in his statement that made me pause. I reconsidered Ivan's comment about police arriving in pairs. Why was this man alone? "I want to see your ID again."

He slid it over the coffee table. I wouldn't know a fake police badge if it had *Counterfeit!* stamped over it, but I rested my hand on the plastic coat and closed my eyes, to see what drifted into my mind. I gained a sensation—a recognition of strength and self-possession. Hidden underneath was a split-second flash of utter fatigue, the sort one associates with huge amounts of unhealthy habits. But that might be me, stereotyping the guy. Maybe he was a teetotal policeman.

"You're smart, Sabbie," said Rey. "I'm here on a bit of a hunch. The man we're interviewing is a puzzle, and I'm hoping you'll be able to help solve it."

"I told you," I said. "I can't divulge anything that passes between me and a client."

"If need be, we'd get a warrant for access to your notes. Your entire system if necessary—electronic to handwritten."

I gave a soft chuckle, which calmed me. "That wouldn't do you any good at all. I don't keep the sort of client notes that would tell you anything."

"You don't keep proper notes? What sort of psychotherapist d'you call yourself?" The man glowered. I could see he didn't like me dodging his questions, so I threw in my chips.

"My business is more spiritually based. I read tarot, offer Reiki healing, that sort of thing. Cliff was consulting me as a shaman." I gestured to my belt of tools, which he'd been careful not stare at. "I speak with spirits, Rey. And, yes, I write down what I bring back. But only the client will understand it. I promise you that."

Rey passed a hand from the front of his scalp to the back. His hair flattened and sprang up again, like new-mown grass. "Why … why do people do it?"

"Because some problems run deep. These might come out as bad eczema, or insomnia, perhaps. But underlying that, there is something harming the person from the inside. I try to get useful answers by working with the person's spirit world."

Rey took a while to answer, which I considered a good thing. As a bloke, a copper, and someone who wore their hair as if they were about to pull on flying goggles, I hadn't put "listening to women" anywhere on his priorities list.

"Okay," he said, finally. "So this guy came to you with a serious problem. A paying customer. And now he's under suspicion for murder. You see, there's a possible cause and effect between these two things. Like he's crying out to be helped. Or caught." He picked up his mug, swilled the slops around, and put it down again. "He must want to be caught, because we found him scrabbling around in the middle of the night on top of the shallow grave we opened six weeks ago."

"Not … " I felt the house become still and hushed around me. "Not where you found that little boy."

"Yes," said Rey. "Josh Sutton."

"I can't believe it. Cliff didn't come across as a …" I couldn't say the word.

"Doesn't your business help you see through people?" said Rey. "I mean, *into* them?"

"Yeah, sometimes. Weirdly, it's more likely to be some sort of artefact that works for me—we call it psychometry." I didn't think I'd bother to tell him what I'd felt when I'd touched his badge. "And when I work with a client, I get to know their spirit world. But I'm not at that stage with Cliff Houghton yet."

I thought about the first journey I'd taken for Cliff, using the personal object he'd brought for me. I'd felt an overwhelming sense of foreboding I hadn't been able to explain … I hadn't tried to, at the time. When I work as a shaman, I close my eyes and let myself down into a different place. It's like sinking into a full tub of warm water. I'm hoping to tap into the deep truths of the spirit world. Sometimes I can feel what a client is feeling, even though they don't know they're feeling it. But without that connection … without the spirit world to guide me, I'm not much better than the next guy at gauging personality. What had I thought of Cliff, the one time I'd met him? Quiet. Perhaps a little too quiet, which did make him feel a little … odd.

I couldn't bear to think that I'd entered the spirit world of a child killer.

My mobile crowed. I jumped out of my thoughts, and the detective gawped at the phone. I didn't think Rey Buckley had a surprisable bone in his body, but there he was, mouth drooping open, as my phoned went *cock-a-doodle-doo!* over and over.

My foster brother, Dennon, gave me the cockerel ringtone as a birthday present after I got the hens. I've had as many embarrassing moments with it as I've had laughs, and I'm pretty sure that was what my dear brother had hoped. Den is only eight months older than me, and when I first went to live with his family at age thirteen, we got up to shed-loads of mischief together. Later, it had turned into nicked carloads of mischief. Joke ring-tones are his settled-down side, although he had his fair share of community orders before he managed it.

I could see who was calling, since I'd entered his number into my contacts. I started with a gentle "Hi" and let Cliff do the talking, which didn't last long.

"Wind-chime door bells and cockerel phones?" said Rey, as I folded my mobile closed. "You kinda like your sound effects, don't you?"

But I was no longer in the mood to barter comments. "That was Cliff, to say he's sorry he's late. He didn't mention why."

"He won't want to tell you."

"He's going to take what's left of his appointment." I suddenly felt as if the temperature had dropped around me. I was trembling like a small puppy. "I cannot believe he'd hurt a child."

Rey didn't make any reply. He was standing as if ready to depart. I noticed that his hands had folded together and that the fingers were lacing and re-lacing.

I threw him a sharp glance. "You don't believe it either, do you?"

"I go by facts, Sabbie," he said. "Facts, proof, evidence. I don't trust hunches."

"Yes you do," I said softly. "Or you wouldn't be here."

THREE

"It was awful," said Cliff. I'd given him a glass of water and he was holding on to it as if it was a healing elixir. The pads of his fingertips were crushed around it, until the surface of the water trembled and slopped onto his cords jeans.

"Perhaps it will help to describe what happened to you."

Cliff downed the rest of the water and spent time examining the tumbler, turning it round and round and gazing into it as if it were a crystal ball. His hands were bony at the knuckles, the fingers long and pale.

"Look," I began. "I've been honest with you. I've told you a detective came here, and what he wanted from me. I think that's called putting your neck on the line."

"It looks bad, I know." Cliff risked a glance at my face. "I couldn't even give a reasonable explanation to the police."

"Why not?"

"Because I don't have one. I don't know why I went there. It was stupid. A stupid thing to do. I just... I needed to..." He gazed towards the window. The blinds were covered by a length of muslin I fell in love with at a sale. It's a rich cream in colour and printed at intervals with the outline of birds in flight. I like the soaring feeling they give and the way the light filters in. It also hides the view of the street, busy with traffic and nosy parkers.

"It *was* a need. I had to see. The case of little Josh had got into my head. The thought of where he was in that desolate, boggy place." He looked up. "My dad used to take me to the wetlands. There's fish in some of the bigger waterways. We'd always take back an armful of bulrushes for Mum. I was going to pick a bunch, but the dog got me first." His mouth twisted to one side, showing his teeth, which lay apart from each other, like gravestones in a crowded cemetery. "They set a dog on me."

"You feel the police violated you?"

"Do I look like the sort of person who would …" He squeezed his lips together with one hand, squashing them between his fingers and screwing them round as if he needed to stop words falling from them. It made my stomach churn. "Do I?"

"No," I admitted. But that didn't really explain why he'd waded through the Somerset marshes in the middle of the night.

"Perhaps we should get on with our session." My voice cracked. "Last time, I asked you to bring something you thought was significant to your problem for me to use."

"Yeah, a silver sovereign. Present from my dad. Like I said last time, I think my difficulties … stem from when he died."

"It must have been dreadful for you."

"It's dreadful even now." Cliff looked up from his examination of the tumbler and shook himself, as if he was desperate to change the mood. "It seemed bizarre, you asking for an object. Like giving something to a tracker dog to sniff. Now it seems ironic." Gingerly, he raised his left arm. "I don't think they treated my bites seriously at the station."

"You should get a tetanus. Shamanic consultations don't offer immunity from infection." I took the empty glass from him. Its entire surface was smeared with the sweat from his fingers. I turned to the desk behind me and laid the glass on its surface. I'd made the desk myself—two cheap bedside cabinets with MDF laid across them. I'd draped the remainder of the winged muslin over this, my only nod to coordinated décor. I needed somewhere to keep things out of sight, so that they didn't disturb the tranquillity of the room. From a drawer I took my notes and the small, flat package that Cliff had handed me last Saturday. It had been the first time I'd set eyes on a sovereign. I tried to hand it back, but he was looking at the floor and playing with his mouth again, so I put it next to the empty glass.

"I took a spirit journey using your sovereign to guide me, as I said I would. I didn't bring much back that first time, but I'm confident things will improve over the next few sessions."

"What've you got?"

"Usually on a first journey, I'm wandering around looking for a 'lead in' to a client's spirit world. But with you, Cliff, I immediately found myself in a small room." I gave a cough and looked down at the printed page of my notes. For no logical reason, my stomach was churning. "I suppose this room was about seven or eight foot square. There wasn't any furniture to speak of, but I sensed I was on an upstairs floor even though I couldn't see out. The window was small and covered in a brown curtain that had been nailed onto the frame. Naturally, the light was poor, but I could see that the room was a bit grubby…" I glanced up at him. "Actually, Cliff, the place was filthy, festooned with cobwebs. There was a pile of untouched food lying on the floorboards, a heap of stale sandwiches, curling at the edges."

I knew I was going to shudder as I read the next words, and shifted on my seat to disguise it. Cliff was watching me intently, while his fingers twisted at his ponytail, playing with it as a girl does. Some of the earth-coloured strands weren't long enough to be caught up, and they fell greasily over his face. I looked back down at my page.

"There was only one other thing in the room—a Hessian sack with knots tied around its rim to keep it open, like you see in cartoons. Something glinted in the sack, but in the dim light I couldn't work out what it was. I can recall not wanting to look more closely, but I walked the few paces over to where it stood and dipped a hand in. I think I had been expecting money, or jewels or treasure of some sort, but a softness caressed my fingers."

I paused. I knew I was stalling. I could not bring myself to go on, and I wasn't sure if that was because it had frightened me, or because it might frighten Cliff.

"What?" Cliff croaked. "What was in the sack?"

"Hair," I said. "Clippings of human hair, all colours from black to blond, some curled, some straight." I gave a light-hearted smile. "Could have been swept up from a barber's floor."

"Barber?" said Cliff. "Sorry, means nothing. I don't use them."

"Whyever not?" I felt as if I hadn't breathed properly in hours.

"I chop at it myself. Avoid the queues, save time."

Cliff didn't look like a man who had to choose between a haircut and catching his flight to Zurich, but I didn't comment.

"That it?" said Cliff. "Is that all?"

I nodded, and my neck creaked. I make it a policy not to tell clients anything that feels bad without being able to give a glimmer of hope or at least some explanation. I had no intention of telling Cliff that, as I had handled the hair clippings, I had been convinced that there had been someone standing behind me who hadn't previously been part of this journey. Typically that denotes some sort of spiritual presence, a guardian of mine or of the client's. But a terror had filled me as I stood in that repulsive room. It had crushed my heart into my lungs and hardened my muscles like quick-dry cement. I could not turn round or even move.

I'd had an overwhelming urge to get out of that place. I'd called to my animal guide and in no more than a flash, the scene changed. I was at my shamanic portal, where I set off for every shamanic journey. In it, a brook runs below a deep, mossy bank, mauve with heather. The water is very fast but brilliantly clear, and you can see the white stones that litter the brook's bed.

When I arrived at my brook, my knees had given way and I'd collapsed onto the grass. A wet nose broke the surface of the brook. I'd gasped, then laughed. A raft of short whiskers and round, loving eyes. It was my spirit guide, an old male otter.

"I don't think I can go back there, Trendle."

"That was enough. You should do no more today."

I had reached out to tickle Trendle behind his small ears, which he loves, but he dived out of reach with one splashing flick of his snakelike tail.

Now, I glanced up at Cliff, still sitting with his gaze on his slightly grubby trainers.

"Yes." My voice sounded artificial in my ears. "That was all." I passed Cliff the printout of my slightly abridged notes. "This is your copy. I'd like you to read it through to see if anything resonates."

He glanced down at it. "I don't think it means anything to me."

"That shouldn't worry us." I was trying hard to be calm and professional, but beneath the bodice of my black dress, my heart was flickering like the candles.

He nodded and stretched his legs out. His ankles were suddenly exposed above black nylon socks, all knobbles and blue veins. He was too slim, and I wondered if he had recently lost weight, especially as it showed in his face, hollowing his cheeks.

"Would you like a hot drink, or more water?"

"You could fill that glass with whisky."

"Sorry, I don't—"

"It was a joke," said Cliff. "A coffee would be great."

I got into the kitchen somehow, and flicked the kettle on. I leaned against the worktop. I felt as if I'd just got out of my bed after a heavy night—fuzzy head, wobbly legs, a sick, empty feeling in my stomach. Maybe it was just my lack of breakfast, but I was glad of this reprieve. I needed to think everything through—Cliff's story, Rey, Ivan, dreams, hens. But instead, I thought about Josh Sutton.

———

Josh had gone missing on Christmas Eve, almost three months ago, now. His family—mum, dad, big brother Branwell, and one set of grandparents—had gone for an after-lunch stroll on the Bristol Downs. Josh and Branwell were playing hide and seek among the bushes, according to the family. The Downs consist of mile after square mile of common grassy space that ends where the suspension bridge spans the river gorge, and it's surrounded on the other three sides by the more opulent parts of Bristol. The Suttons, Josh's family, lived in one of the nearby eighteenth-century terraces; the Downs would be their natural playground. I can remember being taken there as a kid. I lived in Bristol then, and it's one of the nicer memories from my early childhood. Dotted across the grassy acreage are the natural-growing copses of trees and shrubs, a great attraction for kids and lovers alike. Kids, lovers, and rapists, in fact … it's best not to venture alone over the Downs on the way back from a late-night party.

But this was the middle of a Christmas Eve afternoon, and no one was thinking bad thoughts. So when Branwell came over to his parents and said that Josh had got himself so well hidden, he couldn't find him at all, his family thought it was a kid's prank. But even with everybody searching, Josh couldn't be found. By the time police and volunteers did a sweep search of the whole area, hope had already faded. Even the Slamblaster action toy that Josh had been clutching had disappeared.

There is never a good time to lose a child, but surely Christmas and New Year must be the worst. His parents' strained faces became increasingly gaunt as they appeared, time and again, on the evening news. The search was spread over a wider and wider area, but the people of Bridgwater—myself included—still felt a long way away from the tragedy. At the start of January, Josh should have celebrated his seventh birthday. The whole country mourned him on that day. It didn't seem possible that Josh would be seen alive again. A couple of weeks after his birthday, a party of walkers and a dog with a good nose stumbled on his body, left in a shallow grave in a remote part of the Somerset moors. Josh had been found fifty miles away from his home.

———

I gave a start. Cliff was standing right beside me. I hadn't even heard him come across the kitchen, but now he was so close that his breathing had broken into my reverie.

"When a child dies, it always feels personal, doesn't it?" I said. "My nephew is just a bit younger than Josh. Everyone will know a little boy like him. It's an unspeakably compulsive story."

Cliff forced a weak smile. "Thank you for that. I was beginning to think it was just me that was obsessed with the case. I've listened to every news story since he was found, bought every newspaper. While I was in the cells, the police searched my flat. They found all the articles I'd cut out in a file."

"Why? Why did you do that?"

"I was hoping you'd tell me."

"Hot drink first, I think." I made a repeat of the earlier Barleycup and coffee (this time milk but no sugar), and we carried them back into the therapy room. I followed behind Cliff's lumbering gait, which I suppose went with his extra height.

"They never announced how he died," he said, without looking round. "I've read every newspaper report; they never said."

"I hadn't really thought of that before," I said. "I suppose it is rather odd."

"Not as odd as where he was found."

"Because of those other bodies? The ones they found there ages ago?"

"That's right." Cliff returned to the client's chair. The chair is a sun lounger, a little tatty around the edges, so I've draped it with a Celtic knot throw. I can adjust it from psychoanalytically prone to bolt upright, which was how it was now. Cliff's trainered feet were solidly on the floor and he leaned towards me, ready to talk. "The papers can't make up their minds. Sometimes the Wetland Murderer has returned. Sometimes it's a copycat crime."

"I don't remember the Wetland Murders at all," I said.

"They were twenty-three years back."

"Ah. I would've been five. And I didn't live around here."

"I remember," said Cliff. "I was eleven. All these little kids started disappearing. Their photos were plastered over the papers. Everyone got scared."

"The new stories resurrected those old photos, didn't they?"

"They're loving it, the papers. Wallowing. Those killings were... gruesome. Even the children's bones were broken. They were found with the duct tape still over their mouths." Cliff broke off to take a swallow of his coffee and place it carefully on the floor by his feet. "Unbelievable."

I felt the silence grow in the room. Cliff appeared to be the world expert on both these crimes.

"How did it all end?"

"I can remember seeing it on the telly. They found bodies buried on the moors. Matthew, Joanna, Nicolas, and John. Everyone poring over the gruesome details like ghouls." Cliff shifted on his seat, almost tipping the metal frame. He was perched right on the edge of the chair like some flightless bird. It's better to rest back on the lounger, but he seemed unable to relax. "They never found the murderer," he went on, "but after a while, the kids round my way were let back out to play. I guess people thought it was over."

"I wonder what makes someone do something so evil and then stop, all of a sudden?"

"Their consciences, I hope."

I was silent for a while. "You remember it very well. The names and details."

"You could say the whole year is burned on my memory. Dad was sick around then, then he died, and I never felt the same again."

I could see that Josh's death might very well have brought back memories of Cliff's own pain and loss, confusing past with present in his mind.

"In our first session, you said you felt as if something was making you depressed."

"Yeah, well, the doctor calls it depression. But to be honest, none of the tablets he's given me has done anything. It's the mornings, mostly. At least, it always starts as I wake. I feel so … afraid … for no reason. Getting out of bed is impossible. That's why I shelf-stack in Morrison's. I do the night sessions. I don't have to wake up till the evening, and if I'm lucky, the feeling of dread goes away more quickly."

"Can you remember your dreams?"

"No. Never. I don't have dreams."

"Dreams often slip out of sight, but if we write down all the tiny fragments we remember, we can nudge our 'dream memory'."

I took a new softbound A5 book of unlined pages from a pile I keep in a drawer and wrote Cliff's full name in the front. I flicked a few pages in and sketched out the room I'd visited on my journey. I belong to the Mickey Mouse school of art, but even I could draw a cartoon sack. Then I sellotaped the copy of my journey in beside it and dated the entry. I showed him the notebook.

"Each session, I'll describe what I've seen in your spirit world in this book, and I want you to use it as a memory jogger in between sessions. If any thoughts or coincidences happen that take you back to the description of my journeys, I want you to put them down. Add all the dreams you remember. Leave the notebook by your bed and jot down even the tiniest scrap as soon as you wake."

Cliff gave a snort. "Why should I to do that?"

"You've come here because you want to know why you feel so wretched all the time. Dreams are part of the shamanic work we'll do together."

"Okay, that makes sense."

"I want to see you next Saturday," I said, writing the date in the notebook and passing it to Cliff. He flapped it in his hand as if he needed extra air.

"What will you tell the police?" he asked.

"What did *you* tell them?"

He grimaced. "I see your point. I told them mostly everything I've just told you. They've allocated me a solicitor—Miss Smith. She's insisting I should be careful what I say, but I hope I won't have to say anything to them again. Surely they've done with me."

I checked the time on my mobile, which was lying on the desk. I usually leave a good space between appointments—I never know just what's going to happen in a shamanic consultation—but the doorbell for my next client was going to chime at any moment. I offered Cliff a handshake. His palm was hot with sweat. When he pulled away, I felt his hand tremble, as if he'd just received bad news.

It wasn't until after he'd left that I realized he'd forgotten the sovereign—or maybe he'd thought I would need it again.

I reached out and laid one index finger on its cool, indented surface. Sometime during this next week, I would have to travel into Cliff's spirit world again, and I was not looking forward to it one little bit.

FOUR

THE FOLLOWING MORNING, I indulged an impulse and went to the Sunday car boot sale they always hold on Plum Lane—Bridgwater's finest. I had appointments back-to-back from two until seven in the evening, so I reckoned I deserved the morning off. I fed my three sad hens. Juniper, Ginger, and Melissa peered nervously at me from their fox fortress. They reminded me forcefully of Cliff—how he'd turn his lips into a beak and the way the dark pupils of his eyes were tiny, bright dots.

I made the one-mile walk through the houses to Plum Lane, letting the sharp wind blow my cobwebs away. The sale was already buzzing when I got there. I pushed into the browsing, haggling crowds and began to trawl for bargains. Some of my favourite stalls are those I never buy from. I love the philatelist who turns up with albums and cellophane packets of brilliantly coloured foreign stamps, and the chap who sells rusty, archaic, and seemingly useless tools from a blanket laid on the ground, which is constantly surrounded by men of a certain age.

I sifted through the second-hand clothes, treated myself to a Will Smith DVD (he is on my "want to marry" list), almost won a fight over a cut-glass salad bowl, then made a beeline for my favourite stall, a chap who comes once a fortnight to sell CDs at amazing cut prices. Barty (as he's called) will put a CD into his player and let you listen to something new. A beat pounded out and his stall was deep in punters.

I elbowed my way through the crowd and ran my hands along the racks, searching out artists I liked. I felt the close proximity of a sharp warm aura behind me just as my hand lighted on a Pet Shop Boys album. People do that at boot sales—breathe all over you as they try to snatch the bargain you spotted first.

"Bit before your time, aren't they?"

I jumped, despite my early warning device. The CD flew up in the air. With a certain panache, Rey caught it like a discus.

I had no intention of ever clapping my eyes on Detective Sergeant Buckley again, but I'd forgotten how often the hand of fate takes a leading role in my productions.

"Have you been following me?"

He laughed. "We don't have the manpower for that. I like coming here."

I didn't believe him for a moment. I had a feeling that our exchange yesterday had rankled with him. He'd gone out on a limb, despite what he'd told me about hunches, and it hadn't paid off because I wasn't prepared to play his sort of games.

"Want this?" He brought a fiver from his pocket and waved it at Barty.

"Will you stop?"

"Go on, let me treat you."

I snatched back the CD, stuffed it onto the stand, and stormed off through the crowd. I knew he was following; he caught me up, sneaked in front, and held up his hands in defeat. "You really take this self-sufficiency thing seriously, don't you?"

I couldn't help smile at that, or help taking it as a compliment, either.

"Fancy a drink?" said Rey. "There's a couple of tables by the burger van."

It was a sure bet Rey would spend all his time trying to needle information out of me, but I did like his new-mown hair and the eyes that, in daylight, veered on the greenish side of hazel, so I gave a half nod. "Just a tea, please."

"Come on then." Rey hugged himself. "It's cold work, car booting."

He strode ahead. Today he was wearing a worn leather jacket that skimmed the belt of bleached, deliciously tight, unironed jeans. He scrubbed down well, did Rey Buckley. By the time I'd plonked onto one of the cheap plastic seats, he was on his way back from the van, both hands occupied with paper cups. I noticed that he'd left a carrier bag full of purchases next to his seat, an old clock resting on the top. Maybe he did car boot, after all.

I stretched out as he sat down, and under the tiny bistro table my foot nudged against his thick-soled boot. I snatched it back as if Rey were a live cable, which indeed, he must have been—a spark flew from him and shot through the centre of my body. I hid my warming cheeks behind my paper cup while I foolishly focused my gaze on his left ring finger. Naked skin, all the way down to the hairy back of his hand, which meant, in my calculating mind, that DS Buckley was either (a) single, (b) divorced, or (c) a man who chose not to wear rings.

"So, what's your preference in music?" said Rey as he diligently poured packets of sugar into his black coffee.

"That has to be reggae. I have everything Bob Marley ever released."

"Because he's dead?" said Rey.

"What? Why d'you say that?"

"I'd just been wondering what this spirit world you were on about was like. Is it filled with dead people like Marley and Sid Vicious?"

His question surprised me. I'd expected him to badger me about Cliff, not start a philosophical discussion.

"It isn't like that. A lot of spirits have never even been human."

"Whatever do they look like then?"

"Mostly what I encounter is symbolic. Sometimes I see abstract patterns, sometimes stories play themselves out, like allegories. Most of my spirit guardians look as if they come from another world, but sometimes they turn up in jeans and a baseball cap. They usually bring messages I have to interpret. Sometimes what they give me seems complex and coded; other times things fit together through coincidences that jump up and smack you in the eye."

"I can't see how it works. How come I don't bump into these spirits when I close my eyes?"

"Good question." I paused, because the chap from the burger bar had arrived with a sausage and bacon buttie on a paper plate and I was fascinated by the variation in sauces and dressings Rey was lavishing over it. "Most people can enter a trance. Actually we do it all the time. It's that state of mind where we shut off from what's going on around us even though we're not asleep."

"Oh, I've got that one off to a tee," said Rey. "I use it when my mates start banging on about their wives."

I bit back an overpowering desire to ask if Rey had a wife to bang on about. "Part of my job is introducing my clients to their own spirit worlds."

"Could I do it?" said Rey, taking an oversized bite of his burger.

"Yes, sir, if you'd care to book an appointment…"

"I wouldn't have to be ill or something, then?"

"Not necessarily. But I do do a lot of therapeutic work. Most of my clients are hoping I'll solve their problems."

"And do you solve them?"

I thought about Cliff—the enigma that seemed impenetrable and the cryptic symbols I'd been offered. Maybe this time I'd bitten off more than I'd be able to chew. "I guess clients are happy with what they get. A lot of my work is by recommendation."

"So," said Rey, keeping his voice all laid-back, "are drugs involved?"

I grinned. "Not by me. In some places maybe. South America, for instance, or in ancient times, but I like to keep my head crystal-ball clear."

"Strange way to earn a crust."

"That's what it generally is—a crust! But I get by. Lucky I've got a garden full of vegetables."

"And hens," Rey reminded me.

"I fancy getting a goat, but I'm not sure I've got room."

To my surprise, our conversation took off, flapping here and there as conversations do, and finally perching on a fence as we argued the ultimate question.

"Boy bands are sad," said Rey. "They're all adolescents, hoping never to grow up and do proper jobs." There was tomato ketchup on his chin and I weighed up telling him about it or simply leaning over to wipe it off with the flimsy paper napkin.

"Girl bands can't even sing, let alone compose their own tracks," I argued back. "They're fine if all you plan to do is fantasize as you watch them."

"So what do girls do with boy bands, then? No sneaky little fantasies about getting hitched?"

I tried not to look down at my Will Smith DVD. "No, we go and watch them. Gives you a real buzz. I've still got the pics from the Live Earth concert on my laptop to prove it."

"Laptop!" said Rey, wiping his mouth and screwing the last bits of sausage bun into his napkin. "What happened to scrape-a-carrot-from-the-soil?"

"I've got a very generous family. It was my going-to-university gift."

"They do degrees in *shamanism*?"

"Not exactly. You need to study with a master; it's a practical subject. A skill. A gift, I suppose."

We might have gone on all day, but the booters were packing up around us.

"You ever thought about selling things here?" Rey asked as we walked towards the entrance.

"Come early May, I'll be behind a pasting table, offloading my surplus seedlings."

Rey put the flat of his hand on my arm. "I knew I'd seen you somewhere before."

"What, are you saying you've purchased my Pelargonium cuttings?"

"I might, if I knew what they were."

We'd stopped walking. Frankly, my legs were in no state to carry me along the pavement while Rey's hand laid on my arm. It was strong, with straight-cut nails that had no dirt under them. For some reason it seemed to have a built-in device that weakened the person it touched, body and mind. Useful if you're arresting someone, I supposed. I looked into Rey's face and saw the change in the curve of his mouth, the softness there suddenly. I was sure that any second, he would dip his head to my level and kiss me. Then someone jogged against my shoulder as they passed us. I turned to give an automatic apology and when I turned back, he was walking on, the moment broken. Maybe I imagined it altogether.

"Did he turn up, then, yesterday?"

I knew Rey had been choking on that question from the moment he'd spotted me. But he'd managed to keep it nailed down, and I felt he deserved a little reward.

"He did. We had a good session."

"Go away all cured and happy, did he?"

"He had a wretched time when he was a boy—"

"If you ask me, some people just can't cope with life." Rey snorted. "My dad walked out on us, you know, left me to 'be the man', but I didn't see that as something that would affect my life badly. Not then, and not now. Actually, I think it was the making of me."

"You're right." Just for a second, I was tempted to trade "tough times," but I was not in the mood. "Some people can cope with things others can't. We're all different. I have to accept that my client's anguish is how he tells me it is. Otherwise it would be like a surgeon telling a patient he can't possibly be in that much pain from his op, wouldn't it?"

"I'll give you that." Rey fished out his car keys and zapped them at a natty-looking Nissan with sporty wheels. It winked back at us. "I just wondered about your gut reaction about Cliff Houghton."

By the time I was ready to answer the question, we'd reached the car.

"I don't know," I said, and it was the perfect truth. "Not yet."

"Not yet?" Rey repeated, in an optimistic tone.

"You think these are copycat killings, don't you?"

"Whatever that is."

"Don't dismiss my questions," I said, riled, "and expect me to answer yours."

"I asked you for a gut reaction. Hardly the Inquisition."

"I told you, I can't talk about clients."

"Same thing applies to a case—can't say a word."

"Apart from giving me the third degree."

"You'd know if you were having that."

We stood, inches away from each other, seething.

Rey opened the passenger door of his car. "Can I drop you anywhere?"

"I'll walk. I need the exercise." I strode off, heading towards home.

"See ya!" Rey called after me.

I put my hand in the air but didn't look back.

————

I suppose you could say that my fascination with the spirit world can be traced back nine years, to the day my foster mum, Gloria, persuaded me to go to university. I wasn't keen, although I had been trying to sort my future out. I was nineteen, living in the smallest bedroom in her house and running two jobs—bar assistant at Badass and care assistant at a local residential home for the elderly. Neither of my jobs paid above the minimum wage, although I did enjoy them—especially the evening one, which I'd had since the day I'd hit eighteen. I spent most of my evenings leaning against the Badass bar, and I did backflips at the idea that they'd *pay* me to spend time behind it.

I had left school in a great hurry, fed up with the way they kept putting me on suspension for trumped-up mini-crimes they'd got their knickers in a mess over. I'd hated school, especially its petty rules and the way imaginative thinking was stifled (well, my imaginative thinking, anyway). I'd told Gloria I didn't need stupid exam certificates; I could earn my own living and pay her back for the years I'd been eating out of her fridge.

"I don't want nothing," she'd said, "except to see you happy, girl."

"I am happy," I'd said, my eyes smarting with hot brine.

"Bein' angry is not the same as bein' happy," said Gloria, one of her many maxims.

Nevertheless, she had helped me find the job at the residential home. I soon had money in my pocket for most of each week, despite the fact I was the only person I knew who paid rent to live at home. After all, it was the only place I'd ever called home and the cooking was great—except on Sundays, when my foster dad, Philip, made us trail the countryside byways around Bristol with sandwiches in our backpacks. He's still a believer in fresh air and exercise, is Philip, even though he's gone sixty-six and retired.

One evening, as I had been getting ready for my shift at the pub (which always meant a good deal of makeup and hair arrangement), Gloria had slammed a brochure down in front of me.

"Bristol City College?" I'd read. "Oh no, Gloria. You've got me wrong. I have no intention of going back to school."

"You'd better have," she'd growled. "I've just enrolled you in three evening courses. My treat for your nineteenth birthday."

"Ta," I said with heavy sarcasm. "What are they? Flower arranging? Yoga?"

"A levels," said Gloria. "All your favourites: psychology, sociology, and biology."

"*Ologies*?" I'd exploded. "How d'you expect me to do all this?"

"Because you're clever," said Gloria. "You just don't know it. And because you're always banging on about these subjects."

"Yeah, right," I muttered, turning the pages of the prospectus. "Like I actually know anything about any of them."

"You'll surprise yourself," said Gloria.

But the greatest surprise was the one still hiding up Gloria's sleeve. Because to my amazement, my exam results after the evening courses gained me a place at Bangor University, up in North Wales. While I'd been trying to work out if I could afford to study there, Gloria had presented me with a cheque for all the rent I'd paid her over the last three years. She had me weeping all over her soft, warm, loving shoulder.

I had thought it might be nice to stay in a bedroom like the one at Gloria's, so I'd phoned a few landladies, eventually speaking to Rhiannon Howell. "It is just me and Bren here now." The slow richness of her North Welsh accent had powered down the phone line. "Both our girls have babies of their own, and we miss all the mess and loud music, we do."

"Honestly?"

I heard her give a throaty chuckle down the phone and immediately warmed to her. "I hope you like countryside, Sabrina. We're out of the town. Out in the wild, like."

"I'll be okay, I've got my Honda bike." I had imagined that I'd be spending most of my time in the campus pubs. "Oh, and I'm Sabbie."

I hated my full name back then. It reminded me of the mother who'd chosen to die rather than look after me. Plus I thought it was a stupid name to give a baby. I used to imagine that she'd looked down into the cot and called me the first thing that had come into her drug-fuzzed brain. I wanted to forget my earliest years, and I dealt with that by never answering to the name Sabrina.

The plan was that Philip would drive all my things up in the car, and I'd follow closely behind on my Honda. I'd been whizzing around Bristol for a couple of years and felt confident of the trip north. But we'd only just crossed the border into Wales when the rain started to bucket down in sheets.

Bloody typical, I thought, and then I saw the brake lights on the lorry in front of me, and that thought was my last for a long while.

My first memory of recovery was a song in my head.

Later, Gloria had told me I'd been rushed straight to the operating theatre to relieve the haematoma that had caused pressure on my brain. The surgeons did everything they could but were cagey about the outcome. They wouldn't promise when I'd come round, or even if I would. My family sat round waiting. My first response was a lifted hand, as if I was reaching for something. The following morning, I opened my eyes and began a slow recovery.

That was the outside world's version of events. My internal story was quite different. I swam in a dream world. I had no knowledge of time or space. I heard a woman's voice. She sang, sweet and light, of waves and tides, although I never could remember the words or tune. Her song was accompanied by the rush and babble of water. I was floating in that water, high banks on either side, drifting along as if I was a piece of riverweed. No other thoughts were in my head at that time. I couldn't remember my past life and never once imagined any sort of future. I was in limbo, buoyed up by the woman's sweet humming.

Just once, I saw a face: a man's features, an older man, with salt-and-pepper hair that drifted down to his shoulders and a beard that drifted down to his chest. I still remember how his speedwell eyes caught my attention. When he smiled, I saw his teeth had a wide gap at the front and a gleam of gold at the back. Finally he spoke:

"You return to us, Sabrina. Make the effort, love. We're all waiting for you. It's going to be a good life, Sabrina, you'll see. You'll see."

He went on whispering and smiling, and I know I tried to reach him, hang on to him because he was the only thing in my universe at that moment and I didn't want to lose him. I didn't even care that he called me Sabrina. I'd forgotten my name, and the word seemed enchanting on his tongue. When his image began to fade, I opened my eyes because I was so sick to lose the sight of him.

I had not known right then, but this was the strongest spirit world experience I'd had up until that point. I'd only begun to suspect anything at all, when, the following October, Philip once again drove me up to Bangor. The Howells had sent me a get-well card, promising to keep my room open until I made it. It was Bren who opened the door to my knock when we arrived.

"Sabbie!" he exclaimed and gave me a beaming smile—big gap between his front teeth and a gleam of gold at the back.

FIVE

HAROLD STREET IS A narrow road filled with ex–local authority houses, built almost sixty years back in pairs. I'm the corner house, so I've got the biggest plot. There's actually room for a garage—somewhere I could put Mini Ha Ha, my dependable little car, instead of leaving her out on the road at night where she's all exposed and vulnerable. But no chance of that—my landlord's understanding of property improvement is a splash of cheap white paint each time someone new moves in.

Three years ago, this garden was nothing but a mass of unkempt grass, and the only things that grew out of it were rusting motorcycle parts. I've spent hours getting it how I want it. My front door is on the side wall, so that's where I laid enough flagstones to call a patio and put my patio table and chairs. There's a spinster's hanky lawn behind it and flower borders on each side of the path leading to the front gate. When I sit on my patio, I can see everyone walking up and down the street . . . and they can see me clearly over my low brick wall. So many neighbours gatecrashed last summer's parties that I thought about offering games and rides for ticket sales.

The things I'd bought at the boot sale were pulling at my arm sockets by the time I'd finished my mile walk home. I dug into my jacket pocket for keys as I sauntered down the side path. I was deep in thought, trying to work out just what impression I'd left on Rey. A brainless smile was hovering over my lips as I became aware of someone leaning on the side of my porch, and I returned to the real world with a bang.

"Ivan! What are you doing here?"

"Waiting for you," said Ivan. He threw his half-smoked cigarette onto the path and twisted his left shoe over it several times. "Couldn't work out where you'd gone this early on a Sunday."

"Car boot." I lifted my bags as if pumping iron with them.

Ivan stared for several seconds. "You do have some odd hobbies."

"Why didn't you phone?"

"Thought I'd surprise you."

"Congrats, you succeeded."

"You were daydreaming about something, that's for sure. Hope it was me."

I dumped my boot sale booty in the porch but didn't go so far as to open the door. "Actually, Ivan, I didn't know where I stood with you when you left yesterday. I was wondering if I'd see you again."

He grinned. "Babe! You take life way too seriously."

"I do?"

He slid his arms around my waist, catching his kiss on the corner of my mouth. I put my hands gently on the sides of his face, and closed my eyes. Ivan's not the sort to drop a butterfly kiss. He starts out with full passion overdrive and moves up the scale. On Friday night that was a real turn-on, but something had gone missing. I

45

shifted my mouth to his ear and whispered in it. "I'd love to do this, Ivan, but I can't, not right now."

"'Course you can."

"I have to get ready for a client."

He began nuzzling at my neck. I could feel his teeth pretend to bite, sharp as a puppy's. "Don't you ever take a break?"

"Not if I want to pay the rent."

"Ring them up and cancel, sweetheart. I'll pay your rent."

I laughed. "Nice try. But I actually love my work, rent or not."

"When am I going to see you properly?"

"How about Wednesday evening? Come round, I'll cook something."

"Are you telling me you're working every evening between now and then?"

"Yes, Ivan. My clients mostly work too. I'm busiest at weekends and after four in the afternoon."

Ivan shrugged. He nestled his mobile in the palm of his hand. His fingers moved fast over the keys, like the fat legs of some intelligent insect, searching for his calendar. "Yeah, I can come straight from the office, if you like. Six-ish?"

"Make it seven," I said. "I'll probably have to shop for food."

He leaned into me and we kissed again. I wanted to ask him to not turn up without warning another time, but I didn't like to admit how uncomfortable I'd felt when I realized he'd been watching the stupid grin on my face.

"Seen any more of that copper?"

"No, of course not." The denial was out of my mouth before I could stop to ask myself why I was lying.

"What did he want, in the end?"

"One of my clients got himself arrested. It's okay, he's not in any trouble. Mistaken identity, almost."

"That's good. You got me worried. Thought my girlfriend was a known criminal, for a minute."

"Yep, that's me. A price on my head in nine counties."

I watched him lope along the path and waved as the gate clanged behind him. I went into the kitchen and made myself a sandwich. Ivan's parting quip was ringing in my ears—not the *known criminal* part but the *my girlfriend* part. I wasn't ready to consider Ivan anything more than a casual date. We were as different as a ladybird is from a greenfly.

I grinned. *So long as I'm the ladybird*, I thought, munching on a radish.

———

"So pleased to see you, Sabbie," exclaimed my four o'clock. "How are you doing today?"

Marianne Meyer had the faultless English accent of the Dutch, and she was always rather formal in her politeness. She towered over me as I let her in. She bordered on six feet in height, favouring well-cut slacks that glided against the concave curve of her abdomen and floated in a boot-cut around her stiletto heels. Her hair was as silky blond as mine is crinkly black and almost as long. She favoured small, tight tops that enhanced her beautiful breasts. At first I wondered about boob jobs, but now I'm sure that everything she displayed was real. She's just a lucky girl—and that extended to her life. She had a fit bloke who adored her, a big family back in the Netherlands that meant a lot to her, and until recently she'd been accelerating through the cut-throat world of public relations.

Yet she came to me over a month ago in quite a state. She'd taken weeks off work, lying in bed for most of the day, swallowing pills her doctor had prescribed, and trying to puzzle out the extreme reaction she'd had to the news that the firm was downsizing. Yes, everyone had become jumpy about re-interviewing for their jobs, but Marianne could happily tell me she felt quite confident that she'd keep hers. At first I couldn't offer a crumb of help. I'd been completely stumped. Whenever I had journeyed into Marianne's spirit world, everything seemed calm, well ordered. Cheerful, even. Nothing my guides offered me to take back to Marianne had rung any bells with her at all, and her meticulously kept dream diary looked as benign and mellow as Ovaltine, just as her life had been—until the day she'd taken the phone call about the threat of redundancies and suffered a complete emotional breakdown right there in the office.

There were no gaps in her life into which this trauma could have fallen—no messy relationships, no wicked stepfather, no previous job losses, no reason at all that her psyche might have taken this knock. Four weeks into our contract, I was wondering if I'd ever be able to help. I'd cut some old greetings cards into a pile of data sheets and noted down every scrap of information I had on her, setting my record cards out over the desk, trying to make sense of it: the stages of her life, the people she knew, the events of the last year, the symbols I'd brought back from my journeys, details of Marianne's dreams, conversations, memories, repetitions. I'd shuffled them randomly then tried them in various orders, but it wasn't until I laid them in columns that I saw the weight I'd put on Marianne's past— her childhood, her lovers—rather than looking at her workplace. My gut feeling was that her problems had little to do with her job, but I was more than happy to be proved wrong.

I had taken time to spiritually journey to Marianne's office. I had left my brook with Trendle trotting at my side and walked in my mind until I'd suddenly found myself in a confined space no bigger than a box room, nearly filled with a desk of dark polished wood. In the centre of the desk a black telephone sat up proudly as if begging to be answered. It had to half a century old, with a circular dial and a fabric cord. It shrieked an outmoded ring tone … *brum, brum* … *brum brum* … that echoed inside my head like a constant cry of pain.

"Answer it," Trendle had said. I'd lifted the receiver. It was as heavy and cool as a stone. It smelt of chemicals and dust.

"Hello?" I said, feeling foolish.

"Your name is on this document." It was a man's voice, cultured but gruff, as if he'd smoked too many cigarettes.

"Who is this?" I asked.

"Don't tell anyone I called you."

"What?" My voice rose. "Are you a spirit?"

"I suggest you try to stay calm. Panic is your enemy."

"I'm not panicking," I threw back, but suddenly that wasn't true. The receiver was sticky with sweat under my hand.

"Don't bother packing your things."

The lined clicked dead and buzzed in my ear.

I had stood in the silent, close room and felt it revolve around me until it faded from my sight. At last I had something different, something with an edge. I had no idea what I'd been given, but I was eager to tell Marianne.

I gave her a spontaneous hug as we settled down in the therapy room. "How's work going, now you're back?" I asked, as I retrieved the notes of that last journey.

"Things are all right. I feel sometimes wobbly."

"But you manage."

Marianne nodded. I wouldn't have noticed in normal lighting, but in the flickering glow of the candle, I could see that her cheeks were covered with a fine layer of perspiration. "I get through the day."

"Have you heard anything further about the redundancies?"

"Rumours are still flying around the building. But there are many people affected, not just me." She examined her delicately pinked nails. "I don't know why I took it that bad. No one else on the list had such a reaction. I did not know how pathetic I could be."

"Rubbish. You come across as a strong person."

"No longer. When they re-interview the posts, going off sick like that will count against me." Marianne sat on the lounger with her hands folded like tidy napkins in her lap. They didn't fidget, those hands, ever. They exuded utter composure.

"We are going to discover what this is about. Then you can walk into work like the old Marianne and knock 'em flat."

She shook her head. "I lost my nerve. You should never lose your nerve. At Simpson and Grouche, if you lose your nerve, you are as good as dead."

"Dead?"

"Dead in the water, as they say. Washed up."

"Marianne, could you describe your office to me?"

She didn't even blink at my sudden change of direction. She'd gotten used to my often-bizarre questions. "Oh, it is good. Very light, you know. We grow plants in the windows."

I nodded. "You're not cramped for space?"

"No, it is open plan."

I beat a tattoo with my pen on the paper. "Remind me who phoned you that afternoon?"

"My line manager, Will Clyde. He is a nice guy. He sent me flowers when I was off."

"What's his voice like?"

She frowned briefly. "Like … any man's."

"No distinguishing features?"

"Yes, he is Scottish, he has a slight accent."

"Can you remember his exact words?"

Marianne shook her head. "I can't remember much about what happened, Sabbie."

"Yes. Of course. You were in shock—"

"Fit. It was like a fit."

"You collapsed."

"I could not move. Like Lot's wife."

I tried to cast my mind back to my years with Gloria. She'd had a strict Pentecostal upbringing and was always quoting things from the Bible. "Like a pillar of salt?" I hazarded. "Like you'd been petrified?"

"Petrified is a good word," Marianne agreed.

"You don't recall anything?"

"No. Strange, that is, as I generally have a good memory."

I placed the writeup of my last journey in her lap. "Just look at the words in capital letters."

She glanced down. Almost instantly, she gave a sort of hiccup, as though forcing back tears.

"Do the words make you feel a particular way?"

"The same." Her breath was scraping through her throat as if it were closing over. "The very same, Sabbie. The words he used … the list for re-interviewing … that is what he said, more or less."

"Phones are funny things, sometimes," I said. "You can't see the person. It's easy to muddle voices or mix one turn of phrase with another. In the end, it's the words that will have an effect."

She trained her gaze on me. The only indication that I'd rattled her was the way the paper quivered in her hand. "What do you mean, Sabbie?"

"I just want you to consider the possibility that you didn't have that dreadful reaction because your job was on the line. Maybe, sometime in the past, you heard a similar voice, or similar words that really were a threat. To your life, even."

"But, I know that cannot be so."

"You were never mugged, or anything like that?"

"Nothing, Sabbie."

"I'd like you to read the whole report of my last journey. I'll go and make us drinks to give you a moment. The usual for you?"

"Yes, please."

Already, her head was bent. I left her to it and went to put the kettle on. I knew every word of my report almost by heart. It had been the shortest journey I'd taken for her, but it was pivotal. I carried two lemon and ginger teas back in and set Marianne's in front of her. I took a quick sip of mine. Most of the ginger went up my nose, making me blink.

"What do you think?"

"I do not think this is my office. But this man on the phone. The words make me tremble."

I was sipping away at my too-hot tea, as if I wanted to be in sympathetic pain with my client. "It's not your office, of course not. It belongs in the Fifties, or even before. I've been wondering if the reason you can't remember these words is because they didn't happen in this lifetime."

I watched her mouth fall open in slow motion. I waited for her to reject my suggestion out of hand, but she was thinking about it in her usual unruffled manner.

"You think I lost my job in a previous life?"

"No, Marianne. I think you lost your life. Because you were on a document."

"How would I ever know?" she asked. "How would I ever remember such a thing?"

"You *don't* remember. Maybe you never will. But if a voice said the exact words to you for a second time, that might have made you feel as dreadful … as *petrified* … as it did the first time."

She gave a slow nod. "I see."

"Naturally, you might not believe that people have more than one life."

"Not believe, perhaps. But I would consider it." She gave me a smile that almost reached her eyes. "Is there anything I can do?"

"You know, there are therapists who specializing in taking people back into their former lives under hypnosis. I could do this in a shamanic way, teach you to journey for yourself, so your guides can show you some of your previous pasts. But it's up to you whether you go for either of these options."

"I don't want to change my therapist. I like what you are doing."

"That's reasonable." I touched her hand. "Maybe we should concentrate on healing the knock you've taken, so you get back to feeling whole and balanced. I'd like to explain the rudiments of experiencing a trance state. Then, as well as keeping a dream diary, you can enter your shamanic consciousness and work with your own guides and guardians."

"It sounds exciting."

"Hope so. It may be scary too—I'll show you how to deal with anything too difficult."

"I think this will suit me better than hypnotherapy. I like to be in control."

"I'd noticed," I said, smiling at her. "The entire point is to empower you. Get that power you had back inside you." I stood up. "Are you ready for the first step?"

She stood too. "Yes. I am ready."

"See? You're up for anything. S&G would be crazy to let you go." I altered the shape of the sun lounger so that Marianne could fully relax on it. "I'm going to ask you to lay a scarf over your eyes."

Marianne dipped down and unzipped her cherry-red boots. It was like watching a gymnast perform a floor exercise. As she sank back onto the lounger, she said, "You think I will be a good student, Sabbie? I don't believe I have any psychic powers in me."

"You won't need any more than you naturally have. We all have spirit world guides, whether we know it or not. Just let your mind go where they bid it go. You'll surprise yourself." I draped a fleecy rug over her knees and went about setting up a gentle drumming CD. I pulled the wicker chair closer so that I could guide her through her first journey.

"This is encouraging, is it not?" she whispered.

"Yes," I whispered back. "We've moved on today. That's good."

The scarf was over her eyes and her breath was already calming. For the first time since she had walked into my house, I began to feel positive about Marianne and the work we could do together. And that gave me the confidence to believe I could eventually help Cliff.

SIX

"Sabbie, is that you?"

"Cliff!" I barely recognised my client's voice on the phone. It sounded like the guts had been taken out of it.

"I need to see you, Sabbie. Now."

"Cliff, it's Wednesday evening. Can it wait for your Saturday appointment?"

"You haven't heard."

"Heard what?"

"Another child's gone missing."

"What? A child?"

"Yes. Someone has kidnapped a child. Today. They're already saying it's like the Josh Sutton case."

I closed my eyes against his words, as if that would make them less sickening.

"Sabbie? Can I see you? I need to talk to someone."

"Are you sure that should be me?"

"I saw my solicitor earlier and she advised me to carry on as normal. So I plan to go to work. But if I came over now, we'd have a couple of hours."

So many of my clients are vulnerable...needy. When I first set up my practice, I would spend hours with them over the teapot in my kitchen, but now I charge for all my time. This makes me feel like a money-grabbing bitch sometimes, but I force myself to stick to my rule. "Okay, Cliff. We could bring forward your Saturday session. Is that acceptable?"

"That's great, Sabbie. I can't thank you enough."

After he'd rung off, I speed-dialled Ivan's number.

"Babe!" he cried down the phone.

"Ivan, I'm so sorry. I'm going to have to cancel tonight."

"What?"

"Client in crisis."

"Tell them to get lost."

"Big crisis, Ivan. I can't do that."

"Bloody well can. It's principles, Sabbie. You shouldn't put work above us, just when things are hotting up so good..." I heard kissing noises. They did not make me want to squirm, except from embarrassment.

"I'm gutted too, Ivan," I said, and this was true, but mainly, I recognised, because I'd already started to prepare the meal we were supposed to be sharing and now it was going to get ruined.

"I'd cancel a client for you," said Ivan. "Like a shot."

"I honestly don't think somebody's financial portfolio can compare. I won't go into details, but this chap's pretty desperate."

"Right. It is a *he* then?"

I wasn't going to give that remark any sort of credence. "Sorry, I can't do tonight—end of story."

"When can I see you? I'm gagging, Sabbie."

I scanned my plans for the weekend. "What about Sunday evening? We could meet for a drink?"

"I'll have to be satisfied with that, won't I?" Ivan's breathing echoed in my ear, as if he was jogging in an empty room.

"Yes." I tried to make my voice sound encouraging. "What about the Curate's Egg? Eightish?"

As soon as I got Ivan off the phone, I zapped the TV remote. The first feature on the local news was about the missing child. I turned the volume up on the reporter.

Five-year-old Aidan Rodderick disappeared from his school in the village of Morganswick this afternoon. When his mum Stella came to pick him up, staff realized he was no longer on the premises. A police hunt has already been initiated.

Avon and Somerset police say that the boy may have simply wandered off, but they're asking the public to be vigilant and to report any odd occurrences they've witnessed in the last three to four hours. The number to contact is…

A photo of a boy with a rascal's smile and a mess of blond hair popped up on the screen as the number rolled by underneath. *Trusting eyes*, I thought, knowing it to be hindsight's intuition.

The news items moved on. I sat on the sofa, unable to get going, feeling generally out of sorts. At first I thought the news report was affecting me. But when I analysed it, I realized I was still smarting over the phone call with Ivan. Why was I giving this guy houseroom? He had a complete lack of respect for my work and my independence. I punched at a cushion. I couldn't pretend that I didn't fancy him, with his shaggy-dog hair and Italian suits, but I never can trust my intuition when it comes to men who have the hots for me. I sighed, smoothed the cushion out, and placed it at the corner of the sofa with a pat. I was pleased I'd chosen the Egg as a meeting place. There were quiet corners where the live music didn't overpower conversation. I'd be as gentle as I could about it, but on Sunday evening, I was going to have to ditch Ivan.

The doorbell tinkled its song, and I went to let Cliff Houghton in.

———

If Cliff had sounded in a bad way over the phone, he looked a hundred percent worse in the flesh. I took him directly into my therapy room and sat to face him.

There was a silence. I wasn't sure what to say to the man, and Cliff seemed to have lost the power of speech. Finally, I decided to be more forceful than I felt.

"Why are you so frightened, Cliff?"

"I don't know." His hand worked at his mouth.

"Have you got something you're hiding? Something you're not telling me?"

I was expecting—hoping at least—for an instant denial, but instead, Cliff gaped at me, his long legs crossing and recrossing. "Something to hide." His voice was as tight as a wrung-out cloth. "I must have, mustn't I?"

"What is it?"

"I don't know. That's why I came to you. To find out."

I didn't reply. A disturbing thought was busy crossing my mind. I should have phoned the police, as well as Ivan, while Cliff was still on his way. But it was too late to worry about that now.

"I've been thinking about the sack of hair," said Cliff.

"Good. Anything come up?"

"Bits of hair? That's not exactly scary stuff is it? But the picture you drew. It brings on a mood…"

"What sort of mood? Can you explain?"

He shook his head. He wasn't wearing his hair in a ponytail today, and hanks the colour and shape of rats' tails fell over his face. He brushed them back and tucked them behind his ears. Cliff liked his hair anything but shorn.

"Have you been writing down your dreams?" I was expecting an obstinate response and was taken aback to see the pain on his face as he yanked the notebook out of an inner jacket pocket.

"It's not much. I was half asleep."

"That's good," I said. "Best time to write down dreams, really." I flipped through the pages and came to a double-spread of huge, black writing that sloped down the unlined pages. It was hard to decipher, but not impossible.

Man in my front garden, it began. *Shirley tied him to the rose bushes with garden twine. I walked on up the street, scared the neighbours would think it was anything to do with me. When I went into Mrs. Harvard's house, there was a hole in her kitchen floor…*

I looked up, a huge, artificial smile covering my face.

"It's a muddle," Cliff said. "Shirley was a girl in my school. Haven't seen her in years. The garden was hers—we used to go round there in a gang." His cheeks darkened. "You know, play 'mummies and daddies'. But Mrs. Harvard lives up the road from me. She runs a greasy spoon. I've never seen her kitchen."

"Health and Safety'll be after her, if she's got a hole in it," I said, hoping for a smile I didn't get. "Be easy on yourself, Cliff, this is a pretty typical dream. Anyone could have had it." I put the book on my desk. "The real breakthrough is that you had a dream and recorded it."

"I guess," said Cliff.

"How far away from your childhood neighbourhood do you live?" I asked.

"The other side of Finchbury."

"You never fancied moving on?"

Cliff shrugged. "Where would I go?"

"Does your mum live there?"

"Yes, Mum's still in the house I grew up in. She has her friends—Women's Institute, Church Council, that sort of thing. My baby sister's long gone; she's a teacher in Guildford."

"Tell me about your dad," I said, thinking back to the sovereign.

"We had some brilliant times together, until he was taken down by leukaemia. He'd worked at Hinckley Point after he'd finished his apprenticeship in engineering. He left to start his own business. Mum was convinced that the power station caused his cancer. Not that they ever admitted liability." He shifted his position until he was on the very edge of the tubular frame of the sun lounger, his bony elbows digging into his knees. The lounger creaked.

"You miss him still, don't you?" When he didn't answer, I moved quickly on. "We've agreed this is your Saturday appointment, Cliff. And as I haven't yet journeyed for that session, I'm going to do that now, with you in the room. Usually, I get excellent results that way, so it can't be anything but beneficial. Are you up for that?"

"Yeah, I suppose."

I motioned for Cliff to get up so that I could lower the head of the lounger. "Okay, if you could just stretch out, Cliff, I'll cover you with a rug. I'd like you to be warm and relaxed."

"I can't lie down on that."

I was caught off guard, struggling with the ratchets of the lounger. I straightened up and looked at him. His hand was pulling at his mouth. His eyes were wide and suspiciously wet. Hanks of his hair had fallen over his face again.

"Don't worry, I'll talk you through the process before we begin. You don't have to do anything—I'm going to be doing all the shamanic stuff."

"It's not the process. It's that thing." He pointed at my lounger. "I had an accident with one when I was a kid. I fell off. Had to be taken to casualty. It's given me a bit of a phobia."

I stretched my mouth into a smile. My lips felt numb. I had no idea why Cliff's phobia made me feel so uncomfortable. "When you sit on it," I observed, "you almost tip yourself off, you're so close to the edge."

"They're easily unbalanced," Cliff said, reasonably. "Quite dangerous, really."

Yeah, I thought, *just like escaped tigers or shifting sands*. But all I said was, "It'll be a shame if you can't make yourself comfortable."

"I'll lie on the floor." Instantly, Cliff let his lanky body down onto the laminate, seeming not to care that it would be hard and chilled.

I brought over some floor cushions, and he shifted to lie on those. He hadn't taken off his trainers, and I could see grass and mud on the soles. Maybe he'd walked over my lawn. I covered him with the rug.

"Are you sure you're all right down there?" I picked up his right wrist and wound a plaited cord around it.

"What's that?" he asked, staring at the white, brown, and green strands of silk.

"It will join us shamanically," I said. "It symbolises the three other-worlds—higher, lower, and middle planes of existence. All of which I can explore to find solutions."

I turned off the lights but left the candle flickering on the central table, then pressed Play on the CD player. The disc was a recording of myself beating a goatskin drum over and over. Since the lounger was free, I settled myself onto it. The more relaxed I was, the better I would journey. I wound the other end of the cord around my own wrist. Now Cliff and I were so tightly linked, there was no doubt in my mind I would find his spirit world.

"Cliff," I said. "Are you all right about this?"

"I expected them to come for me. I suppose that's the reason I got in the car and came over here. I thought the police would take me in."

"Why—" I broke off, because my throat closed over, paralysed for a moment. "Why d'you say that?"

"Morganswick is less than five miles from Finchbury."

I nodded, trying to stay calm and clear-headed. The thump of the pulse in my ears didn't help matters. "So," I said, grasping the nettle, "where were you at three o'clock this afternoon?"

"Still in bed. I'm working tonight. I didn't get up till four."

"I don't suppose anyone saw you?"

"No one sees you when you live alone."

A grisly thought struck me. Cliff was genuinely obsessed with the murder of little Josh. Was that because his subconscious remembered his part in it? Had Cliff woken up at four, or had he been *coming round* after doing whatever it was he'd done to Aidan Rodderick?

As I struggled with this, I began to wonder if Rey and his chums were moving along the same line of supposition. Why hadn't they already called on Cliff? Had he been watched since he was released on Saturday? Perhaps the police already knew that he'd not left his flat all day. I was sincere in hoping this was the case. As I lay down beside him, a dark scarf over my eyes, my heart cracked like a flag in a gale.

———

The drumming hit my ears, but the singing centre of its note entered my body through my solar plexus. For a moment or two, I could feel my client floating alongside, coupled to me by the silken umbilicus. I let the drumbeat reverberate around my mind and suddenly I felt the soles of my bare feet touch cool grass. I could hear the lullaby of the brook even before I saw it.

My spirit portal. The grass is tightly cropped by rabbits, which are shy, but I often spot them loping out of sight. The heather has a dusty, light floral scent. If I stay still, the choristers—blackcaps, robins, and thrushes—belt out their tunes. At night, when there is usually a cloudless sky showing the moon, a nightingale sings. On the opposite bank of the brook runs a thick line of wild hedge, always ablaze with colour. There is hawthorn, blackthorn, and the autumn gold of field maple. In winter sun, the dogwood glows like amber. I've been starting out from here since I first journeyed with my shaman teacher years ago. The paths that stretch from this place in every direction have been forged by me on many journeys, and I never know when a new one will appear.

I settled onto the mossy bank of my brook, my bare feet dangling in the water. I could feel a tickling sensation. Trendle was licking my toes. His thick coat shone with water.

"Come on in," he said, and I slid down into the dark green depths.

When Trendle guides me into the stream, it becomes bottomless—it reaches into the underworld where shadowy spirits live. Trendle swam beside me as I sank, stems of weed tugging at my hair and ankles.

"Here," said Trendle, and I followed him along a narrow, unlit tunnel of water. I could barely see his fur glisten in the darkness, but I felt the flick his tail on my outstretched fingers. I let myself breathe in— there was no need to hold my breath in the water of the spirit world.

We came out into a muddy lane with high hedges of hazel and ash. The overhanging branches met above my head, winter bare and black. The lane was so gloomy, I had to squint to make out the silhouette of a cottage against the cloud-covered sky.

I knew we were close to the grim little room where I'd seen the sack of hair. I willed myself towards the building until I was standing outside a door, the sort of door country dwellings had in the olden days, with wide, ornate hinges, rusting at their edges. The door's black paint was peeling and smeared with mud, as if someone had kicked at it. The name of the house was prominently displayed on an iron plate.

Brokeltuft Cottage.

I put my hand on the round knob of the iron handle. It was as cold as a summer drink. When I turned it, I heard the clang of a latch lifting inside. The door swung open. Carpetless wooden stairs rose up before me. A passageway led past them, into a kitchen that hadn't been replaced since the Fifties. I could see the gas cooker and the kettle steaming on its hob.

"What … what shall I do, Trendle?"

"Go on." The otter lay along my arm. His coat still dripped from the journey, although I felt bone dry. His voice was in my head. "We have to put fear to one side and probe this world if we want answers." He twitched his whiskers and water drops flew from them.

Step by step I advanced along the passage. I remembered the menacing presence standing close behind me in the little room with the sack of hair. Would I find that presence in the kitchen? The whistle of the kettle became shrill. A girl stepped out of the shadows and switched off the gas.

"Want a cuppa?" she asked me.

I almost sobbed with relief.

"Take sugar?" she asked, appraising me briefly. She was not even my height, just a girl in her teens. I saw her platinum blonde hair clearly. It was dark at the roots and curling at the ends. But, as I often find on my journeys, her face was quite obscured, sort of wishy-washy. I'm never sure why I can't see every detail in a trance clearly, but it is usually so. The girl slammed a cup without a saucer down beside the cooker and opened a larder door. She took out a packet of biscuits and sliced through the packet with a bread knife. The biscuits were thin rectangles, pale brown and studded all over their surface with black dots; little bits of crushed currant.

"Garibaldi biscuits," said the girl. "That's all there ever is. Bloody squashed flies. Makes you puke to think of it." She snapped a thin slab of speckled biscuit between her thumb and fingers. "Go on, help yourself."

I looked down at Trendle. "Is this a gift?" I asked, meaning should I take the symbol back to Cliff.

Trendle blinked once. "For you, dear," he said into my mind.

"Bloody take one, will you?" The girl's voice had changed. She wasn't joking around any longer. "Take it and get outta here."

I thought it wise to do her bidding. I didn't even stop for confirmation from my guide. I ran along the passage, clutching a Garibaldi. The massive front door slammed behind me with a boom.

The light was fading fast into evening. I breathed relief out, and my breath whitened before me. I took a step, scrunching over dead leaves.

"This is Cliff's spirit world, isn't it?" I said to Trendle. "No wonder he feels like he does. It needs cleaning up."

"We can't do anything here today," said Trendle. "Except leave the food as an offering to his guardians."

It was good advice. I crumbled the biscuit as if feeding birds. My fingers felt sticky from the currants. "Surely we can help him? His spirit feels so … shattered."

"You know that Cliff's soul is in pieces. It's going to take a long time to bring them together. Let's walk with caution."

I nodded. Trendle was my conscience, my inner reservations and gut feelings, as well as my spirit friend; I would listen to whatever he had to tell me.

I stared at the hedge on the far side of the lane. There was not a leaf or bud to be seen. I have a hazel tree in my front garden and at the moment it's festooned with glorious dangly catkin earrings, but it was still deep winter in this place. I bent a sapless twig and it snapped off in my hand. "You're not dead, are you?" I asked it. The wind rustled through the brittle branches in reply.

"Nothing here is dead," said Trendle, soft-voiced. "Just debilitated."

In the depths of the thicket was a single, perfect hazel catkin. The branches were rough against my hand as I reached in and let it rest on my palm like a caterpillar, a dusting of pollen staining my skin.

This was the sign I should take back to Cliff, something hopeful for the future. As I thought this, the drumming that was still vibrating at the back of my mind changed its rhythm, calling me home.

———

Cliff had fallen into a deep sleep. No wonder I'd been able to slip so quietly in to his world. Gently, I untied my arm from the braid that connected us and went into the kitchen to boot up my laptop. I recorded my journey, saved the file, and printed out a copy for Cliff. I crept into the therapy room and slipped the folded paper into his notebook. With sudden resolution, I drew a child's representation of the cottage on the back of the paper, concentrating the details into the door, with its round handle and wrought-iron plaque.

Cliff let out a snore, and I dropped the pencil in alarm as the noise exploded into the silence of the room. Yet I didn't want to wake him. He would have to work through the night, so it seemed good for him to catch an hour now.

I scrabbled for the pencil, thinking that I should also draw a representation of the catkin. But I realized I could do better than that. I crept away and let myself out through the front door. It was a drizzly evening. The streetlights splashed Renoir orange over the pavement. I breathed in the cool air. Against the low wall that separates the house from Harold Street, I'd planted a line of bushes—a pretty pussy willow, a Japanese maple, and a corkscrew hazel. At their base, daffodils pierced the soil like green lances, almost ready to open. I stepped over the soil to the hazel. The branches were laden with fine-haired golden fingers. I love to see passersby stopping to touch the catkins or put their nose to the pollen. The occasional delinquent will break off a couple of twigs and carry them away—these are usually elderly ladies, keen to plant them as cuttings. Despite these attacks, my trees are thriving.

As I plucked a single yellow catkin, a cry of anguish arose, as if the young tree wailed at its loss. I sprang around. The noise was coming from inside my house, a low growl that progressed up several scales until it wavered hysterically on a top note. It was a petition for the kind of help no one could offer, and it made my spine jangle.

I rushed in. Cliff Houghton was kneeling on the floor by my desk, vomiting into my waste bin.

"Cliff?" He looked up at me with bloodshot eyes, his pupils tiny pinholes at each centre. I grabbed some tissues and thrust them into his hand. "Come and sit down." I helped him shuffle to the wicker seat and he fell into it, huddled with his arms tucked around his knees. "I'll get you some water."

On the way to the kitchen, I grabbed the bin he'd filled and dumped it by the kitchen door. When I got back to him, he was babbling something incomprehensible. I could see the cold sweat like oil smeared across his face, and he was panting as if he'd run for miles. He gulped the water I offered. The skein of plaited silk dangled from his wrist like broken jewellery.

I bent over to loosen it. With a sharp movement, he grabbed my arm.

"What did you see?"

His tone was urgent; I knew I had to be as accurate as possible. "A house on a country lane," I said, keeping my voice light. "Someone was there to offer me tea and biscuits—Garibaldi biscuits."

"That place," muttered Cliff. "I'd forgotten it. How did I do that? I don't understand." He screwed his fingers to his mouth.

My vision flickered. A gauzy veil fell over it, creating a double-image—a glimpse of Cliff's otherworld self. I stared as his grey eyes seemed to travel back into his head until they were pools of murky water. The fingers round his mouth twisted the skin as if it were rubber. Grotesque growths protruded from his nostrils, green as sea cucumbers, writhing over his cheeks. As quickly as it came, the vision faded. I wasn't able to speak for a moment, but he was still gripping my wrist like an iron band; without thinking, I yanked myself free.

I've been having these "psychic events" since I started to train seriously as a shaman. Despite the turnaround in my life, I was still as bad as ever at picking guys. A loser called Jon was my man back then—or at least, I was his girl. One night, sitting at a bar table, chatting, I saw the film of reality lift from his face. For a second or two, the otherworld Jon was revealed; snarling mouth, over-long canines, bloodshot eyes, flaring nostrils. I was so shocked I dropped my bottle of beer. I thought I'd seen the devil himself.

At the time, I hoped a moment like that would never happen again, but they've increased over the years, and now I welcome them. They are not all unpleasant. I might see angels behind the masks people wear, or the features of a trusting infant, and this understanding helps me work with my clients. Cliff was carrying a form of parasitic spirit. These "intrusions" are the leeches of the spirit world, and they attach to people in extreme circumstances. It didn't mean that Cliff was the architect of appalling deeds. Rather, that he was troubled by shades of dread—that, some time in the past, his soul had been injured.

"It was a bad place," he said. He was talking to himself, though, not to me.

I took a deep breath. "It wasn't all bad. There was some hope."

I looked about for the catkin I'd picked as my returning gift from the spirit world. It lay on the laminate of the floor, crushed underfoot. I bit my lip at the sight, not knowing how to continue.

Cliff pulled at the silk cord. It came away from his arm. He handed it to me. "No. There's no hope now."

———

It was the picture that had released the memory. He'd picked up the sheet of paper and seen the sketch I'd drawn. In the instant he read the name on the cottage door, a memory had flooded into him, not just as images, but as sensations, smells, tastes, pain. He'd cast up his accounts into the nearest receptacle.

"I must have blocked it out for all these years," he said. Saliva drooled from the corner of his slack mouth and he dabbed at it with the tissues. "I've heard of women who do that about bad memories, but I'd never really believed it happened."

"What—What is it … you forgot?"

Cliff was quiet for several minutes. He stared into the middle distance. I wasn't sure if he was still summoning up memories or simply trying to put the ones he had into words. Finally he said, "I'd just turned eleven."

Then I knew. A dreadful sensation flooded through me, a choking feeling that made me want to back off or cover Cliff's mouth with my hand to stop him telling me, and I thought of the way he covered his mouth, as if he too, always had that feeling. To my horror, I found myself saying, "What happened, Cliff?"

"It must have been the start to the summer holidays, because Dad was having chemotherapy, I think. Anyway, he was in hospital and Mum and Rachel were going to visit, but I'd asked if I could go round Greg's." He managed a wonky smile. "I hated going into the hospital. Dad would be strapped to this bag of fluid, which seemed to do him harm, not good, and the pyjamas Mum had bought him specially for the treatments didn't fit him anymore, they hung on his bones. Greg had a tent that his dad let him put up on their lawn. We used to sleep in it, some nights. Thought it was a great adventure.

"Anyway, I think Greg and I built a sort of ramp affair out of planks for our bikes that afternoon. Mine hit a rogue nail. We tried to repair it using Greg's kit, but his dad told us it still had a slow leak. He made me promise not to ride it until I'd bought a new inner tube. He wanted to take me home, but I said I'd be fine pushing the bike. I took my time, though. I was worried I'd get well told off about the tyre. Mum got jumpy when Dad was in hospital."

The story seemed to be going nowhere as Cliff broke off to sip some more water. I knew I mustn't say a word or even move, even though I badly wanted to shift position. I was kneeling on the floor beside him, my knees digging into the laminate, but Cliff had grabbed my hand and was holding it as if it were the railing to a high balcony.

"It was a lovely evening. I can remember now, and that's so odd—like this memory has landed inside my head all in one piece. Even so, I was getting fed up of pushing the bike. I was a mile or so away from home when this car drew up beside me. There was a woman and a girl inside. The woman put her head out of the window and asked if I had far to go. I wasn't going to say no to a lift. Besides, I thought it was just a mum and her daughter." Cliff paused.

"But it wasn't," I prompted.

"No," said Cliff, emphatically shaking his head. "No. No. That's what they wanted you to believe, see? That it was all right, to get in the car." He barked a laugh. "The bike wouldn't fit properly. The three of us got it in somehow and drove along with the boot half open." He paused, as if just realizing something. "That was a masterstroke. They were so careful about the bike… *we'll get it home for you, safe and sound…*"

He breathed a wet, sucking breath. He was close to tears. I hung onto his hand for dear life. "The car drove off. I felt fine. The bike was in the boot. I was in the front. The woman kept looking back at the girl, cracking jokes. The girl laughed more than me. She laughed and laughed. Remembering it now, it might have been a scared laugh, but it never occurred to me that I was in any danger until I saw we weren't in Finchbury. I asked where we were going. The woman said she wanted to show us something."

The glass clunked against Cliff's teeth. He was panting.

"Can you remember faces… anything?"

"It's hazy. The girl felt older than me."

"Did she have long blonde hair?"

"It's hard to see her." He squeezed his eyes shut.

"Did you get out of the car, Cliff? I mean, d'you remember doing that?"

"We pulled up in a lane."

"High hedge, mostly hazel?"

"I don't know one tree from the next. It just felt … " He looked directly at me for the first time. "You wrote *gloomy*."

"It was gloomy. But it felt ominous."

"Yeah," he nodded. "Hostile. Made me want to run. But I didn't run. My bike was in the boot. I didn't know where I was. And anyway, you don't imagine … can't possibly imagine …"

"That people would mean you harm?"

Cliff mopped his mouth with the tissues. His hand shook. "The woman got me out of the car. She had the top of my arm and her grip hurt. I think she must have been hanging on to the girl as well, because she didn't knock. She yelled out. 'Fucking hurry up in there!' I was scared then, struggling in the woman's grip. We were standing in front of the door. The nameplate—Brokeltuft—it's a funny name. When I read it on your drawing …" He searched my face. "How did you get inside me like that?"

I shook my head. I could no more tell him than I could truly have swum underwater with Trendle. "What happened next? Did the door open?"

"I … I can't see what happened. The sensations are … I know it was … a bad place. Bad experience. Can't remember." He released my wrist. "I won't need to, will I? Isn't this enough?"

"It's not over, Cliff," I said.

"I never wanted this. This is a whole can of worms. Think I want these memories?"

"Isn't that why you came to me?"

"I was asking for a solution. Not this … horror!"

"Something terrible happened to you when you were a boy."

He nodded, his head shrouded by his hands.

"Something that's broken your—what I'd call your soul—into pieces. The way I work, as a shaman, is to find these pieces and put them back together."

"Like bits from a car engine?" asked Cliff, in a muffled voice.

"Precisely," I said, although *precisely* was not the best phrase for my manner of working. "And, while we're doing that, I think the other memories will come."

"Oh Jesus," cried Cliff. "God, no!" He shook his head, over and over, his eyes wide with terror.

"But you escaped," I said, chaffing his shoulder. "You saved yourself somehow."

"Did I?" Cliff rubbed his face with a hand, spreading the moisture. "I can't bear to think about what happened." He looked at me, his face appalled. "I want my memory back the way it was."

I could only shake my head. I didn't think that was a possibility.

"It must feel like you've received bad news," I said, looking at the dark rings around Cliff's eyes. He certainly didn't look well enough to do a night's work.

There were a million questions I longed to ask Cliff, but both of us were drained from the impromptu session. I felt he should go home to sleep. I rang the supermarket and told them he was poorly. "Will you be okay to drive home?" I asked, folding my phone closed.

Cliff nodded, too exhausted to reply. Personally, I felt I might sleep forever once my head was on a pillow. But something on the edge of my inner perception was jangling like a toy monkey's cymbals. I raised my head in the silence. A crash echoed from the hall. My chest exploded. I'd left the door open when I fetched the catkin. It had slammed against the wall.

"What was that?" Cliff's gaze flicked around the room.

"Maybe it was the wind," I whispered. But already I could hear footsteps.

SEVEN

THE SHADOWS OF TWO figures hovered outside the room. I gave a girlie shriek. The person already inside my home was spooking me, much less unwelcome visitors.

"This is the police," said a voice.

My fear slid away. "Get out of my house," I screeched. "Get out!"

Reynard Buckley walked towards me. A colleague—a heavily built younger man with a slick of black hair and the hooded eyes of a crow—followed him. They were holding open their IDs in tandem before them, as if the wallets were talismans that would protect them from evil.

"Sabbie," said Rey. "This is my colleague, DC Abbott. I'm afraid your door was open, so we came in. You'll find a constable outside, in case anyone ..."

"I've got a client here," I said.

"Would that be Clifford Houghton?" said Abbot.

They had come for him. I felt my body sag.

"So where is he?"

"Where is he?" I echoed, confused. I turned on the balls of my feet. The wicker chair was an empty vessel. Cliff was gone. My mind was so scrambled I was close to believing he'd become invisible.

The two plain-clothes officers stalked my house. Abbott took the stairs and I heard hard-heeled steps above my head. Rey strutted into the kitchen. I hovered in the hall.

"You've let him go," he accused. "Or have you hidden him somewhere?" He yanked at the handle of the back door, then noticed the bin full of Cliff's vomit.

"What on earth—" he began, but Abbott came thundering down the stairs at that minute, shaking his head. "Nothing up there."

"Sabbie!" Rey strode over, and I backed away from him. "You are going to cooperate. D'you hear? We have a child snatching *and* a murder to investigate."

Finally, I found my voice. "He was here," I said. "I've no idea." Something caught my attention. A strange, low-level sound was emanating from somewhere within the therapy room.

Step by slow step, I reached the desk and lifted the muslin, so that the birds on the fabric flapped and flew. Cliff was hunched under the surface, squashed against the wall, whimpering like a dog. Water oozed from inside his tightly closed eyelids.

I felt my own eyes scald with tears. "Cliff," I whispered. I extended a hand towards him and saw red marks on my wrist where he'd clutched at it earlier. "Cliff, it'll be okay." Cliff opened his eyes as if it was the hardest thing he'd ever done, and focused on me. As he whimpered, flecks of white spittle flew from his tight-closed lips.

"Got him, Gary!" yelled Rey. His trouser legs brushed against my extended arm. I looked up.

"Mr. Houghton didn't kidnap the child."

"You don't know that," said Rey.

"I do know it."

For the first time since he'd entered my house, Rey looked me full in my face. "One of your *spirits* tell you that, did they?"

"And my heart."

Rey didn't reply. He hunkered down, his badge in front of him like a miniature shield. "Mr. Houghton, we've met before; DS Buckley and DC Abbott from Bridgwater police station. Can you come out of there of your own accord, please, sir?"

Cliff crawled out and rose up, swaying on his long legs, clearly unable to take in what was going on. In seconds a couple of uniformed officers had marched him through my house, reciting the rhetoric of their caution. I suppose I had to be grateful they hadn't handcuffed him. I suppose I had to be grateful they hadn't handcuffed *me*.

Once Cliff was in the back of the police car, Rey walked back up the path towards me. He took his time, while I hung on to the door for support.

"I have to interview you," he said, "while the situation is still fresh in your mind."

I barked a laugh. "Trust me, tonight is never going to leave my mind."

"We can do it here or at the station." His eyes were focusing everywhere but on me. I was wondering where the chap I'd sat with at the boot sale, chatting about music, had gone.

"He isn't guilty of murder, Rey," I said, but my voice was so low I doubt he caught the words. Perhaps they were just for me.

"He ran away. He might have assumed we'd want to eliminate him from our enquiries. He should have stayed put. This was the first place we came after his own flat, and bingo, his car's outside."

"Then he didn't run far, did he?" I lurched away from him. There was a buzzing in my head. I got as far as the kitchen and hung on to the edge of the worktop to prevent myself keeling over.

Without warning, Rey was beside me. "Go and sit down," he said. "I'll make you a drink." He pulled a mint teabag out of the box and dangled it in front of me. "This okay?"

"Thanks."

"Sure you don't want me to slug in some cooking brandy?"

"Don't tempt me," I said, wondering in one part of my mind why Rey would imagine I could afford brandy in my cooking. I flopped down on the sofa. My heart had steadied a little, but my legs felt like well-washed ribbons.

"It's quite *bijou* in here, isn't it," said Rey. He started on the drink, with an appealing male hamfistedness.

"You mean cramped."

"No, not at all. It's very clever. You've knocked down a wall, haven't you?"

"That was before my time. It was a kitchen-cum when I arrived. But once I knew I'd use the room at the front for my therapies, I had to find somewhere to relax. The breakfast bar doubles as a computer desk. Then all I did was lay a bit of carpet and pick up a second-hand sofa." I shut my mouth quickly, realizing I was rambling on.

"Yeah, neat." Rey brought over my tea, the bag still bobbing on the surface of the water. He set it on the coffee table and next to it he placed a little hand-held recorder. "We might need this later," he said, but he didn't switch it on. As if for something to do, he rifled through the pile of magazines on the shelf above our heads. "What is *Sacred Hoop*?"

"Shamans' magazine."

"Blimey, can't imagine there's such a thing."

"There seems to be a lot you can't imagine, Rey."

"What's that supposed to mean?"

"Cliff. Why is he your number one suspect? Because he was drawn to a poor child's grave? He could have a perfectly innocent reason."

Rey let himself down onto the arm of the sofa, as if it were a de-marcation zone. "You know it's not as simple as that."

He was wearing the same crumpled suit as last week, but the tie was yanked loose and the shirt collar was smudged with yesterday's neck dirt. I began to appreciate that—heck, I don't know—that Rey was a real person, with problems and pressures. And no one to look after him.

"What I need are your notes on this client."

I looked up sharply. "I've already said—"

"It's humiliating, you know."

"What?"

"Having a search warrant served on you."

"Rey, there is nothing in those notes. Nothing *comprehensible*, anyway."

"Right." Rey flashed a smile. "I won't be able to comprehend this, then." He pulled a notebook from his jacket pocket.

"That's Cliff's," I cried. "Where did you find it?"

"The same place Cliff was hiding." Rey lifted his arm higher, teasing me. "This is admissible evidence. You're not having it back."

"You are insufferable." I grabbed his sleeve, trying to free the book. Suddenly, we were way too close. I pulled back. Rey's grin spread over his face. He was enjoying my discomfort. I slid away and crossed my legs at the ankles. Not that he could see them, under my black dress. "This isn't a joke."

"No." Rey flicked through the book. "So why don't you just tell me. Because if you think Cliff Houghton is not involved with the disappearance of Aidan Rodderick, you'll only be of help to him."

He had a point. "You're infuriating, you know that?"

"Infuriating *and* insufferable? I didn't know I was so many long words."

I tried not to smile. "You don't realize what Cliff has been through."

"I'd realize if you told me." He placed the notebook on the coffee table, a truce. "What's in here?"

"All the symbols I've brought back from my journeys. The first one was a sack full of hair clippings, all different colours. It meant nothing to Cliff. But tonight, we had a breakthrough." I flipped open the notebook to reveal my drawing. "Break*down,* you might say. He looked at this picture and was violently sick."

"Must be an art expert."

I leaned over and gave him a little push. "This is not the time to be flippant." But Rey knew exactly what he was doing. The banter was making me feel more normal, and the buzzing in my head was slowly receding.

"True. I saw the puke. Besides, he stank of it. But he could've been drinking."

"That's your poor policeman's brain. It wasn't drink. It was horror." A tremor passed through me. "His compulsion with Josh Sutton's grave. It's more to do with past events than anything Cliff might have done recently. Cliff was snatched by the Wetland Murderer."

"What?"

"Couldn't you have guessed? With your ability for hunches?"

"Sabbie, none of the victims survived."

"Cliff did. He just didn't tell anyone."

Rey leaned across and took the recorder in his hand. "I don't want to say this, Sabbie…"

I shrugged. "You might as well. It's your poor policeman's brain again. He could be making it all up, couldn't he?"

"Of course he could. Even with conclusive proof of his guilt, a good lawyer could convince a court with a story like that. And Cliff has a very good lawyer."

I gritted my teeth. I was pleased and relieved that Cliff had strong representation. But Rey had introduced a worm of doubt into my mind. I felt a chill wash through me.

"What're you thinking, Sabbie?"

I was thinking that Cliff had phoned to make his first appointment *after* Josh Sutton's grave had been discovered. Was he playing me for a fool? I looked down and discovered that Rey's ample, slightly hairy hand was covering both of mine.

Crying is rather like vomiting, I've always thought. There are times when your body insists on it—no argument—but there are times when you can battle the feeling by breathing deeply or biting your lip. I fought back my tears, but my chest gave a tell-tale judder.

"I'm sorry," said Rey. "I have a shitty job sometimes."

"Would it help at all," I asked, "if Cliff managed to prove that his story was true?"

"It would mitigate things. His legal team would go for 'balance of mind disturbed', I'd think. But let them work these things out. Don't go getting any more involved than you already are." He stood, filling his jacket pockets with the book and the recorder, ready to leave. "You haven't touched that drink."

"You didn't make one for yourself."

"I should get back."

"It's true, then: cops do work into the night."

"Bridgwater doesn't see many major murder investigations, to be fair."

"So long as there's no one waiting at home, tapping their fingers as the supper goes cold."

He pulled a face. "Nah. Supper'll be a nice, chilled lager and a bag of cheese and onion. Been a long time since anyone's cooked for me."

I pulled a face back at him. "That's sad."

"No, it's not. It's fine. Great. I spend all day surrounded by gits— and then there's the criminals. I like it nice and peaceful in the evenings."

He began to jiggle his car keys. Part of me just wanted to go on enjoying his company, but I was equally fearful of being on my own. I could still feel Cliff's turmoil vibrating in the air around me.

Rey must have felt it as well, because he leaned down and squeezed my shoulder, his fingers lingering against my neck. I forced a blithe smile onto my lips and glanced pointedly at his hand. "Is this what the police call a 'collar'? Should I be getting worried?"

Rey smirked. "Hope not, Sabbie. You're certainly not down in the books as our most cooperative witness."

I watched his car roll away, not wanting to close the door against the outside world. My skin felt as if hairy-limbed spiders were crawling over me. I sank onto the bottom stair and swallowed the scream that rose into my throat.

It was a long time before I could move again.

EIGHT

I woke up the next day with a banging headache. Dreams hung like a backdrop to a play, dark images that made no sense without the players.

I checked the diary on my mobile. Living half in and half out of otherworlds, I need the occasional alarm to remind me an appointment is coming up. My first client today was an after-work regular, so most of my day was free, and normally I'd spend it in the garden at this time of year. I scrubbed my teeth and spent several minutes scraping my hair into a ponytail. Sometimes, when I just want it off my face, I wonder why I persist in keeping my hair so long. But when it's shorter, it curls tightly, and I love the wavy black length of it down my back.

Once I'd pulled on my joggers, I filled the bread machine with organic flour, water from the tap, and yeast, and then went out into the early morning garden. It felt cool and slightly damp and the sight of it—the glittering webs that graced the herb bushes, the ghostly batons of my last leeks, and the tiny heads of the early broad beans in their soldiers' columns—made my dark heart feel glad.

The kitchen door leads to a paved storage area, where I keep my tools and winter stores and such. Beyond that it's veggie paradise, with grass pathways so that I can walk up and down between the beds and get to the hen house, shed, and greenhouse. Over by the compost heap, on the remains of a pile of horse manure, is a rhubarb crown hidden by an old metal dustbin that has lost its base. I lick my lips every time I peer in and check on the rose-coloured stalks. And this summer I'm hoping to get my first soft fruit crops—some strawberries in tubs and a few raspberry canes. I checked them all for slugs, tossing these into the hen run as an extra-tasty treat.

The early morning sky was overcast, and a cold wind was coming at me from the east as I released Juniper, Melissa, and Ginger from their fox proofing. Juniper, top of the pecking order now that Saffron was gone, gave my wellies a fond scratch. The three of them didn't seem to be grieving for Saffron, Pettitgrain, or the Cocky Bastard one little bit; in fact, a single egg had been laid, the first since the break-in, so I guessed they were on the mend. I placed their hopper full of layer's pellets at the far end of the run and watched in satisfaction as the three hens ventured towards it. During the fallow season, I let them roam all over the garden, but I stopped doing that when the winter broad beans began to show. Last year they devastated them; you learn by your mistakes. Anyway, they didn't fancy straying too far at the moment. Since the break-in, they barely separated even to explore their personal favourite scratching places, and the three girls were already roosting inside their coop long before dark fell.

They'd taken so well to being free-rangers. When they'd arrived a couple of months after I'd got the keys to the house, they'd had almost no feathers at all and had hidden at the back of the coop with eyes wide with fear of the unknown. I'd got them as twelve-month-old battery hens. The farmer had told me they still had a good couple of years laying in them, but as I looked at them, stuck in their travelling crate, I couldn't have cared less if I never saw a single egg. I just wanted to rescue them from their pitiful existence. They've rewarded me a hundred times over, and not just in eggs. Which made me feel even more guilty that I hadn't kept them safe from the fox. I'd tried telling myself that at least it was a natural death, but that hadn't really washed, and I was still waking up each morning with the taste of bereavement at the back of my throat.

I shut the run door on them and grabbed a spade. Half of my vegetable plot was covered in a winter coat of good horse manure and needed turning over. With each push of my boot, I felt the soft crunch of muck and hay. This had to be the richest, yummiest soil known to plant life.

The garden is where I can let my thoughts roam around a dilemma, and today I couldn't stop thinking about last night. I felt that if the police had real evidence on which to arrest Cliff, everything I believed about my practice would fall apart. I had never been so sure about what the spirits were telling me, about Cliff's innocence. The man had come to me for help, and I was committed to stand by him.

None of the work I do with my clients has any foundation in fact. It doesn't even rely on accepted methods of psychoanalysis. I know that my clients are often so desperate they're ready to snatch at any straw, even false straws. But I didn't begin my shamanic work because I wanted a happy ego trip, offering shallow comfort to people prepared to believe what they've paid to hear. I believe implicitly in the results I get. Time after time, clients tell me that the spirits have not lied, but helped them in their difficulties as symbols and ciphers knit together into the fabric of an answer. Usually, though, my clients are not snatched away by the police before we've properly begun our work.

Two hours later, I heard the bread machine bleeping. I straightened up, wiping the honest sweat from my face and no doubt leaving a trail of honest horse poo in its place. I took a long, hot shower while the loaf cooled. I dried and rubbed some scented oil into my body. It was already nine fifteen and I was starving.

I dipped a Marmite soldier into canary-yellow yolk, drifting off to such a breakfast paradise that when my mobile crowed out, for a moment I thought it was my Cocky Bastard.

"Miss Dare?" It was a number I didn't recognise. "My name is Linnet Smith, and I'm the solicitor representing Mr. Cliff Houghton—"

"Hi, this is Sabbie Dare."

"Glad to have reached you." Her voice sounded so efficient that already I felt I'd never attain her standards. "I believe you know that Mr. Houghton was arrested last night."

"I know all right," I said. "What's happening? Has he been charged with anything?"

"No. My first goal is to get him released without charge. But if that's not possible, we'll apply for bail."

"Has he told you why he's seeing me?"

"Indeed. Mr. Houghton believes it might be useful if we talked. I'd like to arrange a meeting, as soon as possible."

I'd picked up a pen in readiness—it was flicking back and forward between my fingers. "That's fine with me. I'm free this morning. Where are you?"

"Our offices are close to the marina."

"I could be with you in less than an hour."

"Excellent. I look forward to meeting you, Miss Dare."

———

The weather had turned icy. Rain fell in tiny stinging drops, like it was practicing being sleet. People beetled along the wet pavements protected by the slick black wings of their umbrellas. I'd left Mini Ha Ha outside my house and taken the green option, but the bus journey was miserable. The wind whipped around my legs every time the doors hissed open, and the person next to me shook the rain off their fleece like a dog. I stepped from the bus into a puddle, thereby discovering that the patent leather boots that had been a snip in the sale were not, in fact, waterproof. By the time I'd found Hughes and Heaven, Solicitors, I was bitingly disgruntled.

Linnet Smith worked out of a high-prestige office in a converted chapel close to the centre of town. Hughes and Heaven weren't Bridgwater's only solicitors, but they must have been among the most expensive. Miss Smith sat behind her impressively large black desk. No bits of MDF balanced on bedside tables for her. As I was shown in, she rose and extended her hand.

"Please take a seat."

The woman had been unfortunate in the genes department. She had that greasy line down the middle of her face that some women are plagued with, and I think it was sensible of her to wear light makeup— just lipstick and mascara. She had chestnut hair in an urchin crop, and this was a good move also, as it lengthened her neck and showed off her pearl earrings. I shook her hand and sat, feeling guilty over my silent critique. My damp feet were turning me bitchy.

"I may as well get straight to my reasons for asking to see you," said the solicitor. "Cliff has told me that he's undergoing therapy with you."

"Yes." I cleared my throat, more nervous than I'd realized. "Did he tell you what that therapy was?" After my run-ins with Rey, I thought we should be upfront from the beginning. "I'm a shaman."

Miss Smith nodded. "I surfed the web. Sounds bizarre, but Cliff trusts you very deeply."

"We did seem to be getting somewhere." It was good to hear that Cliff still trusted me, because I wanted to get back to work with him once he was released.

"And it doesn't worry you that your client has been arrested?"

"No—well, of course, I'm worried *for* him—"

"Two crimes. And two charges, if they manage to make them stick. Child kidnapping and child murder." She paused, blinking several times, as if taking in the severity herself. I was fixated on the words *if they manage to make them stick.*

"I believe in Cliff's innocence."

"Good, because, personally, I can't think of any worse crime. It makes me sick to my stomach. And I can assure you that is also true of the general public. They want an arrest as much as the police do. They will want my client charged, tried, and sentenced. They are baying for it."

"I've heard of people—well, they look like the guilty person, but it's all based on coincidence, you know?" I thought about how my own work was often based on a series of coincidences and trailed off.

"Oh, I agree. At the moment everything the police have is circumstantial. All they have to go on is that Cliff has been acting oddly."

"He thinks he was involved with a serial killer when he was a kid."

"A strange way of putting it, *involved*, as if he was in some way compliant. Is that what you were trying to suggest?"

"No," I said, frustrated. "I didn't mean it like that. Have you heard of the Wetlands Murders?"

The solicitor gave an audible sniff from across her desk and took her time unscrewing the top from a pen the size of a gear stick. She thought I was questioning her expertise. She'd have to get used to it, just like Rey already had. "Of course I have. It's one of those unsolved cases student lawyers pick at in their spare time." She scratched a note onto a pad. "What is it Cliff suggesting?"

"That he was abducted as he walked home one day."

Miss Smith closed her eyes. "How could a person possibly forget, then suddenly recall such a thing?"

"I wouldn't doubt it. People hide dreadful memories from themselves all the time."

"Of course you're right in general terms—regressed memory, motivated forgetting. I suppose digging this stuff out is part of your job?"

"It's more a case of dealing with whatever crops up. I do have a psychology degree, so I'm not working in the dark if my client has an extreme reaction." I leaned forward, warming to her questions. "But what I do is nothing like hypnotherapy. It's me who goes into the trance, not the client."

"What do *you* know about these murders?"

"Much less than Cliff. I was tiny when they happened. But they were shocking."

"I'll get my researchers onto it—media coverage, police statements, that sort of thing." She looked across the desk at me. "You can see why the police are getting so excited. They will be keen to emphasize the fixation he's had all this time."

"But that's wrong! He'd forgotten about it."

"That's what Cliff told you. He's told me the same—that he had no idea why he's got this collection of news items on the Josh Sutton case. We're going to have a hard job proving that this wasn't a growing obsession, finally exploding into mimicking behaviour, that started with a fantasy he invented when it was plastered all over the TV—what was it—twenty years ago now?"

"More. Cliff was eleven." My voice felt weak. "Copycat crime, that's the theory, isn't it?"

"I'm sorry, Miss Dare," said Miss Smith. She had been doodling on her page of notes, a criss-cross of lines like the webs of a colony of spiders, but now she laid her pen on her blotter. "I know it appears I'm negating your work, when I've just suggested how useful it could be, but I have to keep a clear perspective."

I nodded. She was right. The defence needed to think up all the angles the prosecution might use. "What's happening about Cliff, anyway? You said on the phone that you were getting him released without charge."

"I actually said I was trying. But this is such a serious case, the police are reluctant to let him go. They're searching his flat. If that shows the all clear, they'll be forced to release Cliff today."

"They've searched it already," I said. "It was the cuttings they found there that put him under suspicion in the first place."

"It's routine, that's all. However, I have to tell you that after Cliff's release, he will remain one of the prime suspects."

"Only because they've got no one else." It struck me that people like Cliff were convenient to police investigations. I hated the thought that they might not search for the true perpetrator of the crime because they already had someone who looked nice and guilty. "You don't think he'll end up in court, do you?"

"Not if I can help it. But I need to get my facts ordered as quickly as possible. I want you to tell me everything you've uncovered about Cliff's past. It will help a lot."

"Right. Yes, I see that. Did he tell you about the notebook we keep?"

She nodded. "But he doesn't have it in his possession."

"The police have commissioned it."

"Okay." She flipped the page on a secretarial pad. "Will everything be in there? Everything that was exchanged between you?"

"Yes. Except…"

She looked up from her writing. "Go on."

"I didn't tell him. I couldn't tell him. It was as if…" I stopped. "You're going to laugh at this, but it's okay, I'm used to it."

"Go on."

"I felt evil. In the place. In the spirit place."

"Give me a definition of *spirit place.*"

I gripped my shoulder bag in an effort to stay calm. "The places I see on my journeys—my trances. This one was…"

"Evil."

"Yes."

She sucked air through her nostrils again, but this wasn't so much a sniff as a desire to fill her lungs with good clean air. I looked across the desk at the way she wiped her mouth with a hand. She might have a clipped way of speaking and a suspicious way of eying you up, but she was upset, just like I was, that Cliff had been damaged as a boy.

"You see," she said at last. "This is why you are crucial to us. You might become our most valuable witness for the defence."

"What, me?"

"Absolutely. Don't let anyone tell you otherwise. Your honesty and openness alone would sway a jury."

A little glow of hope flared into life. "Where is Cliff now?"

"He's still in a police cell. Bridgwater Station. If he's charged, he'll be taken to the remand centre. That's in Bristol. But we hope it won't come—"

"Miss Smith, could I see him? I need to ask his permission to work with you."

"Please call me Linnet. I certainly don't want to keep calling you Miss Dare."

"I just need to know he's okay," I said. To my horror, tears erupted into my eyes. I brushed them away. "He was arrested at my house."

Linnet leaned across the desk and patted my hand. A single ring, silver or perhaps white gold, glinted on her third finger, but this was her right hand. Maybe she had once worn it on her other hand. Her touch did comfort me. There had been no one I'd wanted to call last night, mostly because I hadn't felt up to going through it all again so soon after the event. "I must remind you," she said, "as Cliff's legal representation, that if you tell me something incriminating, we're obliged to take it straight to the police."

I looked at her fiercely. "I have nothing of that nature. As far as I'm concerned, this is a horrible mistake."

"Excellent," said the solicitor. She swung her legs out from behind her enormous desk. At a little wall closet, she began to add layers to the midnight-blue skirt and cream shirt. A matching jacket, richly lined, oozed over her shoulders; a silk scarf was arranged around her neck. I couldn't help noticing her document bag perfectly matched the navy shoes and leather gloves. Her clothes were chosen to draw attention away from her early middle age spread and shout out a message about competence. I was beginning to feel sorry for the woman, although, on her salary, she'd hardly need my sympathy.

"Let's go and talk to Cliff," she said.

———

As we scurried through the never-ending corridors of Bridgwater Police Station, I enjoyed a guilty fantasy about bumping into Rey Buckley. I peeked around, half searching for sight of him, half taking in the feel of the place. There didn't seem to be many *police*, if you get my drift; certainly Rey was nowhere in sight. Most of the workers who darted past wore office clothes, and the girl who escorted us was careful of her public image, polite and friendly, in a distant kind of way.

Not at all like Rey. He was old school. He didn't fit into this twenty-first-century police force. Not prepared to be over-polite and politically correct, too keen on hunches.

I shook myself. I had to stop thinking about him. I glanced at Linnet as she quick-marched after our escort. The ring on her finger kept drawing my attention. "Have you been in Bridgwater long?" I asked, hoping to shift, crablike, towards her personal life.

She shook her head. "I came down from Scotland—Aberdeen, to be precise—not long ago. It was where I did my articles. I liked the place, so I stayed on as a solicitor in the procurator fiscal's office. It was a great life. Made coming home difficult."

"I can relate to that," I said. "I came back to Bristol from North Wales after my degree. You think you got rid of all the dross, but as soon as you're back…"

Linnet managed a smile. It wasn't quite a happy smile, but it did transform her features. I love it when people do this—change from homely to handsome with their smile—and I was finally able to see how attractive Linnet might be if she let her guard down. "Yeah," she said. "Good word, *dross*."

"I thought you were from around here," I affirmed. "I heard it in your voice."

"I never completely shifted that West Country twang, even living amongst Scottish lawyers. One wears such things like a badge, I suppose."

"Is that why you eventually came back?"

"Not quite. I had no idea how the intervening years would slice away. It's as if I'd never left … memories flooding back." She looked up at the false ceilings we were moving under. "Set me adrift a bit."

I quickly modified my theory of a broken marriage. She'd come back to pick up the threads of her youth. Maybe a love affair that had burnt or fizzled out while she was still a law student. *Friends Reunited*. Of course. That little website had a lot to answer for. "Sounds intriguing."

She nodded several times in slow motion, as if she was deep in thought. "In Scotland, I was working for the prosecution. Makes you feel too righteous." She grimaced. "Haven't had that problem since I returned."

We were shown into a bare room and seated at an office table. Moments later, Cliff was brought in.

I had been gearing myself up to see him again, expecting him to look the worse for wear. But he was shaved and he'd slicked his wayward hair back with the water from a recent wash.

"You okay?" Cliff spoke first, and his words touched my heart.

"Are *you* okay, more like."

"Don't suppose you're used to police raids."

"Don't suppose you're used to getting arrested with such regularity."

He sat at the other side of the table from Linnet and me, looking down at his clasped hands, which seemed to be glued together. I was relieved. I was going to set to screaming if he played with his lips.

"Good morning, Cliff," said Linnet.

His head jerked up. "Thank you," he said. I wasn't sure if he meant for coming, or for being his solicitor, or simply for acknowledging he was there. "They have to release me soon, don't they?"

She nodded a smile at him. "There's nothing they can charge you with at the moment. And as far as I'm aware, they have not applied to extend your detention."

He closed his eyes and yawned deeply, without covering his mouth. "I'm going to sleep for the rest of the day when I get home."

"It won't be long," I said, looking back at the officer guarding the door. She stared over both our heads, as if not interested in a word we uttered. "I've given them a statement," I added. "I had to go through your time in my house last night, more or less moment by moment." I gave him a big grin. "I don't think I incriminated you."

"They're looking to see if I've got a kidnap victim in my flat."

"Never make a joke about the investigative process," warned Linnet.

I could see what she meant; no one in this police station seemed blessed with a sense of humour, but Cliff jumped at her words. He kept drifting out of his body. A trauma can do that to people. His voice sounded unhitched, as if sure he was part of some elaborately staged practical joke.

"Sorry. Haven't had much sleep."

"I'm not surprised," I said.

"I did have a dream, though." He looked directly at me. "The door opened."

I realized why he seemed so floaty. He was still in the dream. It would have taken a tremendous effort to control his feelings, so he'd risen above them.

"I have to write this down, Cliff, okay?" I laid a pad on the table and scrabbled at the bottom of my shoulder bag for a pen.

"Okay," he said. And then he was silent for long minutes.

I didn't want to put any pressure on his already fragile spirit, but I was sure we only had a short time left before this interview was up.

"Cliff?"

He spread his fingers over his mouth, and suddenly he was talking through them, to no one in particular, the words escaping like trapped flies through a window.

"Why can't we stop dreams? Why don't we know they're not real when we're in them? But this was real. It happened. It happened, real as real." I looked up briefly from my secretarial pad. His face went through a chilling change. "The door opened, Sabbie. The door opened, and there was a bloke. Tall. Big head. Well, I was only a kid. Even in the dream. His cheeks were sucked in. They made him look gaunt, like a ghost. Why a ghost would look like that, I can't say, but in the dream it did. He did. His chin was covered in stubble. His voice growled. I knew I didn't like him. No, not *didn't like*. My feet were drilled into the floor with fear."

"Did he speak?"

"Not to me. He said 'you got one' to the woman."

"You were the first," I breathed.

"No," said Cliff. "The girl was the first."

"You're sure she wasn't part of the setup?"

"How could a kid be part of that?" Cliff looked at me through red-rimmed eyes that hadn't cried. "I don't want to remember any more."

"Are you saying that was the end of the dream?"

"I'm saying I never want it again."

"Don't dismiss this, Cliff. It's a breakthrough."

"There's a blank space in my mind," said Cliff. "I mean, before, I didn't have any idea that I'd forgotten anything, but now I can see that there is something missing. I can remember being picked up in the car, but the house is a blank. There's nothing until … after."

I swallowed. "What d'you mean, *after*?"

"I sort of recall getting home." Cliff stared down at his hands and seemed to almost doze off.

"Cliff," I said, keeping my voice low. "Cliff, tell us, please."

He shook his head, as if to shake the approaching tears out of him. "There's a memory from the summer Dad was ill. I'm in the car with Mum. She helps me lift my bike out the boot. She says it needs repairing." He glanced up at us, and his hand wavered in front of his mouth, as if desperate to tug at a lip. "Now, I realize, it could be … that time." He shook his head. "Weird. Don't know why I suddenly remembered this, but something fell from the spokes of the back wheel. I picked it up, because I liked it, it felt soft."

There was such a long silence in the room that I knew, when I finally found my voice, it would croak out its words. "What was it, Cliff?"

He grinned at me, and his eyes lightened. "It was a catkin. Like a caterpillar or something, all soft and alive. Lovely."

I grabbed Cliff's hand and gave it a bracing shake. "That was a symbol I brought back for Cliff," I explained to Linnet. My heart was trilling with sudden elation.

"This sounds rather implausible—a bit far-fetched," said Linnet. She coughed into her cupped hand and carried on. "You are now claiming you remember taking a catkin from the wheel of your bike, yet you still don't properly remember being held against your will?"

I looked from one to the other. Cliff had read my account of finding the hopeful catkin, and now it must seem as if he'd made up a story to fit in with it. Even I wasn't sure that this new memory was completely authentic.

"Does it matter?" I asked. "These tiny memories might lead Cliff to a proper understanding of what happened. That, somehow, he got away."

Linnet tapped the desk with her massive pen. "If so, I have to say he was extremely fortunate."

"How can you say that? It changed his life!" I clamped my mouth shut. I didn't want Cliff to think that his repetitive job and passion-dousing appearance were a direct effect of those missing days when he was a boy. And I knew that Linnet was still not entirely convinced about me. She wanted me to be of help to Cliff, but I could see that underneath, she was as sceptical about my methods as Rey was.

"My research so far on of the Wetland Murders case history shows that the children categorically died horrible deaths." Linnet was staring at Cliff, trying to get him to respond. "You're saying you were abducted yet survived. I'd call that lucky."

"It was cruel luck," said Cliff.

Linnet brought out a sheaf of papers from her bag. "Let's not split hairs, here." She rifled through them, saying no more, and in the silence, Cliff turned to me.

"Sabbie," he began. "Last time … you said something about … my soul?"

"Yes. I think you still feel bad because while you were in the cottage, the essence we think of as soul broke into pieces. A massive ordeal can shatter a soul and bits of it get lost or hidden in different places."

"You're saying I left my soul in that place?"

"No—it's inside you somewhere. Just fractured, floating all apart in your spirit world. It needs healing, that's all."

"Something needs healing, that's for sure." Cliff took a shuddering breath. "When I get out of here, I want it all back. Can we do that?"

"It will take a long time. But if you feel that you could see it through…"

"I want to try."

We were speaking quietly now, leaning towards each other, so I hardly registered that someone had come in, but Cliff's face suddenly became the colour of my uncooked bread dough. I spun round. Rey and his sidekick, Abbott, were standing with their arms folded. A quip sprang to my lips—that he made a habit of bursting into rooms without knocking—but it died prematurely. Like Cliff, I took in their sombre expressions.

"We're here to interview the prisoner," said Rey to the policewoman at the door.

I wasn't going to be manhandled, or even politely escorted. I stuffed the notepad into my bag and stood up, quickly offering my hand to Cliff so that we could have some small contact before I left him again.

"Will you tell my mother what's happening? I know you'd be kind to her."

My mouth opened and closed.

"Linnet's got her address. Will you? Please?"

———

I had no idea how long the interview might take, but I didn't intend to leave the station until I'd seen Linnet once more. I heard her shoes—stubby heels that must have been just a bit loose—clicking towards the reception area less than half an hour later.

"I've got a couple of things for you," she said. Her face was grey, and I could see a muscle flicker at her cheek. "Mrs. Houghton's details. And my card, my personal number. Please don't hesitate to use it."

"Can you tell me what's going on?"

"The search of Cliff's flat turned something up."

"What? What could they possibly find?"

Linnet rested her leather bag on the bench and sat down next to me. "It wouldn't make a lot of sense to you. It was just a plastic toy."

My jaw slackened with shock. "A Slamblaster figure?" I could see she was impressed, but I was in no mood to be impressive. "I don't understand this. Cliff has nothing to do with these children, I would swear to it."

"Josh Sutton was carrying this toy when he disappeared. The investigating team seem to think that's pretty conclusive. It means that he's now implicated in the disappearance of both the children."

My brain raced. Cliff had a morbid fascination with Josh Sutton's disappearance. He didn't even know why until he saw the picture I'd drawn. I thought about the cuttings and pictures they'd already found in his flat. "Linnet, please, don't you think he could have bought an identical figure?" I was panting. "Insist they do forensic checks on it, Linnet. I bet it's straight out of its packaging."

She shook her head, slow, deliberate. "They've already tested for prints."

"But Cliff *would* have touched it," I blurted. "That proves nothing—"

"Sabbie." Her voice shook. "The Slamblaster is covered with Josh Sutton's fingerprints. I'm afraid they've just formally charged my client with his murder."

NINE

SEEING BREN HOWELL'S FACE in my unconscious dreams after the motorcycle accident was not the first time something strange had happened to me. All through my childhood, I'd fought against the fairies that visited me on the verge of sleep. I hated it. I didn't think of myself as a fairy sort of girl. I was a Doc Martens sort of girl, allergic to pink, and I kept my unintentional encounters secret. When I realized the man who had pulled me out of my coma was a person I'd never met, it spooked me badly, but the Howells were great to me—warm and welcoming, a bit of a laugh, never demanding or pushy. There was no long list of house rules or pressure to join them for meals or outings.

Even so, I hadn't been at Bangor University long before I discovered that the Howells liked walking at least as much as Gloria and Philip did. I was glad to lace up the walking boots I hadn't worn since before my bike accident.

That first time, we drove across the Menai Strait and walked along the headland. Bren started telling me about the ancient geology of Anglesey and the abundance of uncommon plant life, and I nodded politely as he talked.

"Are you enjoying your courses?" he asked, after a while.

"Psychology is fascinating. The psychologists all disagree with each other, but that's quite interesting in itself."

"Indeed, it must be," said Bren. "For you, Sabbie."

I glanced quickly at him. He often made a comment that seemed loaded with unstated meaning, as if he were expecting me to start a conversation about something else entirely. Trouble was, I had no idea what.

Rhiannon was striding out ahead in a pair of brown slacks and ancient but well-soled shoes. Over her arm was a large wicker basket. Philip, my foster dad, always carried a backpack with a thermos and other goodies on Sunday walks, but Rhiannon's basket was empty except for a pair of garden shears. Where was our picnic? I was seriously confused.

Rhiannon was a small lady, ultra-slender, although she served a hearty tea, as the Howells called their main meal. In fact they both looked fit, seeing as they had to be heading for seventy. I was beginning to puff with the pace they were keeping up when Rhiannon suddenly disappeared over the edge of the cliff. I shrieked in horror and raced forwards, pulling up sharp by her basket, which remained on the path like a memorial to her. I looked over the cliff top. Rhiannon was balancing on a small ledge, head and shoulders below path level, snipping at some succulent-looking leaves.

"Samphire," she said, beaming up at me. She shinned up the rock face like a wiry Welsh goat and dropped her find into the basket.

Speechless, I watched her carry on up the path, the basket swinging from her fingers.

"You can run when you want to, indeed," said Bren, as he joined me. "Only, you looked a bit puffy farther back, like."

"I'm fine—"

"You mustn't forget that you've only just recovered from a serious accident."

I shrugged. "It's a year ago, now."

"Thirteen months and eighteen days."

I stared at him in amazement. Even I hadn't calculated the time of my smash-up in such precise terms.

"I came to you. Maybe you can't remember now. Indeed, you've never said anything. But I wanted to help. I could feel you sliding. You were too young to slide over, Sabbie."

We moved along the cliff trail. I didn't reply for ages, but he let me think, not saying anything further. Ahead of us, Rhiannon was examining a patch of tall weeds on the inland side of the track. "Do we need any mugwort?" she called back.

"We're marvelous for mugwort," said Bren.

"Right we are, then." She scouted ahead again, and I finally found my voice.

"Were you really there?"

"You remember now," said Bren, his elfin smile showing through his beard.

"I remember something," I said. "But I don't believe it's possible."

"Of course you don't," said Bren. "Most people don't. They don't believe anything is possible."

"Oh, I believe that," I said. "I believe *anything* is possible. It's Gloria's favourite phrase. Ten years ago I would have laughed if you'd told

104

me I'd be taking a psychology degree. Actually, I'd probably have punched you on the nose, if I'd been able to reach up. But here I am. Yeah, I agree that anything could be possible. Except moving around in someone else's mind."

"Anything except that, eh?" Bren suddenly noticed that Rhiannon was struggling among the branches of a stubby, thorn-laden bush and went to her aid. Carefully, they picked off the red haws and dropped them into a buff A4 envelope.

He didn't bring up the subject again. He understood that it would take me some time to get my head round the idea. For the next mile we formed a convoy spread out along the coastal path, Rhiannon forging ahead, and me dragging my feet behind, thinking deeply.

Suddenly, we came to a lovely cliff-top café, as if the Howells had conjured it out of thin air. We sat in the garden and had bara brith with scalding hot tea.

Although it was November and had rained on and off since I got to Bangor, the day had turned out warm. The weeping willows that surrounded us were bathed in golden light. I can't remember ever enjoying a meal more than that one. While I piled butter on my slices of brith, I asked Rhiannon why she was picking the plants.

"They're herbs, dear. Some for swallowing, some for poultices, and some for burning."

I wrinkled my nose. "Ugh! You could poison yourself."

"They're not for us, not especially. Anyone can come and be treated at our house." Her eyes gleamed, reflecting the late sun. "We haven't poisoned anyone yet."

I'd noticed that the Howells had a lot of visitors. People rang the bell, then traipsed up the stairs into the unused bedroom next to mine, leaving a half an hour or so later. "Are you herbalists?" I asked, thinking I sounded quite clued-up.

"If you like," said Rhiannon.

"We're cunning folk," said Bren. "My great grandmother was a cunning woman and she taught me everything she knew."

"There'll be no one to take it on from us, though," said Rhiannon. "It'll die out when we do. We have no cunning apprentice, you see."

I froze, the slice of brith halfway to my open mouth. "Don't look at me," I said, laughing at my own joke. "The only cunning I know is how to get out of trouble at school."

Bren raised one pixie eyebrow. "That's quite sufficient," he said. "As a start-off, like."

———

I didn't go straight home when I left the police station. I walked around the centre of town in a catatonic state, over the many bridges, staring down into the waters of the River Parrett for minutes at a time, unable to get the least part of my mental capacities up and running. I vacillated from hating myself for struggling with a client who needed more than my skills could offer, to being filled with zeal. I'd heard of people who'd spent their lives trying to prove someone's innocence, only to finally have the guilt conclusively confirmed. I kept coming back to the same moment last night, when I'd lifted the muslin veil to reveal Cliff in his futile hiding place. Why had he done that? Was he thinking they had already found the Slamblaster?

As I walked past the town library, I knew I couldn't let it go. I checked my watch. I had an hour or so to spare. I could go home and eat a proper lunch before my client arrived, or I could do some research. Even though my stomach growled at me angrily, there was no contest.

The Bridgwater town library tries so hard to be stately and elegant, with its pillars and green copper cupola, but it's not very big or extensively stocked, so I wasn't hoping for much. I went straight up to the reference section, where the light filters down so that you feel as if you're inside a lantern. A librarian turned to greet me from the other side of her counter and offered a distracted smile.

"I want to research a series of local murders," I told her. "Can I do that here?"

Her face blanched. "Murders? Local? When was that?"

I grinned at her. "It's okay, it was decades ago. They were called the Wetland Murders."

She tapped at her computer keyboard, but I could see she was taking the poor thing round in small circles. Asking about murders had made her jittery. As the moments ticked on, I became worried that she was trying to raise an arresting officer, rather than a file.

"Would it have been in the *Bridgwater Mercury*? We have those on microfiche, if you have the date." I shook my head at her. Foolishly, I'd never established exactly when the bodies had been recovered. "You're going to have to trawl through a lot of microfiche in that case."

Disheartened, I went to get a reviving coffee from the machine in the lobby. As usual it was out of order and I had to resist the temptation to kick it in rage. I spent a moment or two staring at the walls, trying to gain my temper. I'd just have to come back at another time, armed with the right information.

Without warning, I had one of those little jolts that make you focus in on something you are half looking at. The lobby was

wallpapered with notices and flyers for local events, and pinned between the cello recitals and the am-dram notices, a single word
pinned my eye: *Garibaldi.*

GARIBALDI WAY OPENS TO PUBLIC
A Talk at the Town Hall
*Archaeologist Roberto Garibaldi and his team have recently
unearthed the UK's oldest-ever wooden structures. The 6,500-year-
old staves and poles are thought to be the wooden remains of a
causeway and fish weir installed by Stone Age men who lived in
what was then a salt marsh. There will be footage of the find, and
refreshments will be served.*

This sort of thing is always happening to me—a string of reminders
about the symbols I bring back from shamanic journeys. After Trendle came into my life, I couldn't go out without spotting otters—
everything from DVDs to tattoos. Most of the otters ended up in my
therapy room, except the tattoo. That ended up at the base of
my spine. This particular flyer wasn't new, though; it was several
months out of date. As I stared at it, my thoughts turned back to
Cliff and I realized I should be able to recall his date of birth if I
closed my eyes and visualized his notes. I could work forwards
eleven years from there.

I shot back up the open staircase and collared my vaguely smiling friend with the years of interest fresh in my mind.

"Do you know how to operate a microfiche viewer?" she asked as
she took me over to the files. Again I shook my head, aware I was
looking increasingly gormless. I had an urge to explain about my low
blood sugar. But she was very gentle as she took me through the

technicalities and got quite excited when we finally found our first report of a missing child.

She left me to it then, and I became so absorbed in the gruesome story that when a cough echoed through the silent room, my stomach lurched into my mouth. The articles made for difficult reading—my heart was bounding and my tongue felt dry—but I knew I wanted to take every scrap of information away with me so that I could do it justice. I scrabbled around in my purse and came up with enough change for copies of everything.

I walked along the river from the library. In less than a minute I was faced with the choice of Barney's Café or the Bridge Restaurant. I went for the upmarket option and was soon tucking into a goat cheese salad while I perused my photocopies.

The articles listed the full names of the children found in the moors—Matthew Cladburn, Nicolas Goodland, Joanna Beck, and John Shoreward. At the time of their deaths, they had all been between three and seven years old. Like Josh and Aidan, they had all been snatched from play areas where their parents or teachers had only taken their eyes off the child for a moment.

Cliff wasn't mentioned at all. Was he a trial run that had gone wrong? Did the woman in the car and the man Cliff dreamed of choose smaller children simply because they'd found eleven-year-old Cliff too hard to handle?

I pushed my plate back and wiped the olive oil from my mouth. This story of multiple losses was getting to me, and I still had to face the bus journey home.

As the bus wound its way out of the centre of town, the man in Cliff's dream kept nudging at my mind. He was the essential missing component to the puzzle. Women and young girls did not steal children, kill them, and bury them in a shallow grave—not in any understanding of the real world I'd ever had. *It was always a man*, I thought, *then and now*.

"Please don't let it be Cliff," I whispered.

The rain pattered on the bus window like a lullaby.

———

I longed to crawl into bed and sleep when I reached home, but that was not an option. I had to get ready for an aromatherapy client.

I switched on the local news as the kettle steamed. Cliff's arrest was the main item, naturally. There were shots of his tiny first-floor flat, with uniformed men standing guard behind the ubiquitous blue and white tape. There was a full-screen blow-up of Aidan Rodderick's face, followed by a re-run of his parents' grim and tearful press statement. Finally, the screen was covered with a grainy picture of my client. It was a head and shoulders shot, but I could see it was a holiday snap, taken on a beach. I wondered where they had got it.

I kept glancing towards my bag. Somewhere at the bottom was the contact information for Cliff's mother. I'd promised him I would phone her. I could ring her now before my client, or ring her when I was even more exhausted this evening. There shouldn't have been a contest, but I had to will myself to zap off the telly, and my hand was shaking as I dialled the number.

I'd never spoken to anyone who had just had a son arrested for murder. Even so, I was knocked back by the screech that came down the line as soon as it was picked up.

"GO AWAY! GET OFF THIS LINE!"

"I'm sorry," I said, stuttering out the words. "You don't know me, but—"

"I don't know any of you," said the woman on the other end. Her voice was quieter but still full of fury. "That doesn't seem to prevent you vipers from attacking me."

"Mrs. Houghton." I'd guessed what this was about. All I could do was talk quickly before she slammed down the phone. "I know your son. He might have mentioned me to you. My name is Sabbie Dare."

There was a moment of thought before she came back at me, suspicion uppermost in her tone. "No. My son has not mentioned you. And I'm answering no more questions."

"I saw Cliff today. At the police station."

She let out a sob. "I don't want to speak to the police tonight."

"I was there to give a statement. Cliff was at my house when they arrested him."

She gave a pause. "He never spoke about you."

"I think he might have been preoccupied of late."

"Yes," said Mrs. Houghton. "Yes, he has been, a bit. He didn't tell me he had a girlfriend."

"Ah, now—Mrs. Houghton—"

"He tells me most things. He would have told me. You could be the press. They can pull some dirty tricks."

"I understand that. You don't have to talk to me." I had managed to confuse things further for the poor woman. But she didn't hang up, so I battled on. "Cliff just wanted me to send his love and say he's okay."

I heard her irregular breaths echo into the phone's dark cavities. "He'll be feeling so dreadful, wondering how it could happen."

"I think it's a sort of mistaken identity—"

"Don't say anything over the phone," Cliff's mother hissed down line. "They tap them you know; I've seen it on the television."

I swallowed hard, unsure whether she was losing it or if she might be right. "Is there anything I can do to help?"

"That's nice of you, Sally, it is. You can pray. I've been praying for him every hour since I heard the news. Only no one bothered to inform me, you know. All these phone calls just started happening. They've been driving me mad. It's awful that some reporter is the one to tell you your son's in jail."

I knew that she had begun to cry silently. This wasn't a good time to correct her misunderstandings, either over my name, status, or spiritual path. I had a sudden realization that after she'd put the phone down on this call, she'd be alone, except for the hounds baying outside her front door.

"Is everything … are you all right?"

"Oh yes, dear, of course. I'm just rather surprised to hear from you like this. I really can't believe that Cliff could forget to introduce us. Perhaps we could meet for coffee sometime. Get to know each other better. Without the prying ears. Except I don't think I'm going anywhere very soon. I can't leave my house at the moment." She chuckled, and I silently reminded myself that Mrs. Houghton had brought two children up into adulthood after losing her husband. "You'll have to come to me, Sally, I'm afraid," she continued without missing a beat. "What about tomorrow morning? Would tennish be okay for you?" I fancied she might be scribbling the appointment onto a wall calendar as she spoke. "I'll need to give you my address."

"Actually, Cliff's solicitor has passed that on. Mrs. Houghton?"

"Yes, dear?"

"Take all your phones off the hook. And don't open the door to anyone."

"How will I know when it's you?"

"I'll put my card through the letterbox." *If I can get to it*, I couldn't help thinking.

"Can you send him my love, dear?"

My eyes had begun to sting with sympathetic tears. "I'll try, Mrs. Houghton. I will try."

TEN

MINI HA HA STARTED right away when I clambered into her the following morning. She generally does, but it's always a surprise, because she's older than I am—a 1970s Mini Cooper, lovingly cared for by one previous owner, right down to the original cherry-coloured paint job. I couldn't believe this survivor of a glorious decade cost me less than a five-year-old car. I took over its ownership like I'd been handed a puppy. The local garage adapted it to run on unleaded petrol, and of course, I had to have a CD player fitted. Couldn't do without that.

I slid Nina Simone into the player. I had twenty or so minutes' run ahead of me to reach Caroline Houghton's house, and the growl of Simone's voice would suit the mood of the journey well. The rain had stopped sometime during the night and a mild sun was bobbing above the horizon as I drove towards the Polden Hills.

When I first moved to Bridgwater, I thought it was an ugly town surrounded by a swamp. I guess there's around 40,000 people living here, and most of them are proud as heck of their town, but I couldn't for the life of me see why. Okay, it used to boast of a market and river port, but by the time I turned up it didn't have much at all, not even a swimming pool. More critically, though, I stood out. In Bristol, I'd been one of many mixed raced kids. Here, my skin tones were too dark against the pale, Anglo-Saxon populace.

It seemed daft to move from the city life I knew and loved, but I'd been chasing a boy, naturally. I'd met Marcus in one of the many cafés on Glastonbury High Street. I'd finished my degree, and for several months I had been making the ninety-minute trip south from Bristol to Glastonbury each weekend to learn about the things I'd felt most drawn to—the therapies I planned to offer as my life's work. Learning about shamanism or Reiki in Glastonbury seemed as rational as learning about IT in San Jose.

At first, I'd assumed that Marcus was on the same wavelength, since he'd come to Glastonbury with some mates to have his aura read. It had taken me no more than a couple of weeks to shift all my stuff from Gloria's house into his Bridgwater flat. I was almost twenty-five and knew it was time to grow up and take responsibility for myself. Sadly, I have a tendency to use the most inappropriate men to help me achieve my aims. It had only taken a further couple of weeks to for me to start packing again. On our last night together, Marcus had come back to find me creating a spell in the middle of his living room—wand poised, incense and candles burning. His face had turned, like traffic lights, from red to positively green.

"You've got to stop this, Sabbie," he'd yelled at me as he snuffed out the candles by bringing his whole hand down on their flames. "It's dangerous. It's evil."

"Yeah," I said. "Okay, Marcus. Tomorrow morning, first thing."

Marcus had stomped off to bed, but I'd stayed and finished my spell, magicking up the perfect successful therapy practice—a full list of clients, a working space I could afford, the moxie to go ahead with it all. When I'd finished, it was two in the morning, but still I didn't feel like bed. Instead, I packed my few things. Silently, I bundled my clothes into my suitcase and boxed up my more fragile stuff. I had no idea where I was going, but I couldn't stay with Marcus. As I wrapped glassware in the previous week's *Mercury*, my gaze rested on a blurred photo on the Property to Rent page. I was staring at it, wondering how such a little house had managed to keep so much garden all to itself, when the vision of having a bit of my own land leapt into my mind.

Back then I used to talk all the time about lowering my carbon footprint without ever doing much more than chucking plastic bottles into a recycling skip. I'd looked at the photo of the garden—almost quarter of an acre of good land—and come to the conclusion that Bridgwater might be the place to settle down. Bristol rents were sky high, but around the River Parrett they were affordable, and I'd be closer to Glastonbury, a place I loved but knew I'd hate to live.

I'd cut out the ad and slipped it into my purse, contemplating how magic can work so quickly it leaves you vibrating like a tugged spring. It's three years later, and I still believe that: you don't have to wait for magic; it either hits you in the eyes or it hasn't worked at all.

The first sign for Finchbury flashed past the car. I started to take glances at the printout map I'd lifted from the Internet. My route for Caroline Houghton's house took me through the oldest part of Finchbury, quite close to the medieval marketplace, past the Tradecraft shops and pretty boutiques that now lined the ancient square with its gothic church tower. I drove over the River Cary, swollen from the recent rain, and into a back-street area that seemed forgotten by everyone but those who had to live there. I checked the addresses on the back of the map. Mrs. Houghton was on the other side of the river, but I intended to put in an extra stop before reaching her. I was in the street where Cliff lived.

I locked the car, even though I wouldn't be going far. I was outside a depressing local post office, which surely would be shut down before much longer. Faded cans of food were pyramided as a window display, with cheap children's toys pinned wonkily behind on bile-green plasterboard. A bell rang out as I opened the shop door, a real-live brass one dangling over my head.

"Morning," said the woman behind the counter.

"I just want some stamps." I couldn't bring myself to ask about the tenant who lived upstairs without putting something into the coffers first.

"First or second class? Large package or letter?" She fingered the pages of a worn-edged stamp book.

I was beginning to see why the place looked so deserted. This was not the most friendly post office clerk I had ever bought stamps from. She glowered at me from behind two layers of glass—the bulletproof stuff that fronted the counter and spectacles the shape and thickness of TV screens.

"The chap who lives upstairs," I began and faltered as she gave what came close to the evil eye.

"I should've guessed you're here for that. I knew I didn't recognise you." The woman slammed her stamp book shut. Dust puffed out and danced in the strip lighting. "I want you out of my shop, now."

"I'm not the press," I said.

"You're not official, either." She turned and walked towards the end of the counter, where she pulled back a bolt to let herself into the shop. I backed towards the door. "They've taped it all up," she said, advancing on me. "No one goes up there that's not official. They've left an officer in charge."

I'd thought the brass bell had a merry chime as I'd entered, but as I legged it back to my car, it sounded like the tolling bell of fate.

I checked my watch. It was gone ten. As usual, I would be late for my date, and I fancied that was not the best way to curry favour with Mrs. Houghton.

————

There was no doubting which house Cliff's mother lived in, so I didn't have to check the number. Even though the crowd must have dwindled somewhat since last night, a row of cars was parked tight to the kerb, and some well-wrapped reporters were stamping their feet on the pavement, warming their lungs with cigarette smoke.

Cliff's childhood home was a well-heeled, detached affair. Its porch welcomed guests with ivory pillars and a sunray fanlight, and the picture windows were wrapped around the corners of the house in Art Deco style.

I drove by without stopping and pulled to a halt farther down. I dialled Mrs. Houghton's number into my mobile and got the engaged tone. Naturally. I'd told the woman myself to take her phone off the hook.

There was nothing for it but to brave the mob. As I drew closer, the gang clocked me, surrounding me as I approached the double gates, which were made of foreboding slats of heavy wood, charmingly painted a rich red-brown.

"Are you a friend of Caroline's, dear?" asked a woman in a woollen hat, pulled low. She looked blue around the chin—she must have been standing for ages. "Are you one of the family?"

"D'you know Cliff well?" asked a male reporter, flashing his press badge at me. "Have you seen him? Has he confessed yet?"

I tried not to make eye contact. Surely they couldn't stop me from moving on. I grasped the metal ring that operated the latch to the gate. As I turned it, I realized they had no intention of stopping me—they were planning to follow me right up to the door. I tried to slam the gate shut, but I'm just not made of the right material to cause unnecessary concussion in sentient beings. I fled along the long, wide gravel drive and hammered on the door, forgetting to even look for a bell, then stuffed my card through the letterbox. As always, it read:

SABBIE DARE
Shamanic Healing
Reiki, Reflexology, Aromatherapy
& Tarot Readings

The door took a long time to open. Quite soon, the entire pack of journalists were squashed into the porch with me, opening up new meanings to the phrase *members of the press.*

Finally, through the glass panelling, I saw the undulating image of a middle-aged woman. Her voice, shaky and compressed, floated out.

"Sally?"

"Sabbie!" I yelled back.

The door opened until the chain caught it with a metallic clang. She peered out at me through the gap.

The mumbling from the tight-packed bodies around me grew.

"Mrs. Houghton, tell us if you think Cliff is guilty!"

"What was he like as boy? Was he a handful?"

"You'll want us to publish something you've actually said, Caroline."

"Come on dear, cough up …"

I turned my head round and hollered. "SHOVE OFF! NOW! GO AWAY!" Those anger nodules that grew round my heart when I was a kid come in useful at times.

As I hadn't spoken a word to any of them until that moment, they reacted quite dramatically. They shuffled backwards, falling over each other. A larger, older man was pushed out into the rose bushes, but I tried not to focus on what was happening behind me, because Caroline Houghton had taken off the chain. I slipped into her magnificent hallway.

The woman who faced me could have been Cliff's sister. Her spongy cheeks showed no signs of aging through the carefully applied makeup, although there was a thin line of grey roots at the edge of her blond bob. She was well padded but wore a long-sleeved belted dress that slimmed her bust and hips. A silk scarf was draped around her neck, hiding any chicken-wrinkles.

I looked down at the clothes I'd chosen to wear for this occasion—one of my best "visiting outfits"; a long plain skirt in a shade fairly close to the colour of Caroline's front gate and a warm jumper—but they made me feel dowdy and out of place in this hall, where gilt-framed family portraits hung on the walls. On closer inspection, these did turn out to be canvas-backed studio photos, but I bet they cost a lot more than my weekly earnings.

"Oh yes, I'm *sure* Cliff mentioned you," Caroline was saying, "now I've had time to think about it." A moment before, Caroline had been panting with the horror of the siege at her door, her beautiful eyes, as grey as Cliff's, wide and unblinking. But she quickly regained her poise. This was a woman to whom appearance, in all its guises, meant everything.

She opened a door on the other side of the hall and gestured me into a room of caramel-cream softness. There was a smell of rose petals. The carpet sank under my feet. The sofa I was directed to sucked me down into feather-stuffed cushions. My mouth formed a round "O," but I was too stunned to worry if I looked stunned.

Caroline went straight to the window. She stood behind the half-closed curtains, which had the sheen and quality of an ivory wedding dress, and peered out.

"Have they gone?" I asked.

"Only as far as the gate." She turned to me and lost her balance, toppling against the window. I was on my feet to rescue her, but she righted herself with a military shake of her shoulders. "The coffee's percolating," she said. "D'you like it milky? That's what I usually have about this time, *café au lait*."

"Are you sure you're all right, Mrs. Houghton?" I said. "All this attention. The whole situation must be harrowing."

"You will call me Caroline, won't you?" She patted my arm as if I was the one in need of consolation. "Have you known Cliff for long, dear?"

"Not very long. He—"

"How did you both meet?"

"I'm a therapist, Mrs. Houghton."

"How intriguing!" gushed Caroline. "Is it the sort of new age stuff?"

"A lot of people think that. But it's older than—"

"Cliff needs a steady relationship," she said.

"I agree."

"He was knocked for six when his father died. Did he tell you about his father?"

"Yes. I'm so sorry."

"Had all the treatments, went through the chemo, only to die anyway."

I shook my head, unable to think of anything to say, other than, *I'm your son's shaman,* which didn't feel at all appropriate.

"I think I recovered far better than either of the children. But my daughter's got her own life, whereas Cliff…"

"He does seem unhappy at times, Caroline."

She sat opposite me, her back as straight as a Victorian spinster's. I could only marvel at how she was keeping her composure in the desperate circumstances. I'd sort of been imagining that she would weep all over me; having psyched myself up for that scenario, I felt a wincy bit nonplussed. I was also secretly hoping that she'd bob up again soon and make the drinks. Now she had promised me milky coffee, I was desperate for a cup, and visions of the fragrant, steaming brew—with froth and possibly even cinnamon powder on top— kept swimming in my head. I squeezed my eyes closed for a second.

"It's so nice we've had this opportunity to meet," said Caroline, as if she'd already forgotten about the baying outside her door and the fact her son was right this moment being transported in handcuffs up the motorway to Bristol to the remand wing of Horfield Prison. She got up and walked towards the door, stopping on the way to slide a finely spun glass ballerina along a wall shelf, presumably back to the position it should never have left. "Although I suppose Cliff would have got round to introducing us in the end."

"Mrs. Houghton. Caroline—"

But she floated out of the room. I was left, torn between exploring everything in sight and staying put on the sofa, which seemed to have swallowed me whole. I was glad I chose the latter, because she was back in no time, pulling one of those ornate tea trolleys that look like they're going to tip and spill at every turn of their wheels.

Caroline brought out a couple of side tables from inside a larger one and set them on the Chinese silk rug that graced the area between the sofas with a swirl of pastel flowers. Then she shook out two crocheted doilies and laid them centrally on each table. To this arrangement she added a coaster of filigree silver, on which she placed a bottle-green saucer lined with a circular, quilted paper mat, followed by a gold-rimmed cup brimming with coffee.

"No sugar, thanks," I said, in a hushed voice. This was gentility taken to extremes. I thought only people with butlers behaved like this.

She returned from the tea trolley with matching plate, napkin, and dessert fork. "Which would you like, Sassie? Carrot and cream or plain chocolate sponge?"

"Caroline." It was time to clear up the mess before it tangled into a spider's web. "It's *Sabbie* ... short for Sabrina."

"My dear, what a pretty name." Her lips twitched into a smile, accentuating the fine lines that branched from them like an imprint of trees. I wondered if these lines were caused by pouting; on first impression she looked the sort of woman who might sulk if she didn't get what she wanted. "I'm so glad you came today. I'm feeling under siege, if you understand." I watched as Caroline finally made herself comfy on the opposite sofa and took a dainty sip of coffee, little finger extended.

I delved into my shoulder bag, a shapeless, patchwork thing made of various old coats that probably told Mrs. Houghton all she needed to know about me. "I forgot, in the fuss of getting into your house. I brought you this. Just something to say sorry all this is happening, really."

She pulled off the paper I'd wrapped the package in. "Oh," she said, turning the glass bottle round in her hand. "Why, thank you."

"It's a blend of essential oils in jojoba. You can pour it in your bath or smooth it onto your skin. They should help you relax a bit, that's all."

She pulled off the stopper and gently sniffed. Her eyelids did a sort of ecstatic flutter. "It's divine."

"Caroline. Cliff's been seeing me in a professional capacity."

"Sorry?"

"Cliff's been coming to see me because he's feeling a bit down at the moment."

"Down," Caroline echoed. "That's true. I blame the place he's living. He was so sure he wanted to move out and I didn't stop him, but that dreadful flat would depress anyone. And he doesn't even push a Hoover around. I've started doing all his cleaning. I couldn't bear it any longer."

A thought dropped into my mind. "You tidy up for him? Did you notice his collection of things around Josh's kidnapping?"

She took several seconds to put the top back on the bottle of oil and place it carefully on the table. I knew this was because she had found things at her son's flat that had unnerved her. "People often keep bits of local interest," she said.

"I was wondering if you'd ever seen a toy there. One of those spacemen types."

"No, nothing like that. Why would Cliff have toys? All his old ones are in my attic."

"It's the reason the police have arrested him, Caroline. They found Josh Sutton's Slamblaster figure in his flat."

Caroline opened her mouth, but no sound came from it. Possibly she'd been unable to comprehend the full situation properly until this moment.

I was silent too. I didn't want to interrupt whatever came next. I was hoping that she would reiterate her statement about seeing no such thing in the flat.

Finally she talked. Words flew from her mouth like pigeons from a loft. But she seemed to have forgotten about Cliff. As I sipped my coffee down to its milky bottom, I learnt everything I'd ever wished to know about Cliff's father, from how he could row a boat and throw a line to the gruesome details of his illness.

"He was running his own business when the diagnosis came," she said. "Plastic mouldings. It was really getting established, and he loved the work. Gave it his all. Fourteen-hour days. That changed when he got ill, of course. The only good thing that came out of it was that we all saw him so much more."

"Cliff enjoyed his dad's company, then?" I asked.

"Oh yes," Caroline nodded, her eyes misting with past memories. "Little Cliff looked after his father like a man."

"It must have been hard for him. When his father died."

Caroline shook her head, her over-sized teeth hidden behind tight lips.

"Cliff was devastated by his father's illness. It tipped him out of the boat, as Robin would have said. They both changed right in front of my eyes. Cliff got quieter as Robin got thinner until he was too sick to do anything but lie in bed."

Although the memories must have been upsetting, Caroline seemed to relish the tale. I know this is true of a lot of people, this enjoyment of the macabre, but it made me feel unaccountably angry, and I did a cruel thing, something in the style of the bitter teenager I thought I'd left behind.

"I suppose there's one good thing." My teeth were set like steel traps. "Mr. Houghton never saw Cliff charged with murder." As my odious words hit home, Caroline's face blanched. I struggled out of the sofa cushions and rushed to grasp her hand. I wanted some teacher to give me a hundred lines…*I must keep my stupid opinions to myself*…or slap my knuckles with a ruler.

"I'm sorry," I said. "That came out wrong."

"No!" Caroline pulled out the tissue that was hiding in her sleeve and pressed it to her face. "No." She shook her head from side to side. "No, you're right. I'm glad. I've never been able to say it before, but I'm glad Robin's dead." She pulled the tissue away and looked down at me, kneeling on her carpet in penitence. "No, that's not true. I still wish he was here. He'd be such a support."

"Is there anyone else? Cliff's sister? Friends?"

"Yes, I've got some lovely friends. They made these cakes. I'm in the local Women's Institute, you see, and they're all supporting me, they all say it can't be Cliff, but they're very torn."

"Torn?"

"I know Aidan Rodderick, most of the women in the Women's Institute and Townswomen's Guild do. His grandma is a member, you see." She gave a hollow laugh. "Yesterday, I baked *her* a cake, her and her daughter, Aidan's mum. It's what we do. Just a token. I was baking away, blissfully unaware of what was about to happen."

"I don't think Cliff is guilty."

She gave me a smile. "Oh, no one does, who knows him. It's just a terrible mistake. Terrible, because the real culprit is out there somewhere, with Aidan. That's why Nora has got caught up in the reward."

"Nora?"

"Aidan's grandmother. Josh Sutton's family started a fund before he was … found." She struggled with the word, and all its implications. "Now the *Bridgwater Mercury* has got involved. They want to keep it going for Aidan. Nora's not a wealthy woman, but she's put in some money. She'd give everything to have Aidan back. They live with her, you know, Aidan and his mum. And I was happy to give a donation. I want the real killer found. I want my boy back."

"Of course you do," I said.

There was a pause, as Caroline regained her breath. I watched her lean back, her hand over her breast. As I returned to my feather sofa, something broke through the haze in my mind, a picture on a TV screen.

"Aidan lives with his grandmother? But it was his mum and dad who made the TV appeal, wasn't it?"

She sniffed. "I don't know how that man manages to muscle in on everything. It was very upsetting for Nora. She thought she would be able to have her say—not that she wanted to be on the television you understand—but instead they chose Garth. He hardly even sees the child."

"I've heard that the police ask family members to do these things so that they can determine guilt," I said.

"They interviewed Garth and let him go. Yet they kept my own son, who wouldn't even tug the tail of a cat."

"Did Cliff ever go missing, Caroline?" I had to know. I had to have confirmation of what Cliff had told me. Maybe it was what I had driven here to find out.

Caroline took a breath through her closed teeth. "Well, all boys will, won't they? Run away from home? He wasn't tiny, like Aidan. It's just a game, an adventure. A boy must have adventure."

"Did Cliff have adventures?"

"Just the once. Robin stayed in the oncology ward in Bristol so many times. It disrupted poor Cliff. I think he set off to find his father."

"Did you report him missing, Caroline?"

"Of course I did." Her shoulders shook. Not quite a shiver, but I was sure she hadn't liked my question. "I was rushing between Bristol and Finchbury. I got back one evening and Cliff wasn't around. I thought he was staying over with his friend."

"The one with the tent?"

"That's right. Cliff was always at his house and I thought that was good. He was too young to be hanging round sick people in a ward all day."

"So it wasn't until the next morning…"

"Oh, was I ever frantic when I realized he'd gone missing. The police took the details, started a search." She glanced across at me, over the half-empty coffee cup. "It was a very bad night, that following night. I haven't thought about it for years, though, because mercifully, he was back the day after. I didn't know whether to wallop him or never stop hugging him."

I tried to put myself in the shoes of the woman. She'd had a desperately ill husband and two children to look after. "So he was only missing for one full day?"

"Two nights. He never said who put him up to it, but he was filthy, all scratched and bruised, and his bike was no better."

I remembered what Cliff had said about the catkin. "How did you find him, Caroline?"

"Well, he phoned me from a call box. He was crying, he knew he'd pushed me too far. I got in the car there and then."

"Where was he when he called you?"

Caroline stared at me, clearly trying to recall. "Do you know, I can't remember? Why don't you ask Cliff?"

"He can't remember, either."

"That doesn't surprise me. He never said where he'd gone. In fact, he didn't say much at all, he was very quiet for a time. I had to guess the rest. Sleeping in barns or outhouses and probably getting a bit lost. Dares and things, boy stuff, they never can see when they should call a halt, can they? I expect that's what happened to his hair."

She sliced her piece of chocolate cake into tiny cubes. The silver fork delivered one into her mouth. She chewed with her lips firmly closed and had swallowed the first morsel before I could speak again.

"His hair?"

"He's forgotten entirely, to give you the truth. Some mate of his took a pair of scissors to it. Part of the big adventure. Being commandoes or fugitives, something like that."

I sank back. "Let me get this right. Cliff went missing while his dad was having chemotherapy and he came back with his hair shorn?"

She gave a dry, under-the-bridge chuckle. "We told him it was naughty. He'd had such lovely hair, pale as white gold, and it never grew back the same colour. But I couldn't punish him. And he never told on the friend. He's loyal like that."

She began in polite earnest on her cake. I sat transfixed, watching her chew and swallow. My breathing had shut down, and my heart felt like it was next on the agenda.

"I don't know what you must think of me," she said, dabbing her lips. "But that's the first food I've managed since I heard the news. I must tell Muriel that she makes a lovely chocolate cake." She turned the tissue over and started on the corners of her eyes.

I couldn't reply. All I could hear was the sound of scissors, clip, clip, clipping, and all I could see was cascades of hair falling. Piles of hair, sacks of it, red, black, brown, and platinum blond.

ELEVEN

"OKAY," I SAID. "YOU look nice and relaxed now, Caroline. Just cast your mind back."

Caroline had sunk into the feathers and foam of her chair, her eyes closed, her breathing regular and deep.

I hadn't hypnotized her, not as such. I'd just gently talked her into that half-awake state where brain waves slow into an Alpha rhythm. That's less than fourteen cycles in a second, a light relaxation where things just outside our awareness can drop into our conscious mind, if we let them.

"You're in this house." I imagined Caroline, twenty-three years before, a mum with an ill husband and a missing son. "You're in the kitchen, possibly. The phone rings. Do you remember that?"

Caroline nodded once. "Yes. Made me jump. Cliff had been missing for two nights. I was on edge. I didn't know…" She trailed off.

"Of course. It could be Cliff, but it could be bad news."

"I had a gut feeling it was him."

"So you rush to the phone."

"It *is* him," said Caroline. Her voice was slurring, a good sign.

"You're so relieved."

"Yes."

"He's crying, though."

"Yes. Can hardly understand him … he's upset … his bike's got a puncture … it takes him a long time …" Her voice faded.

"Yes," I say, keeping my voice very quiet. I didn't want her to fall asleep, but I did need to keep her deeply relaxed. "He's not making much sense?"

"He's crying because he's lost. I tell him to look around, see what's outside the phone box … he keeps saying *water wheel, water wheel.*"

"Water wheel," I repeated, encouraging her.

"I think he's talking about his bike, but finally I understand. He's outside the Old Mill."

"You know this place, the Old Mill?"

"Yes. I tell him not to move. I get the car out the garage."

"Is he there?"

"At first I can't see him. He's in the bushes, at the back of the Old Mill. Right in them, him and his bike, tears rolling down his face."

I hated to think of Cliff, stuffed into the scratching bushes, his eyes on the road, searching for the wrong car, the car that might come and snatch him back again; searching for the right car, for his mum.

Caroline had unsettled me. She was an amazing, brave woman who had done the best for her family and ended up—let's be honest here—no more loopy or obsessed than I was reputed to be. We had chatted as the coffee things were promptly cleared, washed, and dried. I did the drying—carefully—while she talked about the flat that she'd helped Cliff move into, and how her hopes for him were slowly being eaten away. How he was still doing the job he'd taken on part-time when he was sixteen after the good grades in his exams had come to nothing. Once the last cup was stacked away, I had asked her to sit down while I told her why Cliff had come to see me. I gave her most of the solid facts, but I couldn't bring myself to tell her about my shamanic visit to Brokeltuft Cottage.

Caroline had been up for having a go with a simple relaxation exercise that can bring things from the back of the mind to the front. Now she blinked a couple of times and opened her eyes. "Gracious. That was rather effective." She might have been talking about a new recipe for blueberry muffins.

"The Old Mill," I asked. "What is it?"

"A pub, dear. It's quite isolated, but excellent food nowadays, although I can't recall eating there back then. It still has a working millwheel, so it's known for miles around."

I gave Caroline a massive hug. "Well done. Rey thinks that proving Cliff was kidnapped when he was a boy will really help his case."

"I do hope so." Her lips curled upwards at the edges. "Who is Rey?"

"Oh—the detective on the case. Detective Sergeant Buckley. We're not really on first name terms—well, we are—but …" I looked her in the eye. "But we disagree about Cliff. I'm determined to prove him wrong and clear Cliff's name."

Caroline hugged me back. "I have every confidence in you, Sabbie, dear."

At least she'd got my name right. That had to be a start.

———

A lot of up-market digital cameras were pointing at me as I inched out of Caroline's sad, flawless house. I put my capacious shoulder bag up to my face and made a bolt for the car. Maybe they'd branded me unfit for interview or something, but a sort of Red Sea parting appeared at the gate and I scampered down the road outstripping my previous speed record, which was probably the three-legged race when I was nine.

I had instructions on how to find the Old Mill printed on Basildon Bond in Caroline's fine hand. I laid it on the dashboard beside me and drove off, glancing at her clear print every few moments. I had to go and check it out while I was in the area. I was sure that this pub could not be far from the cottage I'd seen in my journey. I whispered the name *Brokeltuft* and my heart lurched, remembering the effect that word had on Cliff. A thought had been going round in my head ever since last night. What if this wasn't a copycat crime? What if the Wetland Murderer had returned? I held my breath as the next thought swung through my brain: What if Aidan Rodderick was being held in the very same place Cliff was?

I found myself passing a sign that read MORGANSWICK WELCOMES CAREFUL DRIVERS and slowed for a moment. It was at the primary school in this village that Aidan Rodderick had been kidnapped, only forty-eight hours ago. All sorts of vibrations might have been left there. The thought made me feel ghoulish. I drove on, past school railings veiled by bunches of flowers, their cellophane already damp and ripped.

———

The Old Mill turned out to be miles from anywhere, which felt positive to me. I parked up and went into the pub. It was almost deserted, just a couple of early drinkers cooped into a corner. I went over to them and asked them if they'd heard of Brokeltuft. There was no point in being shy, after all. Neither of them had a clue, and by that time, the barman was hovering, hoping I'd order a pint and a meal, but he hadn't heard of the cottage, either.

"I do know this area well," he said. "If it rang a bell, I'd say so."

"Okay." My eyes were taking in the menu chalked on the fancy wallboard. The food all looked delicious—not cheap but imaginative, especially the veggie option—but the prices were outside my league.

"Well thanks." I dragged myself out, mouth watering.

I did have a plan B, but it wasn't a particularly clever one. Cliff had half walked, half cycled from Brokeltuft to the Old Mill, so they could not be far from each other. Surely, if I drove round for long enough, I would find the cottage. My stomach twisted on itself at the thought. The idea of walking up to that evil front door and lifting the knocker dried my salivating mouth.

Forty minutes later, I'd lost all hope. I'd crawled along every country road in a wide radius. My petrol tank was almost empty. I'd driven past the Old Mill a dozen times, and my stomach was beckoning me back over the threshold. Even recalling the cake I'd eaten at Caroline's had no effect. I would have to start for home before I capitulated and spent my tomato plant money on the veggie option. There were no more roads—no more tracks, even—that I could explore.

I turned the car round and headed back until I reached a farm driveway I'd spotted earlier. A wooden board was nailed deeply into the hedge. The paintwork had faded, but I could just make out the words MIDDLESPRINGS ORGANIC FARM SHOP. Surely a farmer would be likely to know the older cottages around the area. I slid out of the car. Mud squelched over the patent leather of my boots, and I was so busy trying to balance along the grass verge, I didn't notice the woman at the top of the lane until I heard her shout. She was too far away for me to catch the words, but they sounded like "*Stop! Trespasser!*"

My foster dad always kept to the proper footpaths on his map, and he liked to quote the countryside rules at us—always shut the gate behind you, never light a fire, that sort of thing—and it had made me a bit wary about being on other people's property. I looked back towards the car to check the sign. As I turned, I saw something low, fast, and the colour of mud, hurtling towards me out of the corner of my eye. I swung back, far too late, for the creature was upon me: a slobbering, heavily proportioned Labrador. And I was wrong about the mud. He was covered in mud, not coloured like it.

"Stop, Trevor!" The woman continued to yell, as she pummelled towards us. "TREVOR, COME HERE!"

Trevor took no notice of his mistress. He was trying to wash my face with a tongue that felt like a thick flannel—one loaded with last week's slimy soap. He was panting with delight, drool dripping from his spongy muzzle.

"Gerrof," I instructed, giving him a nudge.

"Are you okay?" asked the woman, grabbing the dog's collar, which, luckily, was a thick, bolt-studded piece of leather. "He's just friendly, you see. Oh, look what he's done to you!"

A fetching design of mud dripped down the front of my best skirt.

"I'm so sorry," said the woman, who was now busy clipping Trevor onto his lead. "Not a good welcome to Middlesprings. Most people bring their cars right to the door. Anyway, come and get cleaned up."

"Are you the farmer?" I asked, as we trudged up the drive.

"One of them," said the woman. "It's me and my husband, mostly." She was still having trouble with Trevor, who clearly didn't like the fact his walk had been curtailed and was trying to drag her back down the path. Losing her temper, she flicked the dog's rump with the end of his lead.

"You are a very naughty boy!" she informed him, but he didn't seem to get it. "Sandy Guilding," she added "Sorry, don't think I'm clean enough to offer my hand."

I didn't like to point out that I wasn't exactly scrubbed spotless myself. We reached the farm shop. It was cosy inside, and filled with racks of winter vegetables that smelt of spice and rich earth and made my tummy grumble.

Sandy grabbed a dishcloth from the counter and aimed for my skirt, but I waved her off. "This will go in the wash, it'll be fine," I said.

"In that case, you must have something on the house, to compensate," said Sandy. "A pound of our venison sausages? A couple of dozen of our largest eggs?"

I smiled. "I'm a veggie. And I have my own hens. Although they're not laying since the fox got some of them." Sandy picked up a half-dozen eggs from the counter and opened the box. They glowed like polished topaz in a casket. I shook my head. "I can't. It's like cheating on them."

Sandy laughed. "We'll go for our winter selection, then." She filled a cardboard box with the goodies from the shelves...muddy, odd-shaped carrots, a celeriac as big as Trevor's head, some local fruit, and my utter favourite, curly kale. In the meantime, I wiped the mud off my hands with her dishcloth and cast my eye over the cheesy delights in the cool counter.

"We sell off our excess chicks, if you're interested," said Sandy.

"Okay, I'll think about that." I tried to get her to take a tenner, but she just waved off the note and even carried the box to my car. Well, she was the one in the green wellies, which were a tad more practical than my patent leather.

"I was actually looking for a cottage," I said, keeping my voice conversational. "I know its name, but not exactly where it's located. Brokeltuft. Funny name for a house, isn't it?"

"Mmm," said Sandy. I didn't think she was paying attention, so I waited until she'd stowed the box in my boot and asked again.

"Brokeltuft? Does it ring any bells?"

"No, sorry," said Sandy. "Is it near Middlesprings?"

"It's near the Old Mill."

"Oh, well, that's a couple of miles from here."

I nodded. "Don't worry, it's nothing important."

She splashed up her lane, looking a lot more cheerful than I felt, even considering she still had to take Trevor for a walk, while I leaned against the car and sighed. I had to finally admit that I was not going to find Brokeltuft today. Perhaps it no longer existed. Perhaps it never did.

I was biting into an organic apple from the box when my mobile crowed. I scrabbled for it in the recesses of my bag.

"Sabbie?"

"Linnet!" Her voice set up an involuntary response in me as I wondered what news she was bearing.

"I'll come directly to the point. I have an appointment to work with Cliff at the remand centre tomorrow. I wondered if you'd like to join me."

"Are you sure I'm allowed?"

"You're a professional. I see no reason why you can't accompany me as such." Her tone was formal, but her concern touched me.

"That would be excellent. Thanks for thinking of me. When are you going?"

"Ten thirty tomorrow morning, if you can make it."

"Okay." My brain fizzed at the thought of entering a high-security prison. "What do I need to do?"

"Make sure you are at least fifteen minutes early as the signing in procedure is complex. Bring some formal ID."

Another odd coincidence: I should have expected Cliff to arrive as a client tomorrow at almost exactly that time. Instead, I would be meeting him in a high-security prison. Somehow, though, the thought of seeing Cliff made up for my failure to find Brokeltuft. I'd be able to tell Caroline that Cliff was okay.

An embryonic thought flittered through my mind as I pulled away. *If he is okay...*

"Of course he is," I told myself aloud. "He'll be fine."

———

Cliff looked like someone who had been wheeled out of intensive care. I don't know why I was expecting regulation uniform—arrowed stripes or navy overalls—but he was his own T-shirt and cord jeans. His gaze didn't leave the floor as we came in, as if he was counting the squares on the institutionally brown, industrially thick vinyl. Forty-eight hours since I'd seen him, but it looked as if an alien had abducted him and left a pitiable replica in his place.

"It's good to see you, Cliff."

Cliff nodded at me but did not speak. His hair, loose and greasy, did a successful job of hiding his eyes.

The small room was bare, blank. There was a stack of plastic seats in one corner. I followed Linnet and took one, seating myself away from the table that Cliff was propped at, not sure of what my role was going to be and not intending to get in the way of the work they had to do. But as Linnet spread the contents of her briefcase over the table,

I felt cross with myself for acting out of my depth—like a seaside knickknack might have felt among Caroline's glass ballerinas—and shuffled the chair closer.

"Okay, Cliff," said Linnet. "I've been concentrating on presenting good reasons for bail, so I want to run through them."

There was no response. Linnet glanced over at me, a plea spread over her expression. This was clearly the part of her job she found hardest.

"How have things been, Cliff?" I asked. Cliff gave a grunt. His shoulders remained hunched and stooped. His hands were covering his knees in a defensive posture. "Have you been able to think back at all...remember anything?"

"Yeah, a bit. Being in the car is more like a normal memory now." He gave a growl of a laugh. "Normal! I keep trying to bring back their faces...their names..."

Linnet stopped shuffling her papers and looked up. "The woman gave you her name?"

"I don't think so," said Cliff. "But the girl's name is there somewhere."

I jumped my chair forward another notch. "If you can remember the least part of it, the rest might come."

"Before I started to get scared, we were all joking around, I suppose to keep me from seeing where the car was going. I made a joke about the girl's name—" Cliff's eyes were squeezed shut. "I think there was an A in it."

"Ann? Clara?"

"No...no." I saw a glimmer of a smile. "Don't confuse me."

"You're right," I said. "You shouldn't force the memory. It'll pop into your head when you least expect it."

"I've been worrying about the Slamblaster," Cliff said to Linnet. "Did you get anywhere with that?"

"Not as yet."

"It isn't mine. Nothing to do with me."

"I hear what you're saying," said Linnet. "But I can't stop the forensic process. The police think of this item as their major piece of evidence."

"I don't know how it got there!" Since he'd mentioned the Slamblaster, Cliff had become more and more panicky. His fast breaths were whistling in and out between lips that he was pinching tight with one hand. He was half out of his chair.

"Okay, Cliff," I said, reaching out but not quite touching him. "Miss Smith will find out how it got . . . wherever it was."

"Under Cliff's bed," said Linnet. "According to the data I'm allowed access to."

"Then someone put it there. Planted it there," I said.

I thought Linnet might query this massive leap of faith, but she quietly nodded. "When was the last time you checked under your bed, Cliff?"

"I—I don't know," said Cliff, shaking his head. "Not ever, really."

Something popped into my head, and I couldn't help but blurt it out. "Is there anyone who would state under oath that they had looked under your bed quite recently?" Linnet turned to me and raised a quizzical eyebrow. "I just wondered if anyone could make a statement."

"The prosecution would flatten such a witness in seconds," said Linnet. "*Not* seeing an item isn't proof of evidence."

"No one could do that, anyway," said Cliff. "I don't have a girlfriend at the moment or anything."

"Your mother could. She cleans your flat sometimes, doesn't she?"

His eyes brightened for the first time. "You've spoken to my mother?"

"I saw her yesterday. She sends her love."

Cliff put his hands over his face. "I've brought this on myself, haven't I?"

"Be careful what you say, Cliff," warned Linnet.

"Mrs. Houghton may be able to offer corroborative evidence," I said, pleased with my legalese. "She reported Cliff missing at the exact time he says he was taken."

"Mothers." Linnet gave us both a rueful smile. "Sadly, mothers are of no consequence. Of course they'll swear their child is innocent. Whereas, what you do—now that's interesting."

"Sabbie can really see things, Linnet," came Cliff's earnest voice.

"You certainly seem to have some sort of talent," said Linnet. "I believe that you drew, on a piece of paper, a reasonable likeness of the house in which Cliff says he was imprisoned." I bit my tongue to prevent asking what else I might have drawn on, if not paper. Linnet could hardly help sounding like a lawyer. "However did you do that?"

"I enter a different world, a different plane of life, if you like. With some luck I can communicate with beings that wish to help us poor humans. They're not tied to bodies as we are. They move across time, space, emotions…" I broke off. "Sorry. Didn't mean to lecture."

"No, it's good," said Linnet. "You need to sound credible, authoritative."

I felt as if I'd swallowed several ice cubes. "You don't mean like an expert witness, do you?"

"I think your testimony, if it could only be validated, would make all the difference to our case for the defence."

"But it can't be validated."

"If you and Cliff could continue with this therapy, we might see amazing breakthroughs." Linnet opened her arms, showing the palms of her hands, and I had an image of her in court, the power of her intellect shining through. "Admittedly we don't have long, but how do you feel about working with Cliff right here?"

"That sounds like a freak show. I'm happy to journey for Cliff in my own place and bring you the results, but—"

"Please, Sabbie." Cliff wriggled against his chair as if it were covered with spikes. "You could try."

I gave myself a mental slap on the knuckles. This wasn't about the rules of practice. It was about the murder of a child.

I picked up my plastic chair and moved so that Cliff and I could sit facing each other. Linnet took hers right over to the wall, crossed her legs, hitched her skirt over her slightly lumpy knees, and leaned back.

"Okay," I said. "No different from last time, except we don't have our plaited link, so we're going to be holding hands through this, but otherwise I want you to just relax. It won't matter what you think about—let your mind wander."

Cliff dragged his lips into a smile. "Thanks for this."

"You may not thank me," I told him.

I closed my eyes and felt my mind lift. If I have no drum to guide me into a trance state, I chant a single word in the very back of my mind while I try to calm the front of it. Getting rid of thoughts is one of the main preconditions of the art of meditation. Not easy even in your own bedroom, but here I couldn't silence the welter of images and emotions that were zinging round my head. It was no good struggling to dispel them; a trance has to come down upon you, like a surprise fall of snow.

Suddenly I felt such a pain behind my arms that I half fell out of my chair.

"What's going on?" I heard my voice choke out the words. I opened my eyes. It was clear that nothing was going on in the room. Linnet was still in her corner, and Cliff was staring at me with his mouth open.

"Are you all right?"

I rubbed at my shoulders. The pain had been as intense as a heart attack, rising from my sides, through my shoulder joints and into my arms and neck. It was gone now, but I felt wary of touching Cliff's hands again.

"I think I experienced your pain." I looked at him, but he would not return my gaze. "I can take a guess on how the pain was caused." I pulled my arms as high up as I could behind my back. "If your wrists are bound behind you, then pulled tight, it's excruciating."

Cliff had squeezed his eyes shut. He was breathing fast through his mouth; his eyes had become fixed and blank. I cursed myself for bringing this memory upon him. "Cliff?"

A whisper formed on his grey lips. "Patsy."

"Sorry?"

Cliff's eyes flickered and he was back with us. "The girl. I think that was her name. Patsy." His face cleared as memories winged into his mind. "I can't picture her face at all, but that name feels … real." He looked surprised at himself. "Where did it come from?"

I gave his hand a squeeze. "I'm sorry to bring this back to you."

"No," he said. "You were right. I should be pleased the memories are returning. How can I defend myself with a blank mind?"

"Good on you, Cliff." I turned to Linnet. "That sort of positive attitude will really help, won't it?" But Linnet didn't reply. She was staring at us, her mouth half open. I was pretty sure she hadn't expected such instant results. Actually, neither had I.

"She told me her name in the car. I told her mine. She leaned forward and whispered between the front seats. Like passing secrets." He rubbed his kneecaps hard with the palms of his hands, as if trying to wipe off sweat.

"Can you remember being with Patsy inside Brokeltuft Cottage, Cliff?"

"No." His head shook backwards and forward. "No, no."

"Let's go back to a good memory. How did you get away?"

"I can't remember." Cliff was still shaking his head. I could tell he was beginning to panic.

"Just let your mind go blank, Cliff. Close your eyes and let me do the work for you. See what I can get."

Once I was sure Cliff was calmer, I closed my eyes. I was trying not to pick up his terror. I began the silent chant of a single word... *Ostara... Ostara...* a goddess from another time and place whispered inside my head slowly over and over, more and more quietly, until it vanished like mist from a window pane, leaving an empty space for new worlds.

———

Two perfectly round eyes stared at me out of the darkness. It was Trendle. I let myself fall into those kindly eyes and in the next moment we were standing outside Brokeltuft Cottage, the otter lying along my arm, as always. The building had become dilapidated since I'd last visited. Windows had lost most of their glass and the frames were rotting away. The roof was in disrepair—slates lay at my feet in pieces, and I was standing in knee-high weeds. Trendle had brought me to the cottage as it was now.

"No one loves you," I told it in a silent whisper, and the building creaked on its foundations.

I lifted my hand to try the door handle and a sensation of revulsion came down on me, rasping at every nerve ending.

I felt Trendle's sharp claws dig into my arm. "This time, you're not going in."

"Of course. We must follow Cliff. How did he get out of here?" I turned my back to the gruesome door. Across the lane, the amber glimmer of late sunlight slanted through the hedgerow branches. To my right, the lane dwindled into a narrow track of black mud flanked by shocks of grass, twisting away into a darkness tinged with fog. To my left, it was straighter and wider, as if it might go somewhere.

"North or south, Trendle?"

"The path to the north is for another time."

"Thank the spirits for that. It looks bleak down there."

I set off up the lane. The shoes I'd worn to the prison squeezed my toes and at times sank down into patches of mud. An evening breeze caught my hair and pimpled my neck like a plucked chicken. I tried to imprint the small landmarks on an inner screen. I passed gates and potholes and the rusting heap of a burnt-out Mondeo, the remains of a joy ride.

I lifted my chin and saw that ahead this lane reached and joined with another. A triangle of green was set in the middle of the T-junction, and a wooden signpost sprouted from the grass, two arms pointing in opposite directions. I came right up to it, but the words were blurred and faint. "I can't read what it says, Trendle."

"Never expect too much." Trendle felt heavy in the crook of my arm, so heavy I wanted to lay him on the grass and weep. It all felt so unsubstantial. But of course, it was of the spirit. I reached up and ran my fingers along the engraved letters of the sign. Could I read the imprint like Braille?

"Sabbie? Sabbie! Time's running out!"

I felt an alarming sensation, as if I'd been punched in the solar plexus. I opened my eyes and found Linnet Smith standing over the two of us. I had become bent in the chair, naturally leaning as I moved deeper. My hair was touching Cliff's chest and a thin line of saliva drooled from my mouth onto my hands below.

I stood up and rubbed the drool from my mouth. "Do you realize how dangerous it can be to wake someone abruptly from a trance state?"

"I'm so sorry, Sabbie. But I should get on with the paperwork." She'd brought her chair back to the table. She sat at it and unscrewed her fountain pen. "Did you see anything?"

My mind was filled with cavity insulation foam. "Nothing concrete. Cliff, did anything come into your mind?"

Cliff jerked his head, as if to shake away approaching tears. "I remember a tree. Falling from a tree."

Linnet gave an intake of breath. I turned to her, but she was digging about in her massive blue handbag.

"D'you think this is important, Linnet?"

"What?" She pulled a clean linen handkerchief out of her bag, ironed and pristinely white. She passed it to Cliff. He pressed it, folded as it was, to his eyes. It was lovely that she kept hankies specially for the tears of her clients.

"Do you think that falling from this tree is important?"

"Gosh, no." She gave a dismissive wave of her hand. "Boys climb trees, they fall out. Happens all the time." She turned to Cliff. "You were probably just playing with your mates."

It was a good point, but I was relieved to see Cliff come straight back with an answer. "I used to get the same dream all the time. I'm high up in a tree. I have to get down. They are after me. There's an arm, reaching out. I go down through the tree. I try to stop my fall…" He was panting, his upper lip coated with oily sweat.

"What happens then?"

"Nothing. I wake up. You always wake up, don't you? If you get to the bottom, you're dead. That's what they say, isn't it?"

I looked into the dullness of his eyes. "Sometimes, symbols get muddled. Could the tree have been a signpost? They're both made of wood, after all, and signposts have branches, sort of."

Cliff gave me a skewed look. "No. A tree. A black tree that sighs in the wind." He clasped my wrists, wrenching at my arms. "Did you see a tree, Sabbie?"

I shook my head. But I promised myself I would see that tree. If I could find the signpost, I would find the tree.

TWELVE

WE LEFT THE GRIM slamming metal of the prison. Linnet seemed at least as affected by it as I was. She darted away from the gates as if the screws were after her with handcuffs.

"It's the worst part of my job," she shuddered. "God! To be locked up for life."

"Knowing you were innocent," I added.

She shrugged and looked away. "The law tries to be balanced. Judicial. But it's still a risk. I don't want Cliff to confess to anything that might lead to his plea of innocence being laughed out of court."

"You're talking about his memories of being kidnapped, aren't you? Rey Buckley thought that might strengthen the defence."

"Possibly." She swung her document case from one hand to the other. "The prosecution will be just as interested. We should be cautious about what we include as evidence. Or rather, how we present it. I'm not planning to use his links to the Wetlands Murders unless—well, frankly unless I'm trying to mitigate a sentence."

"Do you think he'll be found guilty?"

"We have to face facts. The fingerprint evidence alone is going to sway the jury. In that case, someone like you—a witness who can make a credible statement—may convince the jury he underwent a severe trauma."

"You don't sound as if you believe him!" My voice hit a seagull shriek as the full realization hit me. "How can you represent him if you don't believe him?"

She looked at me with dull eyes. "This is my job, Sabbie. I represent people who are accused of a criminal offence. Even if they're guilty, they deserve an advocate. It's the bedrock of our legal system."

I had stopped walking. We both had. We stood facing each other across the pavement. "I know he's innocent," I said.

"Is he? He's blameworthy of something. Or blames himself for something. I can see it in his eyes."

"Well, I can't," I snapped. But when I stopped to think if this was true, I had to admit that although the sensations connecting me to Cliff felt harmless, they didn't feel *blameless*. I recalled the intrusions I'd seen crawling out of his otherworldly mouth, and my stomach gave a lurch.

"You don't think there's something disturbing about him?"

"Why is that surprising? He was kidnapped by a sadist. Tortured and abused. That's disturbance enough, surely."

She rubbed her fingers over her forehead. "I'm sorry. Please don't worry. I will represent Cliff as innocent until I'm blue in the face. If you can help me with that, I will be most grateful."

"Of course I will. Anything."

"I've finally been allowed to read the notebook you and Cliff were keeping, I can see that you hit the nail on the head." She put a tender hand on my arm. "Anything that occurs to you, or that comes to you, I want to be the first to know. That way we can make sure the information is used in the best way. Or smothered if I believe it might have the reverse affect. Do you understand what I'm saying?"

I nodded. She was telling me that trusting the police was tantamount to informing the prosecution. We began walking again. I lagged behind, trying to process all the new stuff that was being thrown at me.

I caught her up as we turned the corner. "Linnet. The name Cliff gave us. This … Patsy. Surely we should try to find her?"

She looked up at the grey sky as if the answer might be in the clouds. I could see our cars, parked at the kerbside. I had less than one minute's walk to convince her this was important. "Please, Linnet, say you'll consider it."

"I'm just not sure what good it will do. What will it prove, exactly?"

"It'll prove that this whole thing isn't a fiction Cliff and I have dreamed up together. That's what the police are thinking. For all I know, *you're* thinking it."

She pulled down her lips. "Actually, rather despite my own good judgement, I'm beginning to be convinced by these dreams of yours."

"Journeys."

"Journeys of yours. They do seem to reveal things. Does this girl figure anywhere?"

"Yes, actually." I could see I'd got her attention. Her fingers stopped fishing for her keys. "It was the journey I took the night he was arrested. I walked into this cottage. She was there, in the kitchen, making tea. A whistle kettle on a gas stove."

"Good God." Linnet shook her head as if trying to get her thoughts around what I was saying. "Did she speak to you?"

"She offered me a biscuit. Garibaldi. She said she hated them. Squashed flies. That's what they're called, isn't it?"

"Sabbie," said Linnet. "I know you say you're not asleep, but that sounded like a typically weird dream."

"Was I asleep at the prison?" I tried not to sound defensive.

"I don't know. Where would *you* say you were?"

"I'd say I was within my spirit world, but you're entitled to think that's a load of bosh."

"No," said Linnet. "Not bosh, not really. Something's out there, I'm convinced of that. Ghosts ... yes, they exist, I'd say."

"This is not quite the same as people hauling chains and carrying their own heads."

She resumed the hunt for her keys, her eyes downcast as if she was a teensy bit embarrassed that she'd raised the subject. "Of course not, but when someone dies, they don't always completely leave you, do they? Isn't that a haunting? When you can still hear their words inside your head?"

I took a breath, as a little "Sabbie lecture" on the difference between the spirit world and ghostly spectres formed on my lips, but I thought better of it. We were getting off the track of things.

"Do you have any other suspects that might take the place of Cliff?"

Linnet didn't answer for a moment. I hoped she was thinking my question through, but eventually she sighed. "That's not really my job."

We had reached our cars: my little old Mini, her shiny new BMW.

"Oh come on. If you work with a detective agency, surely you've thought of getting one step ahead of the police."

"For heaven's sake, Sabbie, who else might there be?"

"What about Aidan's dad?"

She looked at me as if I was a rather dim-witted child. "Garth Stanford? I don't think so. If you murder a kid, you do not go on to steal your own son. You'd be putting the finger on yourself."

I shook my head in frustration. "I can't believe the police haven't investigated that avenue. Could it be possible that Aidan Rodderick's disappearance is totally unconnected with Josh Sutton's murder?"

"But it's Josh's murder he's charged with. Unfortunately, Cliff also lives very close to Aidan's school. Naturally, I will be arguing that this is pure coincidence. By the by, what was all that about signposts being like trees?"

"Nothing much." My fruitless search for Brokeltuft had taught me to interpret my journeys with a bit of caution. "Shamans always play with symbols."

Linnet shuddered. Or perhaps it was the cold wind that whipped along this long street with its high-security wall. "Trees and signposts can be gallows, can't they? Let's not take symbols too far. Let's stick to the facts."

———

I reversed out of my parking space and drove through the back streets of North Bristol until I reached a road lined with bay-windowed, terraced houses. Their doors were flush to the pavement, but each had a proud name carved above the porch. I drew up outside the one called Oak Villa. Around the name were carvings of oak leaves and acorns. The stonework was chipped and blackened, but the paintwork was glossy and the leaded stained glass panels above the door glinted in the weak sun.

I stood for a moment, taking in the memories. I'd lived in Oak Villa for eight years, and I still thought of it as my true home. The door opened before I could ring the bell, because Gloria was expecting me, her arms ready for me to dissolve into.

"Come right in," she said. "I've been baking."

I first met Gloria Davidson shortly before my thirteenth birthday. She was cleaning the passage floor in the children's home I lived in at the time, and I saw her as just another new worker I could taunt and wind up. I'd moved through a lot of foster homes and children's homes since the age of six and had learnt one thing more comprehensively than anything else: the less you care about what happens to you, the better. So picking on the home workers and even the social workers was fair game, in my opinion. It's impossible for me to imagine what a horrid child I'd become by that point, but I certainly wasn't being offered foster placements any longer. As far as I could see, I was going to be stuck in The Willows until they were legally entitled to chuck me out.

That day Gloria was pulling the vacuum cleaner methodically backwards and forwards over the carpet. All I could see of her was the pair of extra-large jeans in which she'd managed to cram an extra-large rear.

I leaned against the door and yelled at the kids who were watching the telly one room away. "Come and get an eyeful of this bum! It's gonna win the fat-ass of the year competition!"

Gloria swung round at me and planted the cleaner squarely between us, like a weapon. "You can say what you like about me, Sabbie Dare," she said, her voice earnest. "But you say it to my face. My butt might be big, but it's my mouth that answers back."

By this time, the other kids had joined us, ready for the show. I could throw a classy verbal punch by that age, and I'd already perfected my catfight techniques. I was a wild wee thing, and a new staff member at The Willows was not likely to thwart my constant search for trouble.

Yet I was struck dumb. I stared into Gloria's face. All the things I saw—her strong, full mouth; ebony eyes; tight twists of sable hair, but especially that insipid in-between mid-brown skin colour—were the things that I hated the most about my own looks. Gloria could have been my birth mother, except I could vaguely remember that my mother's fragile skin had been so white it was blue.

Now that I have a degree in psychology, I understand the theories of identity. But back then, I was very confused about where my roots lay. For my first six years, I'd lived alone with my blue-eyed mother. Afterwards, I had been brought up (that was their claim, at least) by white middle-class social workers. I'd never met my father, although I understood that he was black. In fact, I didn't know many black adults and had never bothered to think more closely about my origins. I knew I was of mixed race, but all that meant to me was that I was often the wrong colour altogether, neither properly white nor properly black. Frankly, I was too engrossed in the pain of my present to think deeply about my past.

Gloria might have been the first person I'd ever met in my thirteen long years who had my exact skin tones. She arched her eyebrows as a smile lifted her mouth, and to my shock, I discovered being a shade of caramel didn't mean you weren't beautiful. It was a tough connection to make—that someone who resembled me might be lovely to gaze upon. So tough that for a few moments I didn't recognise the sensation I felt inside. A sort of thawing, an opening of petals. The idea that throwing a smile into the sepia mix could make something wonderful happen.

Gloria had taken hold of my shoulders. Usually, back then, that meant someone was about to try shaking some sense into me, and I can remember getting ready to pull away, but instead, she gently squeezed, as if testing me for freshness.

"You okay, girl?"

"Yeah." Everyone watching had known there was something up. I wasn't using my tongue as a hatchet. In fact, I was trying to copy the smile, although I wasn't very proficient at first.

"Girl," she had said, "you finish this carpet off, and I'll make you all pancakes."

"You're not allowed," said Kelly, who was ten and rigorous about rules.

"We'll see," came the reply. I was about to learn that Gloria could get away with breaking conventions even better than I could. She passed the handle of the cleaner to me, and I heard her whistle as she went into the kitchen. She's been baking for my sweet tooth ever since.

"Is Dad home?" I asked as I walked into Oak Villa.

"No, he's gone down to the caravan to spruce it up for the Easter break. Dennon's out somewhere; looking for work, I hope. But Charlene and the kids are coming for their tea."

This was the family that had melted the ice chip in my heart: my foster parents, Gloria and Philip, and my foster brother and sister, Dennon and Charlene.

"Something smells good."

"It's a fatless sponge," said Gloria. We passed into her kitchen where a massive yellow cake was cooling on a wire rack. She lifted it onto one hand, balancing it like a drinks tray while she sliced it into two thinner pieces with a bread knife. "But the chocolate filling is bursting with fat and sugar, so it's not diet material, I'm afraid."

Gloria hasn't lost any weight since I was first hugged by her—thank the goddess, I say—but she doesn't clean floors anymore. She works part-time as a teaching assistant at the school in Bristol where Charlene's kids go. That's Kerri and Rudi, my niece and nephew. The fridge was plastered with kiddie drawings and I checked them out while she filled the cake. She's in her element with kids around her, although I'm the only one she ever brought home permanently.

"Put Polly on, will you?" said Gloria. I filled the kettle and settled down at the kitchen table, my feet stretched out and my hands behind my head.

Gloria placed two enormous triangles of cake on separate plates and sat down across the table from me. It was as golden as honeycomb and soft chocolate drooled from its middle. I let out a little moan of ecstasy.

"So," said my foster mum. "How's things going?"

I pulled a face. I didn't want Gloria to feel the entire weight of the burdens I had begun to carry around with me. She had to be following Cliff's progress on the TV news, and she'd burst a button if she knew how deeply I was involved. But I did want to pick her brain. "Mum, d'you know anything about tracing people? If you only have a first name and a vague idea about their age?"

To my surprise, Gloria leaned over the table and squeezed my hand. "But you do have enough, you just don't realize it."

"What?"

"You know your own full name and date of birth. If you use that, you'll have traced your family soon enough. I'm just surprised you haven't started sooner."

I blinked, feeling stupid. "I'm not looking for *me*."

"You should be. It's not right to have no roots." Gloria smiled, opened her wide mouth, and slid fatless sponge into it.

Déjà vu. For the second day in a row I'd watched an elderly lady eat homemade cake while I sat frozen with shocking realization. Gloria was right, of course. I had no idea about my parents. I didn't even know if Dare was my father's family name or my mother's.

I gave myself a shake. "Gloria, you're the only mum I need. I don't care about the past. It's the present that counts." Unless, like Cliff, the past nudges at you, ruining your life. "I wanted to find a person, that's all. I don't even know where to begin."

"As far as I understand, if you're looking for certificates—birth, death, marriage—you go to the Register Office. If you want to know where people lived, you go to the Record Office, where they keep parish records, that sort of thing."

"How d'you know all that?"

She grinned. "Wisdom comes with age, girl. So I can guess this has something to do with one of your batty therapies."

I waved my hand in a careless fashion. "A client … amnesia … trying to trace the bits of his life he's forgotten."

"Learn delegation. Let him do it himself."

"It's a bit more complicated than that. He's in prison at the moment—that's why I'm up in Bristol."

"Prison!"

"Honestly, Mum, he's innocent, I know he is."

"*Pshaw*! You should leave that sort of thing to the police."

I nodded. "Of course you're right, but that's complicated too. The detective who's working on the case … Reynard the fox …" I felt a blush warm my cheeks.

"What?" asked Gloria. "*What*?"

"He's a dish."

I watched her roar with laughter. "Girl, you will find trouble even when it's buried six foot deep."

I shivered at her choice of metaphor. "Rey isn't trouble, exactly."

"That'll make a change. You usually pick your men out of police lineups."

"I can't have done, Rey *is* the police. And I haven't picked him. In fact, I wish I could stop dreaming about him. He clearly thinks I'm a notch away from crazy."

"Opposites attract."

"Yeah, well that clarifies *my* feelings, but Rey seems to have his own agenda. I don't know where I stand with him, is the truth."

"I'll tell you where you stand," said Gloria, holding up a silencing hand. "You should make sure that the guy is always a bit sweeter on you than he thinks you are on him."

I laughed. Gloria's knack with matters of the heart was legendary in her family. "Okay. I'll go for that. It might encourage Rey to answer my questions."

I thought about questions. They'd multiplied since seeing Cliff. And Gloria was right. I couldn't answer them myself. But they needed answering, and in express time.

I sprang up from the table. "I have to get back."

"Hey? I thought you'd hang around for Charlene and the kids."

"I'm sorry. There'll be another time. Soon, I promise. But right now—"

"You haven't even finished your cake."

"Wrap it up for me, will you? I'll eat it in the car."

———

I put my foot down all the way back to Bridgwater, but Rey had already left for the day by the time I reached the police station. Gone home to his lager and crisp supper. Instead I was presented with Detective Constable Abbott and taken into a little room where he towered over me like a shadow in a dungeon.

159

Even when they'd been arresting Cliff, Abbott had reminded me of portraits of the Tudors. The square of his torso would perfectly fit into the box-shaped tunics and rucked-up shorts they wore back then. His hair, as black as a villain's, would have looked great curling from beneath a feathered hat, and he had those eyelids that cover the upper half of the eye like a tight-fitting garment. The pupils swiveled away from me when I looked back at him, as if Abbott only sneaked glances when you weren't noticing.

I had the impression, mostly from this eye-avoidance, that Abbott had disliked me on first sight. Maybe it was because of Rey and me. I checked myself. There was no *Rey and me*, and I should be severely worried that I could even think such a thing.

"Sorry to disturb you like this," I said, starting out on the wrong foot—never apologise is my usual motto.

"I don't mind disruptions," said Abbott, "so long as they bring useful information my way."

"Well, I'm hopeful that this will."

"I'm pleased you've come in," said Abbott, sounding anything but. "You must recognise it was only a matter of time before you were interviewed more formally in regards to this case."

"I've honestly told you all I knew about Cliff. This is something that came up in a meeting with his solicitor. We both want you to investigate it." I searched back in my mind. Linnet had said *something* like that, I was sure.

Abbott hadn't sat down. He was shifting about the room, his body language telling me to astound him or go away. I took a breath, tried to get my thoughts in order. So far, rushing back to Bridgwater hadn't gone to plan. I'd hope to sweet-talk Rey into investigating the girl called Patsy. Abbott looked a much harder proposition.

"Directly before the Wetland Murders happened, two people may have been reported missing. One was Cliff Houghton. The other was a girl called Patsy. I'm hoping she had a report filed. You keep Missing Person files that long, don't you?"

"Patsy what?" said Abbott in a calm, bored voice.

"I don't know her second name. Cliff doesn't remember. Perhaps he doesn't even know."

Abbott closed his heavy lids for a second, as if despairing. "You want us to find a missing person—"

"Not necessarily. Just seeing the report details would be a good start."

"I'm sure it would. But at the moment we're investigating a recent murder and an even more recent child disappearance. I don't have time for any of this *is there anybody there* stuff."

"All we're asking you to do is check the Missing Persons lists."

He gave a cold laugh. "Let's just say our resources may not stretch to that. Besides, Miss Dare, I'm confident that you can find this person by merely closing your eyes."

I ignored the sarcasm. "It could really help."

"Yes, help screw up our case." I saw Abbott smile at his own bad joke, and the burning smog of anger that plagued my teenage years smothered me so that I could hardly breathe.

"Fine," I spat. "No need to investigate the crime, once you've framed your prime suspect. And while you're at it, why not harass innocent citizens. Until they bring up evidence, that is, then go right ahead and ridicule them."

Abbott's mouth hardened against his fine teeth. He came over to the chair I was perched on and positioned himself so that when he spoke, his spittle would land directly on my face. I felt sure he used words where spittle might be increased.

"Sabrina Isabel Dare. That's your full name, isn't it? I never liked the idea of bringing you and your charlatan shamanism into this case. The idea stinks. It was the detective sergeant's pitch, but I'm fucking sick of this floating about with phantoms. You might fool your *clients*, Miss Dare, but you don't fool me."

I felt my cheeks burn as he mentioned Rey. "What d'you mean, *bringing in my shamanism*?"

Abbott didn't reply. He walked to the door, opened it wide, and stood like a sentry, waiting for me to pass.

I thought he might toss off a final sarcasm as I scuttled down the corridor, but all I heard behind me was his derisive silence.

———

By the time I'd finished work that evening, I felt completely done in—ready for bed at a quarter to nine on a Saturday night. I poured myself a glass of chardonnay and switched on the telly, but I couldn't concentrate on the shifting pictures and chattering sounds, so I zapped it off and found myself wandering through the house, trying to make sense of it all. I needed to tie down the loose ends that were flapping about in my mind, because I was sure that they were all connected.

"Be sure of this Sabbie," Bren used to say to me. "Everything connects." I'd lived with the Howells for the three years of my degree, and as the time went on, I became more than fond of them; they were family to me, my third set of parents.

I guess losing both my natural parents—my father before I knew him and my mother when I was six—made it okay to have two sets of surrogate parents. Philip and Gloria Davidson had defused the spitfire kid and created someone ready to take their place in the world. But living with the Bren and Rhiannon Howell had changed me even more drastically.

The Howells made me listen when a tree shakes its branches. They showed me how to get drunk just looking at the moon. Bren had taught me the phases of the moon as we worked in his garden, introduced me to a small community of Pagan people hidden by the North Welsh hills. We'd light a fire of split logs in the centre of the garden with its herby flowerbeds. Bren would trace a circle and draw a five-pointed star within it. The magic of the pentangle. Once drawn, Rhiannon called power to us. She used the four ancient elements, as I do today in my therapy room—fire, water, earth, and air. Only when we felt empowered and protected in this way, did we begin the work that went on in our minds. Squatted on a variety of damp-proof seating arrangements, we traced paths to other worlds. Sometimes the sounds of the night and the crackle of the fire were our accompaniment; other times there would be a drum to give a steady rhythm, or a chanter repeating an arcane word or phrase over and over until it stilled my racing thoughts and let the visions come.

At first, I had not believed I would see things. When I did, I told myself it was all my imagination.

"Imagination?" said Rhiannon, when I'd explained how I felt. "What d'you think that is, Sabbie?"

It took me a long time to understand what she meant, especially as, at that point in my life, I was attending lecture after essay after seminar on the psychological workings of the human mind.

"What are the pictures we see in our mind?" I asked my professor. "What happens when we're imagining something so deeply, we don't even hear a friend speak to us from across a room?"

"Ah," he said, gearing himself up into lecture mode. "That is the Alpha brainwave state."

"But what happens?"

"Our brain's electrical impulses slow into Alpha rhythm."

"But what *happens*?"

"You sound like my six-year-old," he said, moving so that his shoulder formed a barrier between us. "She's *why, why, why* all the time. You must phrase your questions more academically, Miss Dare."

I was twenty-four years old when I left Bangor with my honours degree. By then, I had decided I wouldn't be Bren's cunning apprentice. Herbalism was fascinating, but it wasn't close enough to the things I wanted to explore. I was pulled to the very edges of my degree subject, the areas my teachers couldn't tell me about. What are the pictures we see in our mind? What happens when we're in a trance? Why do silly coincidences keep happening when we're concentrating on one thing? Does a spirit world really exist? *These* were the questions running through my thoughts.

I went back to Bristol. The job at the residential home was waiting for me as if I'd never left it. I started an aromatherapy course in my spare time. I knew I only had to wait. Bren had come to me in my dreams when I'd needed him most, and I felt sure something would happen quite soon.

Gloria, on the other hand, had nearly exploded. "Why the devil are you cluttering up my spare bedroom again?" she kept asking me. "You should be using that degree, girl."

Sometimes you've got to nudge the spirit world. In a New Agey magazine I spotted a small advertisement for a therapeutic shaman. At that point, I didn't even know what that was, but I rang him anyway, because something had been bothering me.

"I keep dreaming about otters," I had said. "I'm hoping someone can tell me why. I don't know anything about them. Actually, I've never even seen one alive, but last week, a lady was admitted to the residential home I work at, and she wanted to bring this stuffed animal in a case with her. I thought it would be gross, but it was so beautiful. I wanted to tell her I was dreaming about an otter, but I couldn't quite manage it."

"Just one?" the shaman had asked.

"Sort of. It keeps saying its name is Trendle."

"It's good to take notice of coincidences and connections," he'd said. "You'd better come and see me."

Coincidences and connections. Nudging the spirit world to show itself. That's what I needed to do now, if I was to make sense of Cliff.

I wondered about the way I'd recorded essential words and phrases on pieces of card in a bid to understand Marianne's spirit world. That had seemed to work, sort of. In the spare bedroom were the rest of the Christmas cards I'd saved from last year. I'd kept them with the intention of up-cycling them into new Christmas cards, but hey, it was only March; plenty of time yet.

Half an hour later, there were bits of cut-up Christmas card spread like a hand of solitaire over my kitchen worktop. A single detail was printed on the plain back of each one in red felt-tip. I started with the children, trying to record everything I knew about Josh Sutton and Aidan Rodderick. I listed the four who had been found in the moors all those years ago: Matthew, Joanna, Nicolas, and John. I carried on, including everything that might have a bearing. The words swam in front of my eyes: *Brokeltuft Cottage, Slamblaster, shaved heads and sacks of hair, catkins, cars, kidnappers, trees and signposts. Waterwheel*, I wrote. *Old Mill.* I chewed my pen and used a card to describe the nameless man Cliff had seen in his dream ... *bulky, with a bristling beard and deep-set eyes.* I noted the rest of the players: *Cliff, Patsy, Caroline, Bella Rodderick,* and *Garth Stanford,* even *Josh's family in Bristol. The woman in the car*, whose name I might never know. As an afterthought I included *Gary Abbott*. As an after-afterthought I added *Linnet* and *Rey*, and my own name, on the understanding that everything connects to everything else.

I shuffled the cards around, put them in random order, then in columns and categories. Nothing shouted an answer. I stared down at the cards with their bright red words, perplexed. I'd left something out, but I couldn't see what.

I yawned and stretched. The hens were already shut in for the night, and a good night's sleep wouldn't do me any harm, either. It might help me see connections and coincidences in a fresh light.

———

Even on Sundays, my mobile alarm goes off, in its spiteful fashion, at 6:30 a.m. No change there, then. I groaned, covered my eyes against the bedside lamp, and eventually fell out of bed and into my garden clothes. Yesterday, with all its strange turns, continued to weigh me down. I even had to pull off my joggers and put them on again. The pockets don't work when they're back-to-front.

I was feeding my remaining hens when I heard a gravelly voice behind me.

"Where's the Cocky Bastard?"

On my lawn, hands on her hips, was my foster mother.

"Gloria! A fox got in. Saffron and Pettitgrain too."

"When was this?"

She was glaring at me as if I was at fault. "I'm sorry I rushed off like that yesterday."

"Gave me a sleepless night. I knew there was more to your mood than you were letting on. You should've told me about the fox."

"You don't know the half of it." I ran over to her and flung my arms around her neck. The tears I'd longed for began to pour and pour. I was so glad she'd come, because she's the one person who can make everything better.

We sat on the bench outside my back door while I wiped away tears with the handkerchief Gloria passed me—one of Philip's, as big and bright as a royal headscarf. "You didn't drive all the way down from Bristol just to see me, did you?"

"Not quite," said Gloria. "Philip's still over at the caravan, so I've brought Charlene and the kids down for a seaside break without the seaside weather. I thought you might like to join us for a bite of lunch."

"I'd love to. I've only got one client today, late this afternoon."

"They do a nice Sunday roast in that pub by the caravan park. We might manage a walk."

I glanced up at the sky. "It looks like rain."

"That's never put us off," she said with a laugh.

I thought of my foster father, chivvying his lagging children over mile after mile of countryside. Philip had given me an early love of nature.

"So. You gonna tell me what's up, girl? It isn't just the hens, is it?"

Gloria is the only nonshamanic person I confide in. I know I can trust her to be discreet, but she doesn't pull her punches and makes no secret of her opinion of what I do. She listened carefully while I spilled the beans but was shaking her head before I finished.

"I've been expecting this," she said. "I never stop worrying that your job will attract oddballs like this chap."

"He's not an oddball, Gloria," I said. "Whatever that is."

"Someone who might end up blaming you for all their troubles, that's what."

I shook my head. "It's all too awful for words. Cliff's mother knows the family of the little boy who's gone missing."

"So Cliff must have known them too," Gloria pointed out. "That's not good. That's hardly in his favour."

I thought about that. "It's circumstantial, like his solicitor says—the only sound evidence against him is Josh's toy."

"Sabbie, that's not *sound*. That's iron*clad*."

"I don't think so. That toy could have got into the flat by other means than Cliff's own hand."

Gloria frowned. "I'm not with you."

I pulled off my wellies, stuffed my hands in them, and slammed the soles together to shake off the mud. "Thanks to Cliff's obsession with Josh's death, he was first arrested five days *before* Aidan was abducted. His flat was searched then, and that makes me wonder three things: Why ever would he take another child so quickly, when he knew the police would be watching him? And why didn't that first search reveal the Slamblaster?"

"That's two things," said Gloria.

"I know. I'm coming to number three." I shifted my bum on the bench, as if getting comfy would make my reasoning more concrete. "His arrest was in the paper. I checked back. It was in the local and national press. It was big news for about ten seconds, which surely would be long enough to give the actual killer a bright idea. I think *that* is why Aidan was taken so soon after Cliff's release. It might even be why Aidan lives so close to Cliff. The killer waited for Cliff to be hauled back in, then he went to his flat and planted the toy. I don't think Cliff's fingerprints are on it. Only Josh's."

"Come on, Sabbie. The police would be prodding around that flat in seconds. When would someone have a chance to plant evidence?"

"Cliff came to see me as soon as he heard about the kidnapping on the news. Maybe the killer had time to get in." But I couldn't help remember the woman in the post office ... *they've taped it all up.* Her gothic face loomed in my mind.

Gloria put a warm arm round my chilled shoulders. "Sabbie, when you're caught up—obsessed—you don't think clearly."

"It's a gut feeling. I am *sure* this man is innocent."

"Okay, who would you put in his place?"

"I have a funny feeling about Josh's father. But I don't think the police should discount the original Wetland Murderer. No one caught him, the killings just stopped. Why shouldn't he have started again?" I stared gloomily at the paving stones beneath my feet. Tiny weeds and blades of grass were forcing their way through the crack. A spasm passed through me, and Gloria felt it.

"This is spooking you. Forget it for the rest of the day and come back to the caravan."

"You're right, as usual. A nice rainy, windy walk will blow the spooks away."

I went up into my bedroom. I brushed my hair and plaited it down my back out of the way, then searched for my walking gear. I had no lightweight, breathable rainproof coat with detachable fleece lining, but I reckoned my charity shop find would keep me warm and dry, although it did make a strange crackling sound as I moved and had yellow stripes that glowed in the dark. My walking boots had not been cleaned in, well, *ever,* really. I had a pair of gloves, but they didn't quite make a match. They were a left and a right, though, with a scarf to match the left one. I caught a glimpse in the mirror of a canary-coloured clown. My foster dad, who believed in the right clothes for the job, was going to despair.

I crackled down the stairs, leaving moulded jigsaw shapes of dried mud from my boots on every step. Gloria was in the kitchen, washing my supper things. She gave me another of her glaring looks.

"I was plum exhausted last night. I had clients straight through to almost nine. I just dropped into bed."

"And look at this—all these cards written out here." She waved a soapy hand. "That's what I meant about becoming obsessed."

"I did that last night—I was trying to get my thoughts in order." I shuffled them some more. "Something's missing. Stupid thing is, the more missing it is, the harder it is to spot."

"You see?" said Gloria. "You're worrying about him, getting involved with him, draining yourself."

"I just I feel so inadequate."

"You should keep out of things as much as you can. Even so, you're gonna be called as a witness, sweetie."

"I realize that. Miss Smith has asked me—"

"Not for the defence! Lord, once the prosecution gets wind of you, they'll tear you apart. And if I was a juror, as far as I can see, everything you've told me so far would only convince me he was as guilty as hell."

I slapped my gloved hands over my eyes. "It's a mess. There are too many imponderables to take in all at once."

Gloria grabbed my brush and dustpan and began to sweep the kitchen floor. "So let the proper authorities get on with it."

"You mean Rey, don't you—will you stop doing my housework, please? I'm perfectly capable."

Gloria had disappeared under my breakfast bar and humped the box of veg from Middlesprings Farm onto the surface. "What in heck is this?"

"A freebie. I haven't managed to eat much of it yet."

"Eat it? You haven't even put it away!"

"No, well, I have been busy."

"It's going off, left in this box. Look, the curly kale's yellowing." Gloria bustled around, stuffing vegetables in the fridge and filling my empty fruit bowl.

"Take some with you," I said, coming over to help her. "There's too much for me."

"They've left a load of flyers in the bottom," said Gloria, pulling out a sheath of notices and shuffling through them. "Craft Fayre, dog training classes ... Lordy."

"Trevor must be going to those," I said, smiling. "He's the reason I got the free food."

"Farm open day, Stone-Age Centre ..." Gloria dropped them into my hands. "You want to put them in the recycling?"

A word caught my eye. My body froze. I stared down at the paper in my hand.

"Garibaldi," I whispered.

I had found my missing word.

THIRTEEN

I REALIZED I WAS holding my breath. In my head, I heard Trendle chuckle. *You never listen to me,* he said. *It's enough to make an otter despair.*

I must've looked very strange, because Gloria came over to me. "What's wrong?"

I passed her the flyer. She could see I wanted her to read it aloud. I needed the confirmation.

"*Stone-Age Visitor Centre,*" she began. "*Great for all the family! Sit by the fire inside our rebuilt Neolithic roundhouse, have your face painted with woad, make stone-age musical instruments, walk the replica Garibaldi Way—the oldest man-made path in the UK. Tea Rooms and children's play area.* Great idea, Sabbie, we could take Rudi and Kerri."

I was no longer listening. The smell of that gas hob was in my nostrils, the steaming kettle, the tea, and Garibaldi biscuits. *Bloody squashed flies. Makes you puke to think of it.* I'd asked Trendle if they were a gift. *For you, dear,* he'd replied. And I'd ignored him.

My heart beat like a crazed drummer at a festival. It seemed that the Somerset Moors constantly revealed things hidden within their black heart, both fair and foul.

Garibaldi. A plate of biscuits and an ancient track. Probably nothing more than a silly coincidence that would turn me into a fool, but shamanic journeying thrived on such connections. I could not ignore the clue that Middlesprings Farm had handed me.

"Sabbie?"

I blinked. Gloria was gripping my hand, making me feel like a screwed-up thirteen-year-old again. "Nothing," I said. "Could I borrow one of your walkers' maps?"

She sniffed. "Not coming back to the caravan, then."

"I can't let this go. That cottage where Cliff was kept has to be somewhere."

"You think you're gonna find this poor snatched baby inside?"

"Am I mad? The police aren't going down that road at all. If there's even a chance that..."

"You're as crazy as chicken and banana pie. Not that that's ever stopped you before." But she grinned and fetched her collection of Ordinance Survey maps for me.

I smoothed out the appropriate map while Gloria did a bit of light dusting and pretended not to be interested in what I was searching for. It took me a while to pinpoint the road where the Old Mill stood. Only a few miles away, the Stone-Age Centre was marked by a little tourist legend. All around these two landmarks lay the enormity of Somerset moor and fen, mile after mile of low-lying land. Somewhere within their damp acreage was a vile tomb that had held four children twenty-three years ago and one small boy only months ago.

I had to find Brokeltuft Cottage before another child could be buried in bogland like a dog.

The doorbell chimed as I was poring over the map, and before I knew it, Gloria was letting Ivan in.

"I do believe you're Rey, aren't you?" I heard her say, in a motherly voice that made my stomach squirm.

"No," said Ivan, his face clouding. "I'm Ivan."

"Sorry!" Gloria grinned. "I'm that bad at names. But you are the detective, isn't that right?"

"I'm not the detective," he said. "I'm Sabbie's boyfriend."

It struck me that everyone wanted me for their girlfriend—or their son's girlfriend—except the one man I had the hots for. "Sorry Ivan," I began. "I thought we said—"

"I'm sorry too, babe. I just had to see you." Ivan took a couple of wide strides past Gloria the doorkeeper. He took my chin between a tight thumb and finger and kissed me on the mouth.

"Yow," I said and pulled away so fast that I fell onto the staircase behind me. I badly needed to toss out some sassy line that would tell Ivan that he (a) couldn't keep turning up like this, (b) was not allowed to pinch me, and (c) had never made promotion to boyfriend. But I was sprawling over the bottom step in a glow-yellow coat and odd gloves. All that came out of my mouth was a sort of low-grade swearing, as I struggled to get up.

Gloria stepped into the breech. She reached for her jacket, which happily was hanging on the banister knob, and dragged it on. "Time to go, Sabbie." She turned to Ivan. "We're just off to a family lunch." She cast a glance at my appearance, clearly stumped. "And then a walk along the coast."

"Brean. Very nice there, but windy." I'd found my cool again. "I'm sure we were supposed to meet up this evening, Ivan. Eight o'clock wasn't it?" I turned to Gloria. "Ooo, we must go. Don't want the meal to spoil."

I tucked my arm in Ivan's, and he had no option but to come with me up the garden path until we were in front of his Audi S4, a sleek silvery model less than a year old. I suppose financial advisers have to walk their own kind of talk. I let him give me a peck on the lips, but only because I didn't want to explain things right that minute.

Ivan looked at me oddly but let it go. "Pick you up later, then," he said and drove away before I could argue.

"Where did you find *him*?" asked Gloria.

"Out clubbing," I said, trying not to sound like a sullen teenager.

"Isn't twenty-eight a bit old for clubbing?"

"No more than almost sixty is a bit old for walking."

"He's a trophy collector, Sabbie."

"You don't even know him."

"I don't have to, girl. I've met his sort many a time."

I exploded. "What d'you mean, *sort*? He's just a guy, Gloria. He's fond of me, is all."

"The wrong kind of fond."

"Come on. I know my way around bloke territory." I'd temporarily forgotten that I was planning to ditch Ivan. I've never liked interference in my social life, probably because it didn't hold up under close scrutiny. "I'll see who I please."

"Of course you will. You always have." She began the march towards her Daihatsu.

"Mum!" I had to call after her. She was the one person I needed to love me unconditionally.

As if she realized this, she came back to take me in her marshmallow embrace and plant a kiss on my cheek.

"That guy's sniffing round you like a fox sniffs round a rabbit." She has to have the last word, does Gloria, but I wish she hadn't reminded me about the hens.

I waved until her car was out of sight.

———

It was still not much after ten a.m. as I drove clear of Bridgwater. Mini Ha Ha was soon navigating the narrow bridges that crisscrossed the waterlands of Somerset. Everywhere water shone like mercury—from rivers, canals, and rhynes, reflecting the light covering of clouds above. Reeds and withies bent in the breeze as if to acknowledge my presence.

I would only be satisfied that Brokeltuft Cottage was nothing more than an illusion when I'd exhausted all avenues. I grinned. I was starting to sound like a police officer. In that fine old tradition, I gave myself the third degree as I wound round the country lanes. I was searching for a cottage that I'd only seen in the spirit world of a man now held for murder. Even if it did exist, what was I hoping to find there? Was the malevolent mind that had buried bodies of children on the Somerset Moors so long ago beginning all over again? Was he using the same house to hide in? Was he inflicting his sadistic techniques on a new generation of children? Was that the reason the police had not released the details of how Josh had died? Or had a sick killer got off on a sick joke by burying Josh in the same place as the Wetland Murderer victims?

The B roads became narrower as I drove deeper into the countryside, and I dropped my speed. Signs for the Stone-Age Centre were beginning to pop up at turnings, and I doggedly followed them until I could see the gateway. My tyres crunched over gravel as I pulled up in a little car park. The centre was not very big, and from where I stood I could see the thatched wattle and daub roundhouse and the slightly more contemporary tearooms. Despite the greyness of the day, the place was teeming with weekend visitors. Kids streaked about, dipping into the dark interiors, their faces painted an alarming blue. Gloria was right—this would be a lovely place to bring Charlene's two.

I paid my four pounds fifty for a ticket and a site plan and began to drift around. It didn't take me long to find the Garibaldi Way. In a corner of the site was a plot of peaty grass, and beside it stood a cave woman having a bad hair day. She was chillily clad in hand-sewn leather tunic and shoes, and in her hand she held a stone-tipped spear.

"The Garibaldi Way?" I asked, as I squelched through the peat.

She shook her spear at the bog. A run of cleverly fashioned wooden trackway led through it. "More than six thousand years old. Constructed before humans had begun to properly farm. Around here, the Neolithic people exploited the reedswamps for their natural resources. They relied on wild food, and the staves you see halfway along the track is a weir they built to catch fish."

"Gosh," I said, surprised. "It really doesn't look thousands of years old."

The woman laughed. "It's not. It's a model."

I nodded, feeling rather daft. "Of course, you can't have kids storming over the real thing."

"It's not just that. The actual remains had to go back under the bog, or they would've rotted away."

"Right. But those are around somewhere, I suppose?"

"They're actually not far from here."

I should have guessed. The spirit world never makes things easy. "Could you direct me?"

"I can, but you won't see anything. Though there is a plaque, just to commemorate the discovery. In fact, the track runs for over half a mile through the marshes."

"But you can't see the track."

She dazzled a smile. "You can see it here."

"I'd really like to see the plaque." I pulled Gloria's map from my pocket and rested it on the glass-covered display board. The woman tapped at it with one woad-painted finger.

"Turn off this road at the next left-hand junction and follow the signs for Bartonbeck Tip. The Garibaldi Way is down a little lane immediately after the turning for the waste tip." She looked up, keen to impart more wisdom. "It was when they extended the waste tip that they found the causeway. You'll have to follow the lane on foot, it's not passable, it peters out into bog, so go carefully."

"I will," I said. I meant it. These were truly uncharted waters. As I negotiated Mini Ha Ha out of the car park, rain started pattering against the windscreen and all the families disappeared into the tearooms.

I kept below twenty. The soft brown of bulrush heads and the glint of water followed me on both sides of the unmarked road. I pulled into the side just after the turning for the dump and doubled back on foot. The lane had been almost invisible from the car, but it did have a sign saying GARIBALDI WAY, 200 METRES, nailed to the fence. I set out, keeping my eyes peeled for anything that might resemble a plaque.

When I found it, I felt a real thrill, as if I'd completed a quest. A quaint plaque of slate attached to the trunk of an old oak. It told the story of the discovery and detailed the items that were now being displayed at Glastonbury, as well as directing me back to the Stone-Age Centre. I nodded to myself as I read, but the thrill that had run through me was seeping away, until it felt like the words were mocking me. I rammed a fist against the tree trunk. It might as well have been a brick wall.

I closed my eyes, in the hope that Trendle would speak to me. A robin sang, but nothing came. I didn't even have any idea which way the half-mile of track led—it was invisible under the boggy soil. But I couldn't admit defeat. I strode into the trees in what I hoped was the right direction. After only a few metres, my walking boots sank into reed bed. I yelped. Water was oozing over my socks. I scrambled out and went back to the road. The wetter the ground became, the less likely I was to find a cottage.

For the first time, I looked at the narrow junction across the lane, where lorries had left a mire of churned mud as they turned up to the waste tip. I stared at the shape the track formed with the lane. A stillness settled. The robin stopped singing. I had been so intent on finding the plaque that I'd walked right past a little triangle of green grass. And from it, like a bare tree with just two branches, rose a wooden signpost.

For several minutes I could go no closer. I could only gaze and wonder. I had witnessed this place in a trance. Logically, I knew that this was because it had got lodged somewhere in Cliff's forgotten past, and that Trendle had led me to it as a good spirit guide should. But I couldn't help being dumbfounded at its sheer reality.

Finally I stumbled over to the grass triangle. The signpost pointed two ways. The first indicated the road to the waste tip and read: BARTONBECK TIP: ½ MILE. The second indicated the way back to my car and made me bark with laughter: MIDDLESPRINGS FARM: 2½ MILES. Sandy Guilding probably did know this place, at least vaguely. But that didn't matter, because she'd tossed the information I needed into my box of free veg.

I looked about me again. The only path not signposted was the continuance of the lane I was on. I remembered the cave woman's words: *it peters out into bog.* As if to prove this, a ROAD ENDS sign stood as warning, half tucked into the scrub.

My boots were stubbornly refusing to move. "Oh, Trendle, Trendle." I repeated his name for comfort. *Go on, then,* I heard him say into my head. *I'm with you.*

I began to walk. I felt as if I was returning to a place I'd visited long ago. The memories from my journey at the prison were not perfectly accurate, but the general impressions were there. The sun was bright behind its canopy of altostratus, as if trying to burn a hole in the clouds. The previous rain had left large puddles that smelled, as I splashed though them, of iron and rotting weeds. Catkins softly swayed in the slight breeze.

Slowly the cottage came into view. It grew from imagination into memory, from distant miniature into full reality.

The tensing in my stomach surprised me. Every tiny hair that lined my neck and spine was standing to attention. My flesh felt covered with scales. My pace slowed to nothing. The relic of a building stood before me—a country cottage.

I had done something I'd always known was possible but had never quite believed in: I had used my spirit paths to locate an object on the physical plane.

FOURTEEN

THERE WAS NO DOUBT this was Brokeltuft Cottage, but it was hardly more than the empty husk of the original house. The black paint of the front door was entirely gone. The iron nameplate was missing, the screw holes where it had once lived torn and rotting. It looked as if it might crumble if I touched it. Although *touch it* was the last thing I wanted to do. I looked longingly to where the track led onwards, the path to the north, as Trendle called it in my last journey. In the spring light it looked almost welcoming in comparison to this malevolent dwelling.

"Trendle?"

You found it, Sabbie!

I walked up the short front path. I laid my gloved hand in the centre of the door and pushed. It was not locked or bolted from inside. It screeched over a stone-tiled floor and then stopped. I leaned my shoulder on it, then my back against it, but the gap, just enough for me to get my hand through, would widen no more. I put an eye to the opening. I could see grey light, like a fog that hangs around in abandoned places.

Some time ago, someone had come here with planks and nails and a pot of paint. The downstairs windows had been boarded up and the words DANGER—KEEP OUT painted across the boarding. Whatever was in the way of the front door must have been there even at that time, as they hadn't bothered to board that up. I stared at the words for a moment or two, waiting to see how they affected the more rule-abiding side of my nature, then shrugged and traced the path around the side of the house.

I had to scrunch through a wasteland wilderness. Brambles were the predominant feature, but the thorns couldn't get a purchase on my plasticky coat—it was like wearing steel plating. The high swathes of nettles had more success. They seemed to lean forward and deliberately brush the thin sliver of skin that showed between my coat cuffs and my gloves. I stuffed my hands in my pockets and took steady step by steady step. A smell of fungus rose as I walked, as if the pathway had become mouldy with lack of use.

I turned the corner of the house. I was in the back garden. I pushed through the thigh-high weeds until I reached an ancient back door. You could see the plank work in it. This door did not budge at all. It must have been bolted from the inside.

I beat my fists against the wood, then turned and leaned on it, frustrated to the point of tears. I hadn't taken in the rest of the garden; I was too caught up my desire to gain entry to the house. But after a moment or two, I realized that a strong presence was in this place. I stepped out onto what was once the lawn.

At the far corner of the cottage stood a massive tree. Its solid trunk sprouted into powerful branches. I struggled through overgrowth until I could touch its deeply fissured bark, as black as coal tar. The tree was bare of leaves, but from the end of each twig hung long catkins with soft green bells, like unfastened necklaces. Instantly, I knew this was a black poplar. I'm no authority on trees, but Rhiannon frequently used such a tree for its healing qualities. She thought the black poplar was darkly magical but with genuine good intentions, and as I leaned against this one, I felt the truth of that. It had aided Cliff in his greatest time of need. He'd fallen through its branches and escaped from the torment of the Wetland Murderer.

I stared up until my neck cricked. Twenty-three years had passed and the poplar had continued to stretch and grow since the house was abandoned. It was pushing heavily against the wall of the cottage like an undefeated sumo wrestler, and one branch had smashed through an upstairs window and crept over the sill.

I reached up to a low branch, cupping my hands round it and fixing the sole of my boot on the trunk. As a kid, I'd been a champion climber of trees. I was taller now and supposedly stronger, but I soon discovered that my childhood ease among the branches had been replaced with short breath and a locked jaw. I clung to that first branch like death, unable to move, until suddenly the rhythm of climbing came back to me and I was off.

In minutes I was sitting astride the branch that fed through the window. I took a rest while I examined the frame at close quarters. I could see shark teeth triangles of glass still imbedded in brittle putty, and my heart sank. I would have to get rid of them, or climb down again.

I eased forward. The branch shifted as my weight pushed against its narrower end. I felt my seat dislodge. The sensation of ice-cold fear for your life tore through me. I grabbed at twigs to steady myself. The unmown grass was a long way down, and I was a lot heavier than Cliff had been when he'd fallen through these branches.

Centimetre by centimetre, I crawled towards the window until I was close enough to touch it. Pulling the sleeve of my coat down, I grasped the hem so that my fist was covered and bashed at the teeth of glass through this armour. Just once, a vicious point sheared across the back of my hand. The blood oozed, slow but livid red.

The cut was a warning. I wrapped a tissue around the site and eased every single bit of jagged glass out of the crumbling putty before I dipped my head through the frame. The branch held my weight because the windowsill was supporting it. With slow care I lifted my legs into the room. On the inside of the windowsill, the branch quickly bent and drooped, sickly with lack of air and sun. I slid off, landing on the bare floorboards with a yelp.

I was in a small room with a low ceiling. Cobwebs hung like the hammocks of grey ghosts from every cranny. The walls were papered with such heavy-duty Anaglypta that thick layers of grime clung to its moulded swirls. The floor was layered with dust and I was lying in it.

I peered around the room, trying to tap into its essence. All I could feel was the bounding of my pulse. The room was almost empty of furniture. A cane-bottom chair lay on its side, the cane seat ripped and missing in its middle. A single mattress lay in one corner. I stared at the wall a metre above the mattress. Screwed through the dusty wallpaper was a thick metal ring. The sort that's used at country markets to keep bulls from wandering.

I froze through to the core of my body. This had to be the epicentre of Cliff's appalling experience—the place I'd seen in the first journey I'd made. I stepped closer. The ring was made of silver steel and as thick as my finger. It had been driven deep in, but even so, I could see the plaster disturbed around its root. Something or someone—maybe more than one someone—had tried to drag it from its mooring. But each attempt had failed; it was too deeply imbedded. As I put my hand out to it, a slight movement, a rustle in my ear, made me glance at the mattress. Its contents were exploding, wadding and springs spilling out through the torn cover. With escalating revulsion, I realized that some form of rodent had made this bed into a nest.

I ran, powder flying up from the floor as if this was the surface of the moon. I tried not to breathe in or look back, but I felt my skin prickle.

On the upper landing, I stood for a moment. My voice crackled from under-use. "Aidan? Aidan? Are you here?" This would be a terrible place to imprison a small boy, but I had to check it out. The boards creaked beneath my boots, warning me not to trust them. I passed two more bedrooms. Neither contained anything more sinister that a single dead sparrow lying on its back in a corner.

When I reached the top of the stairs, I discovered what had been barring the front door. Most of the treads and banister rails had collapsed through the stairwell and lay in a pile below. The landing stopped dead where the stairs had once began. I stamped my foot in frustration and dust and grit showered through the opening, snow-flaking down to the ground floor.

I could get down there, I told myself, dropping onto my haunches.
You are kidding, my saner self replied.

I turned so that I was facing belly-in and slid a leg over the unprotected stairwell. I eased the other after it until I was balancing on my arms. I'd always heard this was the way to fall the distance of one storey. Once you're dangling from the tips of your fingers, your feet are less than a metre from the ground below. But my rib cage was lodged on the rim of the existing floorboards. Allowing my body to slide down so that I would be holding on with outstretched hands seemed an impossibility.

The boards creaked at me in alarm as nails were drawn out of antique holes by my weight. Regardless of my desire to get to the ground floor, I was about to reach it in double-quick time. My coat zip caught on a protruding nail as my grasp slipped. For a couple of seconds I was swaying in midair, like some insect that had flown slap-bang into a web. My coat had protected me in the garden, but now it became a menace. I felt the zip give and remember too late that the dangling arms trick should only be used in case of emergency—fire, that sort of thing—not just because you fancied it. There was a shriek from the ancient wood as a floorboard sprang loose and flew out into the stairwell—the board whose nail I was hanging from. I landed in a heap on the red and black tiles of the hallway and the board tumbled down on top of me.

I groaned feebly, but no one was going to come to my rescue. My knees were smarting, so I rolled up my trouser legs to examine them. They'd taken the brunt of the drop and were raw and stinging. Ah, now it's in circumstances like these that a knowledge of herbalism comes into its own. I took another tissue from my coat pocket, spat on it, and dabbed them better. I checked the scratch on my hand. The blood had stopped oozing, but the cut looked angry. I gave mental thanks to Gloria, who was severe about things like tetanus boosters.

For long minutes, I stayed on the floor—not because I was unable to get up, but because the dread feeling I'd first sensed in the upstairs room had followed me in my descent. Anyone coming close to this place would have felt the sad cloud of melancholy that lay over the cottage. It was no wonder it had never been claimed or resold. Not even knowing why, people had given it a wide berth until it had fallen into complete disrepair.

When I finally overcame the sensations of foreboding that kept me pinned on the floor, I headed towards what was still a recognisable kitchen. Around the hard edge of the grey stone floor stood a kitchen dresser and a grease-coated New World cooker. A ceramic sink was fastened to the wall, but when I tried the taps, no water came from them.

"Hello?" I shouted. "Anyone here?" I felt silly, listening for tiny noises through the drear stillness, but I wasn't going to leave until I'd searched every closet big enough to hold a five-year-old boy.

I heaved back the rusty bolt on the kitchen door and stomped through the overgrowth of garden, grateful to be out of the rank house. I discovered what must have once been an outhouse, but only ivied bricks of fallen walls remained. Reluctantly, I went back into the cottage.

There were two other main rooms downstairs. The back room was as forsaken as the upper storey. The one at the front was lined with rugs, eaten away by rodents and unrecognisable under their weight of dirt. The boarded window cast a grim darkness over everything.

On one wall was a sideboard. On another, a dining table. In the middle of the room was a shabby maroon sofa. I took cautious steps towards the sideboard and kneeled to click open the tiny doors. It was stuffed with filthy plates and cups, the old pale blue type with fluted edges. I breathed in, tasting ancient dust. There was no boy hidden here.

I called out with a sudden urgency. "If you're here—I'm a friend— I'm here to help—try to make a noise!"

Foolish girl, I thought, sounding uncannily like Gloria. *You are the first person here since they boarded up the windows. All this yelling is pointless.*

I got up from my knees and brushed down my jeans. It was time to go, and I was glad.

When I'd called out to Aidan, I'd been hoping for a creak or a tap or a grunt. What I heard was not a noise at all. It was a lifting inside my head, as if I'd just knocked back a couple of double gins. A sort of hushed tinnitus.

"Trendle?" I said and found my voice was unsteady.

Sabbie, Trendle hissed in my head. *It's okay, Sabbie.*

Something was making me tremble like a beaten dog. I stumbled backwards until my shoulders hit the wall. There was a spirit presence in this room. I had no idea what or who was with me here, but I was not alone, and my call had brought them out. The sofa was shimmering as if the room had a heat haze. I couldn't take drag my eyes away. The back of the sofa undulated as if it was a flag in a breeze. The effect was so hypnotic that, without warning, I was walking with Trendle, the trance coming down upon me in a moment of time. I could feel the plaster of the wall behind me, but also the cool air of another world chilling my face. The room was visible as if through a dusky net curtain. There was a muted hum in my head.

"Where are we?" I asked.

"Same place, different plane of existence." To my horror, Trendle's voice didn't rise above a whisper. "Don't worry. Nothing can hurt us."

"What? What can't hurt us?" In the dim and flickering light, I saw Trendle beside me now, fully formed and stock-still. His short claws dug deep into the dirty pile of the rug. His fur was standing on end all over his body—my own hair prickled my scalp. I was in the room as it must have once been. A television in the corner fizzed with electrical snow. I kept staring at it, terrified to know what else might be in this previous room.

"You must look," said Trendle.

"I don't want to look," I sobbed at him.

My eyes were pulled towards the sofa. The shimmering body of a woman was sitting at one end with her legs crossed. They seemed painfully thin, emerging from under a tight skirt, one stiletto dangling from her toes. I could not make out her features—she was filled with a hard light, like an overexposed photo taken by a trembling hand—but I could see that one arm was stretched along the back of the sofa, and as I followed its length, I realized that a second blurry outline was manifesting, shifting and changing until a fully human form had joined her. This creature had risen into my trance from somewhere indefinably drear and dark. A thickset form, sitting with his legs splayed out as if just coming round from a nap. His face was lean and closely shaved, as was his head, while the woman's hair sprouted wildly from her head, creating a halo in the incandescence about her.

As soon as the figures became substantial, I knew I must not lose this moment, which I'd fallen into without intent. I was drifting between the substantial world and a zone of dream and illusion. I had called these shadow beings to me; if I let them fade, I might never regain what I was witnessing now.

The woman extended a thin arm towards me and, dimmed but distinct, I heard her words.

"Help us."

I could not move. Her voice transfixed me. My chest cavity was crushed in a sort of vise; blood rushed in my ears like the beat of giant wings. Without doubt these were the spirits of unspeakable people.

They were asking for my assistance. I could not possibly help the killers of children.

Bile gurgled at the base of my throat. "What are your names?" I asked, silently.

"You can call me Kissie, darling," said the woman. She had to search in her memory for her name, as if she'd not thought of it for a long time. "We're Kissie and Pinchie." She looked at me in such an openly inviting way that I felt my spine contract. The man pushed her, and she swirled up into the air for a moment.

"Shut up," he hissed.

"No, I won't. I want to tell it." Her voice vacillated as if the spirit world connection was weak.

A horror gripped me. I felt my rib cage rise and fall as my breathing panicked. My jaw was open so wide that a dentist could have pulled a tooth. "Stay calm," whispered Trendle.

The woman began to speak. Her voice was low and rasped as if she'd smoked too often for too long. "All that blood. All that blood!"

"Fat lotta help you were," said the man.

"I fell asleep in front the telly. *Coronation Street.* Too much port and brandy. All that blood down your T-shirt. You cried out."

"Wake up, you stupid bitch!"

"You never said that."

"I couldn't fucking speak. I had a bread knife sticking in my chest."

"You tried to speak. But blood came out of your mouth."

"Stupid bitch. You could've saved me."

"I couldn't've! It was too late. I couldn't move. The knife came out of you dripping blood. I couldn't stop it. Too quick. Outta you and into me. Hardly hurt. Right into me belly, once, twice. Coughing.

They were fighting on *Corrie*. Couldn't hear 'em prop'ly. Couldn't breathe. Couldn't see."

"Stupid bitch."

"Stop swiping at me."

"What does it matter now?" I asked them, suddenly exasperated at their bickering.

They broke off and stared at me. "We want to go," she said. "But we can't. We can't leave. We're still attached."

"It's all your fucking fault," said the man. He raised grizzled hands and put them firmly around the woman's neck, rocking her back and forth. She pummelled him with blows.

I had never seen creatures of the spirit world behave in such a ghastly way. They were embodied with hate. I could not bear to watch them. Both my hands were clamped against my open mouth, stifling my breath. The grappling figures were engaged in a silent dance, one attempting to strangle the other, twisting together faster and tighter until they were a single, indistinct outline. As they faded before my eyes, the woman raised her voice in desperation. It pierced my mind like a knife on a plate.

"Help us!"

I heard her cry long after she'd disappeared altogether.

———

It felt dark in the cottage. My throat was dry and foul and my skin ached. The physical proximity of spirits had brought me this vision. *Help us*, she'd cried. *We're still attached.*

The faded spirits had gone without making the confession I'd hoped for. They'd left me with a burning desire to find them again. I forced myself to go over to the sofa. I lifted cushions, as if the spirits of Kissie and Pinchie might be hidden below them. A spider with thin legs, abnormally long even for a spider, ran up my arm. I gave a high, quavering scream and flung the cushions to the corners of the room.

You're perfectly safe, girl. I always hear Gloria's voice in my head when I'm being silly. *Wait until there's something to scream about, for goodness sake.*

The only other thing beneath the sofa cushions was a woman's plastic hair slide, pale blue with a zigzag of glitter running through it. I picked it up and stared at it. A single strand of platinum blond hair was trapped in its teeth. In this bare and abandoned place, the slide was the first thing that might be part of the story Kissie and Pinchie had started to tell. I slid it into my back pocket, wondering what else I might find in or under the sofa. I rested my hands on the nearest of its arms, stuck my bum in the air and pushed. The sofa squeaked as it rolled and the cheap mat below caught in its casters and slid away with it, revealing the floorboards.

They were a mess—previously pulled up and slotted back down. Some had been sawn through. The sawing was inexpert, even to my eye, which lacked sawing experience. The boards didn't fit properly any longer.

Why would people saw through their floorboards? I wondered.

I hooked my fingers over the splintery edge of a board and pulled. With an echoing cry, it came away, revealing the cobwebby blackness beneath.

A smell of must rose up. Something pale reflected in the murky daylight. For a moment I thought I was still in a half trance, still seeing spirits. I grabbed at one loose board after another and they came away like slices of cheese. I knelt, cautious of whatever was under the floor, and peered into the hole I'd made.

Pale, curved strips lay in the bowels of this room, resembling two hollowed mounds. They looked like the wrecks of upturned miniature boats. I had to bend closer; I had to be sure what I was seeing.

Then, with a shiver of abhorrence, I *was* sure. My body tensed like steel wire, every muscle quaking uncontrollably. I took a step back, then another. When finally I was able to turn my eyes away, I ran from the room, uttering sounds that built into a juddering yell.

Now you've got something to scream about, dear, I heard Gloria comment in my head.

But I didn't take any notice of the thought. I was too busy running.

FIFTEEN

I DROVE STRAIGHT HOME from Brokeltuft Cottage, hitting sixty until a speed camera flashed me and I prayed to the spirits that it had run out of film. But when I opened my front door and threw myself in, I felt no better. What had I been speeding for? So I could pour myself a gin or two or five in the hope I'd blot out the half memory of what I only thought I'd seen? Put on the kettle and have a nice, reviving cuppa? Call the cops?

I slammed the front door shut and leaned against it. I was trembling as if I'd contracted some ghostly infection. From my coat pocket, my phone let out a crow. I jumped as if it was Kissie and Pinchie, keen to have another ghoulish conversation. "Get a grip," I hissed. Nevertheless, my voice was a hoarse crackle as I put the phone to my ear.

"Hello?"

"Sabbie? You okay?"

"Ivan," I said, breathing out.

"Still all right for tonight?"

"Oh, tonight." Meeting for a drink had been my idea. Now it looked like a really bad one. "Sorry, but I don't feel up to it anymore."

"'Course you do."

"No, I've got to—"

"Sabbie, can I come in?"

"What?" I turned round.

"Just let me in, babe," said Ivan, and I heard the words echo from my phone and through my door. Ivan was outside, his phone still to his ear. "You've been gone a long time."

That was when the enormity of my day hit me. A feeling of chill went through my body and black spots filled my vision. I took whooping gulps of useless breath. I felt Ivan grasp me under my arms. He got me out of my coat and boots and onto the sofa. I let my head fall back and noticed with sudden intensity that there was a dirty great crack in one corner of the ceiling. I laughed at the absurdity of it all, bellows of laughter followed by whoops of breathing in.

Ivan found the half bottle of white wine in the fridge and poured two glasses. I should have asked for water or chamomile tea, but once the wine was poured I couldn't resist the first slurp. Or the second, or the third.

"You shouldn't be allowed to work with the sick or wounded," I said to him. I was proud to be making weak jokes, but my flaky voice gave me away.

"What the fuck d'you mean?"

"Wine in the afternoon. Enough to flatten me."

"That looks nasty," he said, touching the cut on my hand. "Was that the fox again?"

"No, it wasn't a bloody fox!" I didn't realize I was crying, until I tasted the salt in my mouth.

Ivan found the kitchen towel roll and sat down beside me. He dabbed my hands and face with it, kissing each place as he worked. The kisses felt wet on my face, as if he didn't really want to dry my skin it at all. "You've got to tell me what is wrong," he said. "You're my baby now." He drew a lock of my hair away from my eyes. "So, what's this all about?"

"Oh, I stumbled across a derelict cottage. I've always had a thing about ruins." That bit was true, at any rate.

"Sabs," said Ivan, and I scowled at the diminutive. "You didn't go somewhere you could have got hurt, did you?"

His tone grated, but I ignored it. Blokes need to think they're protecting their women. It's part of the knight errant image. Tamper not with it, or you tamper with their egos, and then where are you? I decided to leave out the bit where I was swinging from the ceiling by my coat zip.

"There were loose floorboards. Something underneath. Put there." A convulsion passed through me.

"What d'you mean, *put there*?"

"It was a corpse, I think."

"*What*?"

"Sorry—that makes it sound like rotting flesh and a pool of blood. I saw what might have been the rib cage, you know? Just white bones." I didn't mention the fact that there had been two rib cages, side by side, like cathedral effigies. I caught his eye, feeling reticent now. "It was probably an old basket or something. I didn't wait to take a closer look."

"Baby!" He rubbed his cheek along my neck. "You really freaked yourself."

"Okay. I admit that."

"Did Gloria see it?"

"Gloria?"

"She must've been there."

"Uh—no. She wasn't with me by then."

"She never was, was she?" said Ivan. "I could see she was lying. Covering up for you. It's that detective, isn't it? He's dragging you into trouble."

"No, Ivan. This has nothing to do with Rey. I was on my own. That's why I'm kind of jittery."

He turned away from me, as if thinking about things. "I should have been with you," he said, at last. "I could've taken care of things, called in the right authorities."

"And what are they, for Old Mab's sake? The County Council Department for the Removal of Skeletons?"

"We ought to report it. What if some kids go exploring and see what you saw?"

If I was honest, I hadn't thought much about the practical steps of what to do with my discovery. "I'll report it in the morning."

"Come on, babe, I want to help." He thrust something at me. It was his mobile.

"You want me to ring the police now?"

"Yeah. And while you're on the phone, tell that dickhead copper you want nothing more to do with him."

I choked on my second glass of wine. "I don't have to do that. He's already told me."

Ivan frowned. "Did you come on to that prick?"

"Stop it, Ivan. I've had enough today."

He leaned into me again. His retriever fringe brushed my skin. I put the flat of my hand on his arm and felt the gym-pumped muscles under his shirt, but nothing sparked in me—no sensation of attraction at all. Blonde and hunky though Ivan was, he no longer turned me on.

"Ivan," I began. "I've got a client in a bit. You've been really kind, but you have to go now. I need to get my head together."

"That's all you ever say. Go, go, go."

"You shouldn't be here at all. We were supposed to be meeting tonight."

"What d'you mean—*supposed*?"

I knew I had to tell him. There was no time like the present. I slid my wine glass onto the coffee table. "This isn't working, Ivan."

"God yes, baby, yes it is. You're the most amazing thing that's happened to me in ages." His voice was muffled because he'd buried his mouth into my hair.

"Ivan, please stop that."

"You're beautiful, Sabbie. A beautiful, sexy dream, all for me."

"No, I'm not." I hate rose-coloured compliments. I never believe them. I know I'm not the least beautiful. Sometimes, mostly if I look at myself at the end of the day (decidedly not the start of it), in a subdued light, when I'm wearing my prettiest nightie (the only bit of silky stuff I own), I can see that I am better than I was when I was a kid. My face seems to have settled now that it's fully grown, and I like the way my hair is—long and kinked but glossy enough to shine when I've brushed it. But I am not beautiful. I am not even cute. Interesting is the most I'll admit to.

I gave Ivan a push, and he shifted off me. He pulled a comb out of the pocket and ran it thought his hair, James Dean style. "I'm going to arrange it so we can spend more time together."

"Ivan, that's not possible. I'm afraid it's not what I want at all."

"Don't be afraid, babes."

"Please, Ivan—"

"It'd be excellent if I had a key."

"Not to this house." I hadn't realized Ivan was anywhere near that serious about me. "We don't have that sort of relationship. In fact, I don't want us to have any kind of relationship."

Ivan didn't seem to be listening. "I hate hanging around, waiting for you to get back from God knows where. And God knows who."

I didn't bother to deny his suspicions. I was too busy watching the light dawn inside my very slow brain. "D'you mean you've been lurking outside my house? Is that why you're always here when I arrive back?"

"That's the point, Sabbie," he said. "Arrive back from where, exactly? From finding dead bodies? I don't think so."

I stood up. To my horror, I wobbled slightly. The vino was having an effect. "I want you to go now, Ivan. I'm finished with you."

"Hell, Sabbie, we've only just got going."

"No, Ivan. I'm sorry, but it has to be over."

He grabbed my arm while I was still off balance. I toppled onto the sofa and in a blink he was on top of me, his weight pressing against my body. "No?" He cocked his head to one side, as if humouring me. "No? C'mon. I know what a woman means by *no*."

I felt my jaw tighten. Ivan really had to learn to listen to people, or he was going to be selling the wrong hedge fund or something. "I'm not going to argue, Ivan. It's over. I was going to tell you so anyway." I kept my gaze on him, so that he'd know I meant it.

Ivan brought his face down onto mine, heading for my lips. "Poor baby, all shook up," he said.

I gave him a shove. He wasn't expecting it and rolled off the sofa onto the floor. He looked so startled and ludicrous that I couldn't help but laugh. The wine mingled with the earlier shock of corpses. I dissolved into hysterical giggles.

Before I realized what had hit me, Ivan had pinned me down. His body pushed me into soft upholstery. I wriggled like a beetle on its back. "Get off me," I said. He'd already pulled my jumper up above my bra and started sucking and biting at my breasts. I felt a pain across my back as he tried to yank my bra off, his fist knotted in the lace between the cups.

I fought back, my hands ramming into his chest. He lifted his head and stared at me. "No one pushes me around," he said. His voice was cold and a chill shot down my spine. I stopped thumping his shoulders and stuck my fingers directly into his eyes, like you're taught at self-defence classes. He didn't like it. He cried out, something akin to the *argh!* noise you see in strip cartoons.

"I want you out of my house now," I yelled at him.

I should have said that a lot earlier. I should have told him to go instead of laughing at him. It was too late now. He knocked my hands away from his eyes as if they were skittles. He forced his palm onto my forehead and leaned his weight on it, so that my head crushed painfully into the hard arm of the sofa. I felt him yanking at my jeans, pulling at the button. The zip scratched as they shifted down my hips. I felt the rush of air on my skin and his hand delving down into the bit of lace I call knickers.

For several precious seconds, I could only think about how I'd managed to get myself into this position. I had no defences left. He was heavy on me, and hurting me. He didn't look at me as he ground at my jeans and dug his knee into my thigh. His wine breath felt like the heat from an exhaust. I could not understand why he should force me to have sex with him when only last week we'd been passionate lovers. But when I managed to twist my face, I saw that his eyes were unfocused and his mouth was a grim line, as if he was concentrating on something important that obliterated reason.

He was branding me, as if I was a newly acquired mare. He was making me his own.

While all this had been going on in my head, I had automatically made myself limp. I waited until his hand began to grope for his own zip, then coiled my muscles and put every particle of fear and disgust into my next move.

I sprang at him, using the back of the sofa as support. I wrenched at his shoulders and kicked with my feet. Thanks to the miniature size of my two-seater, Ivan slid towards the floor and I wriggled out from under him, all flailing arms and banshee wails. I ran to the other side of the breakfast bar, where I stopped, gripping its edge. I was no longer afraid. The clatter of my heart was due to white-hot anger.

"Get out."

He stood up, but he didn't reply. He turned his back on me, as if he was modestly adjusting his trousers, but I'd already noticed that this was a ploy with him, a way of wriggling out of discussions he didn't want to have. "You need to lighten up, babe."

"If you don't get out of my house now, I will report an attempted rape."

"That should turn the detective on."

"Ivan—"

He smoothed down his hair with his handy comb and that seemed to help calm him. "I'm sorry, babe."

"Ivan, what you just did then—"

"You started it."

"Yes, well, you frightened me."

"I wouldn't hurt you. You know that."

"JUST—GET—OUT!"

Ivan walked slowly towards the hall, really taking his time, but I allowed him that, I didn't want to risk another attack. At the kitchen door, he turned back, and I saw real sorrow on his face.

"Sabbie, I don't want to lose you." He sounded so contrite I had to clamp my teeth together so that I couldn't retract my words. I heard his footsteps pause at the door, as if deliberating whether or not to come back in, and my heart did one of those stupid lurches, reminding me in plain terms how terrified I had been.

As soon as the front door clicked shut, I ran to it and bolted it fast. Somehow, I managed to get back to the sofa. I was trembling as with cold. I curled up on the cushions, my head on my arms.

I tried wiping Ivan out of my mind, but then Kissie and Pinchie filled it. I knew that I had to tell the police what I'd seen in the cottage, but I wasn't so sure about telling them what had just happened in my own house. I fancied the police would laugh at my stupidity, rather than fill out a crime form. Right that minute, I really couldn't take the sarcasm and suspicion I knew the police—Rey, or surely Abbott—would throw at me.

I began to pull the protection around me that I draw on when I feel bombarded by threatening spirits—a silken, silvery cloak with a voluminous hood. Its imagined softness fell over my head and shoulders, and within its folds, I closed my eyes.

————

In the light of a dim lamp, someone was brushing their hair. They were brushing it from the back to the front, stroke upon stroke, getting rid of knots and tangles. Shoulder-length, mouse-brown locks fell over the person's face, masking their features, so that I could not see who this was, or even if it were man or woman. Except, a man wouldn't brush his hair with such care, would he? I stared at the hand that held the brush. It was strong and yellow in the lamplight. The brush I could see clearly; it was made of polished wood and fine, soft bristles. Each time it passed through the hair, it left a path of smoothness with a soft shine. When it passed through once, it caught at something and dragged it out, so that it clattered to the stone floor. It was a blue slide that glittered in the glow of lamplight.

———

The doorbell chimed for what might have been the second or third time. My heart thudded and I felt hot and sticky. My eyes were full of grit. I must have fallen into a deep sleep.

I moved down the passageway as if towards the cage of a wild beast, touching the wall for support as I crept closer. I imagined Ivan leaning on the porch, probably whistling a nonchalant tune, possibly even holding an overnight case.

The spy hole was in the door before I rented this house and until now, I'd only used it to play the infantile game of "turn your mate into a goldfish," but now I put my eye to the glass lens in earnest.

Marianne was outside, as slim and grey as a heron in her trouser suit. She was here for her Sunday appointment. Flustered and heavy-eyed, I let her in, trying to remember what we'd done in her last session. Yes. We'd talked past-life regression, and I'd given her some shamanic starter exercises.

"Sabbie!" Marianne had never seen me in street clothes, and certainly never seen me look such a mess.

"I'm sorry," I said. "I'm feeling a bit out of sorts."

Marianne smiled. "I know what I must do," she said. "I will make tea."

She moved around the kitchen, her linen slacks swinging at the hem. I watched her, unable to speak, my head still caught up with Kissie, Pinchie, Ivan, and the sorry feeling the hair-brushing dream had given me.

Two steaming mugs were placed on the breakfast bar. I pulled myself onto a stool in slow motion.

"You looked troubled, Sabbie," said Marianne. "Can I help?"

I was touched. "It's mainly a chap I met a few weeks ago. I've seen him on and off. Well, that's the trouble. He's still full on while I want to call it off. Actually, I've just chucked him. Turns out he's overpossessive...jealous." I stopped, unable to add *and aggressive*. I could feel tears behind my eyes. I tried not to blink because I didn't want them to run down my face. I turned from Marianne and shook them away, but she reached out and squeezed my hand, her pretty pinked nails hiding my grubby broken ones.

"Are you all right. Really?"

"Yes." The more I thought about it, the more I became certain Ivan had only intended to make a rough sort of love. I'd started the pushing and shoving—really, all Ivan had done was respond in kind. Men are stronger than they know—that was all it had been. Less than an hour had gone by, but already the memories were beginning to grow hazy around the edges. I shook myself. "I'm fine, Marianne. I'm not hurt. Ivan can go boil his head for all I care." I took a deep breath. "How are things with you?"

"I have been working very hard since last week," said Marianne in her precise way. "You are a great teacher."

Even in my fuzzy state, I was able to slam down on that. "The greatness is inside you," I said. "It's what our spirit guides will show us if we allow ourselves to look."

"I've enjoyed journeying for myself, rather than expecting you to do all the work. I have met some helpful allies."

"Good," I said, trying to keep my mind on what she was saying, forcing Ivan straight to the back.

Marianne drew a notebook out of her bag. Although I had, of course, given her one of my stockpile when she first arrived, that had soon been substituted for a far more feminine version. Her book was bound in pink faux suede with a pattern of glass jewels on the cover and smooth, ivory pages between. I could see that she had made an abundance of notes since she was last here.

"There is a long-haired cat with beautiful ginger fur who calls herself Slatterly." She giggled. "Have you ever heard such a thing? Together, we've had many adventures." She turned a page. "It is a lot of fun, is it not?"

I nodded. At that moment, I had almost forgotten what fun felt like, and it was good to be reminded. "What's this sketch here?" I asked, pointing.

"The last time I met Slatterly, she took me to such a peaceful place. We came to a still lake and on a tiny island in the middle was a baby—a foetus, really—all curled up with its umbilical cord feeding into the earth of the island. It felt calm and right."

"What d'you think it might mean?"

Marianne looked down at her book, taking a moment to think. "I wondered if this baby was me. I asked Slatterly not to take me back into a previous life, not just yet anyhow, and she hasn't attempted to do so. But I thought perhaps she had taken me back to the beginning of this life, to show me how I had recovered from the previous one—how pleased I had been to be born again."

I nodded. "That sounds good. Has it helped?"

"Yes. Things feel much better at work. The telephone no longer bothers me. And my boss."

"Will Clyde?"

"Yes. I can hear him speak without a shudder. Even about documents." She gave a little laugh. "Slatterly has been helping me feel more confident about my work. I can see that Simpson and Grouche is not the only firm I could work for. In a way, it may be time to move on, even before the redundancies are announced."

"Sounds sensible," I said. Her newfound energy was beginning to restore mine. "I ought to go and change, Marianne, so that we can move into the therapy room and have a proper session."

"I think not. We should not work if you are feeling out of sorts. Instead, you can tell me all that is wrong with you."

I let out a stifled laugh. "Apart from man trouble? Don't ask! I've got myself caught up in stuff that doesn't concern me, and I don't think I'm handling it well."

"You know what you would advise me?" said Marianne.

"No," I replied, struggling to keep the surprise out of my voice. "What would I advise?"

"Seek aid from your guardians."

"Yeah, okay. Well, I've done that." But I realized this wasn't completely true. Lately, I'd been so caught up with Cliff's awful inner world that I'd neglected my own. I grasped her hand. "But you're right, Marianne, that's great advice—tremendous wisdom. I'm so proud of you. You're clearly gaining skills that are going to help you time and again in the future."

To my horror, Marianne's eyes filmed with tears. "You think I come towards the end of our work together?" Out of her elegant handbag came a pack of paper hankies. She extracted one and dabbed at her tears without unfolding it, carefully avoiding her mascara.

"One or two more Sunday sessions and then you'll only need an occasional checkup from me."

She sniffed and placed the tissue neatly back in the cellophane pack. It seemed like a magic trick, but I saw it with my own eyes, so I had to believe it could be done. "Not only the work will I miss, but you. You have become like a friend."

I grinned. Sometimes I'm rather relieved when I discharge a client, but I knew I'd miss Marianne. I just couldn't believe that a career girl with a model figure wanted to be bosom buddies with a woman whose only nail covering was dirt. "You can always pop in for a chat, when I'm not working."

"I come and make you tea?"

"Please do." We hugged. Swathes of warm affection passed from her into my chilled interior. It made me feel ready for anything.

After Marianne had gone, I took one of last year's aubergine moussakas out of the freezer and stuck it in the oven on a low heat, then got under the shower. I spent twenty minutes scrubbing as if I'd been in a nuclear zone, until Ivan was no longer sucking at my skin. As I threw my jeans into the wash, something fell from the pocket. It was the blue slide I'd found at Brokeltuft Cottage. I turned it over in my hand. I had seen this slide in my dream. But nothing seemed to link it with anything I already knew about the cottage. On the other hand, the strand of hair was still caught up in it. I had to consider that this might be a valuable piece of evidence. Or it might just make DC Abbott wet himself with laughter.

Tomorrow I'd visit the police station, make a statement about what I'd seen, hand over the slide. See Rey, perhaps. Or Abbott, ready with his thumbscrew and his rack. But for now, I wanted to take my client's advice and journey just for myself.

———

The blackness of my closed lids filled with moving coloured shapes; spirals and twisted teardrops, convolutions of cream and white flecked with mud brown. I thought of paisley, or doodles on a telephone pad. The patterns swirled and whorled in time with the drumbeat that thudded at the back of my head. I could hear a roar, as if there was an open mouth within the coils and curls. The white streaks loosed themselves from the dark rolling core as the shapes thundered on, all hooves and flying mane. The smell of brackish water came into my nostrils... fish... damp autumn forests. I was tumbling over and over until my head spun.

"Trendle?" I asked. "What's going on?" I felt short, damp fur under my fingers and the warmth of his elongated body. "What is it? Galloping horses?"

"Almost." He spoke into my ear. "White horses."

Then I saw clearly. The roll of waves. "We're at sea?"

"Not sea."

I tried to widen my vision. We were being swept along between high banks, pushed downstream at a great rate, carried along on a spring tide.

"Get me out of here, Trendle."

"Hey," cried my otter. "Just enjoy!" He leaped out of my arms and began to play, diving and leaping from above the rolling waves. "It's a bore!" he squealed. "It's a bore, but it's not boring!"

I know that we'd become a partnership, my otter and I, because by nature I am a playful person, just like Trendle, someone who tends to see the happy side of things. But sometimes his sunny nature is way too inappropriate. The water was rushing into my mouth and eyes, and he was being no help whatsoever. I splashed out, trying to head for the bank. I could see low branches stretching into the river. I thrust out my arms as I was hurled along. A branch smashed into my ribs, knocking the air from me. I clung to it, coughing and spitting. I could feel the rush of the bore dragging at my legs and hips, working to loosen my hold. The force was persistent. I felt my grip slide away.

An arm, white and slender, came from nowhere. The fingers slid around my wrist. A woman was leaning out from the bank, supporting herself by the uprights of the tree. Her strength was enough to lift me clean out of surging waters. I felt myself dangle from her one arm, then my feet made contact with the slip of mud. I fell into her breast as I tried to scramble up the bank. She lifted me again and placed me on the path that ran alongside the riverbank. I gazed at the woman in awe.

She wore a diaphanous cloak that swirled around her body, covering her hands, feet, and most of her head. There were eddies of blues, greens, foamy creams, blacks, and browns within her coverings. The fine flowing cloth masked her features. Surely this was a goddess or other high guardian.

My heart fluttered. I made a deep bow. "You are the Lady of the river below us," I hazarded.

"Did it persuade you of my might?"

I cast a glance towards that boiling body of water, racing against time, as if on a mission. "Too much. I came on this journey for healing and found myself battling for survival."

"That is something I love well in Sabrina Dare. She is a survivor."

"What are you saying? That I don't need to be healed? But Ivan—"

"Yes, Sabbie. There are threats in your life at the moment. More than one."

I took a step forward, but without seeming to move, the Lady was the same distance from me as she had been. "What wisdom can you impart, Lady?"

Maybe the tone of my voice was just a little sarcastic. I hadn't meant it to be; I did know I was in the presence of an Old One. Still, she reacted in the instant. The shimmer of her cloak dazzled my eyes as she turned on the spot. When I could look again, she was gone, and with her, all the scene before me.

I was back in my dream. Only now I was not dreaming. I looked around. I was in that most hideous of places, the kitchen at Brokeltuft Cottage. The figure still sat bowed on a low chair, brushing and brushing at their hair, as if they had brushed without stopping since I left the dream.

"Who are you?" I asked, raising my voice, trying to gain control of this journey. My heart was racing as if I was still battling in the water; my breath was coming in fast gasps.

My words created a reaction. The hand stopped brushing. The figure parted the sheen of hair with both its hands. But it did not part. It fell, like a wig, to the floor, revealing what was beneath.

I cried out in revulsion. The obscene shine of the scalp was made more grotesque by scabs and blisters. The nose was blotched with red and so big that turned on itself until it hung over the mouth. It dripped slime.

"Are you Kissie?" I hissed. "Or Pinchie?"

The creature shook its head, but not at me. It hadn't heard me at all. It was preoccupied to find itself in such a dreadful state, as if it, as much as I, had expected a beauty to emerge from the mane of hair, not this…horror. It tried to shake off the grotesqueness of its appearance, like a dog tries to rid itself of burrs, scratching the skin of its cheeks, pushing and pulling at the bulbous nose. There was no relief.

It swept the hair up from the floor and tried to cover its pockmarked scalp, but the wig would no longer fit. The creature threw the wig at me and wailed in anguish. The gaping hole of the mouth showed blackened teeth filed to sharp points. I smelt the fetid odour of its breath. The cry grated on my ears.

"Please," I called. "Trendle!"

Instantly I was on the soft grass beside Trendle's brook. My knees trembled so much they couldn't hold my weight, so I curled into a ball and lay, with my eyes closed tight, until the call-back sign came from my CD player.

SIXTEEN

"So," said Rey. "You are finally prepared to make a statement."

I'd arrived at the police station at just after nine in the morning and was swiftly ushered into an interview room. Abbott and Buckley were sitting on either side of a small square table, with me between them like a prisoner. I didn't respond. I refused to respond to such harassment. I'd told Abbott as much on Saturday.

"How is Cliff?"

"He's in the remand wing of Horfield Prison, Sabbie," said Rey.

"Yes, I know." I didn't bother pointing out that I'd asked *how*, not *where*, he was.

"Are you happy if we record this conversation?" DC Abbott placed a finger on the recording equipment and spoke into it, detailing the date and who was present at this interview. A tiny tape spun round and round, hissing like a snake. "The information you're bringing," he prompted. "Is it relevant?"

"Yes … no …" I looked down at my hands and forced them to relax under the table. "I don't know. You'll have to make up your mind about that."

"But you can give us information?" said Abbott.

"Yes," I said and, in a sudden fit of anger, added, "*sir.*"

"It's okay, Sabbie," said Rey. "We're all on the same side."

Abbott said nothing, as if he wasn't sure Rey was right.

"This may not be of any relevance at all." I fished out the envelope that contained the glittery hair slide and let one finger push it across the table.

"Is this something Cliff has given you?" Rey picked up the envelope but didn't open it.

Finally I could see how their minds were working. "This isn't about Cliff." Instantly, I realized that wasn't perfectly true. "This *starts* with something that Cliff—that I …"

I trailed off and in the silence that followed, I watched the miniature spool revolve inside the tape recorder.

"Sabbie?" said Rey. "Just tell us what's on your mind."

"I don't know where to begin."

"Start at the beginning and just keep going," said DC Abbott. I was instantly reminded of Alice in Wonderland. So Abbot was the Knave of Hearts, was he? Perhaps because I was thinking of rabbit holes and strange, reversible worlds, I did exactly the opposite of what he advised. I started at the end.

"I've found two bodies," I said.

———

For a long time after I'd finished, they sat me in a sort of visitor's room, a place with no windows, but it did have softer chairs and an ancient coffee table with a pile of magazines, reminding me of trips to the dentist, weighted down by a glass ashtray.

I stared at the ashtray for long minutes. *Trust the police to proffer the means to disregard the statute book*, I thought, wishing that I were still a smoker so that I could (a) pass the time, (b) soothe my split-end nerves, and (c) blatantly flout the law.

I was glad that the hair slide was at last in police custody, because I'd hated having it on my person, especially after the journey I had taken last night.

I was still in a sweat about that. Nothing had seemed right. I had taken last night's journey to soothe my bent and broken spirit, but instead I'd confronted a fickle river goddess who had sent me to the place I hated most in the entire spirit realm.

After the call-back from the CD, I had sat up on my sun lounger in the darkened therapy room and made notes on all I had seen and experienced on that journey. But when I'd reached the part where I had to describe the creature in the kitchen at Brokeltuft, my pen stopped of its own accord. I had wanted to write *witch*, but Rhiannon and Bren were witches and they only ever did good with their work. This creature was not of their ilk. This was a black witch, and I had not ever thought to encounter such a thing in my spirit world. Because of this, I was still angry with the Lady of the River. I would not trust her again if she came to me.

Hours seemed to pass before Rey reappeared, carefully closing the door behind him. He laid a thin cardboard folder on the coffee table and sat down in the chair next to mine, one of those old-fashioned winged things, with rough brown upholstery that had gone shiny at the edge of the seat.

"Did you find them?"

"Yes," said Rey. "Two bodies. Skeletal remains only."

For some stupid reason, I felt as though someone had swung a body kick into my midriff. "I've been hoping I'd found the hulls of boats."

"No. No."

"They looked like hulls of rotting boats."

"Sabbie." Rey touched me gently on the arm, as if to wake me. "You know these are bodies, that's why you came to us."

My breath fizzed from my lungs. "D'you think they're Kissie and Pinchie?"

"Who?"

"That's what they told me they were called."

"However would you know that?"

"I just said. She was desperate to communicate." Boiling fluid filled my veins as I recalled the slow rasp of her voice. "I'm glad those people are dead. They were hardly human."

"Wait a moment here," said Rey. "Let's see what the pathologist comes up with before we start down that track. Dead bodies are usually considered victims of a crime, not perpetrators. Even so, we would love to wind up that old case. I'll check to see if those names were being bandied about in the Eighties and Nineties."

I felt all pumped up. "You're finally taking my information seriously, Rey, thank you so much for that."

"We take everything seriously, even the whacko phone calls." Rey was jotting notes into a pad. "Even the half-truths."

"Sorry?"

"No one could have found those bodies if they hadn't been given a few clues."

"I did have clues. From my journeys."

"And the names? Who gave you the names?" Rey stuffed the notepad into his jacket pocket and opened the folder on the coffee table. "My colleagues—"

"You mean Abbott."

Rey ignored the interruption. "Any day now this might become a double murder investigation. Dead kids make the blood run high in this department. We need to know how you found the cottage."

A sort of buzzing welled up in my head. Being proved right about something wasn't necessarily a good thing. "You think Cliff told me where the cottage was."

Rey said nothing. He just set his gaze on me like I was a nut and he was the nutcracker.

"If that's what you want to believe, nothing I say now is going to change your mind."

"Detectives aren't the most trusting of people," said Rey. A glimmer of a smile tweaked at one side of his mouth, as if he wanted me to know he was sorry about that. "And you do say some crazy things."

"They only sound crazy because they're out of context," I began, but Rey moved smoothly on.

"Take this notebook of Houghton's." He shook his head in despair. "Reads like a bad horror movie most of the time. Sacks of hair? Whatever's that about?"

"If you took the time to hear Mrs. Houghton's story, you'd know. When he disappeared as a child, he came back with his head completely shaved."

"The disappearance she reported to the police?"

"Yes. She thought his mates had done it for a dare, but honestly I don't . . ." I trailed off. Rey was smoothing out papers from the file he'd brought with him.

"Summer holidays, wasn't it?" he said, glancing up briefly. "Clifford Houghton, aged eleven years, three weeks. Reported missing by his mother. Returned home uninjured within forty-eight hours."

"You've got the report," I said.

Rey shuffled the papers. "June the twenty-ninth, just weeks earlier. Disappearance reported at Taunton Police Station by parents Diane and Arnold Napper. Patricia, commonly known as Patsy. File closed, as she never returned. Can't blame her, looking at the address." He let a photocopy drop onto the coffee table.

I felt my mouth gape. "How did you know?"

"My colleague informed me of your visit, of course. You think we sit on our asses?"

"He said he had no intention of doing anything about it."

Rey grinned. He was enjoying my surprise. "The two bodies you've just discovered rather changes things."

"You've just spent the last ten minutes explaining why you aren't interested."

"I've never said that. But I have to pose questions. If this missing girl was taken by the murderer, why did we never find her body?"

"It could be anywhere, Rey."

He gave a brief nod, as if to concede this. "Okay. But if Cliff was abused in any way, why didn't his parents come back to report the full story?"

I thought about this. "He was trying to protect his mum. His dad was in hospital at the time…" I trailed off, confused by dreams and fantasies, truths and trances. "You're never going to believe anything I tell, are you, Rey?"

Rey hunkered down in front of me. "Not true."

His eyes were directly across from mine, and in them was something that disturbed him. "What?" I begged.

"Plastic carrier bags, Sabbie. Stuffed under the floorboards and placed on the bodies of the two victims. Gnawed through, of course, so the contents had fallen all over the skeletons." He shook his head, as if the image distressed him. "They were clothed in it. As if their spines had grown fur."

The memory of the gently rustling, squeaking mattress came back to me. "What?" My voice was weak. "What!"

"Carrier bags of hair. Until forensics have done we won't be certain, but human hair, I'd guess."

"They shaved the heads of all their victims," I whispered. "And kept it. Is that what you're saying?"

Rey gave me a lopsided smile. "You wrote about hair, sacks of hair. How did you know so early on, before, as far as I can see, Houghton had confessed to his early memories?"

I reached out for the photocopies. Rey got up and walked over to a pin board on a wall, as if the notices were suddenly of great interest. He'd made the copies to give to me, but he didn't want to witness the fact. "You should go home," he said, without turning round. "Get some sleep or something."

"I can't afford to do that. I have clients. If I don't work, I don't eat."

"Apart from eggs," said Rey. He glanced over his shoulder, and his eyes, green as a sprite's, wrinkled wonderfully.

———

I hadn't dared tell Rey that I had a visitor's pass for Horfield Prison the following day. He'd probably think I was still interfering in "police business," but I badly wanted to see if Cliff was doing all right.

Visiting started at two p.m. and I skipped lunch to make an early start. I couldn't have eaten anyway. Some form of butterfly had hatched out in my stomach and was fluttering round, taking up all the room. I'd never known a prisoner before, despite my reprobate past, and this time round I didn't have Linnet's hand to hold.

After queuing outside the visitor's entrance along with wives and mothers and other assorted loved ones, I decided that the prison system went out of its way to humiliate people connected with its inmates. I could feel my shoulders hunching and my eyes following my feet as I shuffled down the line towards the bag search. I thought it might be bullet-proof glass and telephones, like it is in films, but the visitors' room for remand prisoners was a spread of cheap tables and plastic chairs.

Cliff was sitting at the far end of the room, bent as an old man. I took the chair on the opposite side of the table and realized they were bolted to the floor. To prevent use as missiles, I supposed. I stretched my hand across to him. As soon as I touched his skin, he spoke.

"I didn't do it."

"I know that, Cliff."

"Yeah." He risked a tiny, piercing look into the very heart of my eyes. I would have lurched backwards, if the plastic, bolted chair hadn't stopped me. There was a glint of crazy in them, anguish that could not be quenched. "But no one here does."

He kept his voice down. There must have been twenty tables in the room, most of them occupied, but people spoke in quiet tones, apart from a woman at the far end who was losing it big time.

"It makes you crazy, this place," said Cliff, as if he knew what I'd seen in his eyes and needed to explain it.

"You're not crazy, Cliff."

"I think I've always been mad."

I found I was trembling. In the course of four days, Cliff had changed. He'd become a convict. "Have you seen your mum?"

219

"No. I can't see her. She'd only cry. I can't watch that."

"But she wants to support you."

"You and Linnet are doing that. Linnet's working so hard. She says the only real evidence is Josh's toy, and she's trying to prove that it could have been planted in my flat."

"That's great! What's she come up with?"

"My landlady," said Cliff. "She has a spare key."

"The woman who runs the post office? I've met her." I hoped my voice didn't tell him I'd taken an instant dislike to her.

"Linnet thinks she might have a grudge against me."

I felt a tiny seed of hope begin to germinate inside me. "Do you think that she let someone into your flat?"

"Mrs. Gale? She'd never do anything like that. She wouldn't give a person a second-class stamp unless they paid up-front. She has her position to maintain."

"So how is Linnet going to make this work?"

"It's what she calls a 'counter argument'. Any opportunity that the toy could be put there by someone else would make a jury see things differently." His voice sounded stronger as he said the words, but he didn't look up or unfold his arms from a permanent self-hug that reminded me of the pull of a straightjacket.

"I don't understand."

"She's going to put Mrs. Gale on the witness stand and get her to admit that she's never liked me."

"Counter argument." I tried to keep the smile on my face. I had trouble with the image of that cross-examination; transforming a dour-faced woman into a credible witness for the defence. "Tough call!" I laughed, challenging him to laugh too. "Cliff, I'm so sorry I haven't been of help."

"You tried your best."

"But now you've *got* the best. Linnet. She'll look after you."

He rubbed his fist across his eyes. "Since that time. Even though I never remembered what happened. I sort of knew."

A robotic hand gripped my stomach and twisted. "Knew what, Cliff?"

"That the trouble wasn't over."

My hands covered my stomach, protecting it from the internal grip. "What d'you mean?"

"I don't know. I think those people have followed me all my life."

"Those ... the Wetland ..."

"Yes. Like they were inside my head. They got inside my head and I didn't even know they were there, but they're there all right. They've ruined my life."

Caroline had said the same—Cliff never became the person he should have been. I took a breath. "There's a couple of things I've been researching. The name you remembered, Patsy. You were right. A girl disappeared before you did. She was never found. I've got her details, and I'm going to try to find out more about her."

"I told you," said Cliff. He did not sound surprised. "She was the first victim."

I gave a solemn nod, as if to acknowledge her demise. "Do you think the other two names will come back to you? The woman and the man?"

He shook his head, not as a negative, but to shake thoughts out of it, like a dog shakes water from his coat.

I said, "I think I know their names."

"What?" His fingers wandered up to his lips and jerked as if they were rubber. I fought back the temptation to gently pull his hand away, as if he were a small child.

"Some of the signs that were in the journeys we did together, they led me to Brokeltuft."

"*What?*"

I leaned over the table. "I found it, Cliff. It's derelict now. But your tree is still there; it got me in, I went inside." I broke off. The news was too much for him. He began to shake like he had a fever. Sweat broke out on his face, which was stony white. "Cliff," I said. "It's all right. They're dead. They're dead."

"Jesus." He looked away, then back at me. "How d'you know?"

"I saw them, the bones of them. They came to me as spirits. She … the woman … spoke to me."

"Kiss," said Cliff, his voice rising up over the other hushed mumbles. "*Her*, and *him …*"

"Quietly, Cliff," I said, my voice a whisper.

"God—oh God in hell!" wailed Cliff. "Kiss and Pinch—oh Jesus Christ!"

I could see that he'd alerted the officers on duty. One stepped towards our table. "Cliff," I whispered, "calm down, or they'll take you back to your cell. Calm down, please."

He nodded frantically. "Yes. Calm. Yes. Not easy in this place." But he was calming, his voice back to normal. The officer stopped, although his gaze was now permanently on Cliff. "I keep having dreams. I wake up yelling out. They don't like that."

"The officers?"

"The men."

I looked closer at him, at the sallow skin of his face. There was a bruise on one temple, and what I'd thought was a shaving mark looked suspiciously like the sort of wound a ring would make.

"Can't they separate you from the other men?" I asked.

"Not all the time."

"Tell me what your dreams are about," I said, desperate to move the subject on. If I knew for sure how the other men were treating Cliff, I would never be able to report this visit back to Caroline without her seeing it in my face.

"I'm on a sort of moorland. I hear the sound of hooves. I look back and there's this horse pummelling towards me. Pitch black horse, and the rider all in black. I take to my heels, but I can't run—"

"That awful slow-motion thing," I whispered, not meaning to interrupt. "Like your legs are tied to the floor."

"Yes. But he catches up, leans off the horse, and clamps a hand on my shoulder. I try hard not to look at him. It's like my face is forced round ... and it's him."

"Pinchie?"

"Yes. I know because I feel that fear. The shock that stops your heart. Then I wish he really had scared me to death and I'd never woken back up to all this."

"Please don't lose hope," I whispered. "Please don't give up."

He lowered his head into his hands. I thought he was about to cry, but after a moment, he spoke again. "All he did was laugh. Bloodcurdling laugh. It shot through me like a pain. I woke up straight away. But, you see, that's the problem, the waking up."

I swallowed. I had no need to ask what he meant. I understood. The dreams were jogging the memories, and that was where the true horror lay.

"It's all coming back," I said. He nodded, over and over, his hands still tight to his scalp, the hair grating under his fingers, a small repulsive sound.

"They had a sun lounger. Turned it into a *contraption*. A place of torment. Pushed you down on it, held you down, belt across the chest, stop you moving, belt across your neck, stop you breathing. Head and

223

legs bent back, on your stomach, on your back. They called it an operation."

I turned my head away and closed my eyes. No wonder Cliff had hated lying on my lounger. Without meaning to, I let out a moan.

"That's right," said Cliff, suddenly fierce. "You moan. Moan for me. Why not? I did. Moan, cry for my mummy, scream … but they didn't want tears. Or screams even. They wanted white fear. You know what that is? White fear?"

I nodded, once. The terror that silences your mouth—numbs your brain. Stops your heart, finally, if you're lucky.

"They were terrible people," I managed.

"Oh God! No one in this world more evil. Ever. Worse than cruel; cruel people want to make you cry. Not them." He flopped back, exhausted.

I thought about Rey, how he wasn't convinced Cliff had been part of the Wetland Murderer cycle. If he could hear this, surely he'd understand. But then, wouldn't he still say that none of this was relevant to his enquiry, except to bring Cliff into it? *They are long dead, Sabbie…*

"Did they," I struggled with a sensitive way of asking, "leave marks on you?"

He nodded once, a slow up and down.

"I just ask because your mother never said."

"Mum never saw. Well, I was gone eleven. I was never going to show her what they did. And I was lucky, I guess. I wasn't in that house more than two days. The others … they weren't so lucky."

"Matthew," I whispered. "Nicolas, Joanna, John. And Patsy." By the time Cliff left the clutches of Kissie and Pinchie, Patsy Napper must have been damaged beyond repair and destined for an unmarked grave.

"It was her who got me out," said Cliff.

It came out of the blue. I felt my spine tense. "Can you remember what happened?"

"I remember it was always dark. They pinned the curtains across the windows, nailed into place, I suppose. Thick, dark curtains. The second night, the door opens to my room. I don't make a sound. See, I've already learnt that doesn't help. She comes over with scissors in her hand. I know it's her, but that doesn't mean I trust her. I hadn't even seen her since I'd been in the car. She's in jeans. So am I—the clothes I'd come in. She cut through the stuff they'd tied me with, ripped up sheets, I think. Then she went to the window and yanked at the curtain. It fell down in a cloud of dust. I was still on the bed, paralysed, sitting up looking out into the night. It was drizzling.

"She hissed at me. 'Can you climb trees?' It seemed a daft thing to ask. I just gawped. She pulled up the sash window and pushed me towards it. She didn't say 'hurry up,' or anything, but I didn't need to be told. I got onto the sill. The end of one branch was just brushing the pane right above my head. I had to pull at the thin end of it, yank it down, slide my hands along it, and try to shinny out of the window."

His voice was muffled. I had to strain to hear each word. I was hardly breathing as I listened. I could see the images so clearly. I'd been in that bedroom, seen the mattress and the metal ring.

"My heart is racing. I'd never climbed as high into a tree as I was when I went out that window. But somehow I land on the branch, somehow I keep my hands around it, wriggle towards the trunk. The girl hisses 'fucking hurry up'. It shocks me. None of my friends swear like that. She's waiting for her turn. The leaves drip rain. The branches are wet. I cling on for my life, but my fingers are slipping. The entire branch is bending under my weight. I hear the creak—the crack. I don't understand. I look up and see her mouth open in horror. Then

225

I'm flying. Just like in the dream. Still hanging onto the branch. It's falling with me. I think it gets caught on a lower bough, because something slows me. I land flat on my stomach in wet earth with the wind out of me and the palms of my hands stinging, but I get up straight away. Right in front of my eyes is my bike. They'd thrown it onto a pile of rubbish in the garden. The back tyre's soft, but I'll get away quicker on it. Anyway, Mum would slaughter me if I didn't bring it back."

Cliff grinned. It wasn't a very humorous grin and it certainly didn't light up his eyes, but I smiled back at him in some sort of hope.

"She helped you escape."

"You don't understand. I think she planned to get through that window. When the moment was right. It must've been the only route out of that house of terror. Then I turn up and, well, she decided it was now or never, or maybe they'd taken their eye off her, now I was there. She took her chance, but she let me go first."

"Of course," I said, keeping my voice low. I could see the window in my head, see the darkness outside, feel the chill of the rain as it lashed into the room. "Of course she did. You were younger. You didn't know what was going on."

"But I broke the branch."

"Your weight broke the branch. Hers would've too, wouldn't it?"

There was silence between us. I wondered why Patsy hadn't just thrown herself into the tree, even though the bough had broken. Was she already too terrified? Or too brainwashed? Or were Kissie or Pinchie stirring? I wondered about the scissors, the clean cut through the bindings. I tried not to imagine just how mad they would have been, but clearly Cliff could imagine. The memories were returning.

"She gave her life for me."

"One life saved. Isn't that a good thing?"

He looked up. His eyes were raw from broken sleep and tears. "She didn't mean to give her life. But now I know that she did anyway, it makes me feel..." His jaw moved, teeth grinding.

"You *will* get out of here," I told him. "You won't be found guilty, not by twelve ordinary, honest people."

He shook his head. "It's not the injustice. I never expected justice. Now I remember about Patsy... well, I don't honestly want justice. Someone must pay. Because of the little boy."

"Aidan?"

"They think I've got him somewhere. But I've got no idea where he is, or what he's going through."

I nodded. We would both be having the same sleepless nights, wondering about little Aidan.

"He's been gone five days. That's too long."

Cliff was right. Time was running out and no one was getting any closer.

SEVENTEEN

THE MISSING PERSON FORM that Rey had photocopied gave me tiny glimmers of information about the girl who might have been the Wetland Murderers' first victim.

Twenty-three years ago, Patsy Napper had been fifteen and living with her parents, Diane and Arnold Napper. I had the date of her disappearance and the date when they closed the case. And I had her old address—a high-rise block of flats in Taunton.

I tried to reckon out the chances of finding Mr. and Mrs. Napper still at the same address. How long did people live in one place? Most of my various friends moved round a lot, but Gloria and Philip had lived in Oak Villa in Bristol since Charlene was born, and I knew that Bren and Rhiannon had moved into their little house outside Bangor the day they were married.

I had no clients booked for the whole day. My Reiki client had cancelled by text, adding to my sense of overall failure. But the glimmer of weak sun that warmed the spring morning brought my spirits up; that and the stupidity of my hens. Juniper and Melissa are usually satisfied to stay in the hen run while I clean it out, but if the door's left ajar for even a second, Ginger will escape and be off on some intrepid adventure. I found her in my kitchen, kindly pecking breadcrumbs from the corners and not so kindly leaving a trail of muddy hen-shaped footprints over my kitchen floor.

Magic, according to the shaman I trained with in Glastonbury, is a combination of the power of will and the power of coincidence. If you want it, you must make it happen. I really wanted to find Patsy's family, although I hadn't actually got round to asking myself why or wondering what I'd say to them if I did find them.

I lit a candle and burned some rosemary oil with frankincense—the first for memory and the second to open my mind to the spirit world. I asked my guardians for a boon...a little bit of luck...a chance to find out what actually had happened to Patricia Napper twenty-three years ago.

Taunton was our nearest big town and offered a night life that Bridgwater could not provide. But perhaps surprisingly, a few of my clients took the half-hour drive over to keep appointments with me. There are alternate therapists in Taunton, but maybe I have something they don't. Hope so.

Twenty-three years ago, the Nappers had lived on the other side of the town, in the centre of what was reputed to be the worst housing estate in Taunton—what used to be called a sink estate. When the Wetland Murderer was hunting for small children, it must have been heading towards its most sunken status, but it had grabbed itself by its bootlaces and started to haul itself out of the mire. Four 1960s tower blocks rose up at me, monolithic in height and and shape. They still belonged to the local authorities and had recently been painted; one in salmon pink, one in a soft yellow, one in sky blue, and the final one in a sort of khaki shade, as if it needed camouflage.

The address for the Nappers was way up inside the khaki tower block. I saw the warden as I parked my car. He was tending the rose bushes that grew around the front of the complex.

"Nice day for gardening," I called out, eager to pass for a bona fide member of the visiting public. He doffed his hat in a jovial manner—a bright red baseball cap he was wearing back to front—and went on wielding his gardening shears.

I walked around the massive walls. The block was called Watchet House, Watchet being a harbour-side town on the coast to the north of Taunton, so I guessed that the other blocks were also called after local seaside places. Maybe to bring a feeling of salt air and fun days into the minds of people who lived in faceless corridors that oozed depression and limited opportunities.

As I reached the entrance, I had one of those tiny sparks of memory. Me and my mum had lived in a tower block like this. It must have been in Bristol, where there are high-rise flats all over the city, but I'd forgotten about it until this moment. I must have been quite tiny, maybe three or four, because I could suddenly recall just how high the walls had loomed and how I'd run along the corridor that seemed to go on forever, looking for our door. I had stronger memories of living in basement apartments and even sleeping on people's floors, but at one time, we must have been council-housing tenants.

I shook the memory away. I hadn't asked for it and didn't want it. I was here for my client. I pressed the buzzer for number thirty-four, where hopefully Mr. and Mrs. Napper were still in healthy residence. I waited and buzzed again. If they lived here, they weren't at home to callers.

Deflated, I wandered in the direction of my car. I decided to go into town and window shop, then come back in an hour or two. The warden had finished his pruning and weeding and was trundling a wheelbarrow away from the beds.

"You okay there, missie?" he called out in the bur of his Somerset accent.

I shrugged. "I was hoping to catch the people who live at number thirty-four. That is, if the people I'm looking for still live here."

He pulled the cap from his silver hair. "Who wants 'em?"

"Ah. My name's Sabbie Dare. I've never met Mr. and Mrs. Napper. They don't know me." I chased around for a good excuse to be visiting. "I'm sort of asking after their daughter, Patricia."

The pretty fib slipped off my tongue. I wasn't expecting any sort of reaction, but the warden's face took on a transformation. His ruddy colour turned to grey and his lips thinned into a straight line.

"I be Arnie Napper," he said. His eyes were sombre and shocked, with a wary element deep down. "You never knew my daughter. You wouldn't call her Patricia if you did."

"Patsy," I said. "She was Patsy." It was a confirmation for me.

"My daughter ain't been around since you were a babby." Arnold Napper lifted his wheelbarrow and marched past me, his eyes on his pile of cuttings.

I skittered after him. "I'm sorry. I didn't mean to upset you. I'm desperate to find someone I can talk to about Patsy." It was hard to keep up with Arnie's long, fast stride. The barrow tilted this way and that as it bumped along in front of him. He was going so fast that I almost careered into him when he stopped in front of a galvanized bin.

He twisted off the lid and I took my opportunity in both hands, literally. I scooped a large armful of the clippings, rose thorns and all, and tossed them into the bin. "Won't this take ages to compost down?" I asked.

"It's for burning."

"Oh."

He watched me empty his barrow, a bemused smile beginning to smooth out the lines of irritation. "Like gardening, do you?"

"Love it," I said, flinging the weeds in after the thorns.

As soon as the barrow was empty, he grasped the handles in his firm hands, the backs of them as brown as hen feathers, and marched off again, moving into the shadow against the wall of the flats.

I did not follow. I stood still, watching him go, my hands already beginning to prickle with scratches. Will I ever learn? I had craved a boon from my spirit guardians, but it looked as if they'd chosen to show me that half-truths could cost me dear.

Arnie manoeuvered the barrow to turn the corner of the building. He had almost disappeared from view when he looked back at me across his shoulder. "I'll put the kettle on, eh?"

————

Arnie's apartment was over-warm and filled with the ticking of the mantel clock. It was crammed with the memories of his life, but there wasn't a dirty cup or speck of dust to be seen. Local papers were tidily piled on a table in the hall, under which his slippers were lined up alongside a pair of polished brown brogues. Arnie untied the laces of his trainers and pulled them off. He swapped them for the slippers. "Just me, now. Me wife's been dead these twenty years."

It was clear he lived alone. In the living room, the one easy chair was positioned directly in front of the telly. By the side of the chair was a trolley that vaguely resembled the one Caroline pushed crustless sandwiches about on, but this held everything that Arnie might need in his day—crossword book, newspaper, ashtray, cigarettes and a pile of cheap lighters, a biscuit tin decorated with red and yellow roses, a half-full glass of diluted orange squash drink, and a half-full (but definitely not diluted) bottle of Three Bells Scotch.

Photos placed into cheap certificate frames adorned the wall above the gas fire. The most recent was a wedding picture with an almost identical groom and best man. Photos of babies in cots or on shawls were dotted around, some very new, some with faded colours. A girl laughed down from a farm tractor, her legs long and her shorts short. For a moment I thought it was Patsy, then I did my sums and realized it had to be her mum at about the same age. Finally, there was Arnie, alone and clearly still in his teens, his uniform cloned with all the others in the passing-out parade, his shoes as glossy as the ones under the hall table.

He saw me looking. "Cyprus. Somerset Light Infantry." He sniffed. "Better get that kettle on. How d'you like your tea?"

"As it comes," I said. "Milk, no sugar." I wasn't sure whether or not to stay where I was, but he continued to talk to me while the taps hissed and the kettle clicked on, so I wandered into the glistening kitchen. I'd've thought the cooker had never been used if it hadn't been for the overpowering smell of artificial cleansers.

"Army were the making of me. I made sure my two boys went into the armed forces straight from school. Derek went into the Grenadiers, and Richard took to the sea. They were twins, meant I lost 'em both together, only months after our Patsy walked out. Before that they were a right worry, heading for the clink! I dragged them off to the recruiting office kicking and screaming. That did the trick. Gives you a sense of discipline, see. Both married now. Brings their kids to see me. Little imps, they are." He nodded to himself, and I had an image of small children chasing in circles around the tea trolley.

"You don't have many photos of your daughter."

"That baggage." He sloshed a small amount of UHT milk into two large mugs before pouring in a liquid the colour of molasses.

Arnie motioned me into the winged chair and pulled a hard-backed seat from the miniature dining table for himself. He was an old soldier, so I didn't quibble. I placed my mug down, its contents straining at the sides, and tried to summon up the right words. I couldn't sit and make small talk until he knew why I was here. But I had no idea how Arnie would react to the things I wanted to discuss with him. "What do you mean, she walked out?"

Arnie coughed into his fist. "She were getting to be a handful, the minx."

I gulped back a brave sip of tea. "Was she destined for the army too?"

Arnie gave an almost pensive shake of his head. "She weren't really like the twins at all. Broke the mould, she did. Always writing stories and making up games. Used to wonder if she did take after me a mite, 'cause I reckoned if I'd've been born different I'd've made something of meself." He blinked a couple of times, and I was sure that he'd turned slightly pink. "The boys were never going to amount to much—no discipline to them, only boisterous bother—and me wife were a lazy git. Sorry to speak ill of the dead, but that's the truth of it. She liked her drink, did Diane. Well, we both did, but I could take mine, if you get me meaning."

"And Patsy?"

"Patsy were different. Mind you, she were a bossy bugger from early on. But soon as she hit her teens, she changed. Makeup plastered on and a yard of flesh between her jeans and whatever passed as a top. And that mouth! Teachers saying that she'd lost her promise, our Diane tearing 'er hair out about drugs." He glanced up at me, suddenly, as if he'd forgotten I was in the room. "Vanished, she did. Cleared out one day and never did come back."

"She went of her own accord?"

"She went of her own bloody-mindedness. She were nowt but fifteen, and she turned her backs on us, never gave any of us a second thought."

"Didn't she leave a note, anything like that?"

"No, but she nicked 'er mum's suitcase and twenty quid out my wallet. Even so, I went all over the estate asking. Got soaked through, more than once, and I was thinking … she's out in this, somewhere, stupid chit."

"She hadn't gone to friends?"

"They'd caught no sign of her, thought she might've got the bus to Bristol, or London." He stopped and slowly shook his head, staring into his mug. "We'd had trouble with the boys, but it felt worse with Patsy, because we did all wrong, see? After she went, I wished I'd paid her more attention when she were a good little girl. If I'd got to know her earlier, when it mattered … well, it might've helped, that's all." He shrugged. "Don't know why I'm telling you all this. Haven't thought about it in years."

"Yes," I said. "I'm sorry to haul it all up again, I really am, but—"

"See, she never did know. Never had chance to tell her. Weren't that sort of family, is the truth."

"Never knew what?"

"That we were proud of her. Loved her. That I didn't mean to be so quick with the flat of my hand. One row, I brought her eye up in a bruise. Didn't know my own strength." He swallowed, and continued in a quieter voice. "Didn't know my own anger. It were okay with the boys. I dunno, they sort of expected it. But Patsy—she came home one night pissed on drink and I slapped her full across the face. And she screamed at me. She said we hadn't ever loved her, so why should she care what we told her to do? It felt too late to say I'd been scared off by the way she'd answered back.

"She ran off into her room. She'd had the little box room since we'd moved into the flat and I guess at her age it were a mite too small for her, but what could we do? Anyway, it went all quiet. I were congratulating meself on winning. All I wanted was me little girl back. The one that got on with 'er homework." He suddenly stopped, as if his lungs were heaving for air he wouldn't let them have, lest tears came alongside. "Are you going to tell me who you are, missie?"

"I'm the therapist of Cliff Houghton."

"Who?"

"He's been on the news, lately."

"I don't watch the news," said Mr. Napper, his voice grumpy with displeasure. "I like the football channel."

I pointed to the *Taunton Herald*, lying on the bottom self of the tea trolly. "It's local news. The man who was arrested for the murder of Josh Sutton."

His eyes widened. He'd expected anything but that. "That little boy?"

"That little boy, and the one that's still missing."

"You've lost me," he said. He was shaking his head, but his eyes had narrowed. I didn't think I'd lost him as much as he was letting on.

I didn't want to open old wounds or create new ones, but I had to tell him.

"I don't think Cliff has anything to do with these kidnappings, but he's caught up with them because he has a memory of being kidnapped himself twenty-three years ago. He is sure that someone—a girl—was being held captive in the same place, by the same people."

Arnie rubbed a hairy forearm across his mouth. I saw a washed-out tattoo, a curling, naked woman with ankle-length and suitably positioned locks of hair. "What d'you mean?"

I shook my head, as if in warning. "I'm trying to piece things together. My client started remembering all this from his past. He'd blocked off awful memories about being kidnapped as a child." I shuddered. "And tortured. But then this girl helped him get away. Her name was Patsy."

"Patsy?" Arnie's eyes had begun to water. "Sounds far-fetched to me. Who would take kids like that?"

"The Wetland Murderer."

His mouth opened, the bottom lip hanging like a slug. "Them bodies in the peat bogs?"

"Yes."

"But all of them were babbies. Our Patsy weren't never found out there."

The reflection in his voice made me look at him. "When they found the bodies, you did wonder, didn't you?"

"Of course I bloody wondered," said Arnie. "I were there when they dug 'em up."

———

Arnie had pulled out the bottle of Three Bells and filled his empty tea mug with whisky. He took a long time over the first few swallows, but I stayed silent, pretending to sip my tea.

"It were our Diane who made me go to the police," he finally began. "Guilt, you might say. She never forgave herself for not sticking up for Patsy during our rows, but she was usually too hungover to bother. After the police took the details, I said to our Di, 'When she gets back, I want her to find you dry. I want you to give up the booze. You do that, I'll never hit her again'. To her credit, she did try for a week or two." Arnie sighed and drained his mug and lifted the bottle. I bit my lip. I didn't want to comment, but I wasn't keen to sit with an inebriated Arnie Napper.

"Sure you won't?" he asked me, swinging the bottle. There was not much more than a last slug at the bottom. I let him fetch me a glass, thinking that even if I didn't touch it, at least Arnie would lose the chance to down it himself.

"Funny thing, kids," said Arnie. "When Patsy were born, I loved the pillow her head lay on. By the time she'd got to her teens, I could've smothered her with it. But it didn't take long after she'd walked out on us, it got so I was desperate to see that sullen face of hers. Then it got so I was frightened that I'd never see it again.

"It must've been months before the other children went missing. They never came back to us, the police. I went to them and said I'd like to sign up to the search team. They have this kind of look, don't they, cops? Like it'd be a great job, policing, if it weren't for the crime. They said it'd be unlikely, finding Patsy. She 'didn't fit the scenario.'"

"But you joined the search parties?"

"Lot of good it did anyone. We were concentrating on the wrong areas. As soon as the bodies were found, the peat bogs seemed the obvious place."

I'd already noted from the cuttings in the library that the Wetland Murderer had stolen the tiny victims from a wide area, so it was understandable the police would take a long time to find their grave. "How were the bodies discovered?" I asked.

"There were a bad drought that summer." He flicked a glance at me. "You won't remember, but the bogs dried up and summat began to show through."

"And you volunteered?"

"Yes, I went," said Arnie. "The bogs are a dreadful place to hide a body. They needed a bloody regiment to lay tracks and manhandle the equipment."

"But they didn't use the army."

"No. They used us. P'raps they thought it would keep us busy—we were mostly the fathers of missing children."

The thought saddened me. Building a track through the wet to retrieve your buried child. The final thing you could do to relieve the suffering.

"They were just dumped. *He* never had to do any digging; they'd've sunk beneath the stagnant water. It's all black because of the peat. There's a lot of willow growing over the moors. Where they were hid, them babbies, massive trunks were coming out of the water, growing there for years, I'd say."

"All four bodies buried at once?" I asked.

He shrugged. "Looked like it. No doubt there's some report that can tell you for definite."

"But how could he have got them there? Isn't it remote?"

"Not remote, exactly. Peat is what they farm. There be paths all over. But there aren't many souls about." He took a swig of Three Bells. "Know my thinking? He used a barrer."

"A what?"

"A wheelbarrer. They were only little 'uns, after all. You wouldn't think anything of someone wheeling a barrer in that country place."

"It must have been dreadful. Having thoughts like that."

"It's what killed our Di," said Arnie. "She went back to the sherry big time; drowned in it. She were my second wife. First one went off with some bloke, and I hope he's making her life a misery. I gotta be a bad judge of women. Never wanted to bother again, that's for sure."

Arnie took time to swill his whisky round and round, as if he was regretting pouring the last of the bottle for me. I picked up my glass and took a tiny sip. I could see how the burning at the back of the throat might feel like a sort of salvation.

"Me heart was in me mouth when they pulled them black bones out of the wetlands," said Arnie. "But our Patsy were too slippery to get caught. She could blag her way out of any trouble, even the worst. I think the cops were right. Long gone. Nothing to do with any of that business."

I nodded in what I hoped was a sagacious manner. It was not for me to tell Arnie how to deal with the dreadful news I'd brought him. In my heart I knew I had a match—Arnie's missing daughter had been in the car the day that Cliff was stolen away.

She'd already become a victim of the Wetland Murderer.

———

I had to pass Hughes and Heavens on my way home, so I drove into their parking lot and asked at reception if I could speak to Miss Smith.

"Have you an appointment?"

"N-No. I thought I'd just pop in."

The receptionist gave a thin professional smile. "I'm afraid she's very busy." She picked up a receiver and talked into it. Of course Linnet would be busy. I'd have to leave a message. I tried one out in my mind: *I've found the missing victim* was impressive but untrue. *I've found Patsy Napper's father Arnold* was a bit of a mouthful.

"Okay," said the receptionist. "Miss Smith will see you."

I strode into the office. "I've found Arnie Napper!"

From the other side of her yacht-sized desk, I saw Linnet's face open with surprise—mouth, eyes—the lot. I felt extremely good about getting ahead of her in this way, and I knew my face was beaming.

Linnet cleared her throat. "You ... sorry?"

I plonked myself on the client chair, sticking out my legs. The sadness of the interview had left me. I glowed in triumph. "Sorry, Arnold Napper is Patsy Napper's old dad. I've been with him all afternoon."

"God almighty."

"I know. Although that particular deity had no part in the process."

"You're saying you found him through some shamanic technique?"

"Actually, he was still at the address he was at when he registered Patsy as a missing person."

"Even so. I could use your investigating skills."

"You won't believe what he's told me, Linnet. He even went to the burial site when they brought out the bodies." I gave a laugh, sheer exultation. "I guess it sounds a little grisly."

She bent over the desk and scribbled a note. "From what I've been told, you're having to get used to grisly."

"Oh," I said. "You've heard that I found those bodies."

"More investigative technique?"

"Actually, that was purely shaman's luck."

"Well, I must say, excellent work."

"Thanks." I swear my chest actually puffed out. I know my cheeks were warm. She was silent for half a minute or more, as if she felt she'd been too effusive with her praise, although it was a bit late for that. I watched her finish her notes and close the folder.

"Look," I began, "Sorry, I know what you're thinking—I said I'd bring anything to you first. But I had to tell the police."

"Definitely." Linnet rose and came round to me. She looked tired, as if she'd been up since dawn. "Definitely well done. I hope you've made notes about this missing girl, because I want all the details."

"Actually, no. It wouldn't have looked polite to flip open my pad in front of Arnie Napper."

"Look, Sabbie, it's gone five. No harm in packing up for the night a little early. Fancy a drink?"

She did that thing at her closet, swinging jacket and accessories from peg and shelf. She picked up her document bag and led the way past the thin-lipped receptionist and across the road into the Admiral's Landing. The bar staff seemed to know Linnet quite well, because she raised a hand as she passed the bar, walking straight on to a corner table. Moments later, a dish of a barman brought a bottle of rather nice Shiraz and two glasses.

"Hope you like red."

I didn't like to say that I was more of a crisp white girl myself, but when I sipped the drink she poured me and the curranty, peppery tangs burst in my mouth, I wondered if I was missing out.

"Mmm, nice," I said, putting down my glass. I felt my eyes pop when I looked at hers. It was empty, all but the ruby glow at the bottom. She poured a second and sipped more slowly. "You're quite a heavyweight," I said in awe.

"Comes with the territory." She sipped again. "Tell me all. It'll help you fix the memories before they fade. Tell me how you found that place, the … bodies. It must have been grim."

"Yes." I looked across at her.

She gave me an encouraging smile. "Go on. Spill the beans."

I started with the signpost and the poplar tree—she deserved to be filled in on the journey at the prison—and soon I was running on without thinking quite what I might say next. It was so lovely to talk to someone who wasn't silently thinking I'd flown over the cuckoo's nest. I even told her about Ivan.

"I know I'm never going to see him again, but maybe you can help me. I can't work it out in my own mind. Was he trying … would it have been rape?"

"Without a doubt," said Linnet. "You should have contacted me straight away! Never mind if it didn't fully happen, that was due to your courage and quick thinking. You can still press charges, if you want."

"Goddess, no." I shuddered. "Let's forget it. I haven't told you what happened today yet." I started describing my search for Patsy, the way Arnie's story had unfolded over tea and whisky. She listened in silence without taking a single note. When I'd finished, Linnet topped up both our glasses, silently evaluating the new data.

"Interesting, Sabbie."

"Sad, really. It made me think how we will all look back at the end of our lives and regret our mistakes, and how we'll still make them because we won't know they *are* mistakes until we're old."

"What was his mistake? He pushed his daughter out, but he wasn't responsible for what happened next."

"It was something about love. He could hardly bring himself to use the word. Too soppy. But it tormented him, I could see it did, that he'd never told his daughter how much he loved her."

"Loved her so much he'd—what was it—slapped her in the face?"

"He didn't understand about teenage girls. She'd changed overnight. And love can be very strange—domineering, possessive. Sorry, I'm back to Ivan. Must be the wine." I took a consolatory sip, because I was way behind Linnet and not the least bit squiffy, which was just as well—my car was parked outside the solicitor's office.

"Waffle as much as you like, Sabbie; I'm off duty here. But I have to ask: Are we taking this new development to the police? Because we should, I suppose."

"You mean, they'll twist it all round?"

"You can rely on the fact they are keen to build up a case for the prosecution. It shouldn't work like that; they should treat all information with impartiality, but I'm afraid they don't."

"They want their first guess to be right. Well, some of them do. Rey Buckley, he thinks outside the box—"

"Leave this with me. I'll make some inquiries before we go any further." She tackled her glass, shifting the line of red by several fingers. "So let's recap. This girl left home of her own accord and was reported missing by her father."

"Both parents. But the mother died."

"And the exhumation of the corpses?"

"I think he had this gut feeling she'd be there. Even so, he told me Patsy was too clever to get caught … he was unable to express what he really felt. Arnie's sort of 'soft centre, hard exterior', you know?"

"Sounds like you got on with him."

"I did. I'd go back. I feel I'll have to, after … if there is an *after*. To tie things up."

"There's always an *after* in my experience."

"As a professional, do you get gut feelings about things? Can you guess how cases'll turn out?"

"Not always. The ending can come as a shock. But more commonly, you've evaluated the odds and are going for the best result within them."

I suspected she'd already evaluated Cliff's odds. Was she going to recommend he plead guilty? I shuddered. There was no mitigation for child killers—they went down for life. I tried to straighten the thoughts in my head, but before I could ask her about this, she began to talk.

"It's the nasty shocks that stay in the memory. I'm in a hardnosed profession, but I don't mind admitting things sometimes get to me. I was remembering a case I had in Aberdeen. The victim, the way she'd been treated … well, she would never bear children, let's put it that way."

I blanched. "And you prosecuted this man?"

"Yup." Linnet gulped at her wine, as if all the shock endings had choked up inside her over the years.

"Successfully?"

"He got the result he deserved. His victim watched justice being done. But these beasts—monsters—they leave scars that are impossible to recover from, ones not on the body. Flashbacks, constant apprehension. But this victim had physical repercussions."

"You couldn't do anything to help her."

She shook her head, fast, once and looked across the room, studying the décor.

The image wouldn't leave my mind, either. "I'm not sure if I'll ever have children, but I'd hate to know I never could."

"Have that ripped away from you." She took a fast swallow of Shiraz and laughed suddenly. "Make you want a child all the more, probably."

"Is that what happened? To that man's victim?"

"No idea. I left Aberdeen after a line of gruesome cases in a row. I fancied a change. Thought about my roots. Sent out a few feelers and came up with Hughes and Heaven."

Whatever she thought about her strong constitution, the wine was getting to her. Her lips were pale, almost white, and her mouth was beginning to move involuntarily, the stage before you start to slur your words.

"It's our gain."

"Actually, Sabbie, take a tip from me: never try to find your past. Worst thing you can do."

"All I know is that you're working hard to do your best for Cliff."

She grinned, emptied the bottle into our glasses, and raised it in the air, without turning round. In seconds, the dishy barman had left a replacement on the table.

"Whoa, I'm driving!"

"I tend to take a taxi. Drop you off, if you like?"

"Better not. I've got an early start, don't want to overdo it."

"How nauseatingly dull you are." For a moment, I thought she was being bitchy, but then she flicked on a grin that gave me a momentary glimpse of the person underneath the proficient façade. "We've done nothing but talk about me. What about you? We've probably got a lot in common."

"I dunno. I was a bit of a late starter. I bet you were fed through some posh school and straight into university. Hot house and all that?"

She shrugged. "Don't worry. I took a well-earned gap year."

"Blimey, I don't blame you!"

"And it turned into three years. South America. It's an amazing place. Very cheap. Very cheerful, in an odd sort of way. You can get lost in it. I liked it, anyway. I didn't get back until I was twenty-one."

"So you were a mature student, like me?"

"I believe it only benefits a person. There's more to life than being force-fed qualifications."

"How true. Well, I should know, took me ages to get going."

"What? You're a mere kitten. Loads of time left for you to carve out a career *and* have babies."

"I did say I wasn't sure yet about babies. My sister's got two, so I make do with them."

"And me, two nephews. I adore them."

"Hers are a boy and girl. They're pickles, but I only see them in small doses."

"I'm the same," said Linnet. "I love their company, even when it's exhausting—kids are like grownups but without the veneer of polite society, don't you think? All you want to do is make them happy, but it's never that easy." She looked down at her hands, turning her silvery ring. "Anyway, it's too late for me to have babies of my own. I'm off the chart."

"Nowadays, there isn't a chart, is there?"

She straightened her back. "Okay. You can see into the future?"

"Actually, shamans tend to see into the past—"

"Past, future, what the heck. Tell me what you see about mine."

"I couldn't." I shook my head, laughing. "Not unless I began working with you."

"Couldn't? Or won't? You never get a sudden glimpse?"

"Not often."

"I don't understand how it works. Does it happen when you're just sitting with someone, or brushing past them in the street?"

"Actually, it's quite random. And it's all mixed up with what I learnt about psychology at Uni—body language, that sort of thing."

"I think I see." She leaned back in her chair. "Go on, tell me what's coming off me at this very minute."

What I was getting was that hotshot Linnet was already fairly pissed, but I kept that to myself because I was beginning to covet the feeling. I hadn't got drunk on a girlie night out, where you giggle over nothing and talk about men's dangly bits, for a long time. "The vibes are rising…" I twitched my fingers like a sham medium. "The vibes are saying…that the ring on your right hand means a lot to you."

Her reaction was instant. She wrapped her left hand around the ring. She was clutching the finger so tightly that, even in the low pub lighting, I could see the tip of it turn red then blue. "You're right." Her mouth gave a tight smile. "Go on. Tell me more."

I leaned right over the table. "You have a past lover. You came back to find him. That's why you left Aberdeen."

A laugh hiccupped from inside her. Then another. She was dissolving in giggles. "And have I found him? Or maybe her?"

"I don't know. I don't think so."

Linnet covered her face with her hands until the laughter subsided. She wiped her eyes with her fists. "That was a guess—right?"

"Yeah. Well, it gave you a laugh. You don't look as if you get enough of those." I raised my glass to her. "Oh hang it. How about I take you up on that offer of a taxi. I can jog back in the morning to get my car. It'll do me good."

Linnet pulled her mobile out of her bag and switched it off, signifying that her business day was at an end. "Great," she said. "Let's get down to some serious drinking."

EIGHTEEN

I WOKE UP ON Thursday morning in exactly the state I deserved. I lay on my back for a minute, remembering the night before. We'd both got slaughtered, Linnet and me. That woman had a committed attitude to partying. We'd stayed at the Admiral, as they do nice food, and Linnet said the tax man would foot our bill. We shifted closer to the big screen to watch a game. Linnet had got keen on footie while in Aberdeen. I don't know my off-side from my off-centre, but by the end of the evening I was yelling and singing along with everyone else—I was pretty good friends with Shiraz, too, although right now, with the strange way the ceiling was behaving, the idea of taking even one sip of its rich redness made me feel like puking. I rolled out of bed and stared at the carpet instead of the ceiling.

Get going girl, said Gloria's voice, far too loudly, in my head. *Get that bread machine on, then get out in the fresh air.*

The greenhouse lifted my spirits, little green shoots bobbing under the spray of my watering can. The hens were looking their cheerful selves again, and they'd hidden two bronze eggs in their straw. I cradled them in the palms of both hands, walking with care as I took them into the kitchen.

I was downing a big glass of water straight from the tap when the doorbell sang at me. I checked my watch, terrified that it was already time for my first client. But at ten to eight, it was probably nothing more exciting than parcel post. I wasn't even looking properly as I opened the door.

"Sabbie," said Rey, swinging round from scrutinizing the side path.

I held on to my lip muscles, forbidding them to light up into an embracing smile. "Detective Sergeant," I said, and inclined my head like a geisha.

"I thought I'd catch you early..." His gaze swiveled from my grey, shadow-eyed face down my grubby, malodorous, and shape-less garments, each a total passion exterminator.

"You'd better come in."

"You look a little bit... wasted."

"I don't stay in doing macramé every evening, you know."

"Macra—" He shook his head, a grin struggling for supremacy. I led him into the kitchen.

"Actually, you could do me a massive favour, if you're going back to the station, and give me a lift. I've left my car by the marina."

"Right! So you do have sensible brain cells tucked under that mane of hair."

"Just a few. Probably countable on one hand, but—"

"Sabbie, I've come to let you know the results."

"The results?"

"The pathology results on the bones you found."

I heard myself gasp. His words had swung me back to the moment when I'd levered up the bare boards.

"I've brought a copy of the report with me." Rey rested his briefcase on the carpet and sat down on the sofa while he shuffled through the files it contained. "Certain things are beyond doubt. You discovered a man and woman. They were both fifty-plus at the time of death, and that's estimated at between eighteen and thirty years ago. They were deliberately placed side by side under the floorboards in the cottage. So either this was a suicide pact with intervention from a third party, or it was murder."

Rey silently skimmed through the pages of the report while I leaned against the sink, reeling from his words.

He glanced up. "Sorry. I'll summarize first—the pathology report has given us this—two people died around the time of the Wetland Murders, and in a locality close to where the bodies were discovered; very close. Whether or not they died of natural causes, they didn't put *themselves* under the floorboards."

"What about the hair you found?"

"The problem with that is we won't have any DNA stored on the original victims—too long back, I'm afraid. But it's only too clear that it's from several different sources."

"Some of it will be Cliff's. That will be conclusive, won't it? And I bet you've got his DNA already."

Rey gave a nod, stiff to the point of reluctance. "We've traced ownership of the cottage. At the time of the murders, a local businessman was renting out a few of these country properties. Apparently, the final tenants did a runner, and the owner died in his seventies only a year or so later. It's my guess that the cottage hung around as part of an inheritance for a long time, until it was too run-down to bother with."

"It's that all right."

Rey turned the pages, quick, flicking at them. "I'm just trying to find the relevant bits. Here we are. *Cause of death difficult to establish conclusively. A single trauma in the male victim—an abrasion on the fifth left vertebro-costal rib, indicative of a knife stab…*" he glanced up. "Straight between the ribs. Either someone knew what they were doing or just a lucky stab."

The knife came out of him and into me. I would never forget those words.

"Intruder?" I asked.

"Or *intruders.*"

"Sorry?"

"There is nothing substantial to clarify who these people are, but the dates and location suggest this must have something to do with the Wetland Murders. If a child murderer lived in this house, the logical assumption is that these are further victims, killed, perhaps, because they'd discovered the truth."

"But…wouldn't someone need to have gone missing?"

"People go missing every day of the week. It's only children we can actively investigate. Adults have a right to disappear."

"Patsy disappeared."

"Neither of these bodies is that of a fifteen-year-old, but we will continue to look."

A tremor passed through me. "What, pull up all the floorboards?"

"Forensics will take that cottage apart brick by brick. And the garden."

"Those bodies are not victims. I heard them talk. It was horrid. They were Kissie and Pinchie."

Rey scratched at an eyebrow. "Oh, whatever, let's run with it, you found them after all. I'm sorry to say that the obvious motive for killing two ruthless sadists might be that someone escaped their clutches and returned. Cliff admits he was in that house and got away. It's looking possible that he has a very long history of murder."

"Typical! So convenient to pin every dead body in sight on the same person."

"We examine all alternatives—"

"Cliff didn't kill the Wetland Murderers, Rey. He was just a puny kid." A better theory flashed into my mind. If a parent of a missing child had gone searching...found that cottage of horrors. Who wouldn't attack the people who tortured your child?

But then I thought about Arnie. I had assumed I'd tell Rey about Arnie but found I was clamping my jaw shut. He had been at the wetlands when the bodies were exhumed, but I was sure there was nothing more hidden behind that story. I'd caused Arnie enough grief. The thought of him being hauled in for questioning made my knees lose their strength. I snatched at the kitchen surface to hold myself up.

"You're in shock," said Rey. He got up. I felt, rather than saw, his approaching figure. My body tingled, as if he'd caught me in a ring of magnetism. His hands came down onto the corners of my shoulders, where the bones lift and round. I tried to control my breathing, which was rising to Watt's steam engine levels. The gentle touch of his warm hands slid around me until I was leaning into him. I could smell the aftershave he'd sprayed on earlier that morning, even pick out the sandalwood and vetiver. I rested my forehead on his chest, as comfortable as my own pillow. The warmth of his face was right above me, and I knew he had brought his lips to within a millimeter of my hair. A butterfly kiss, a secret one that I was not supposed to know about. I lifted my arms and rested them on his back, subtly pulling him closer.

"Sabbie..." he said, his voice hushed and trembling.

Into the slow-motion encounter came a persistent bleeping. I hadn't put Rey down as the jumpy sort, but his clavicles hit his ears and he bounced away from me.

"What the hell is that?"

I managed a grin. "My bread machine." The magic moment was over, and I didn't think we would regain it. "Fancy some breakfast?"

———

I was impressed with Rey, who clearly knew his way around a cafetieré. He made the coffee while I knocked the loaf out of the tin.

"Got the breadmaker from a boot sale." I hoped I would remind him of that happy Sunday morning we'd spent, which now seemed a long time ago. He was standing so close, his presence was making the hairs on my skin stand erect. "It was still in the packaging," I waffled on, hardly knowing what I was saying. "Don't suppose they'd worked out why they should stop buying their sliced white from Sainsbury's. Their loss is my gain—the bread tastes like angels' wings."

"What—feathers?"

I stuck my tongue out at him (just the prettier half inch), put the steaming loaf onto a rack to cool, and put a pan of water on to boil for the two eggs I'd collected earlier. I dashed upstairs to slip into something more clean. I took a few deep breaths and sat on the bed, trying to think. My whole body had fizzed when Rey held me. I'd managed to fool myself into believing we were in a mutual state of flirting. But now I knew it—I was falling for the guy. And probably, he would never fall for me back.

I gave the eggs three and half minutes then lifted them out of the rolling water and dropped them into eggcups. Neither of us spoke as we tucked into breakfast. Finally, Rey pushed away his empty plate. "A rocket's been going round the station since you found that cottage."

"What d'you mean?"

"Both investigations—the original one and this one now? We should have found those bodies ourselves."

"You mean the police—"

"Never entered that cottage."

"No one would ever have known there were bodies down there."

"So how did you know?"

"I felt it, I guess."

Rey didn't reply. He swallowed the rest of his coffee and set the mug down with utmost caution. I took the silence as a go-ahead.

"Whether the bodies are victims or killers," I said. "It is definite, isn't it? Brokeltuft was the epicentre—"

Rey was pushing at the handle of his empty mug with one finger, turning it in a circle. I saw the picture of Bugs Bunny followed by the words *What's up Doc?* over and over like a mini movie show. "We still have no idea how closely these two sets of crimes are linked. I'm not part of the investigation into what happened at Brokeltuft. We've had to draft in more officers and hand most of this over to forensics for now." He was addressing the mug, as if it was the least threatening listener. "My team must stay clear about its brief: Josh Sutton and Aidan Rodderick."

"The children buried in the moors back then were around the same age as Josh and Aidan."

"Okay." Rey glanced up, and I could see that the detective inside him could not resist picking at the puzzle. "We seem to have established that the original murderer started by enticing a teenager. No doubt she's a handful, so next time they go for a younger boy. It does make sense—a sado-sexual motivation was verified by the autopsies on the four original victims." My face contorted at his words, but he didn't notice. "The boy escapes, and the girl's giving them so much grief, they do away with her. She might not have been the only older victim. There is a time gap between Cliff and this girl being reported missing and the snatching of four smaller children."

I thought about this. "Maybe they deserted the cottage for a time, in case Cliff reported his ordeal to the police?"

"Maybe."

"So, you agree with me, then? The two bodies are murderers, not victims?"

"Your average murderer doesn't usually go for decomposition under their sofa area. Which is why the garden has to be dug up next."

I was thinking about Cliff. How he'd returned to his home and never even told his mother. He'd got into trouble because those brutes had shaved his head, but he still never told. "Little Josh— did he have his hair shorn? If he did, then it's a true copycat crime."

"I'm sorry, I can't give you that information."

"The public don't know very much, do they? They don't even know how Josh died."

"We need to keep some facts quiet. It's the way the investigation operates."

I went rigid. "You're just waiting to find the body of Aidan Rodderick, aren't you? You've given up before you've started."

Rey looked stymied by my outburst. "You should take a look inside our incident room. The guys are working into the night, every night."

"But you're not getting anywhere! You're fixated on Cliff, and on where I get my information from." We were leaning across the breakfast bar, almost touching. The air was charged. "Sometimes, the spirit world knows things. You think Cliff told me where the house was, but he'd forced everything out of his mind. He was just a *kid*. A lost kid."

"Okay. I'll give you that. Besides, why would Houghton want to lead to you to these bodies? The discovery reinforces his connection with the original murders and only makes him look guiltier." He showed me big, creamy teeth. "Which is why we've got him banged up."

My temper flew away from me. "Right. You've got him banged up. But no sight of Aidan. Does Cliff look to you the sort of man who would sit quietly in a cell while a child slowly dies somewhere?"

Rey's eyes flashed. "Don't you cross-examine me, Sabbie. These people have a substratum inside them. They hide all their evil in it and go walking around the world as if nothing is amiss. They fool most people. That's why we go on *evidence*. Evidence is how we compile a watertight case and get justice for the victims, and the evidence against Houghton is damning. It would be nice to get a confession from him, but frankly, we don't need it."

"It's just…" My voice had left me for a moment. "I can't sit here and do nothing. The whole of the county—the whole of the *country*—must feel the same about Aidan at this moment, but I think I could help! I feel I ought to try."

"Try to what?" said Rey, not bothering to keep the scorn out of his voice. "Find the missing child?"

"Yes," I said in a tiny voice. "It's why I went to Brokeltuft."

Quite suddenly, Rey got up from his stool. For a moment, I thought he was going to walk around the breakfast bar and take me in his arms again, because he was swaying on his feet as if trying to resist some inner temptation. He glanced at me, almost shyly.

"Josh died from paracetamol poisoning."

I gazed at him, afraid to speak. Telling me this secret felt more intimate than our almost-kiss.

"The modus operandi could not have been more different from the first set of murders. Josh still had all his hair. There wasn't a single bruise on his body. The only similarity was the place of burial."

My mind was racing. "So … was he alive all the time he was missing?"

"Pathology think so. They're placing time of death days, perhaps hours, before he was dumped."

"For Old Mab's sake!" I focused on the grim line of his mouth. "Does that mean—"

"Yes. Aidan could still be alive. Unless …" He lifted his briefcase onto the breakfast bar and gazed at it, as if not wanting to continue.

"Unless what?" But I knew already, just as Rey did. Little Aidan's body could already be hidden, undiscovered. No one could say for certain that the child was alive.

"The entire murder team would laugh until they'd wet their seats if they knew that I trust your judgment," said Rey. "And I don't know if I do. I only know that it was me who dragged you into this case. I didn't have to come knocking on your door when we found Houghton on the wetlands. That was my call, and the team is not going to let me forget it. None of them know I'm here."

"Oh," I said, my voice full of breath. I remembered what Abbott has said—that Rey had deliberately chosen to use me, almost as bait, at the start of the case. I looked over at Rey, burning to confront him with this, but the words never left my lips.

From his case he brought out a small package, triple-bagged in heavy-duty polythene, with a red label sealing the final fold like a wax signet. He placed it on the kitchen worktop, carefully away from our crumbs and coffee stains. I stared at it. I could feel my chest rise and fall like a Southern belle in a Civil War movie.

"No one can know I'm leaving this with you," said Rey. "Ever. Do you understand?"

"Wh-what d'you want me to do with it?" I asked. The packet filled the room with significance.

"I don't know," said Rey. "Do whatever it is you keep telling me you're so good at, for God's sake. My mobile number is on the seal. Now. D'you want that lift to your car?"

NINETEEN

BY HALF PAST ELEVEN, I was back home and ready for my Reiki client. The therapy room vibrated with candles, incense, and soft music, and thoughts of Cliff Houghton and Aidan Rodderick were lodged as far back in my mind as I could get them. In reality, both were lost in dreadful places they could not escape.

For an hour, I passed my hands over my client, feeling the heat radiate from them. This energy doesn't come from me any more than the messages and gifts I receive from journeys to the otherworlds come from me. I'm just the adapter. When my client rose from the bed, his eyes had found a focus they didn't have when he arrived, and that pleased me more than I could let him know—it meant that I had transformed myself from someone helping the police with their murder enquiries into a complementary therapist. I filed his cheque, updated his notes, and got ready for the next client.

For lunch I picked a bunch of the baby salad leaves I was growing on my kitchen windowsill and piled them on top a slice of today's loaf, grating a bit of cheddar over them. I spread mayonnaise thickly on a seond slice, rammed the two slices together, and bit down into the oozing mix. It hit the spot, immediately reviving my energy.

Upstairs, I showered and tugged my black dress over damp, bare skin. I brushed my hair until its kinks were temporarily dispersed. It felt heavy as stage curtaining when I moved my head.

Already, I was between worlds, held there, floating in the viscous ether, neither Sabbie nor spirit.

In my therapy room, I opened the file drawer. At the bottom was the furtive package Rey had left with me this morning. I weighed it in my hand: no more than a gram, but as heavy as pain; a white plastic figure with a scarlet sash around his middle and a wand as long as his arm, ready to discharge the blaster ray.

Josh's Slamblaster.

Somehow, I was surprised to see it, as if I might have dreamed Rey's presence in my house and his covert motive for arriving.

I chose a sixty-minute recording of double drumming. I let it start before I settled myself on the lounger and pulled a scarf over my face. The Slamblaster lay on my solar plexus, triple-wrapped in its forensic packaging.

———

It was nighttime at my spirit portal, which didn't surprise me. I stood quietly, gripping Josh's toy in my hand. A smell of riverweed was in the air, and I heard a slurping splash from the stream. Trendle scrambled onto the bank. His sleek body shone in the light of a waning moon; water droplets sparkled as he shook his coat dry.

"Good evening, Sabbie."

I thought he sounded a little formal, as if there was something wrong—some way I'd offended him that I'd forgotten but he had not.

"I need to find the place that Aidan is hidden. Can you help me, Trendle?"

"This is always my one endeavour, to help you."

"I think Josh was there before him, that's why I've brought his toy." I held up the Slamblaster and gawped at it. It was now the length of my arm. I dropped it in horror.

"Sabbie." Trendle's voice was urgent. "I am here to counsel you."

"I need counselling," I agreed.

"This *thing* you have brought is not a spirit. It's only a memory of a boy's love for his toy."

I began to understand what was wrong. Trendle did not agree with my reasons for the journey. He considered this his first job—a sort of triage service, where he sniffs out bogus motives and methods.

"Untrustworthy," he said, his voice low, as if he didn't want to be overheard.

I gathered my arguments, keen to persuade him, but something rammed against my left shoulder before I could speak. I sprawled down, my face hitting a stone that jutted from the grass. I stared at it in horror. Things often appear suddenly in my portal, but not things of danger. I got to my knees and saw blood dripping onto the stones. I'd bashed my nose. That shouldn't happen. I looked up.

The Slamblaster was now as tall as a young boy—as tall as his owner might have been. He stared at me with glowing red pupils. His mouth struggled to speak, but the plastic lips were permanently sealed and no sound came from him. Of course. The toy saw me as a threat—after Josh's experiences, he must consider every new adult a threat.

"Please! I mean Josh's spirit no harm." I scrabbled to my feet. "I must visit the place where Josh was kept, so that we can find the poor child who is held there now. Is this possible?" I didn't think I needed to add that it was important.

The Slamblaster nodded creakily, as if nodding was as alien to his muscles as pushups would have been to mine. He was growing all the time; now he was as tall as me. His purple-gloved hand closed over my arm. His grip was tight enough to make my fingers tingle. He turned on his jointed body and crashed through the trees that lined the brook, pulling me with him. We were in a dense forest of oak and beech. There was very little light and the ground was deep in bracken, but the Slamblaster was so tall now that my feet didn't reach the ground as he yanked me along.

Trendle leaped onto my shoulder. "Tell that thing to let you go."

I shook my head, impatient at his reproach. "This might actually give us some answers for once."

"Get out of its grip and let me deal with it."

But I didn't want that. Rey had asked me to do this, and I was determined to provide him with a result.

I felt a great tug on my arm as my dress caught in the tree roots that twined over the forest floor. I fell onto my stomach, squashing Trendle's long, soft body beneath me. He gave a squeal of pain. The gigantic toy dragged me up, and Trendle turned tail and fled through the trees. That brought me to my senses.

"Stop!" I yelled. "Stop, stop! Let go my arm!" Finally, the Slamblaster seemed to register my distress. He turned to me. His red eyes were as large as spotlights. He grasped my thigh and arm and slung me over his shoulder. A long trail of a scream came from me like vapour from an exhaust as I sailed into the air and landed, breathless, on the toy's plastic jacket. I dug my knees and fists into it, but the Slamblaster didn't even react. He just stomped through the forest, each stride taking us ten or more metres, as he continued to swell and grow—soon he was so tall that I had to cover my head with my hands to stop the topmost branches of the trees whipping against me as we stormed on.

Suddenly the Slamblaster came to a juddering halt. His hold on me faltered, and I yelled in terror as I felt myself slip. I gripped at the plastic bolts sticking out from his ludicrous helmet. We were no longer in the forest of trees. We were on the edge of a ravine that seemed to slope down and down into a chasm.

I had to take charge of my journey. I let myself float from the creature's shoulder. My feet landed just as the Slamblaster began to storm down the ravine. I tried to follow as best I could under my own steam. The floor was littered with small rocks and larger boulders, but the massive figure had no trouble with them. He powered stones out of his way with a kick from his boot and lifted larger rocks in both his purple-gloved hands, sending them crashing down the path ahead. I slipped and slid behind him.

The bottom of the gorge was filled with potholes and pitfalls, its air thick with sun-baked dust. Not a bush or tree afforded shade or the promise of fruit. There was nothing but the road ahead, bordered on both sides by a gorge so steep and so high that the sky above was no more than a channel of unnatural blue. It was hard to look up, anyway, for the sun bore down on us with blinding intensity. I could feel it burn the back of my neck. My armpits prickled with heat, but I didn't dare take off my black dress in this fierce sun. Every muscle in my body ached—the back of my calves especially. Tiny round balls of gravel cut into my bare soles.

"Trendle," I gasped. "Don't desert me." I was truly sorry that I hadn't taken his advice. That was what my spirit guide was for, after all—to guide me safely through otherworlds.

Suddenly my otter was back, trotting beside me. We picked our way forward through the stones. I was trying not to twist an ankle or take the skin off one, but Trendle's legs were so short that his stomach was scraped over the rocky ground. I couldn't bear to think of his paws all ripped and bleeding as my own feet were. I picked him up and cradled him.

"I lost my senses. I didn't start this journey for the right reasons. I was puffed up with the idea Rey Buckley had asked for my help."

Trendle looked up from his position along my arm. His eyes were black and molten and full of love.

"We could float like hovercrafts," I said to him.

"That would be cheating," said Trendle.

Trendle was right. A little five-year-old boy walked a far more difficult path than this. If we didn't experience this journey in its full intensity, we would never be able to face Josh's spirit.

I understood well enough where we were headed. This was Josh's last road—the path to his death.

"You are a most honourable otter," I whispered.

Trendle put out his tongue and licked the back of my hand, where I'd scratched it climbing in the window to Brokeltuft.

———

When the sun dipped behind the rock, I knew something new would happen. The Slamblaster had reached the end of the gorge, which was blocked by its own high sides. A tiny sliver of light filtered through a narrow crack. The Slamblaster was far too big to squeeze through it. He beat his plastic fists on the rock and his sealed mouth writhed with frustration. We had to be very close, now, to Josh's spirit.

Without a backwards glance at my robotic companion, Trendle pushed through the slender breach. I followed, crawling on all fours.

We found ourselves in a busy street. Traffic roared past me, hooting as I almost fell into the road. The rocks melted away, and behind me was a house, a stone-built structure three stories high. It looked strangely familiar, but I couldn't think why. My eye was drawn to the dormer window at the top. Was this where Josh had spent the last days of his life? My stomach clamped as I looked up. I was not sure I wanted to meet Josh Sutton or hear his story.

A gate was set into the wrought-iron railings around the house. I clicked it open, and it dissolved in my hand, leaving me clutching air. The scene was becoming distorted, as if someone was bending a photograph and snipping at it with scissors. The roof was chopped smaller and smaller until I could no longer see the attic window. I kept my eyes focused on the front door, wide and glossy with bottle-green paint with its number placed centrally just above my eye level—73—in polished brass ironware.

I took a fast step forward. Snip by snip, the house was shrinking. Its roof, its garden, its windows were all disappearing until all I could only see the front door. A feeling of dread overwhelmed me.

"A door," I said to Trendle. "Is this the symbol I'm to bring back? I brought a door back for Cliff, and that was the start of everything."

I ran the length of the path and lifted my finger to press the bell. The door faded before my eyes, the last of the photograph snipped away.

As if the entire journey with the Slamblaster had been some sort of dream, I was back with Trendle at the brook. He slid into the water and floated on his back. Unlike me, he no longer seemed disconcerted by the terrible journey we'd taken. I thought about apologising, but it didn't feel it was the right thing to do.

"Why do things always end up with doors?" I asked, but I saw the answer myself. "Because they are portals."

A change in the sound of the drumming came clearly into my ears, calling me back. An hour had passed since I lay down on the lounger in my therapy room. My body had been there all the time. My nose wasn't broken, my feet were not bleeding, and my black dress wasn't coated with dust. But my heart thundered along, singing in my ears like the beat of the drum. I pulled off my scarf and stopped the CD, then reached for paper to record my journey.

————

"That's all I saw. I didn't get the name of the street. I could try again, but I'd like to give it twenty-four hours before I do. Can I keep the Slamblaster that long?"

"Sorry."

Rey leaned forward and put the package in his document bag. Barely half an hour had gone by since I'd pulled the scarf from my eyes, but here he was, sitting on the wicker chair in my therapy room. He'd achieved a personality remake since the morning. I no longer recognised him as the bloke I'd shared eggs and hugs with. I managed a wonky smile, trying to even up the feelings that were swilling around the room. At that moment he had all the command and conviction, and I had all the insecurity and trepidation.

As I'd described my journey to him, his eyes had developed this gauzy film. I realized that he didn't want to hear about a giant Slamblaster. I pushed a notebook into his chest. "See for yourself."

A full-half minute passed before he opened the notebook and read my account. "Feels like your imagination to me," he said, without looking up.

I didn't respond directly. "It was a hard journey. Protracted ... exhausting. But I didn't get any feelings of dreadful pain." I glanced up, sensing the heat of tears in the corners of my eyes. "I'm glad to say."

"I'd told you how the child died." The words felt dragged out of him. "You already knew it was painless."

"Rey, I'm simply relating what took place—"

"Look at the house you've described ... *well-kept, attic window, posh suburb.* Don't you realize what this is?"

I went to stand next to him, pretending I needed to read. But standing close to a seething Rey didn't have quite the affect I'd anticipated. My heart was thumping blood around my body, turning my skin a tender pink. I noticed something as I read my words. "I've left out the number I saw on the door." I reached across to take the notebook and correct the omission.

With a swift movement, Rey's hand flicked out like the tongue of a reptile, pinning my wrist. The book slid from his knees onto the floor. Sometimes lovers cannot wait another instant to caress each other, but this was no lover's touch. It felt about as tender as steel, although he wasn't hurting me.

"Seventy-three," he said.

Thoughts spun through my head. They'd made an arrest at number seventy-three. Aidan Rodderick was safe. Cliff was free. "You've found the house. You've found him!"

"No, Sabbie. This house isn't where Aidan is, if he's anywhere at all."

I realized I was leaning backward, pulling away from the grip around my wrist, breathing fast through my mouth, in and out. I straightened my back and snatched my arm away, circling it with my other hand, as if nursing it back to health. "Stop playing games with me, Rey."

"I have a feeling that the team would say you were playing games with me. If they had any idea you were doing this, which they don't, thank God."

Finally my confusion found form in anger. I scooped the book up from the floor and threw it at him. It hit his chest like a kite. He caught it and smoothed out the pages.

"You're perfectly right, Sabbie. This is number seventy-three, Edward Villas, Clifton, Bristol. You might've seen it on the telly dozens of times. In fact, I'm sure you *did* see it. You remember now, don't you?" He appraised my open mouth, his own gaze impassive. "This is where Josh Sutton lived with his family before he was snatched and put to death. They stood TV reporters outside it, they had cameras waiting for the family to emerge." His mouth screwed in distaste. "Vultures."

My legs buckled. I sank down onto the edge of the sun lounger. I knew he was right—it was all too easy for a journey to get confused with what is already in the deeper recesses of the memory. But it was pointless trying to defend myself. I had failed Rey ... I had failed Aidan.

Rey stood as I faltered and sagged. "I didn't hold out much hope, Sabbie. In fact, I'm pleased with this result. It's proved conclusively that the things you get from this ... spirit place ... are not consistent. Or reliable."

I looked up at the hard line of his jaw and the glitter of his eyes. "I've only tried to be of help."

"I'm going to ask you politely. Keep out of my investigation. Allow the professionals do their job. We're about to have a major breakthrough and I can almost promise you that it won't be long before we find Aidan."

I could feel my pupils expand with shock. "Breakthrough?" I echoed.

"Houghton has agreed to be interviewed by a psychological profiler. A few nights in the remand wing has helped him see sense. I'm confident he'll give us all he knows." The line of his mouth lifted into a smile of triumph. "He's about to confess to murder."

TWENTY

THE SOFT CHINK OF Christmas sleigh bells drew closer. It was Caroline Houghton's tea trolley. I was back in the dustless gleam of her lounge. Across from me, taking up quite a slice of sofa, was a lady in her late fifties, a dumpy woman in a tartan kilt—a garment that did nothing at all for her figure—teamed with a twinset in a sort of apricot colour. The chink of china stopped as the door swung open and Caroline drove her contraption into the room.

"I hope you two have been getting acquainted," she said.

The tartan lady nodded both chins vigorously. "Oh, we have. It's been so interesting. I've never met a shaman before."

Last night, after Rey had left, taking the triple-coated Slamblaster with him, I felt about as worthless as the garden spade I'd had to chuck out after it lost its handle. A spade with no handle ... a shaman who didn't listen to her animal guide. *Throw them both in the bin*, I'd whined.

It was lucky I had an evening free of clients, because all I had wanted to do was curl up on the sofa and eat chocolate. But first I had rung Caroline—I'd needed to give her a selected version of my visit to the prison, and I felt sure that her matter-of-fact tones would calm me down and focus my attention. She'd certainly sounded more upbeat than I did, remembering that her son had been locked up for a week. Over the phone, she had told me that a member of the family liaison team had arrived in time to forewarn her about the news of the Wetland Murderers' bodies before she was confronted by it on the telly. I hoped that it was Rey who'd set up the visit. I hoped that because I really needed corroboration, right then, that he had any sort of soul.

"Did you have a hand in finding those evil people, dear?" she'd asked.

My cheeks had pricked with heat. "That information wasn't supposed to be released."

"It wasn't. It's just my hunch."

I'd heard my breath whoosh down the line as it crackled between us. "I only wish I could help in any way to locate Aidan, but my attempts so far have been useless. Worse than useless, really," I'd added, as I recalled the gunshot sound of Rey slamming my front door behind him.

"Sabbie, dear. Are you free for coffee tomorrow? There's someone I'd like you to meet." Her voice was so composed I wondered if she was trying to enroll me in her Women's Institute. "It's Nora Rodderick," she'd continued. "You came up in conversation, you see."

"Aidan's grandmother?" My antenna shot up above my head, waggling like cobras summoned by a flute. "Are you absolutely sure she wants to meet me?"

"Yes, dear," Caroline had said. "She really does."

I didn't bother with breakfast before I left for Caroline's; I already knew her morning coffees were served promptly at ten with rich pastries.

And true to form, Caroline was building her little towers of tables, place mats, saucers, doilies, and finally the green and gold cups before pouring the steaming liquid, adding the right amount of sugar and milk to each one from memory.

"I wondered if I'd have to shoulder my way through newshounds again," I said, watching her with awe. "But there's only one bloke left now." I'd been momentarily tempted to feel sorry for him, huddled inside his dog-eared sheepskin coat against the cold.

"He's the worst." Caroline shuddered. "He follows me right up to my garage, screaming questions at me every time I go out."

She settled the coffee pot onto her trolley and walked purposefully across to her window. She didn't cower behind the curtains today. She stood full centre and shook a fist at the solitary newshound who lingered by the gate.

"Look," said Nora, holding up one of my brown glass bottles. "Sabbie has given me this!" There was the vestige of a Devonshire accent in Nora's voice.

"I had one of those, they're lovely. Use it in your bath."

"Well, I'm very grateful." Nora Rodderick recrossed her ankles. She'd been doing this every half minute or so. I wondered if the slight change in position was a substitute release valve, letting off an invisible charge of pressure from within. She seemed immensely calm to me, but perhaps that's how people under strain behaved within range of Caroline's influence. Or perhaps it was something to do with being in the Women's Institute—a remnant of the wartime spirit that kept up the home morale. One simply didn't show one's feelings, even if one was melting with tears.

"We pray daily for him," she said. "The whole village. The school playground is a riot of colour—bouquets on every railing. I believe that keeping him in our thoughts will keep him alive until he's found."

She opened the handbag on her lap and delved in. I assumed she was searching for a tissue to keep the tears at bay. What she brought out made me blink. It was a laughing Buddha, carved from wood and painted in glowing colours, maroon and gold and indigo, then lacquered to a high gloss. It fitted snugly in her hand.

"Aidan had this in his satchel when…" She hesitated, then smiled. "Funny, how they've gone back to satchels, isn't it? Some of the children have a sort of big zipped-up pencil case for their pictures and things, but Aidan has a satchel. He's so proud of it."

She was struggling to keep her grandson in the present tense, willing him to still be alive.

I was staring at the Buddha in horror. With the experience of the Slamblaster fresh in my mind, I never wanted to work with an inanimate figurine again. "It's… it's not really a *toy*, is it?" I faltered.

"He has a thing over this," said Nora. "Stella brought it back for me from her student travelling days. She did visit a lot of interesting places, before she had Aidan. Anyway, it used to grace the dressing table in my spare room, the one we made into a nursery. He was eighteen months at the most when Stella found a job. Well, she didn't want to be a drain on me, and I encouraged her independence. But little Aidan cried for his mummy something dreadful." She placed the Buddha in the centre of the coffee table, where it chuckled at us in silent, macabre mirth. "He took a shine to this, started carrying it everywhere, called it Buddy. I remembered what Stella told me when she brought it back from Thailand, and I turned it into a story. If you rubbed his fat tummy, he'd send you good luck. We used to rub Buddy's tum each morning as Stella went out the door and wish she'd come back safely. Of course, she always did."

Nora retrieved a lace-hemmed hanky from her cardigan sleeve as tears welled up and overflowed from eyes as red as wounds. With the amount of crying she must have done lately, I was surprised she hadn't gone over to man-sized tissues, but old habits die hard.

Without speaking, Caroline passed round fine china plates, each with a tiny pastry cup filled with custard, soft fruit, and whipped cream. These must have taken hours to make, and I reckoned I could dispose of mine in less than a minute.

"Try to eat," she told Nora. "To keep up your strength."

"Oh, you're right, of course. Stella needs me." She picked up the fruit cup and took a valiant bite. "And Aidie'll be back, you'll see, tumbling over the furniture and upsetting the flower vases!" She put the pastry down, as if the tiny morsel she'd taken was going to last her some time. "Did Liz bake these? I recognise her light touch."

"An institute member," Caroline explained, turning to me. "They're being so kind to us both, aren't they, Nora?"

Nora nodded. "Stews, bakes… they sent me over the winning floral arrangement yesterday."

"You've been friends a long time?" I was touched by the camaraderie of the two women, the victim's granny and the accused man's mother.

"Oh yes, years," said Nora. She looked at Caroline, who'd perched herself on one end of the three-seater, now that we had been fed and watered. "And we've all known Cliff since he was wee. No one round here believes he did it. No one."

There was a tremor in her voice. I thought of my own determination to clear Cliff's name. None of us *knew* he was innocent. It was all gut feeling. As Rey had said, it was proof that counted. Proof or a confession. I cleared my throat.

"I can't promise that I'm going to be any help at all, Nora." I wanted her to be let down now, before her hopes were raised too high.

"Caroline's told me how you've been supporting Cliff. And she said you had a hand in finding that awful place out on the moors."

"Yes. That surprised me as much as anyone else." It was the truth. As the days went on, I was beginning to believe I might have dreamed it all, and Rey's scepticism encouraged this process.

"I understand that you can't contact Aidan," Nora was saying. "Well, of course you can't, but I wondered if… because his Buddy was something he loved… oh God, he'll be distraught without it!"

I didn't speak. I could think of nothing to say that would soothe this woman's pain. She blew her nose with her bit of lace, and continued. "I'd just like you to try. I'll quite understand if… "

There was a long pause in the room. I thought about the body of Josh in its shallow grave, and how his Slamblaster toy hadn't been placed there with him. And when I finally took the Buddha in my hands, a sensation flashed through me. The images weren't visual, but the symbols that came into my mind made me feel uneasy. I lowered Aidan's precious Buddha gently into my lap. I didn't want to drop it, not even onto the deep pile of Caroline's silk rug.

"What happened on that afternoon," I began. "To the satchel, I mean. Did he have it with him?"

"He took it to school. But when he disappeared, it was in the classroom."

So the Buddha had been nowhere near Aidan's captor. Strange, then, that it shot such despondency into me. Or was its psychotic grin disturbing my balance?

"So different nowadays, though," said Nora, dipping into her handbag again. I held my breath, concerned what would emerge from it this time. An envelope; inside it a photo. "In my day we had to sit behind our desks for the school photo. Two children at a time, sitting behind a double desk, and then they cut the picture down the middle so it was only you. But now, well, look at this."

Aidan was at the very top of a climbing frame, his legs dangling through the bars, his face mischievous as a pixie. He was brim full of the climb, his socks half down, his shoes a bit scuffed, his hair all messed.

I looked up at Nora. "He's wonderful," I said.

"I know. That *is* him—captured perfectly. He has a thing about that playground equipment. It was made for him. In fact, he's a bit of a problem at school. Not 'settled,' the teachers say. If he's missing from class, they know where to find him."

"Out on the climbing frame?"

"He's been told off and warned off I don't know how many times."

I looked back at the photo. It felt as if Aidan winked—*was winking*—at me. Always up to monkey business. A little monkey.

"We warned him against strangers," she said, her voice rising. "Stella was insistent. I think he must have been offered chocolate, he's a sucker for that."

I passed the photo back. "This must be so difficult to bear."

Nora nodded, taking shaky breaths of the floral-scented air. "They wouldn't have heard his screams," she said. "It's what I've been thinking since the beginning. It's only one class, for all the five- and six-year-olds, you see. The juniors don't even have the same playground access. And they'd have been clearing up from painting. I help in the class from time to time; I know how loud things can get. All those little darlings, having fun." She tried to turn a sob into a chuckle. "I can't sleep for thinking about it. But that makes me feel better. My suffering isn't a hundredth of Aidan's."

Caroline got up and went to sit next to Nora, her arm around her friend's shoulders for long minutes, while sobs wretched out of her. I mostly looked at the Buddha, who seemed to be telling me I was a callous fiend to put Nora through these questions.

Even before I picked the Buddha up, I'd guessed he'd been nowhere near the abduction site. Tucked safely at the bottom of the satchel hanging on a school peg, he wouldn't hold any of the terror of that moment. So why did he impart such an aching sadness?

After a while, Nora spoke into her palmed hands, which were shiny with tears and saliva. "I needed a proper cry," she said. She was the sort of woman who would be embarrassed about showing her feelings before strangers, but I think she already had begun to consider me as a friend. "I've been holding things in a long time."

"It'll do you a world of good," said Caroline.

"Nora," I began, "there's something in the Buddha. Was Aidan going through a difficult time before he—You mentioned he hadn't settled at school, for instance?"

"He can be a bit wild, but he loves his class. Runs in through the door of a morning. Of course, it's just as well, because Stella needs to go to work in the day. She's a one-parent family, you see."

I recalled the TV appearances, Stella's frightened, tear-struck face, alongside the grim visage of Garth Stanford.

"Doesn't Aidan see his father?"

"He has him for the odd weekend, yes."

"Does Aidan like Garth?"

"He seems to. I've taken him to visit myself and I can't deny that he fair raced away from the car when I dropped him off."

"The police have interviewed him," Caroline broke in.

Nora nodded. "He was one of the first, I think. But they let him go." She looked directly across at me. "Stella had this dreadful relationship with Garth when she was at university. I could tell that he was...how can I put it? He isn't the man I'd wish as the father to my grandson. He's not stupid—he got his degree—but he's done nothing with it. Nothing with his life. A waster is what I'd call him. Far too self-ish to want to snatch his son and have to tow him around with him."

"The police don't seem to be thinking along the lines of a simple battle of parents," I agreed.

"We don't know that for sure, though." There was a slight quaver in Caroline's voice. "We don't actually know anything about Garth, do we?"

"Caroline, love," said Nora. "Garth is a waster, no doubt of that, but he's never been cruel to Aidan."

I remembered what Rey had said yesterday. *These people … they hide all their evil and go walking around the world as if nothing is amiss.* I could see how Caroline might clutch at the straw of Garth, a seemingly far more likely suspect than her own son. Rey's words might fit either of them equally. Even so, I went over all the details Nora had given me so far.

"No one heard Aidan scream. What if he didn't cry out at all? If he'd seen someone he knew and trusted at the edge of the playground, he might not even have thought about returning for his satchel."

"I'm sure Garth wouldn't hurt him," said Nora, an obstinate look on her face.

It struck me that although Nora had taken a strong dislike to her daughter's college romance, she was going to defend the father of her grandson, as people tend to do when their family is threatened. She'd made up her mind that evil had come down upon them from outside.

"*You'd* know," said Caroline, turning to me.

I was pulled from my thoughts. "Pardon?"

"You'd know if it was Garth or not. Soon as you looked at him. I'm sure of it." She got up and loaded the tea trolley. "This has all gone cold. Shall I make some fresh?" She trundled out, shutting the door behind her. I imagined her standing over the kettle to weep.

I looked across at Nora, wondering how she would react to Caroline's outburst. "That's not how it works. I'm no better at gauging character than the next person. I have to have access to someone's spirit world to know anything more."

Nora struggled up from the feather-depths of the sofa. She came across to me slowly, as if the floor was strew with hazards. She contemplated Aidan's Buddha for a moment before lifting it from my lap as if it were Aidan himself.

"Anything," she whispered. She kissed its merry cheek. "Anything that will find my darling. Any tiny thing." Her eyes had a halo of tears. "I'd like you to meet Garth. Please. For me."

TWENTY-ONE

GARTH STANFORD LIVED LIKE a traveller, except his multihued van was not going to travel anywhere. Some time in its history, it had lost its wheels. It was half out of sight from where I was standing—on the other side of a five-barred gate—but I could certainly see that it was balanced on breeze blocks. I hung around the gate as if I was on a stakeout and dived into my bag for my mobile.

"Caroline?" I hissed into the phone. "I've found it."

"Clever you!" came from the other end. "Nora said it was hard to find."

I glanced back at the van. "Once seen, never forgotten, I should think."

"Now, you take care."

"I'll be fine."

"You must ring us again as soon as you're out of there."

"If he lets me in at all." I'd been hoping we might give Garth a ring, to ask him if he was available, but Garth did not have a telephone, and now I could see why.

"If you haven't rung in half an hour, I'll ring you. If I don't get a reply, I'm alerting the police."

I blanched. "Don't do that, Caroline! I'm not exactly popular with the police at the moment."

"Keep in contact, then."

"You have to give me some time. Promise you won't ring me until later."

But I didn't trust her not to call, and I didn't want it to sound as if we'd set this up between us, so I put my phone on silent mode. This cloak and dagger stuff wasn't at all appropriate. I just needed to get to the bottom of the dismal feeling that had come off the Buddha.

Getting into the field was going to be my first challenge. The track leading from the gate had been used by farm vehicles and was deep in mud. I clung to the fence, sliding from one patent leather boot to the other until I finally reached a bit of field that came up to trade description level. Grass, in other words. Feeling as conspicuous as a pheasant in season, I squelched in a straightish line, skirting the fire pit dug in the grass, surrounded by odd-shaped, heat-blackened stones. Soon I was close enough to make out that the splash of colour by the back door was a pot of spring primroses.

The van was tucked up against the far hedge between a couple of massive sweet chestnuts whose branches overhung its roof. Originally, the van had been an unpromising off-white colour, but its paintwork had been re-created with spray cans to depict a glorious, bright green, fire-breathing dragon. The windows were hung with bits of net curtain, which meant that the closer I came, the more easily the occupier could spot me, whereas I couldn't even tell if he was in.

I took a razor breath and rapped on the back door. From a distance, I heard a creak of metal against metal.

"Yeah?"

I put my head round the side of the van. Garth Stanford stepped out of his driver's door, jumping the short distance to land squarely. He was a tall man, as lean and berry-skinned as my beloved Bren, and with even more beard, if that was possible. His hair was a wild, unbrushed corona of bronze and on his nose was the oldest pair of spectacles I'd seen in a long time. Even Arnie had better glasses than these. They were a huge, black, horn-rimmed affair, held together with bits of duct tape.

Garth was dressed in a single garment, an ankle-length kaftan of faded orange. He wore no shoes and I would've placed a bet that he wore nothing underneath the kaftan, either.

"Can I help you?" His voice had the deep, slow warmth of bamboo chimes.

I put my hand on the side of his van, in a sort of honouring gesture, but I couldn't think of a thing to say that wasn't incriminating. It occurred to me that if I did nothing more than shake his hand, I might get what I'd come for. I busied forward, arm outstretched.

"I'm Sabbie Dare."

He stared at the hand in the way the cows in the next field might have stared at the fence, but he didn't move.

"Let me start by saying I'm not the police or the press." I had a strong feeling that everyone connected to Aidan would be fed up with both these agencies by now. "Or the council," I added, searching round for other possible irritants in Garth's life. "Or the farmer."

The eyes behind the glasses trapped me in their gaze. "Don't tell me who you *aren't*."

I let my hand drop to my side. I was doing badly. "Nora Rodderick told me how to find you."

"How is she?"

The response caught me off guard. "Oh, well, desperate, I suppose."

"I gave up on desperate some time ago."

I studied the mud that coated my boots. "I'm so sorry."

"What does Nora want?"

I looked through the lenses of his glasses, right into his eyes. They were a clear, honey-edged brown, guileless and filled with sorrow. "It's about Aidan." My voice was all whispery.

"In that case," said Garth, "you're welcome to come in."

He turned and climbed back into the van, a length of bronze-haired shin showing beneath his kaftan as he pulled himself up. I scrambled after him.

I was expecting to find myself up against the front seats, but everything had been removed—seats, steering wheel, gearbox, partition. There was nothing about this van now that made it a vehicle. Instead, the interior had been turned into a surprisingly spacious one-room accommodation. Garth's bed was a mattress tucked in behind the back doors and raised from the floor, caravan-style, to allow for storage underneath. Along both sides were overhead shelves stacked with books, tapes, potted plants, and a mismatch of crockery. On top a small chest of drawers was a cardboard box of vegetables and a shabby portable radio. There was a tape playing inside it—something from a different place and time, maybe ancient Greece, maybe Mexico City. Wherever he could, Garth had draped throws and scarves and other fringed things, giving the metal interior a feeling of softness and colour.

"Take a seat."

I looked around. The choice was eclectic—a chair straight out of the Sixties, with wooden arms and a sagging cushion; a beanbag covered in big yellow sunflowers; or a set of canvas camp chairs, folded against a wall hanging of another dragon, this time with ochre scales and eyes of burning coal…a bit too much like the massive Slamblaster for me. This was a symbol he clearly identified with, yet I couldn't see anything fire-breathing about Garth. I plopped down onto the beanbag.

"Nice music," I said.

"Helps me relax," said Garth. "I'm trying to stay calm, see."

"I guess it's hard."

"I'd like to kick the sides of the van in."

"You don't look to me like a van kicker."

Behind the glasses the honey brown eyes closed, briefly. "It's having nothing to do. Not being able to help in one single way."

I was reminded of how Arnie had volunteered to find the missing children—how all the parents must have done so. Garth struck a safety match and bent to light a gas burner. He placed a whistle-kettle onto the half-hearted flame. "Drink?"

"Oh," I said, startled. "Thank you."

He didn't offer me a choice but spooned something from a tea caddy into a small white pot, pouring water on top as soon as the kettle whistled. The lid chimed into place. Every action was self-possessed and measured.

"This is a peaceful place to be," I said. Actually, I loved it—loved its simplicity.

He nodded. "It's good."

"You travel about, or just stay put?"

Instantly, this struck me as a stupid question. The man literally had no wheels. But Garth gave it his reflective consideration.

"I guess we're all looking for the place to settle. Never thought that would be me. But I like being close to Aidan and Stella."

"Only, finding somewhere to live alternatively…"

"Yeah. Can be hard. The council have tried to move me on."

"They'd have a job," I quipped.

"I'm lucky. I've found a friendly farmer."

"He lets you stay?"

"I get the pitch, rent free, if I lend a hand when they're at full stretch."

"Oh, good exchange of energies."

"The farm job makes me an 'agricultural worker'."

"Great!"

"It's an organic farm." He gestured to the box of vegetables, which I assumed was part of the exchange of energies. This was a man of as few words as possible.

"I've turned my garden over to organics," I said. "Hens, vegetables, that sort of thing."

Garth gave the pot a slow stir and poured a straw-coloured liquid into two chunky mugs. He handed me one and made himself comfortable on the floor, sitting cross-legged.

The scent of the tea wafted up from the mug. "Mmm," I said, sniffing. "Mint, chamomile, Melissa, something fruity... haws, perhaps?"

"Rose hips. You know about herbs?"

"I used to live with herbalists." I took a sip of the tea and felt its warmth and flavour slide into my stomach, relaxing me. "And I've got most of these in my garden. I ought to get round to blending them more than I do."

"So, did Nora send you here just to remind me I'm useless and hopeless?"

I shook my head. It was getting hard, being in the middle of so many people's utter pain. My hands were around the mug, comfortably warm. I felt relaxed and at home. The lemon balm in the tea, the smell of incense in the van, and the music were all drifting around my mind, making me forget why I'd come. It would have been nice to talk about permaculture for the rest of the afternoon—anything to avoid the subject of a missing son. Maybe I could even convince myself I'd be doing Garth a favour—taking his mind away from his agony.

"You know I've come here about Aidan," I said, as softly as I could. I waited for Garth's response. His body rocked to and fro, his mug in his hands. "But it's more about the man they've arrested." Suddenly, I knew I was going to tell Garth everything from the beginning, from the moment Cliff had walked into my therapy room for the first time and I had seen anguish and mystery in his eyes.

Halfway through my story, I absentmindedly put my empty mug down on the floor, and Garth refilled it from the pot.

"Something wasn't right about Aidan's Buddy," I finished. "When I touched it at Caroline's, I felt a despondency that couldn't have had anything to do with the kidnapping. So I suppose I came here to ask you if you could shed any light on it."

I realized how my agenda had changed. I had no intention of trying to work out where Garth had hidden Aidan, or if he'd killed Josh. As far as I could tell, he'd find it difficult to sever a stick of barley or dig up a carrot.

In the dim lighting of the van, I saw his otherworld image. It was lifting slightly away from him with a sort of repressed compulsion. It explained to me how Garth was managing to cope with the calamity that whirled around him. He had risen above it; he had risen above the howling world.

"I'm sad to think my son was sad, even before … what happened."

"What I got was more everything not being right."

"Things weren't right," Garth agreed.

"Oh?"

"If Aidan had had his way, he'd be with me now. Out here, where a kid can run and climb and eat off a wood fire."

"Are you saying he'd choose to live with you over his mother?"

"What? No." Garth shook a laugh out of himself, the first I'd seen. "No, Stella used to dig this life too. But her mother wouldn't have it. They wanted Aidie to go to the church school in the village. Come home and play on a computer. Have nice friends to tea."

"To be fair, that's not quite how Nora told the story."

"You have to make up your own mind about that." He looked down at the herbal dregs in his cup, then back up at me. "Stella was always torn. She loved the travelling. We used to spend every summer going from festival to festival. Then she finished her degree and inherited a bit of money from her grandmother and we took off. India, Thailand."

"The hippie trail?"

"You can look at it like that, if you want. You can say we trod in the footsteps of a lot of other people. But we did it for ourselves, to work out what we wanted from our lives."

"And for you, that was …"

"The simplest life I could possibly find. The joy of never harming a living thing. The wonder of waking each day just to appreciate that the sun has risen and the season is moving on."

"Yes," I said. "I can see the attraction in that."

"Can you? Stella lost that feeling. We came back to England because she knew she was pregnant—that *we* were pregnant. She insisted she wanted to be near her family for the birth. Before we knew it, obstetricians overran us with their epidurals and caesareans. I think we had our first row ever."

I didn't interrupt, but I had trouble imagining Garth in a row of any description.

"She moved back to her mum's. I went off for a bit. I missed the birth. I never forgave myself for doing that, but I didn't feel part of things with her anymore. There'd been a takeover bid."

"I'm so sorry."

Garth went back to his gentle nodding. The tape clicked off and the otherworldly music stopped. The silence extended into a Zenlike stillness.

Garth moved around the van while I finished my second mug of tea. Carefully, he put the cassette into its battered case. He threw some herbs on a charcoal burner and a scented fog of smoke curled into my nostrils. When he came and sat down again, something had changed in him.

"You're quite a shaman," he said.

"Thank you."

"I don't just mean the Buddha. I was thinking of what you said earlier—the way you found the cottage."

"The police don't believe that had anything to do with my work. They assume Cliff told me."

"I don't assume that."

"I've no actual idea what happened. It was a trail of coincidences and twists of fate. And an image that came through strongly while I was holding Cliff's hand in the prison."

"So to pick up directions, you need to be close to the person who could give you them."

I shrugged. "I was fool enough to hope that I would find Aidan when I found the cottage, but it hasn't been used since the Wetland Murders."

"Is that the point of all this? You think you'll find Aidan?"

When Garth put my secret hope into words, it made me splutter with embarrassment. "Don't think—I'm not trying to race the police investigation—anything like that."

Garth leaned back, balancing on his spine. "Makes no difference to me who finds my son, so long as he comes back to us whole."

I looked over at him for a long time. Mostly, I was contemplating the word *whole*. Aidan had been missing for a week. Even if he were alive, he would be changed. I began thinking about Josh. How the little boy from Bristol had probably trodden the same path and seen the same sights as Aidan had in his stead.

"I—I shouldn't tell you this," I stuttered, "but I did have the opportunity to work with something forensic." Garth shifted his position, his eyes concentrating on me. "But Josh's spirits didn't lead me anywhere."

"You touched something of Josh Sutton's?"

"That's what I'm saying. But it was a world away from what I got when I held Cliff's hand."

"Have you thought about where Josh Sutton is now? Physically, I mean."

"His body?"

"Yeah. In some morgue, perhaps? If they let you touch this forensic thing…"

I shook my head. "Cliff told me. He knows every detail of the case." I took a moment to work things out myself. "Josh was taken on the twenty-fourth of December last year. He was found on the eighteenth of January. His body was released for burial shortly before Cliff had his second appointment—that's only a couple of weeks back, but I think the family were planning immediate cremation. His ashes might be scattered anywhere."

For a few seconds, I'd seen a sort of rising of hope in Garth, but it withered and died as I spoke. His head bobbed down onto his chest. "He was missing for less than four weeks when he was found dead."

"The body wasn't hurt, Garth." I shook my head. "That is no consolation at all. I'm sorry I said it."

He looked at me with hardened, dry eyes. "We're clutching at straws, aren't we?"

I don't know why the image came to me at that moment, unless Trendle conveniently helped it bubble to the surface, but I saw Cliff in my mind's eye as I had when he'd told me the story of his first arrest. The bulrush he'd picked for his father's memory.

"I guess straws are better than nothing," I said.

———

It was gone lunchtime when I got home. I was starving, but I didn't intend to sit down to a hot meal. I sniffed around the fridge. Gloria had left a plate of her spicy veg pies for me, now three or so days old. I grabbed one and some fruit from the bowl to go with it and switched on my laptop. While it was booting up, I went over the photocopies I'd brought home from the library, cross-referencing the site of the burials with my walker's map. I took a sharp intake of breath. The shallow graves were hardly more than a mile from Brokeltuft Cottage.

This latest crazy idea of mine had to be the most extreme of long shots. Neither Garth nor Nora had asked me to do anything further, but I had to try, and, as I didn't have appointments to keep, now was the time to start. I clingfilmed a couple more of the little pies and lowered them into my backpack on top my bird-spotting binoculars, map, torch, phone, purse, gloves, scarf, and a bottle of water. I laced up my mud-caked boots and locked the door behind me. The day was cold and there was a dampness on the wind. I doubled back through the side entrance and shepherded my flock of hens into their fox-proofed house. It was March, and night wouldn't fall until almost six, but I had no idea when I would get back.

Leaving Bridgwater, I got snarled into traffic, then spent unnecessary time trying to get close to Brokeltuft, but the police had blocked the lane off at the top, by the signpost on the grass triangle. I examined my map, looking to get to the burial site from the opposite direction, driving up and down the country lanes to find the closest walker's path. Finally, I parked on a remote B road, pulling in close to the hedge that ran along its flank. I stared over the flat, green fields punctuated with willow and shimmering with water. I checked my watch. It was three-thirty in the afternoon, but the heavy cloud cover produced a premature feeling of dusk. If I was honest with myself, I did not want to be here.

I followed a footpath arrow that led to an iron gate. It creaked on rusty hinges as I pushed my way through. The metal burned like ice into my hands. I fished out my gloves and pulled them on. I reckoned I was only half an hour's tramp from my goal. I shifted my backpack onto my shoulders and set off.

The Somerset fenlands had once been fresh lake mingling with salt sea. Early farmers, desperate for more growing room, had reclaimed every clod of earth I trampled on. They'd gained their fields by digging the rhynes, ditches, and canals that stretched in every direction. Even so, my boots squelched as I headed over the field towards the first of many wooden bridges.

This place felt more and more like one of those children's maze puzzles. I was zigzagging across water meadows, blocked in on all sides by ditches—some holding clear and fresh water, some reeking and stagnant. And where there weren't ditches of water there were hedges—pussy willows in fluffy white bud and hazels shimmering with catkins and scratchy thorn bushes bare of leaf and shiny from the damp air.

I tramped on, seeking ways to cross water, until I had been walking for well over an hour on this tortuous route. I sat down on the elevated bank of a rhyne, my legs dangling over the edge high above the soft-moving water, and ate most of Gloria's pies while I looked at the map. If I gave up now, I'd be back at the car before the sunset. But I didn't want to give up. I wasn't far from Josh's resting place. I had to go on.

"Is that what you do?" Nora had asked. "Just by closing your eyes, you can talk to the dead?"

It's difficult to describe what happens to me. People are expecting a snappy sound-bite response, but that would be too simplistic.

Most people can feel the "difference" between a graveyard and, say, a park. The veil that separates the living from the dead is thinner in some places. I think I'm just a fraction more sensitive than most. I pick up... well, for want of a better word, I'll call them vibrations... that other people only half feel.

Garth had said, "It might be the only way to find Aidan. The police don't have a clue," but that wasn't true. They had plenty of clues; the only trouble was, they all pointed directly, and most conveniently, to Cliff.

I got up, brushing down my rear. I missed the company I used to have on country walks with the Davidson family... Gloria's pleasant chatter, Philip's solid back moving constantly in the right direction, and the wicked laughs I'd be having with Charlene and Dennon, plus whatever dog it was at that time. Being together made the walks fun and easy. Being alone in these vast wet fens as gloom grew was unnerving. Early evening shadows were already closing down the colours, taking the greens and silvers to shades of grey.

I pushed through a thin line of trees and came upon the peat bogs. These stretched out before me, miles of grassless land as black as a seam of coal. Acres of the peat had been dug out to a depth of several metres, and the recent excavations were already filling with water. The lines were mechanically angular—thin, straight paths led between this scourging of the soil. There was no choice but to tread them, even though my mind was screaming at me to go back. The paths were slippery and narrow, with an invisible drop on either side. It was like walking around the edges of massive ink-filled swimming pools.

When I lifted my chin away from my footsteps, I could see I was drawing closer to the long-abandoned areas, murky water held together with sedges and bulrushes. These bogs went on forever, impossible to tell one blackened hellhole from the next. I had no idea how to find the location I wanted.

I turned a full circle, skimming the horizon. Far away into the west, an ancient clump of willows sprouted out of the bog. The trunks were glossy black against the reddening sunset. Each branch, thick as a Sumo wrestler's leg, skimmed the water's surface before turning upwards to the sky. The patterns they formed brought symbols to my mind—cages and gallows and rune signs. My skin goosed up along my arms.

Where they were hid, them babbies, massive trunks were coming out of the water, growing there for years...

Without a doubt, these were the willows Arnie had described to me. I pulled my jacket close about me and raised the collar against the wind. As I marched towards them, I saw the faint outline of police tape on thin metal poles, inadequately closing off the area.

The sun was slipping below the horizon like a thief in an alley. I had hoped I wouldn't need my torch, but now it drilled a swirling vortex into the space ahead, illuminating the path with its paltry light.

The slurry surface of the abandoned bogs gave me the clearest indication of where the path lay. I leaned forward as I walked to get the maximum light from the beam. The wind was whipping up and darkness was falling. My cheeks and nose felt numb. When I looked up again to check my progress, the willows had gone.

I stared in horror. I wasn't used to such dark magic. The grey horizon was hiding their silhouette. A gurgle of panic, like quickly swallowed porridge, rose in my gullet. The trees were somewhere ahead of me, but I hadn't thought to take any sort of marking of where they lay—which of the many paths I needed.

My boot slid off a clump of slimy leaves. It filled with bog water. I clutched at the air, struggling to keep my balance, and the torch fell from my grasp. I watched in dismay as it sank beneath the oily sheen.

My eyes stung with tears, and the wind instantly chilled them into ice. This was a dreadful place to be at night. Cliff must have been in a bad state of mind to attempt the journey across the marshes. Some compulsion had kept him going. For me, it had to be the thought of communicating with a dead child, left to rot out here. An unwelcome thought inveigled its way into my mind: There *is* no child out here; the body lay under the willows for but a few days before it was removed to a cold, white room. *You won't find Josh's spirit here*, I thought. *You're a fool to try.*

"Trendle," I whispered aloud into the wind.

You need me at last? his voice came in my head.

"Trendle, I'm sorry."

You didn't listen. You went your own way.

"I had to see where the Slamblaster would take me."

It was a false witness, Sabbie.

I wiped my eyes with the fingers of my woolly gloves, and bent gingerly to tie my boots tighter. "What about now? Is this the right way?"

Trendle didn't reply, but as I straightened up, the clouds skidded away from the moon and her ethereal light shone out between them, only a few days away from full. A waxing gibbous moon, aching with her pregnant form. Her light brushed the willow branches with a coating of ghostly snow and made my route between the bogs a silver path. I strode on, keeping my mind focused.

I heard the burial site before I saw it. The police tape cracked in the wind where it had blown free of its moorings, like banners at a fete. I sped towards the sound, crying from relief.

The police had covered the area surrounding the investigation site with plastic walkways and wide tarpaulins. These were already slimy with mud but were a respite to my legs, which were aching and trembling from the strain of feeling their way.

The forensic work was complete here—the crucial evidence gathered, the visible and microscopic traces of the crime documented, examined, and stored. There was nothing here now for those who looked for proof in the physical world. I made my way over the tarp to the clump of willows. The trunks rose out of what looked like deep water, their shapes contorted, as if something had tortured them, preventing straight growth. The branches stretched over my head. I reached up and touched them. They had stood at this site for generations. They had seen too many things—the devastation of the land, the hiding of small bodies. And yet, they stood here now, bearing testament to the way the world continues on, no matter what.

I had wondered how I would connect with Josh without disturbing any spirit presence that remained from the Wetland Murders a generation ago. Now I knew. I would attempt to communicate through the willow. He had seen it all and would aid me. He would prevent my mind from searching wildly and in vain.

I sank down onto the tarp under the branches, getting my back against the wind. Cold seeped up into my trousers, but at least it was dry. I pulled off my boots and socks. One foot was squelchy from its dunking, the other hot and sweaty. I dried them with tissue, wrung out the wet sock, and draped them both over the shoes to air out for a while. I tucked my bare feet under my thighs, legs crossed yoga-style. Balancing my weight gave me more purchase on my mind.

Nothing mattered now except the journey I wanted to make. I gave myself up to it. In this dank, foul place, surely the barricades between the worlds would be shot with holes I could crawl through in my mind. I closed my eyes. Images came and went until my mind felt ready to face my spirit portal. I began the chant that would let me sink under ... *Ostara ... Ostara ...*

I felt myself shudder, just once—from cold or from fear of where I was about to go. Just once. And then I was gone.

TWENTY-TWO

MY MIND WAS FAR from the dankness of the moors. I'd slipped into a deep trance and moved into someone else's world on a shamanic quest that might have taken me minutes or more than an hour. I'm not sure how long I had been away when into my spirit world came the sound of drumming. I thought I was in my therapy room. I thought this was the call-back sign on my CD. I kept my eyes shut for a moment, so that all the images I'd encountered between the worlds would be imprinted on my brain. I tried to recall who my client was and why I'd journeyed for them, until I realized I was shivering with damp and bitter cold and that my journey had been to the grave of a child.

I opened my eyes. I was sitting in a hard vortex of light that came directly from above. It wasn't drumming that had brought me back; it was the guttural sound of helicopter blades.

I sat on the tarp, my gloved hands over my ears, unable to block out the manic, brutal clatter of the chopper. I stayed absolutely still, legs crossed, my chest pounding through my double layer of jackets. It was probably the same protective impulse a rabbit has when caught in headlights, but it saved me from darting away and sinking into the nearest water.

I was only half out of my trance, and the battering of sound and light leached into my dream state. I could feel the beam behind my orange eyelids as if extra-terrestrials were trying to lift me into their spacecraft. But the first voice I heard didn't come from above.

"Stand and place your hands wide of your body. Stand and place your hands…"

The words were standard procedure, the tone aggressive. I opened my eyes a slit and saw a man in uniform outlined against a beam of light.

I stumbled onto my senseless legs. The officer came forward like a dream creature. Some way beyond us, ethereal colours floated in the night sky, a brilliant, moving sequence of blues that my still-dreaming brain connected to the fen-spirits who inhabited these watery places. I dreamily shoved my feet into my boots and pocketed my socks. I followed the officer out of the peat bog until both of us became more upright as we reached solid ground.

The helicopter took off, and the silence sang in my ears as we strode forward without watching our feet. Suddenly the fairy lights were in front of me.

"A police car!" It was the first thing I'd said, the shock finally bringing me out of my dream world.

"Move on, miss," said the officer.

The car door opened, and a woman stepped out. Although she was in standard cop gear of trousers and jacket, I could tell she was a woman by the fine lines of her cheeks and the way she moved.

My overwhelming feeling was relief. I don't think I could have crossed the marsh again, not until dawn, and I might have been frozen solid by then. The whole expedition was badly planned—

laughable really—and I was sure that the officers involved in my rescue were chortling silently at my stupidity. I looked at the officer who bundled me into the back seat. He was thin-faced, his hair springy beneath his cap.

"I can't thank you enough," I said, my voice hollow. "I know I've put you to a lot of trouble."

"Don't thank us," said the woman officer, glancing round at me from the driver's seat. Her eyes were like ball bearings. "We're not a rescue team. You are under arrest."

"Sorry?"

"Didn't you hear me caution you, miss?" said the other officer.

"I—no—what have I done?"

"That's what we'd like to know, miss. What you were doing in a police-cordoned area without permission."

The driver completed a proficient three-point turn and eased the car along a narrow lane. I could sense her looking at me through the rear-view mirror. "Just remember that anything you say can be used in evidence."

An idiotic scene passed though my head. I was standing up in a court of law. The judge was placing a black cap on his head. *The evidence against you is of your own making…* I shook myself. I wasn't fully out of the dark and terrible place I had visited in my trance. It takes me a while to come round, but usually I'm alone in my therapy room, not under police escort.

"I don't know how this works," I said, half to myself.

"You'll be offered legal representation, don't worry."

Outside the car, dark bushes waved in the night wind. I rested my head back and fought a sudden, desperate need to sleep, blinking awake as a house loomed into view, alone on a dark lane. I felt every muscle in my body tense. We were passing Brokeltuft. Forensics had shrouded it in a white garment, protecting their intimate work in its bowels. I closed my eyes against the sight and Trendle's words came into my mind: *The path to the north is for another time.* Had he always planned that I would find the graves under the willows?

"There is not much true evil in this world," Bren had said to me once. "Mostly, what we think of as wrongdoing is just nature taking its course." But I was sure that everything Brokeltuft stood for was true evil in its darkest form. Out in the moors, I'd stepped into a mist of suffering. I'd experienced the hurt of a kidnapped child so profound it had scored tears down my cheeks without my knowing it. The horror of capture and captivity, the fear of an unknown future, the longing for home and loved ones, and the unfairness, the confusion of it all were implanted on my mind. This mist had encircled me, pulled me down, tied me in. Truly, I had been rescued by the 'copter's beating wings.

Josh had left me one single, recognisable image, along with those sensations. And I had no idea what it could mean.

By the time we'd reached the station, I was anaesthetized from cold and shock. They took my backpack from me and listed its sad contents, down to the screw of clingfilm I'd wrapped around the crust of pies, and my mobile deep at the bottom. It was still on silent, of course, which meant I wouldn't have heard it while it was in my backpack. The officer swiped it from my uncooperative hands.

"It's my duty to ask you if you want a solicitor with you during your interview," the sergeant said as he bagged up my property. "If you don't have one, we can supply you with the duty solicitor."

My brain was still fogged. Linnet had become my friend and I knew she'd want to help me, but did I need help? I was in a state, all right, but there was only one person I wanted to hear my story. His face had not left my mind since he'd left my house. I was desperate to see him one last time.

"I believe I can make a phone call."

"Who d'you want to ring?"

"DS Reynard Buckley."

———

It is impossible to sleep in police cells, I have now discovered. I'm not good with hard, narrow, or confined spaces. They fairly terrify me, truth be told. The sounds from outside the cell kept my eyelids wrenched wide open and the smell within it was on a par with playground toilets, along with the scrubbed-off graffiti. The hours went more slowly than a snail trail across a carpet, and I feared the walls were just as slowly closing in on me. I couldn't even tell what the time was. I'd been interviewed for what had seemed like hours. I told them about my connection with Cliff. I told them why I went to the site. Then I shut up.

As the two arresting officers prodded at my story, I saw them exchange cautious glances with each other, probably their shorthand for *this one's a got a leak in the think tank.* Even though it must have been clear to them that I was telling the truth, albeit a pixilated version, they weren't going to release me. And hours later, here in my cosy little cell, I was still beating myself up. Thoughts tumbled round in my head all night, like clothes caught in an everlasting wash cycle. I drifted into sleep while kneeling in front of a washing machine, pulling each item from it, stained and grubby. The T-shirts bore slogans that crushed my heart. *For Sale: Useless Shaman—Stupid and Reckless.* I kept thrusting the laundry back in the drum, but there was something wrong with the cycle; the controls were complicated, I couldn't see how to set the thing going again. The door of the machine suddenly screeched wide and a vise gripped my shoulder.

"Sabbie?"

"I can't get the marks off."

"Sabbie? Wake up."

My body trembled from lack of sleep. My head was burning, but my feet and my back were freezing. I opened my eyes. The light was full on in the cell, and Rey was standing beside me. The one blanket they'd allowed, previous owner a horse, had fallen to the floor. I rubbed my eyes and cheeks with the flat of my hands and groaned. The smell of the cell pressed in on me.

"Sabbie," said Rey, again. "What's going on?"

I struggled into a sitting position. "I ache all over."

Rey picked up the blanket and arranged it around my shoulders, dapping at it as if trying to keep it in place. The touch was so gentle, I had to stare hard at the concrete floor to keep my composure. I badly wanted to cry, and I kept the tears away by barking at Rey.

"Are you here to grill me? Because I'll let you in on a secret: I'm not up to it."

Rey turned to where a uniformed officer hovered by the cell door. "Give us five." The door clanged shut, and we were alone.

"You look appalling."

"Thanks." I showed him my tearless eyes. "You should try a night in police custody. Works wonders if you need an ego reduction."

"You didn't listen to me. I asked you to remain detached. Actually, I told you to detach yourself entirely. The next thing I know, you're crawling over a murder site. Since Cliff became our prime suspect, we've been keeping a careful eye on the place. He could have an accomplice, after all."

"But it wasn't like that, and you all know it. I was only trying to help. Why did I get banged up in here?"

"You're a civilian, Sabbie. One of those damn dumb civvies who think they're of more service than they actually are. They get in the way—knock our enquiries off course—become a danger to us, not to mention to themselves." He scratched at his thigh, as if the cell's infestations had jumped ship and started biting him. "I've known members of the public to obstruct us so badly, we've lost our chance of getting a suspect to trial."

"You're mad at me," I ventured. "You told me to keep out of the investigation, but I just couldn't do it."

"That's clear." Rey laid a hand on the bunk for a moment, as if testing the paltry mattress.

I couldn't help looking at the back of his hand. It had a worn, veteran appearance, as if it had seen many a thing. I wondered how many women that hand had caressed.

"I guess you are my millstone." Rey hooked a smile onto his face. "But you kept quiet about the Slamblaster. I should thank you for that."

"Can you tell me about Cliff?" I asked. "Did he see the profiler?"

"He did." Rey frowned and remained silent. A flutter of optimism rose in me.

"He didn't confess, did he?" Rey pouted like a small boy refused candy. "The profiler isn't sure about Cliff's guilt—that's what's happened, hasn't it?"

Rey paced round the cell. It didn't take him long, but I could see he spent the short time thinking. He came to a halt in front of me. "If I tell you something now, can you keep it to yourself until the press release the details?" I nodded violently. "We're going to bow to pressure from Cliff's legal team and let him out on bail."

"Oh! Rey, that is the most wonderful news." I punched the air. "It was his one bit of good luck, getting Linnet as duty solicitor."

He frowned at me. "Luck? Duty? She's his family's solicitor."

"I'm sure Cliff told me she was allocated—"

"Ah, but you see, Sabbie, you shouldn't believe everything a murder suspect tells you."

"So Cliff's family is paying for legal representation?"

"Through the nose, I should think."

"Good. Caroline can afford it. Does she know he's being released? She'll be so relieved."

"Don't get carried away. We've agreed to release him only on the strictest conditions."

I didn't need to be told what those conditions were. I could see exactly what the plan was. "You're hoping he'll lead you to Aidan."

"He's not uttered a word to help us find that child. Letting him go is worth a try."

I shook my head. "He's not going to lead you anywhere."

"Got any better ideas? Something call to you out there?"

"Yes, as a matter of fact. I don't suppose you want to hear it."

Rey eased himself onto the hard bunk, choosing his spot with care—an arm's length of don't-touch space between us. "I hardly know what to make of the things you say."

"You will never believe in what I do, not after what happened with the Slamblaster. I'm sorry there were false leads with that one. I do understand that I blew it."

"Shut up, Sabbie." His face was screwed with emotion. It wasn't hate or contempt, as I'd feared. It was sorrow, and around its edges was guilt. I had begun to think of Rey as one of a kind—a bit of a rebel, but the sort of guy people could rely on. Old ladies who'd lost their cat, young women in police cells. But something was driving him at the moment that had nothing to do with his policeman persona.

"Rey?"

"The picture of Josh's house. It was a false lead, you're right." He stared at the thick, strong-bolted door, as if hopeful someone would come and rescue him. "We tricked each other, I guess."

"No," I said, "that's not so—"

"I didn't give you Josh's toy. D'you really think forensics would sanction that? Not in a million years. I bought a Slamblaster from Toys 'R' Us and bagged it up." He turned half away from me, as if in shame. "It was necessary. I needed to prove to myself that you really are a damn dumb civvie." I could hear Rey's breath, a fast noisy rate that suggested a rise in blood pressure.

"Trendle told me! He said it was untrustworthy!"

"Who the hell is Trendle?"

"You read my report. You know that I was warned." Tears were threatening like rain clouds, swelling my throat. "You were right all along. I saw that house on the TV."

"I'm not proud of myself, Sabbie."

"You must really hate me."

"No!" Rey thrust out ungainly fingers and knotted them into my cold ones. "Not at all. But I'm a copper. I can't allow myself to trust you." He turned away, and I heard him whisper under his breath: "To trust anyone."

The brief connection of our hands had left me juddering, as if I'd been rammed against an immovable object at speed. I wrapped the blanket tighter around me and stared down at the shine of the ceiling light on the floor. "All I can do is tell you I'm not lying. Even when I'm wrong, I'm telling the truth about what I see in my mind. Can you accept that?"

"Yeah, I guess." His voice had gentled. I shifted so that I could look him in the face.

"But you don't want to hear what happened out there on the moors. You're afraid."

"Don't talk tosh," said Rey. He tried to laugh, but I knew I'd hit a nerve. Rey Buckley couldn't be afraid of much, I was sure of that, but the spirit world unnerved him. I grabbed his sleeve and held it tight. Before my cautious side (which is pretty nonexistent anyway) could stop me, I had to make him listen, despite his prejudice.

"Josh's spirit was there. His last impressions. His last feelings. It was like bathing in them. It was unendurable." Rey's eyes widened—I had his full attention. "I was given one clear vision while I was out there. Just one image, Rey. In all the time I sat in that ice-cold darkness, absorbing this child's absolute terror. Only one positive symbol. I know it's crucial, because it kept returning. A sort of tunnel. I had the feeling that Josh had stood in front of this structure, a massive arch edged with knobs of steel. Then a dark tunnel leading away into blackness."

I looked him in the face, trying to get a fix on his shifting gaze. "That's what I saw. I know that Josh saw this as well because the feeling was terrifying. Like … like jelly. Like knowing the worst would happen—an unknown worst."

We sat next to each other in this absurd situation, his large shoes resting on what appeared to be an old urine stain. I didn't say anything more. I'd told him the core of my journey, the place I had travelled to. From the moment I'd seen the mouth of the tunnel, I'd known that this was the most important vision I'd ever had.

Finally, Rey spoke. "You might have seen a tunnel like that somewhere. In your own past."

"No. I'm sure. This time it's genuine. I think Aidan is hidden inside some sort of tunnel."

"Even so, what help can that be? There are too many tunnels in Somerset." For a moment, he sounded genuinely regretful. But his voice changed subtly, as he went on. "This tunnel. Would Cliff know where it was?"

The words exploded out of me. "You still believe I'm hatching plots with Cliff! How can I convince you he never told me anything suspicious?"

"I deal in facts, the harder the better. Yeah, you're about as legit as they come, but you can't persuade me that Cliff isn't our killer. He's got you under his spell, and that means I have to disregard anything you say that might lead us away from Aidan."

"I took you to the bodies of two murderers, Rey! Surely that tells you something?"

Rey shook his head. His eyes were sad. "The perfect red herring, finding that cottage. We're not one whit further on. But the case might start going somewhere when Cliff is let out and takes us on a walkabout. And maybe he will lead us to some remote tunnel, but that won't be anything to do with you. You're going to go home and forget all about the case. I mean it, this time, Sabbie. Leave this to the professionals."

———

I was released with a caution just after lunchtime. They showed me into a washroom, but soap and water wasn't going to rinse away a night in a cell. I was issued with a cheap red plastic comb and spent a long time trying to drag it through my hair. It was a good meditation on time spent wisely. Finally I had my hair up in a high pony tail and at least looked my normal self, even if I felt like a felon as I pocketed my possessions.

I walked out of the station on the shaky legs of someone who was recovering from a bad bout of flu, supported by Caroline Houghton on one side and Nora Rodderick on the other.

"What are you to doing here?" I'd asked.

"We've come to collect you," said Nora.

"Like they do on films," said Caroline with a tiny chuckle.

"But how did you know?" I'd secretly planned to not tell a living soul about my idiotic escapade, certainly not the entire Finchbury Women's Institute.

"Didn't they say?" said Nora. "It was us that alerted the police."

"But we didn't mean to get you arrested," said Caroline.

"You forgot to ring us back when you left Garth's. We rang you several times, but you didn't answer and we started to worry."

No wonder Rey thought I was such poor sleuthing material.

"Eventually we drove round to Garth's van. He was quite helpful. We had a long chat and we worked out what had been in your mind. By then, it was pitch black outside. We had to dial 999."

"We rang the station again this morning and they said you were being released."

"We thought we ought to help you get home."

That was something else I'd been worrying about all night in the cell. I could barely recall where I'd left my car. Caroline and Nora seemed like spirit angels sent just to help me when I needed it most, and I gripped their arms tightly. "I'm so sorry about this. My head feels like the contents of a charity shop sack."

"I quite understand," said Caroline. I was sure she did—her castoffs were far more likely to go in that direction than mine.

"It's just shock," I added.

"It may be more than that," said Nora. "In my mother's day, people who strayed out onto the moors had to be nursed back to health with hot poultices and steam inhalations." Her voice dropped. "Those that survived."

For some reason, this reminded me of Rhiannon, made me wonder what she would have treated me with. I felt as if the spirits of that place of death had slipped into my soul and sucked the energy from it.

"You did what you did for *us*," said Nora. She patted the back of my grubby hand. "We're humbled at your bravery."

"Stupidity," I said, "according to the police. I was lucky to get away without a conviction. I've been a clown, haven't I?"

I was helped, like an invalid, into the back of Caroline's car. I asked for paper and Nora passed me the road map. On the back inside cover, I drew the tunnel I'd seen in my trance. A man-made, perfectly proportioned arch, with massive bolts, each one elegantly engineered into a smooth, silvery dome, assembled at regular intervals around the steel-clad opening.

"Do you recognise this? Are there any disused train lines anywhere around here?" I said, passing the road map back.

Nora shook her head. "Maybe the police will know?"

"The police aren't interested," I said. I was cold to the bone. I suspected that Nora might be right—the only gift I'd get from a night on the marshes would probably be some awful bacterial infection that would turn my skin yellow and my innards to water.

The previous day seemed light years behind me as we drove around Somerset lanes, searching for where I'd left my car. Finally we found it, almost passing it by, it was so well pulled into the verge. But at least it was quite safe.

"Are you going to be okay getting back?" Nora asked. "Are you sure you wouldn't like me to drive your car home for you?"

"I've put you to too much bother already," I told the ladies, and as they protested, showering me with offers of hot meals, I realized I meant it. If I let them help me any further, I'd just get embroiled with the whole thing all over again. What I needed to do was take Rey's well meaning, if wounding, advice. I was going to ask the Wraxalls next door to feed the hens and drive up to see Bren and Rhiannon. I needed to drink their potions and sit by their garden fire until I was whole again.

Nora waved the sketch at me. "We're going to search for this tunnel the length and breadth of Somerset if we have to. Be in touch."

The image of them both searching made me remember my promise to Linnet. As soon as I got home, I would ring her and tell her about the tunnel. She wouldn't disregard it like Rey. Her private eye would probably find it at least as quickly as two middle-aged ladies.

I hugged both of them hard, saying that everything would turn out okay, even though I couldn't see how that would ever be. I clambered into Mini Ha Ha and they waved me out of sight.

I couldn't wait to get home.

TWENTY-THREE

EVEN SO, THINGS DIDN'T feel quite right as I stood on the pavement outside my house, locking Mini Ha Ha. A warning sensation behind the solar plexus. I put it down to my low condition, but as soon as the front door clicked shut behind me, I knew there was something wrong in the house. There was an aura of suspicion about the place and a smell of mistrust. Oh yes, and the telly—which I have to say was my strongest clue—was blaring out some gormless afternoon programme. I hadn't left it on.

I let my backpack slide to the floor and eased the door kitchen open. I had to scan the room twice before I saw Ivan, resting in comfort on my sofa, his left ankle balanced on his right knee.

"Where have you been?" he demanded.

The accusation threw me. I'd been about to say, *What're you doing here?* The words faded before they could reach my lips.

"I said, where have you been, Sabbie?" He shifted position, putting both feet on the ground and leaning forward, one hand punched into the palm of the other. "I've been waiting for you all fucking night. All fucking night and all of this morning."

"You've been here since yesterday?"

"Too right I have."

"How did you get into my house?" I heard my voice falter.

"That's not the issue here. The issue is you, Sabbie."

"How did you get in?"

He raised his fisted hand. My spare set of keys dangled from the fingers. I rushed forward and snatched them from him. There was a heat behind my eyes. "I told you. I don't want to see you again. Ever. I said no, Ivan, and you didn't listen."

He grinned at me. "Women always say no and mean yes."

"For your information, this girl means no. You tried to rape me. I could've had you carted off to a police cell. And I can promise you that is one place you would not like."

He didn't reply. Without taking his gaze from my face, he stretched a hand over the side of the sofa. I could see his laptop case lying against it, but he wasn't reaching for that. I was looking at a gun. A rifle as long as my arm. Its butt was of glossy yellow wood and along its length was a complicated sight of polished steel.

I took a breath to steady myself. "Did you get that from your loft?"

Ivan smiled. His eyes lit up. He lifted the gun onto his lap as if it were made of crystal glass. "I'd forgotten what it was like to use it. I took it out for a practice run. I'm still pretty good."

That smell I'd detected in the hall was much stronger now that I stood in front of its source. It was the overwhelming odour of control, of the power that certain things give certain men—money, authority, or, in this case, the clout of a loaded weapon.

"The fox has gone," I managed. "There's no need for a gun."

His eyes were sharp as slivers of glass. "Isn't there?"

My whole body became ice cold. "You haven't been shooting at my hens, for old Mab's sake!"

He chuckled. "Don't be daft, woman. Why would I want to do that?"

I shook my head, unable to respond. I leaned against the kitchen worktop. My legs felt gelatinous, unable to support me. "I want you to take that thing out of my house. Now. Take it away. Please."

His face hardened. I could feel my words bounce off it, as if his skin had toughened into steel.

"The gun isn't the issue, Sabbie."

"What?" My heart stopped its racing and stood still. If he raised the air rifle now, how badly could he hurt me with it?

"You need to tell me this instant," he said. "You need to be honest. Have you been with another man?"

I closed my eyes. Perhaps I hoped he might disappear, but when I opened them again, he was waiting and I hadn't answered. The only answer I could think of was, *Are you crazy?* But that didn't seem like the right one, just then.

"There isn't any man in my life at the moment," I said at last. "And that includes you, Ivan."

"Of course I'm in your life. I'm here, aren't I?"

"Without an invite. With a gun."

"Sabbie, babe. All I'm asking is where you've been. That's the only issue. Where you have been ... *all night.*"

It was like he was on rails, his head caught up in a single obsession. I knew I couldn't reason with him. I knew I shouldn't anger him. I gave him a big, artificial grin. "If you must know, I've been locked in a police cell."

I picked up the kettle and took it to the sink. Every particle of me was on high alert. I could feel the roots of my hair prickling. But I filled the kettle and put it back in its base as calmly as I could. I pulled off my damp outer clothes and shoes and dropped them by the back door. "It's been a long and stressful night."

His forehead furrowed. "You're in trouble with the police?"

"I think I *am* the trouble. I'm the sort of person who has to poke their finger into all the holes marked Do Not Insert."

I saw his eyes shift their gaze around the room, as if he didn't know what was going on. As if he had to check in the dark corners to make sure he was in control.

"I've got to have a hot drink," I said, reaching for a mug as the kettle clicked off.

"Great. Got any decaf?"

With a gun across his legs, I was kind of expecting Ivan to draw a hip flask from his pocket. The sudden normality in the midst of all the insanity made a stupid chuckle well up from my queasy stomach.

"What's so funny? I don't see proof that you've been locked up for the night." He grimaced. "Might have been knocked up, not locked up."

"Don't you remember the bodies I found under some floorboards?"

"They were real?" squeaked Ivan, destroying his hard-man image. "You never said."

"You were the one who told me to go to the police. Which I did. Now they've discovered that two people were buried in this derelict cottage."

"What?" Clearly, it wasn't the direction Ivan's mind had been taking. "They think you murdered someone?"

"Not exactly." I tried to shrug my shoulders. "I'm sort of helping them with their enquiries. In fact, I'll have to go out again, in a moment."

Ivan smiled. He was swallowing the story. I'd half forgotten that I was telling the complete truth. He pulled a pack of cigarettes out of his jacket pocket and lit one. Ivan knew that I don't let people smoke in my house—we had that conversation the very first night he was here. The gesture was to tell me he was now in charge.

I didn't say a word. I turned to the worktop, poured water onto coffee, and turned round again to hand the mug to him. He was standing, his expression alert, and the gun was in his hands.

"You're not going anywhere, sweetie," he said. Smoke filtered down his nose. I thought of Garth's dragons. "Not without me. And I'm not going anywhere. I think it's time for bed, don't you?"

Stupidly, I lost it. I screamed at him, flinging the cup of coffee across the room.

"Get out of my house!"

The coffee sloshed across the floor, so luckily the mug was pretty empty when it hit his chest. I watched his mouth form a round O as slowly as a dream.

I couldn't move. I just stood there, the coffee pooling on the floor between us, ready for the gunshot and the pain.

The pain came all right, like an explosion in the head, centred across my left eye. I waltzed across the room until the worktop stopped me.

He'd hit me with the butt of the rifle. I put my hand to my face. The blood on my hand blurred as my vision faltered.

"You do as I say." The words sounded garbled and echoing. "I am sick of watching you play ice bitch. That is not how it should be with us."

I felt him grab my arm as I slid down the cupboard doors. He half lifted, half pushed me onto the sofa. His image loomed over me, but it was as if he was standing behind frosted glass. He bent and

317

dabbed my forehead with what looked like my dishcloth. The sensation was exquisite—the icy chill cut through the throbbing, but the weight of the cloth added to the pain, making me yelp like a puppy.

"Oh babe," said Ivan. "You're going to have a shiner." It was like he was congratulating me—or himself.

"Ow," I hissed. "Stop that."

He stood back, keen to obey, and the cloth dripped bloodstained water on my trousers. "Maybe we should use ice," said Ivan.

"Use ice?" My voice sounded faint and slurred, even to me. "How about using some sense?"

"I'm sorry, Sabs." He bent and tried to kiss me. I wriggled away from him. "You don't ever have to be scared of me, sweetie. I won't hurt you."

"You just did." My head was pounding too badly for me to raise my voice, but that was no bad thing—I was finally learning that you lost your temper with Ivan at your own peril.

"Never again," he said, sliding his arms right around me. I didn't have the energy to push him away. "Never again. You know you belong to me now. I wouldn't hurt my girl."

"I'm bleeding on you," I said. "I think I need stitches."

I had to get out of the house. But the suggestion that we go to casualty made him jumpy. He kept dabbing at the wound so gently that tears rolled down my cheeks. I could feel myself trembling uncontrollably. I felt as if I'd just had some sort of coronary event—my forehead was ice cold and my vision was all over the place. Ivan wrapped his arms around me and pulled me up.

"Shh, shh, it's okay. It's going to be okay." He was forcing me along, using a shoulder to push me in the direction of the stairs. My mind wasn't completely clear. There was a singing at the back of my head, but I knew I should not get into bed with Ivan.

I turned to him and tried to open my eyes wide with trust and appeal.

"I've got to see to the hens."

"Oh, Sabbie, fuck the hens, can't you? Just this once?"

"I've got to check they're all right. It's the afternoon and they haven't had their breakfast yet." Desperation was clearing my head rapidly. "It won't take me more than a minute, honestly."

Ivan was sufficiently nonplussed by my insistence for me to pull away from his grasp. Behind me, leaning against the hall wall, was my backpack. Both my mobile and my car keys were in there. I was desperate to have them close to me again.

I slung the backpack over my shoulder and marched towards the kitchen. A microsecond later, Ivan was behind me. I felt his big, angry hand grip my arm, swinging me sideward. He seized the backpack and thrust me away from him. I lost my balance, clutching at the radiator as I watched him unzip the bag and tip the contents onto the floor. He grinned at me as he pushed my keys and my mobile into his jeans' back pocket.

"You didn't mean to run out on me, did you?" His voice was shaking with emotion. "You know I can't allow that."

I looked up at him. I was so shattered that I longed to curl up on the floor with my eyes closed. Let Ivan do whatever he liked with me. Being cared for by a dominant person suddenly felt like the most appealing option—even if that included the occasional beating.

Ivan took a step closer and repeated his words. "YOU KNOW I CAN'T ALLOW THAT."

The words hit me like the air rifle, one syllable after the other, but the onslaught gave me the strength to think ahead. I gave him a wonky smile, the best I could summon. "There's some stale crumbs in there I was going to give to the hens."

I pointed to the crusts of pie in their ball of clingfilm. He picked them up and handed them over in silence, as if slightly humbled. I fled through the kitchen. My coat was crumpled by the back door where I'd lobbed it earlier. I cast it around my shoulders against the drizzly day. Ivan was on me again by then. He did that thing that blokes love to do, he hugged me from behind, cupping my breasts with his hands. I was still coming to terms with the constant alterations in his character—one moment domineering to the point of extreme violence, the next moment tender and amorous. I could not understand how I had been so deluded that I'd allowed this monster into my life for one second.

But this was not the time for analysis. This was the time to put on the performance of my life. Caught up in my palm were the spare keys I'd taken off Ivan. He'd forgotten about them, and so had I—they'd fallen into the folds of my coat as I'd slung it onto the floor and now I was trying to keep them from glinting or chinking. I felt Ivan's hands slide downward from my breasts into the pockets of the coat. He fished out bits of chewing gum wrapper and a used tissue, examining each item in turn.

I turned round to him and planted a kiss on his furrowed brow. I recognised that I was playing this part for my life. He began kissing back properly. The touch of his lips made my stomach lurch. I summoned a bright smile.

"There might be eggs! We could have omelettes! I'm starving, aren't you?"

Ivan thought for a moment. "I guess I am," he admitted.

No doubt beating up your supposed girlfriend can give you quite an appetite.

"Why don't you open the bottle of wine in the fridge," I went on, summoning every ounce of my seductive powers. "I'll be back in two ticks."

He looked confused, which I reckoned was a good sign. I saw his gaze swing around the room again, searching out those dark corners. Then he grinned at me. "Good idea."

I stood, quaking, waiting for him to move away. He seemed unsure, as if he didn't quite trust me, but couldn't work out why.

"Wait a moment."

"What?" The word escaped me with a terrified gasp.

From his back pocket, he pulled the keys he'd snatched from me in the hall and unlocked the back door, swinging it wide open for me. He looked like he wanted to go with me, watch me all the way.

"Get some glasses out, Ivan. You know where they're kept. And the corkscrew's in the cutlery drawer." Actually, it was hanging on a butcher's hook with my cooking utensils—I hoped he'd have his head buried in the drawer long enough for me to make my escape.

I exited the kitchen and half pulled the door shut behind me. I didn't go anywhere near the hens. I chased around the side of the house, trying desperately to be fast and silent. The coat fell from my shoulders and I left it behind. The front gate was in my sights when I heard Ivan's voice.

"Sabbie?"

He was not calling from the kitchen. He had stepped into the back garden. His voice was clear on the afternoon air and filled to the brim with fury.

"SABBIE!"

I leapt over the front gate. I had no idea I was able to do that. I landed badly, and a pain shot from my ankle into my calf. But I was getting used to pain. I flung myself across the pavement, making ready to thrust the car key into the lock. By the time I was inside the car, Ivan had already vaulted over the gate with a lot more agility than I had. I put my trembling finger on the door lock and pressed. Ivan reached the car and wrenched at the passenger door handle. I didn't look at him. I was trying to get my old car to crank into life. The engine turned, slowly but surely. I put her into first and lurched forward.

The jolt of the sound of breaking glass made me yell out. My foot slid off the clutch. I kangarooed to a stop. Ivan had swung a bottle of wine at the passenger window. A massive spider's web of cracks stretched across the glass and Ivan was thumping his fist into the centre of it, time after time.

TWENTY-FOUR

THE WINDOW SEEMED TO be holding. I was lucky not to be covered in slivers of glass. I was lucky that Ivan's hand was not yet through the window and grabbing at my ponytail.

I restarted the car. I could hear my breath, coming in one-second beats, shrieking like a steam train in full throttle. The engine turned over at the same moment that the passenger window shattered. The bottom of the wine bottle shot into the car. I did nought to thirty in seconds, Mini Ha Ha's engine whirring at the strain. Well, I'd just leaped over a gate; the least she could do was a supporting act.

I heard a thump on the boot. I looked back. Ivan was standing in the middle of the road, roaring at me.

"Come on!" I screamed at my Mini. We took the corner of the street on three wheels—maybe two. I had no idea what Ivan was doing right then, I was too busy looking for traffic. But as I hurtled up the road, I managed a quick glance in the rear-view mirror. Ivan was in his car and heading towards me. My luck wasn't going to hold.

My mind flashed back to that odd feeling I'd had as I'd arrived home. I had caught sight of a silver car parked outside the Wraxalls, but I hadn't made the full connection. Perhaps if I'd taken a closer look, I would at least have been forewarned. But, deadbeat, I'd stumbled towards my house with no idea what waited for me inside.

Ivan's car gained on me as I tore down the road, the headlights boring through the dullness of the afternoon. I swerved onto the next side street, frantically searching for further turnings. I knew this part of the town a lot better than Ivan. It was the only advantage I had.

I was reminded of my least favourite reoccurring dream. I'm escaping from something that threatens—usually of an official nature, a knock on the door, a uniform spotted through a window—and I retreat over garden walls and fences. Often I'm carrying something indescribably precious that the faceless officers badly want. I hide it in a pocket, and sometimes the dream turns nasty when later the pocket is empty. In these dreams, I twist and turn through gardens, lanes, and back streets until a feeling of doom descends upon me.

Mini Ha Ha hurtled through the car-lined streets of Bridgwater, their surfaces damp from earlier rain. My eyes strained on the road ahead, alert for dogs, children, and bikes. I headed towards the centre of town, where I could get lost in traffic. For a second, I wondered if that dream of mine was precognitive—that all these years, I'd been dreaming of this madness. My gut was in a nightmare knot and the line of sweat on my upper lip was the sweat I licked off in the dream. But I knew that the dream came from a time long ago. It's not me who's running away, it's my mother. And the precious object, held tightly in her arms, is me.

I hung a right onto Packard Street. For the first time since I started swinging around the back streets, there was no silver streak behind me. I turned too quickly, slotting myself in front of a Sainsbury's van. The driver hooted at me. I raised a conciliatory hand in response.

Up to now I hadn't thought what I was doing apart from getting Ivan off my tail, but now I was in town, I had to ask myself where I was heading. Should I go to the police? I had a nasty cut on my temple, which surely would be proof enough of what had happened. Then I wondered if I ought to make casualty my first stop. The wound felt very tender. I'd be walking round with a beacon of a bruise for a week or so—an excellent reminder that I had a weakness for the wrong sort of men.

I indicated right for the police station, checking my side mirror. In a flash of silver, I saw an Audi powering up the central lane. It gained on me until I could clearly see Ivan's fiendish face through the windscreen.

I felt a shock of tension move up my spine like a lance. The Sainsbury van driver hooted at me again. I took no notice of him. Ahead to the left was an exit road for the A38 out of town. I pulled the car into it, not even considering indicating, tyres screeching on the slippery surface as I tried to down shift and control my direction before I hit the kerb. I saw Van Man shake his fist at the incompetence of women drivers, but he wasn't scaring me. All I cared about was that Ivan was stuck in the middle lane.

"Think, Sabbie girl," I urged myself. "Get a plan." I needed to find help. I was too proud to land myself, shaking and beaten up, on any of my friends. Marianne would be horrified at what I'd let myself get caught up in. Anyway, in my heart I longed to be wrapped up in Gloria's squidgy and welcoming arms.

I powered up the A38 towards Bristol, the March winds blowing ice through the broken window. A mile or so and I could get onto the motorway, then I felt sure Ivan would be lost for good. I glanced down at my speed and my chest imploded inside my rib cage. My petrol dial was kissing E.

I slammed my fist on the steering wheel. The horn beeped at me, as if I'd hurt it. How stupid—I'd used all my fuel up trying to find the burial site yesterday. I had no money, no phone, and very soon I'd have no car. I badly wanted to cry, but I was too angry with myself.

At that moment my gaze fell on a scrap of white, stuffed between the dashboard and the windscreen. Linnet's card, professionally printed in bottle green. *Don't hesitate to use it.* Those had been her words, and her card had stayed tucked onto my dashboard until the spirit world had revealed it to me at the moment of most need.

I swung into the next pub car park and hid in the overflow section behind a nicely bristling pyracantha. I grabbed all the small change dotted around the car and went to find their pay phone, which turned out to be on the wall next to the Gents. Taxi firm cards were stuck all around it with ancient Sellotape, like a wreath to the inebriated. I punched in Linnet's mobile number. After a fifteen-second, stomach-churning wait, she answered.

"Linnet Smith speaking."

"It's Sabbie."

"Hi!"

"I need help." My voice came from the back of my throat, as if it was being strained through thick muslin.

"Do you want to come and see me tomorrow? I could fit you in—"

"No! No … it's Ivan."

"Who?"

"Remember I told you about my boyfriend—well, he's not my *boyfriend*—he's got a gun so I can't go home—"

"Calm down." Her voice sounded thin and distant, as if she was speaking from another country. In a moment of panic, I imagined her back up in Aberdeen. "Try to explain."

I stuffed in the last of my change. "I thought he was going to blow my face off!"

"Have you contacted the police?

"I was hoping you'd be the best person...oh Linnet, my money's going to run out so quickly..."

"Where are you?"

An infantile sob hiccupped out of me. "About five miles north of Bridgwater. Pub called the Arms something or other. I've no money and my tank's nearly empty, and..." I couldn't bring myself to say *I've got nowhere to go,* but she must have heard the desperation in my voice.

"I'm not in the office today. I'm working from home."

I felt tears sting my eye. I wiped at them with my sleeve and it came away smeared with blood. "What...should I do?" There was such a long silence, I thought she'd gone. "Linnet?"

"Okay. Don't worry. Sounds like you're in the Wheelwright's Arms. You're no distance from my house." She barked out a staccato of directions. "He's not still following you, is he?"

"No, I lost him in the middle of town." I put the receiver down gently. The bloke coming out of the loo did a double take at my beaten-up face—his hand was still fiddling with his zip—and I turned away, quickly shielding my bad eye with one hand.

"You okay, miss? Sorry, it's just that you look..."

I probably *did* look something—traumatized—crazed with fear. It was a good job he couldn't see my car. I began to run, the pub door swinging behind me.

I pulled out onto the road, muttering Linnet's instructions. *Drive back towards Bridgwater until you see the B road for Muchum Middling, take the first left off it, signposted Hartley's Wood. I'm about a mile down that track.* Every muscle in my body was screwed as tight as piano strings. Very soon I'd be off the main road and safe. I was hovering at the turning for Muchum when a silver Audi shot past me, heading away from Bridgwater.

They say in books that terror turns your guts to soup. I felt it happen. Every organ inside me was in shutdown. My hands and knees vibrated as if the car had gone into spasm around me. I hung the corner on two wheels and powered along the B road. First turning, first turning—moments ticked by and there were no exits, nothing, not even an open gate into a field. Had it been Ivan? Had he seen the way I was heading? I stormed down the road to Muchum. I had to keep away from Ivan. I felt sure he would kill me if he found me. My foot was on the floor and the engine was roaring in third when I saw the turnoff: a single-track road with a Forestry Commission board. I rounded the corner and killed my lights just in time—a full beam shone against the heavy twilight cloud cover. Ivan had doubled back.

Doubts crowded my mind. I'd chosen this road in a sweat of panic. Was this Hartley's Wood? The lane was narrow and winding. Branches loomed high on either side of me, obscuring the sky. I rolled on through the wooded gloom without lights, almost without power, winding round two half bends in the road.

I saw a flash of headlights behind me, between the trunks of the trees. I lifted my foot from the gas pedal but remembered just in time not to hit the brake, causing the lights to flash red. I pulled on the hand brake and clicked open the door with more stealth than I needed. I didn't think I could be seen, but I desperately needed to see—to make sure. I crawled into the hedgerow and peered back towards the B road. The pale opal gleam of a silver bonnet was nosing its way into the top of the track. I stopped breathing. Would he spot Mini Ha Ha? I glanced back at her. She was surely obscured by the winding lane and its high tree cover. The silver car was stationary, fifty or so metres away. I was sure it was Ivan, sniffing after me like a psychotic terrier, checking every junction. I shivered among the weeds, trying to get into his twisted mind. He'd seen me indicating for the B road, but he couldn't know where I was now. He had to decide between checking each turning and driving on in the hope of catching me up. Finally, the streak of silver slid away. I almost keeled over in relief.

The air had a damp chill to it now, since the sun was going down. I got back in the car and rolled her forward again. Ten minutes down the track, a long gravel driveway turned off it. I parked in sight of it and got out of the car, breathing in the damp air as if I was deprived of oxygen.

At the end of the drive, I could see a house. It was of red brick and had a low, sweeping roof with scalloped tiles. Two tall chimneys seemed to grow from the foundations like stovepipe hats. A cockerel swung in the wind from the apex of the gable. I was trying to work out just how many of the ex-council houses in Harold Street you would have to sell to match its worth, when I had one of my "moments."

A veil lifted from the building, revealing a gingerbread house straight out of a German folk tale. The cottage had an otherworld image, just as sentient beings did. My stomach knotted for a second, then I smiled. It was an old place, miles from anywhere. Why shouldn't it have chocolate finger windows and Liquorice Allsorts chimneys? I figured this was the safest retreat from Ivan that my spirit guardians could possibly have found me.

Linnet must have spotted me, for she hurried across the gravel. "My God, Sabbie, your eye!"

My body had begun to shiver uncontrollably, a final reaction to Ivan's onslaught and my flight. "Pretended to do the hens and jumped the gate…Chardonnay everywhere…" I was sobbing so badly I probably made no sense. "Ivan…he's like a terrier…gone now…sure of it."

"What hens?" asked Linnet. She put her arm around me and we stumbled together towards her house.

"Sorry, sorry, don't know what I'm saying." Even so, I remembered to untie my walking boots, which I'd been wearing since I left the police station, before I stepped onto her thick pile carpets.

"Come and sit down." Linnet ushered me into a vast kitchen. There was a bijou glass table in one corner. I sank onto one of its steel-backed chairs. The kitchen was resplendent with costly materials, glass shelves so thick they were almost green, marble working tops, and wooden items that glowed with golden light—everything from the fruit bowl to the massive butcher's block that stood central on red flagstones. This was a chef's dream kitchen, yet it felt unloved, as if still searching for its dream chef.

Linnet passed me a tissue and I dabbed it over my sore cheeks and blew my nose. She went to the steel sink and filled a glistening stainless-steel kettle. "You need a cup of tea," she said.

"Paradise," I admitted. "Cures everything, doesn't it?"

"Not everything," she said, tossing tea bags into large mugs. "I'll drive you to casualty once you've warmed up. Have that wound dealt with."

"It's not as bad as it seems."

"Even so. If I'm to act on your behalf, we need to have that wound witnessed and documented." The kettle gave an artificial whistle and she made the tea. "You haven't told me anything coherent yet, Sabbie. But once we've got you settled at a refuge, you can see my colleague and start compiling a case against—what was his name?"

"Ivan Sadler."

"He may have previous offences. You'd be surprised how many of these possessive types do." She came over with the tea. Steam lifted from my mug, enticing me to wrap my fingers around it and sip.

"What did you mean," I asked, genuinely puzzled, "about a refuge?"

"I've been surfing the web since you called, checking up on facilities for vulnerable women. I'll print some things out for you."

She disappeared, leaving me to finish my tea. I was bone tired and ached all over. I'd become a *vulnerable woman*. The thought filled me with shame.

I pulled myself out of the stainless-steel dining chair and shuffled off in search of her. I still felt a bit wobbly, but I did not intend to stay in a refuge, not even for a single night, and I needed to tell her so. I found her in a room that felt entirely functional—Linnet's home office. She was bending over a Macintosh, tapping the keys. "I'll just bring up this site."

"Oh, great," I said, forcing myself to sound cheerful. Outside, a maniac I'd invited into my bed was roaming around, searching for me in the growing darkness, but I didn't feel welcome here. Last time we met, Linnet and I had been booze buddies, but today she had hardly caught my eye. She might be at home, but her brain was at work, and I knew it wouldn't be long before I was lacing up my walking boots in readiness for the drive to hospital. "I don't know if I should press charges," I told her.

"Why wouldn't you want to?"

"Because I'm in a bit of trouble myself. Yesterday, I went out to the shallow grave on the moors and they slung me in jail overnight."

She slammed the return key and turned to me, her face fierce with incomprehension. "You are never going to let this alone, are you?"

Her reaction was identical to Rey's. I'd been planning to explain about my trance at the grave, hoping she'd want a description of the tunnel, but she was not ready to listen.

"Yes," I said. "Yes, I am. There is nothing more I can do, I see that. I've made up my mind. I won't need those details you're printing out."

"I don't recommend you go directly back home."

"I was planning to spend a bit of time in Wales."

"That sounds good. So long as you stay in touch. I don't want to jeopardise your use as a witness." Linnet smiled, but it was impatient round the edges, reminding me that I'd pulled her from some important work, arriving unannounced and fraught.

I was beginning to wish I'd had enough petrol to drive to Caroline's house, rather than Linnet's. I would now be sinking into a bottomless sofa and being offered sweet, milky drinks. I was sure that somewhere here was a room filled with comfortable seating, coffee tables piled with magazines, and logs flaming out heat from an inglenook hearth, but this office was not it. Even the fire, inviting though it pretended to be, was a simulation of the real thing. It burned from a central point, red and yellow flames that gave out heat without warmth. It was one of those aseptic gel fires, perfect for the girl-about-town-with-country-cottage.

"You've got a nice house," I said, resisting the urge to tell her how I longed to sample one of its bedrooms. "What's it called?"

"It doesn't have a name," said Linnet.

"That's a pity. It's like something from a fairy tale."

She smiled across at me, her hand still cradling the mouse. "Thank you. It was called Keeper's Cottage when I bought it, but I took the sign down. I'm not a keeper."

"No, but how does the postman find you?"

"All my mail goes to the office."

I took the final swallow of my tea and dumped the mug on the stone mantelpiece, stretching my hands towards the lukewarm fire. I didn't think the ultra-modern design of the fireplace did anything for this low-beamed room. But it was stunning—any TV home décor team would have given their eye teeth for the look she'd created. Circling the ruby and ivory of the flames were thick bands of the blackest cast iron, studded with fat knobs of satin steel. It was a formidable fireplace, but it overwhelmed the small room, like placing a marble statue in your loo.

"Okay, Sabbie, here's some info on your rights as a woman unable to access your own home."

Something was knocking at the back of my mind, like a thought waiting to be let in. I'd overlooked something about the tunnel I'd seen in my trance out on the moors. It was a child who passed it on to me as an image. A child on a nightmare journey towards death. His tunnel did not have to be massive, or deep, or even frightening in itself. Josh had been sick with terror; anything he saw that made no sense to him would be scorched into his thoughts. I swung back to gape at the fireplace.

As I stared, it changed subtly, the way that optical illusion game changes from being a vase to two people kissing. Just for a second or two, it wasn't an *avant-garde* heating accessory.

It was a dark tunnel, studded with shiny metal bolts.

TWENTY-FIVE

I FELT AS IF my head had been held under water until my lungs burst. I spun round, my mouth drooping and my eyes straining wide, desperate to know if Linnet had heard or sensed my distress. She was still leaning over the back of the office chair, having chosen not to sit on it, her right hand on the mouse, her eyes on the screen. But she *had* heard me gasp.

"You all right?"

I kept my eyes averted from her. "I can't help think Ivan's going to turn up any second."

"I thought you said you'd lost him."

"I had. But after I phoned you, he caught up with me again."

Her hand slid away from the mouse. "Let me get this straight. Are we about to be invaded by a gun-happy troglodyte?"

"No, don't worry, he's got no idea where I went. He's halfway to Glastonbury by now, I should think. No doubt he'll think I've got friends there." I was gibbering, hoping that talking about Ivan would keep my monstrous suspicions of Linnet from showing in my eyes. I glanced back at the fireplace. On second examination, I felt even more sure this was what I'd seen in my trance. I gazed round the room, trying to work out why Josh Sutton would have ever been here. For one moment, the awful agony of an answer sprung into my mind. Cliff had kidnapped the boy. He had gone to Linnet for help—family solicitor, Rey had said. And, for some reason, she had taken his side. The speculation was so overwhelming, so appalling, I felt my legs give way. I stumbled toward the computer desk, clung to its edge. Linnet had told me she'd come down here from Scotland because of some man. Could that be Cliff?

The printer made a throat-clearing noise as it began to cough out pages from the Net. I barked a small shriek and felt my body jerk off the ground.

Linnet laughed. "You *are* jumpy."

"It's all getting to me." I let my hand rest over my bad eye. "Could I have a glass of water?"

As we went back towards the kitchen, I sneaked glances into the rooms we passed. Was this a place that one could secrete a child?

She took a crystal glass and filled it from the door of the fridge. I took a sip, my teeth rattling against the rim.

Not Cliff. I had believed in him implicitly from the moment I'd met him, and I wasn't going to desert him now. "Not Cliff," I said without meaning to speak aloud.

"Sorry?"

I faced her. "You once hinted that you thought Cliff was not innocent. Not *altogether* innocent. What did you mean by that?"

"Ah, yes, Cliff. Are you up to discussing the case?

I nodded, hoping Linnet could convince me that I had got my wires tangled—or my tunnels jumbled. I thought back to the Slamblaster journey. I'd been wrong before. I badly needed to believe I was wrong about the fireplace tunnel. I snatched at her hand. "Tell me."

"I'm pretty sure that I've secured Cliff some bail."

"Oh, I do know that. Rey told me. How d'you do it?"

"Sabbie, you have to think like a copper in my job." Her eyes were gleaming. "Nothing is being gained by keeping Cliff locked up. The police could be said to be complicit in Aidan's death, if he's ever found. I've suggested they release Cliff, untagged but constantly shadowed, to see if that brings about a conclusion."

I stared into her face and all I saw was a solicitor who was chuffed at the turns the case was taking. "That's good," I said. "Brilliant."

"I'm also compiling an argument that Josh Sutton's death was not copy-cat. It's clear that little boy had been comfortably housed, fed, and watered…cherished, even. Where, precisely, would Cliff have hidden him?"

"I see where you're going." I was thrilled. "Cliff doesn't have access to anywhere like that."

"Apart from his mother's, of course. But we will request forensic run-down on the house. To verify Josh was never in it."

I clutched my glass. "This is all so positive!"

Linnet gave satisfied smile. "I was hoping you'd come with me to ask Mrs. Houghton if we could allow the team in."

"Yes, of course. Although, I guess you know her at least as well as me."

"Sorry?" said Linnet.

"You're the family solicitor."

She frowned, as if puzzling this out. The she smiled and nodded. "Yes, of course."

I sank onto one of the steel chairs as relief washed through me. I couldn't remember any thrill ride I'd ever been on that felt quite like the roller coaster of the last twenty-four hours. The bitter cold of the graveside…the vision of the tunnel…a night in a police cell…the news about Cliff…Ivan…and now my massive, sinister assumptions about Linnet's house, which were probably so off-centre that I'd make the biggest idiot of myself ever if I ever admitted them to a soul.

The distant chugging of the printer stopped. Linnet turned her head. "That's your information."

She paced from the kitchen, but I was waiting for my heart to slow down a bit. I was beat up, knackered, and befuddled. My blood sugar was in my boots. I needed to wake up and think clearly. I went over to the sink and turned on the cold tap. Water fizzed into my cupped hands and I threw it over my face in a desperate attempt to get on top of things. My mind was exploding with contradictions and puzzles. I felt like I was sniffing around on the edge of a labyrinth, with the answers hidden at the middle. Linnet probably thought she'd let a mad woman into her house.

Splashing my face did nothing to clear my head. It just made my wound sting and my jumper wet. I swung round the gleaming kitchen, searching for a towel rail—something in solid gold, no doubt—but towels seemed to have been overlooked. Everything went in the dishwasher, of course. I began pulling at drawers—there was an entire column of them near the massive, glossy cooker. The first two were cocktail-making requisites. Well, a girl should have a hobby. The next held fluffy orange dusters, so I thought I might be nearing the end of my quest. The next drawer was filled with over-the-counter medication. I shoved it shut and searched on, alighting finally on a drawer of J-cloths. My hand froze over the pile. I slid the drawer closed so slowly, so quietly, I might have been in a museum. I opened the drawer above it once again.

I was staring at a neat row of Calpol bottles, most still in their boxes. My body chilled as if the kitchen had become a freezer. I lifted a bottle out and read the label. *Calpol—paracetamol for children—easy to swallow and nice to taste*. I exhaled, half expecting to see a fog of steam come out of my mouth. The coincidence was too strong, too shocking.

I heard her heels clip over the quarry tiles. I turned my stunned gaze upon her. She was bearing a sheath of copy paper, holding it out to me, her mouth half opened, ready to speak. She looked at the bottle in my hand and saw everything that was in my mind.

Her reaction was instant and effective. She dropped the papers, and they fanned out over the blood red of the tiles. She came at me. She grasped my wrist with the perfect amount of force and speed, pulling me towards the floor. The only thing I had time to do was cringe. My knees buckled, an action she encouraged with the toe of one shoe. I had no resistance in me. I sprawled on my front over the scattered papers, until *COUNSELLING AND FINANCIAL AID FOR WOMEN IN DISTRESS,* was the only thing I could see. I felt Linnet's knee in the small of my back. I pushed against her with all my strength. Suddenly, we were face to face, her dark eyes boring into mine.

"Where is he, where is he?" I screamed. I was sure now, as we writhed over each other in this catfight on a kitchen floor. Linnet knew something deep and dark about this terrible crime. Something or someone had drawn her into a web of cruelty, kidnap, death. "Is he dead? Is Aidan dead like Josh?"

She didn't reply. She was too busy trying to restrain my arms, pin me on the ground. She was panting. She was older and less fit than me. The only real advantage she had over me was the surprise element. All I had to do was spring the surprise back. I looked into her eyes, but they had narrowed to slits as she concentrated on holding me down. I began to fight with every cell in my body, kicking with legs and knees, jamming my elbows at her.

Nothing made any sense. Why would Josh have been here, to gaze in terror at the fireplace tunnel? Why would Linnet attack me because I'd found a bottle of medicine?

"You fed them that stuff!" I yelled, the realization of it hitting me like a blow. "You poured it down their throats!"

That made her react. She stopped trying to pin me down and stared at me. Her jaw was tight, she spoke through clamped teeth. "Only when they cried. To help them sleep."

"What CRAP!"

Slowly, I was gaining the upper hand. She stretched away from me, grasping for something. I had my chance to wriggle free. I pushed up enough to see what she was trying to reach.

It was a chopping board. It came down on my head and with it, came blackness.

TWENTY-SIX

FUCK.

Coming round was like being fast-forwarded through a film noir. I was in a fog of shadows. My head hurt like hell; a plane was revving for takeoff inside it. As soon as I realized I was not going to lose consciousness again, I longed to do so.

Fuck, fuck.

I was on a cold, hard floor. Something bit at my wrists and ankles and prevented even the smallest movement. My vision was all fuzzed up and a chunk of memory was missing. I saw Ivan's face in my rear-view mirror again, distorted by a back and front windscreen. I'd escaped from him, hadn't I... hadn't I?

Fuck. The word echoed like surround sound, and a thud accompanied it each time, soft but determined; a soft *fuck* thud.

"Fuck." Not inside my head at all. Someone else, able to express how I felt—confused, damned, fucked.

I creaked my head in the direction of the voice. I tried to call out. *Help.* That was a good word. *Help me. I can't move, can't move.*

341

Nothing happened. My mouth was welded with dried saliva.

I dragged open eyelids like graters. A pair of legs, hazy at first. Two fawn legs with thickish ankles, glossy with Lycra. A pair of plain court shoes. The sort of shoes one wears in court.

It all came flooding back.

"Fuck. Fuck. Fuck!" Linnet was standing beside her butcher's block. In her fist was a kitchen knife, the blade as long as her hand, the shaft a single continuous piece of stainless steel. She gripped it as a child grips a spoon and stabbed it so deeply into the soft wood, it took a moment to work it out again, twisting both ways before it gave.

"Fuck." She stabbed again.

My eyes were feverish hot. Pain shot though my head with every pulse beat, but I couldn't stop staring. She'd brought a chopping board down on my head and now she was playing with a knife. A croak came unbidden from the back of my throat, and the shoes turned on the spot so that the neat navy toes were pointing at me.

"You took your time," she said, as if passing out was an Olympic sport.

"Help me." My voice was under the earth, but Linnet seemed to understand.

"Fuck you, Sabbie Dare. You've as good as fucked me." She prised the knife from the block and stabbed again like a darts player hoping for the bull's eye. *Thud.* "I was going to help you. But you couldn't stop yourself from sniffing around. Now I've got to sort you." The shoes turned away, the voice dropped. "Got to sort you... got to."

Sort me? I looked at the knife. It quivered in the block. Sort me? With that knife? With the anger that fizzed across the kitchen floor, the posh quarry tiles so cold and so hard that when you were forced to lie on them you trembled? I was trembling up to my teeth. My entire body was a gigantic tic.

342

I tried to shift. A wriggle, a turn, a chance to escape. Several degrees of pressure tugged at my body. I was shaking on a bone-cold floor inside coils of rope. My knees were bent and my arms were pinioned behind my back, forcing me onto my side. She had tied me up. She meant to sort me all right.

"It was going good," muttered Linnet. She thrust a finger at me, as if practicing for the point of the knife. "Perfect plan. Fail-safe. Indestructible."

"Nothing is," I said and coughed.

"No." She turned back to her block and took her anger out on it. "Fuck!"

I couldn't work out what was happening. I didn't get it. I didn't get *her*. This was Miss Smith, partner at Hughes and Heaven, who'd given me her card and told me to come to her house. She was helping Cliff, she had *fought* to get him out on bail. She loved children, said how it turned her stomach, this hideous crime.

Something had come roaring from deep inside, roaring to her surface, transforming her into a woman who swore like a drunken teenager and played darts with twenty centimetres of chromium steel and had to sort me because she was fucked.

She was fucked? *I* was fucked. I'd seen the tunnel... I'd seen the drawer full of Calpol. No one kept that much Calpol. This woman, this defender of the accused, had brought Josh Sutton, seven years old and sobbing—crying, trembling like I was, tied, perhaps, like I was— into the room with the tunnel fireplace. She'd fed him Calpol. She'd said so. *Only when they cried.* She'd wrecked his young insides, poisoned his liver so eventually he died from a sticky mixture. She'd killed him sweetly.

After Josh, Aidan.

"Linnet." My throat contracted, my teeth chattered. "Linnet…" It was hard to talk. When I moved my tongue, it rasped against the roof of my mouth. I needed to ask: *Where is Aidan? Is he here? Is he dead, or only just alive, or is there time? Is he already gone, dug into the peat like Josh?*

"You've got him," I managed. "Haven't you?"

"Ah, so clever. All those powers. Weren't a lot of help to you were they? Not in the end."

"Josh told me." My voice floated out, as grey as a ghost. "He came here. He stood in your office, in front of that horrid fireplace…"

"Okay," said Linnet. "Look, I don't care if you had some sort of *visit* from little Josh or not. Although you promised to come to me with anything new." The navy shoes clipped until they were side by side in front of my face. It was almost as if they were doing the talking. "You did seem to know things." A single laugh burst out of her. "It doesn't harm me, what you know or don't know. Look at you."

Look at me, indeed. Fucked.

I longed to cry out, *But I don't know anything!* I thought back to the record cards Gloria had found on my working top. *Something's missing,* I'd told her. Now I knew the truth of that. I tried to shuffle those cards again, in my befuddled head, add in the things I'd learnt since yesterday, but I couldn't hold onto the data. My mind could only concentrate on the rope and the throb in my head. How would she sort me? With that knife? You can slice a person, or jab, and it hurts, it's all pain, but it doesn't kill, does it? Not a kitchen knife—unless, like Rey had said, you get the blade right between the ribs, the intercostal-somethings—a *lucky stab.*

You were abducted yet survived. I'd call that lucky, Linnet had told Cliff, but he'd said, *cruel luck,* and here I was, cruel luck on me, this time.

Linnet loomed over me like a nightmare. I was desperate for water, desperate to run from this place. But I was even more desperate to know if Aidan was alive, where he was being kept, and how she'd got caught up in this. "Who is it?" I asked. "Some man?" In my mind I whispered, *Please don't let it be Cliff.* "Who has made you do this? Because I don't believe you would do this evil thing for yourself…" I trailed off.

She was still standing so close her court shoes were nudging the wound that Ivan had given me. I could feel it puffing up and she was pushing the point of one shoe into the swollen flesh above my eye. My voice broke with despair. "You're not evil, you love kids, you told me about your nephews."

I had to survive this, if only in case Aidan was still alive.

"Shut up," she said and fairly drove her shoe into my swollen temple. I cried out, a sharp sound in my own ears, but a thought had already lodged in my mind and the pain seared it there, made me yell at her. "You don't have a nephew, do you? You were talking about Josh. And Aidan!"

"They're closer to me than nephews," she said, as if correcting me.

I stared at her, gob-struck. "How dare you! You've ruined all these lives and you talk like that? Like you *love* these children?" I was shaking with the horror of it. I breathed deep through my nose to keep my stomach contents down.

"You don't know how much they mean to me." For the first time, she sounded less than sure, and I came back at her quickly, while my brain cells were still up to it.

"I know what you said in the pub. I remember you said it was not easy to make them happy! Well, no, Linnet, not when you tie someone up and feed them poison!"

"I did *want* them to be happy."

345

"You killed Josh. You murdered him, innocent and seven years old. And little Aidan? Have you done the same to him, you bitch? You bitch!"

In a flash, her mood turned. "Shut up about them!"

She brought back her blue shoe and used me like a football. Pain shot through my head and I was back with Ivan and his rifle butt—I screamed across my dry throat and tried to turn, roll away from her, as if she couldn't've walked around me. But I couldn't turn, because when I tried to move my legs, I felt the pull again on my throat. My ankles were bound directly to my neck. If I moved at all, I'd strangle myself.

I felt my eyes shoot open as comprehension grew.

Linnet *did* know what she was doing. She *would* sort me. I *was* fucked.

Clip, clip. Her loose heels faded as they reached carpet. She had left me. I felt my body sag. My mind was going to sag to, if I didn't struggle hard to keep it in thinking mode. The relief of not having her shoes near my head was quickly replaced with the dread of not knowing what she was doing now. She'd been out of control when she kicked me, but out of control and close felt better than out of sight. My breath left me as I thought about what she might be planning. Maybe she had gone to wherever Aidan was, was with him now. I tried to breathe again—*slow, come on, slow*—but it was hard because my head pounded where she'd beaten me flat and throbbed where she'd kicked Ivan's wound, and my throat was tight with the rope around it. I felt something warm run down my face. *I must be bleeding*, I thought, then realized it was tears.

"Stop it," I hissed. "Stop it. Come on, you're a survivor." It was what the guardian I'd seen by the tidal river had told me, the Lady of the River. I had not trusted her for she'd sent me back to Brokeltuft, the last place I'd wanted to go, and the creature with the hairbrush was there, becoming more and more repulsive as the journey progressed.

It was stupid to think of this now, when I had so much to try to work out, but I couldn't help it. In the river journey, I'd gone in search of healing—I'd asked the Lady for wisdom—Trendle hadn't stopped me, he knew of the evil that had happened inside Brokeltuft. I'd been taken there to see … the hair slide falling, the wig slipping, the face changing … this was a spirit gift that I was only just beginning to understand.

Down the side of that sofa. Not Kissie's style of slide, not at all. Not a child's slide, either. A teenager's sparkly adornment with the platinum blonde hairs still caught in the fastener.

Witch, I'd called her, the wigged woman, and regretted it because I know many modern witches and they're all benign. It was only in ancient times that witches were thought to be evildoers. Bitch, I'd called Linnet. Evildoer was too much of a mouthful when you're tied up.

Where did she learn to tie people up like this? The child murderer's manual?

People can have two sides to them. On one hand you had Linnet, defender of the innocent, and on the other you had Linnet who buried a little boy in an infamous grave as if she wanted him to be found. I'd drunk wine with a woman filled with sadness at the cruelty metered out to a victim; I'd seen the same woman viciously stabbing a knife. Between the ribs, that's what Rey had said. Vicious, heartless, lying, desperate, dangerous. Obsessed. I choked as the rope pulled a little tighter across my neck. My legs were really hurting, holding them in one position. Cramping pains shot through my calves and thighs and I was sobbing uncontrollably, even though I knew I should not let Linnet hear me cry or do anything that might tighten the noose.

The image of Linnet taking little Josh's body to the burial site flooded into my mind. Why there of all places? And how could she know where it was? You could do the research, of course, or interview someone like Arnie Napper. Or you could have been there to watch the first bodies lowered and be only too grateful you were still alive.

Two people. Poles apart. Like, here's the good advocate, and there's the witch who lives in the gingerbread house—who I saw in the cottage, where I was sent by the grace of the river goddess—where I saw hair fall away from a good woman's face to reveal, scalped and livid...a monster.

Like, on one hand, you had Linnet, and on the other...you had Patsy.

TWENTY-SEVEN

THE TEARS HAD DRIED on my face and I was still and silent, watching her through half-closed lids as she *clip-clopped* around her Dom Perignon kitchen. She was a million miles—a million pounds—from the little flat where her father lived. It was as if I'd turned to the back page of a puzzle book and read the answer. Everything fell into place.

I'd arrived at her office and announced that I'd found Arnie Napper. No wonder she'd downed bottles of Shiraz. She'd never gone to see him herself, but she'd picked my brains about him. Arnie would have been so proud of his Patsy, if he'd met her a few years ago.

I'd asked her if she'd come back to Bridgwater because of a man, and she'd taunted me... *him, or maybe her.* But now I knew. It was him *and* her: Kissie and Pinchie.

We'd spoken about death and she'd asked, *Isn't that a haunting? When you can still hear their words inside your head?* I'd told her Cliff had forgotten everything and she'd said, *How could you forget something like that?* She hadn't suddenly recalled Brokeltuft. No, she'd held the evil she'd witnessed inside her for quarter of a century. I already knew how those people had affected Cliff. I couldn't start to imagine what they had done with a girl who had been with them for longer, who had watched Cliff come and go from the cottage of horrors.

I'm supposed to be good with body language, but nothing in the way Linnet held herself hinted at a different past. She'd *become* the person she now was, completely.

If only I'd touched her ring. If only I'd reached out, in the Admiral's Landing, as I had already drawn her attention to it, and brushed a finger across the silver band. What might have flashed across my mind at that moment?

I risked a glance at her. She was at the fridge door, ice was clumping into a glass. I heard a glug of fluid, imagined water sliding over the ice. I swallowed grit down my birdcage throat.

"Linnet? Could I have a drink, please?"

One step at a time. Get her to remember I was a person, not a threat. That's how it was done. I'd read it in a Sunday supplement, I was sure of it. Kidnappers did sometimes release their victims. She'd been my friend once. Hadn't she?

"A drink?" said Linnet. "Good idea." She sounded as chirpy as a hospital visitor. No more *fucks*. While she'd been out of the room, something had changed in her. She bent down beside me, kneeling like a concerned professional beside a wounded victim. She took my head between both hands and turned it so that I was staring at the ceiling.

"Drink this," she said, a satisfied sound. I saw what she was doing seconds before she upended a bottle and rammed the neck into my mouth. A burning sensation filled my throat as whisky poured down. I clamped my teeth and turned my head away, struggling to get air into my lungs. She grabbed my ponytail and jerked so hard that I screamed out loud, my mouth ripped open by the sheer traction. Fiery liquid filled every cavity. Colours and white light flashed across my vision and the detached, warm feeling that they say comes when you're about to drown overwhelmed me. I did not want to end my life drowning on whisky. I don't even like the stuff.

Without a thought, I began to struggle. It was a primitive urge to get free. The rope around my neck tightened. I gagged, forced myself to lie still. A drip of sweat ran into my eyes. I focused on slow breaths.

"Clever knot, isn't it?" she said from above. "You lie still now. Stay still, stay alive."

I spluttered, heaved, and coughed. She looked ready to talk, now she'd rendered me unable to breath. Maybe that's what she wanted. A silently received confession. It was my way in. "You were tied up." I wracked out another raw cough. "Like this. Long time ago. Weren't you. *Patsy.*"

Silence. I had no idea how she would react. I braced myself, like I do at the dentist, ready for pain—the final plunge of a knife into the ribs.

Still silence, not even a *fuck*, just the clinking of ice. She was on the whiskey, enjoying it a damned sight more than I had. What did that mean? Shiraz for the pub, whisky for the house? Or whisky for planning? Or whisky for executing a plan? But the ice was rattling. I'd rattled *her.*

"I am not Patsy," she said, but the voice was rough, a Patsy voice. "I got rid of that name because the sound of it made me sick. I mean *sick*, as in aversion therapy. I couldn't be that person anymore."

I was struggling to get air into my lungs, my eyes streaming. I wanted her to start at the beginning. "Your father told me. You walked out of your home. Walked out of your family."

"I'd decided I hated them all. I wanted a different life. The big metropolis, all that excitement. I reckoned I was worth more than a rundown flat in a rundown area."

"But then you met Kissie and Pinchie."

I heard a half-sob break from her and another gulp from the glass. "I hitched a lift, that's all. They promised to take me to London."

"They were bastards," I said.

Her knees gave way and she crumpled down the edge of the butcher's block until she was sitting with her fawn legs stretched out beside me. I thought her lips seemed tinged with blue, but perhaps it was the reflection of her shoes. "What they did. I can't describe it."

A long shiver travelled through me, like ice sliding and melting. She *had* described it, I was sure of that. That night in the pub, she'd done a lot of talking. As if she wanted to lay clues for me to follow. As if, underneath everything, she wanted at least one person to know. The person she thought might know anyway. I'd been slow about it, but I was getting there. "They left you unable to have children."

She nodded, her head bowed. "Each day. Hours of it. I'm screaming... they're laughing."

"You struck a deal, did you? With those two killers? 'Spare me and I'll help you'?"

"You think I was part of it?"

I didn't answer. I was too busy trying to breathe.

"It wasn't a choice!" she yelled, as if I was an obtuse student. "They forced me! Each time, a little child, screaming, dying. Then they'd force me into the car again. Made me go out and help them get another." She downed the rest of the glass. "Let me explain. It was fucking awful. Fucking hell on earth. There were four bodies in the outhouse. Pinchie had stolen a van—he always nicked a fresh one, then dumped it. It had to end. Had to. Someone had to stop them."

The silence grew long between us. She was willing me to say the words.

"You killed Kissie and Pinchie."

Linnet's face drained until it was as white as bones. She bent close. Her mouth smelled of whisky. "Do not call them that. Do not do it. Do not give them the appellations they would choose. Call them by their names."

"I don't know their names," I croaked.

"They were Terrance and Veronica Campion."

She turned away. It was almost too much for her. She had gone back into a world I could not even begin to imagine.

"You used the bread knife. You hit a rib. It was in the report."

"I've never seen so much blood," said Linnet, without turning round.

"And put them under their own floorboards. They must have been heavy. Why do it anyway? No one knew you were there." She only shook her head in reply, so I gave the first answer that came to me. "You wanted to bury them with the hair. Their trophy."

She turned back to me, her eyes flashing. "The first ritual. You'd be tied to a chair. Kissie used the knife. Chunks of flesh sometimes. Them laughing, you screaming." She looked away from me and swallowed hard, as if bile had climbed into her throat at the memory. "Then they were gone. From the world. From my *life*, I thought. And in the outhouse, four little bodies, full of maggots."

"You put the children in the moors?"

"They deserved to be at rest. I did it at night. I drove down to the bottom of the track. I used to hot-wire cars, you know, in my mad moments of rebellion, so driving Terry's stolen van was no sweat. Dragged them to the peat bog. Dropped them in. They sank away from me. There was this tree with a loose branch. I used it to stop their bodies floating up again. I even said a little prayer. Just, *Be at peace, rest now.*"

Lost in her own story, she had calmed. We could've been sitting across a table in the Admiral's Landing, the way she was talking. I knew this was the time to ask—*please untie me, Linnet. Bring water, set me on my feet, set me free.* But I saw how she rubbed and twisted at the ring she wore on her right hand, and the wrong words slipped out.

"You took that ring from Kissie's hand."

Her lip curled. She rammed a fist—the ringed right hand—down into my bruised face. It stung like a swarm of bees. "It won't come off!" I heard her yell. "*They* are on my hand day and night! For ever and bloody ever!" She punched again like she was plumping some un-loved cushion. I lay gasping like a reeled salmon. My eyes welled with tears; it seemed she was underwater, floating somehow. Her voice came from far away.

"For a long time, it was whispers. Or in my sleep, nightmares. Them, coming to me. Like wraiths. Real but not real. Yearning, they were. More. They wanted more and more. In my head their voices were shouting over the voices in my office—even in court. I couldn't do my job properly—couldn't hear—couldn't do anything. Even sleep. Didn't eat, drank too much."

I heard Cliff's sobbing voice. *They got inside my head and I didn't even know they were there, but they're there all right, they've ruined my life.*

"It got bad. Their voices. Unbearable." Her words burst in on me. "They wanted me to do it on my own so they could watch and enjoy. Watch from their grave." She paused for a moment. Her head was in her hands.

"They wanted you …" I prompted, not understanding.

"They wanted me to have a child." I heard one curdling laugh. "*They* wanted me to have a child? *I* wanted to have a child. I wanted a family. A husband, a litter of beautiful sons and daughters. Like a normal woman. They had no idea how much I wanted a child. But not like that. Not like they did it."

I'd met the spirits of Kissie and Pinchie. I didn't doubt that, somehow or another, they had been haunting Linnet since she killed them. I saw her lips mutter something. She was talking to them, even now. I saw her fists tense as they invaded her head. She began to scream, her mouth so wide I saw the fillings in her back teeth. The cries came, as if she had not recognised the full horror of what she'd done until this moment. "They—never—stop. I am sick of it! I came back to tell them. Tell them to SHUT UP!" Her eyes were blazing. Her breath as ragged as mine. "SHUT UP! Leave me alone. LEAVE ME ALONE!"

"You came to Bridgwater to tell them to go away? But everything was all right in Aberdeen, wasn't it? Why risk it? Why come back?"

She put a hand over her mouth. "They've always been too strong for me. They forced me to go to the grave. They made me remember. MADE ME DO IT."

"Don't you care?" I couldn't help ask this pointless question. "Don't you ever think of the parents, grieving for their children?" When I looked at her, Linnet was hazy, grey in colour. My mind was distracted with pain—my head throbbed and stung, my bent legs sang agony through my body. I gasped with every breath as the rope tightened round my windpipe. I was sliding away from things. My mind was closing down.

"Please. This flex is choking me … killing me … please?"

"Why should I be merciful? They never were." She bent over and slid a finger through the loop around my neck. It didn't help. I started to gag. My eyes were wide, sweat stung as it poured into them. I was going to pass out. If I didn't, I was going to vomit, inhale it, and die right here on her kitchen floor. I was staring at her, pleading with my eyes.

I felt, rather than saw, the bottle in her hand. I read her mind. Whisky fumes rose in my throat. She yanked at my ponytail again, but I was ready, my mouth clamped shut with the last of my strength. She pinched my nose, squeezing with her fingers. Like you do for medicine. When a child refuses their medicine. Hold their nose. *Open your mouth for your Calpol, darling, it will help the pain.*

She brought her mouth close to mine. Her voice was a whisper of menace. "You thought I was 'part of it', did you? You have no idea what being 'part of it' was like."

Without further signal, she went over to the block and forced out the solidly rammed knife. Her shoes clipped back. The kitchen lighting glinted yellow on the broad blade. She knelt at my feet. "I asked you, didn't I?" She flashed a rue little smile. It made my spine crawl. "I challenged you to guess about me—find out what I was thinking. And you did. Clever little Sabbie Dare." I felt her slice the knots at ankles. She lifted the line that was around my neck and I felt the pressure give.

I stretched out my legs. The absence of pain was almost a sensation in itself. I could breathe again. "Thanks. Thank you."

"Get up."

"I … I can't."

"Get up. You can do it." She was looking at me with a new expression on her face. I'd been stupid enough to think she'd freed my legs as a sort of reward for guessing right. But she had her own reasons, nothing to do with my discomfort. I was frozen with fear. She had a plan, something new. What had her twisted mind come up with? Was it time to sort me? I tried to get my thoughts on track. Keeping ahead of her was my only hope...okay, not a great hope. Not a hope at all, really.

"Get up!" She rammed the toe of her dreadful shoe into the wound on my head. Pain detonated inside my head. "Now!"

It took several attempts. She'd tied my hands behind my back with the same rope that was now falling around my ankles. I had to flounder upright like an ungainly bird with clipped wings. My legs throbbed as blood flowed through them. I swayed in front of her.

"Come here," she said, gesturing to the butcher's block as if it were a sacrificial altar.

I felt stronger on my feet. Almost instinctively, I shuffled away, glancing round the kitchen. The doors were shut. They didn't even need to be locked; I couldn't get through a shut door without hands. Anyway, where could I go with my hands tied? The answer my heart gave was *anywhere away from her.* I took another penguin step, and found myself on my face on the floor. I'd tripped over the lengths of rope that were coiling round my feet.

"Get up and come here." Her voice was on the edge of patience, but I ignored it. I was concentrating on what I'd figured out. My bonds were loosening. I wriggled as if struggling to get to my feet, but I was secretly examining the rope. She'd wound it round and round my legs, and now she'd cut the bindings at my ankles, it was falling free, trailing across the tiles behind me.

I tried to work out how I'd been tied. Had she started with the noose at my neck, taken the rope to my ankles, tied it tightly there, then tied up my hands? When she'd bound me, I'd been out cold, harmless, and she had been in Patsy *fuck* mode—desperate, panicked—concentrating on the noose thing, to scare and control me. But now she had a new agenda. She wanted me on my feet, she'd cut the rope deliberately. She'd cut the rope, not thinking about the original knots.

She came towards me. I scrabbled to my feet and shuffled uselessly away. She grabbed my wrists behind me and yanked. Pain overwhelmed me. It was the shooting agony I'd experienced in Horfield Prison, when I'd put my hands on Cliff's. She'd learnt all the tricks from Kissie and Pinchie. A sound wailed round the kitchen and back into my own ears. My scream.

"They started up again," she was saying. "I heard them plain. *Patsy take another… try again, Patsy… get it right this time.* They wanted the full bells and whistles. *Patsy take a child… abuse… rape… torture it to death.*"

No marks on Josh's body. That was what Rey had told me. He didn't mention if that included the marks of rope around his wrists or neck. How did she keep them from running away if she didn't tie them?

"But I couldn't hurt him." Her voice was steady. "I didn't even cut his hair."

"You've never been able to tell anyone, have you?" I kept my voice low, kept my pain to myself. "But now you have, you'll feel better. You won't want more babies to die. It's only Kissie and Pinchie who want that. You're a good person, a lawyer, trapped by these terrible people, their ghosts—ah!"

She pushed my Weeble-Wobble body and I skidded across the floor in my socks, squealing like a piglet. We were heading for the butcher's block, where the knife lay. She let go and I crumpled to the floor, gasping. The pain in my shoulders had gone as she'd released me, but my hands were tingling with slow life. When she'd grabbed me, the bindings had slipped a little more.

I had very little time left, and one final throw of the dice. "Linnet." I gave her a crooked smile. "I know a way to be free of them."

"Be free?"

"Yes. They will never stop haunting you. They'll always want another child, another death. But if you give yourself up..."

"Give myself up?"

"Yes."

"To the police?"

"Think of the relief, Linnet."

"What, walk into the station and say, 'it's a fair cop, guv'?"

I could not reply.

"You really do know *sod all*, don't you, Sabbie?" Her eyes had steeled—they were somewhere—*someone* else entirely. She put a tight fist around my ponytail and heaved. I followed the line of the pain, up onto my knees. I was staring across the surface of the butcher's block. She yanked my head onto it. My neck felt ready to break; it was stretched and exposed as my cheek was pressed down onto the sawdusty surface. I tried shifting my legs, but they slid from under me and I was held on the block by the length of my hair, my knees floating handbreadths from the ground. I squeezed my eyes shut. I didn't want to see the blood if she cut at my neck.

"Stop it, Linnet," I choked out, into the wood. "Just stop it all. Do yourself a favour. You're up shit creek."

I heard her chuckle. "Shit creek? That's where you are right this minute."

"Let it be over." I was whispering, words fast and foolish, like a prayer. "Let it be over for you...for me...for Cliff. Let it be over for him too."

"Be over for Cliff?" She sounded incredulous. "Why should I ever let it be over for Cliff?"

I stopped muttering. Her words cut through my fear. Why had Linnet taken on this case, when she knew all along that Cliff was as innocent as she was guilty? *Not altogether innocent,* she'd argued. I felt my eyes shoot wide open. I had betrayed Cliff, thinking for even one second that he might be involved with Linnet. But he *had* been involved with Patsy. I could see his pale face, in the prison visiting room, the story of his escape. *I got in her way.*

"You freed him." It came out as a groan. In my mind I heard Cliff, as the memories came to him. *I wriggle towards the trunk. The girl hisses 'fucking hurry up'.* "You let him go and stayed behind."

Chilled steel lay on my neck. My bones liquidised inside my flesh.

"I stayed behind," she hissed. "And all that night, they kept me tied— feet to neck. I was a stupid young girl, so I struggled a lot. By morning I was half dead, slowly strangled. Thanks to your precious client."

"The tree—couldn't take his weight." I felt the blade in Linnet's hand move. My breath was coming in tiny gasps, like my lungs were bellows. "How—how could you blame him?"

"He never even looked back."

"Linnet. You both survived. Why not just be—glad."

"He went free, innocent, forgetting everything. I was left, murderess and accomplice. That what you wanted to hear? I was their accomplice. After Cliff escaped, they nearly killed me in all the ingenious ways they had, then, hey, guess what we did? We all went on holiday. Terry nicked a car and we all went off for a nice little summer holiday. Weymouth, I think. Ain't that cute?"

"They thought he'd tell the police."

"I wish to God that he had! I would be free now—they would be doing thirty years." The blade trembled, pressed closer, dug into my flesh. "It's his turn. He's had a lifetime without them breathing down his neck. It's his turn."

My thoughts spun. I saw her plan. So simple. Tomorrow morning, thanks to the efforts of his lawyer, Cliff would walk free. No, not free. Surveillance. The police, watching the wrong suspect, watching Cliff when they should be watching Linnet. Suddenly, I wanted to shout out, as if I could warn him, or warn Rey Buckley. *Don't watch Cliff! Don't watch Cliff!* I could see it, as clear as if it had already happened. Aidan's body, left for Cliff to find, easily discovered. Or worse. Another child snatched, when surveillance went wrong, for just an hour. No one was watching Linnet. It had been going great. But I'd fucked it up—fucked the plan by finding the tunnel.

There was a violent sharpness, a long scratch at the crease of my neck. The knife's flat, cold blade slid upwards. A moan oozed from my lips. I tried to stop myself from peeing. The roots of my hair tightened, resisted, then sprang free. She was scalping me. She wanted me to know all the agonies, all the cruelties she'd suffered, starting with this one. I gritted my teeth against the pain as the knife sawed along my skin.

"Don't do this. Don't do it!"

"I have longed to do this. Forever. Longed to."

"Don't do it, don't do it! Don't kill me, please don't kill me, you can't kill, you can't, you can't kill me, Linnet!"

I didn't realize that I was crying until the tears began to drip from my cheeks and chin.

"I *have* killed," Linnet spat back at me, as if I'd insulted her. "I can fucking kill. As you will find, when the time is right."

Panic swilled over me like a scald of water. It had taken me all this time to realize how dangerous Linnet was.

I was as much her victim as Josh, Aidan, and Cliff.

TWENTY-EIGHT

WHAT DO YOU THINK *is in there, Ina?*

Only one person had ever called me that particular nickname. I was seven or eight, and I can't recall the face, can't remember the gender. I must've known the name at the time, but it's gone. When that memory slips in, through some unguarded back door in my mind, I think of *that person* as Ina ... not me. Ina the Vile. Ina—pitiless, callous, vicious. Ina, who technically never laid a finger on me or any other child at the home or foster house or wherever it was. No bruises, no split lips to tell the tale. Ina used terror warfare that only worked on those still young enough to believe that horrors unseen, demons and monsters from dark places, could overcome the miracle of love.

I do recall, in the recesses of my mind, that Ina had many diabolical tricks. They were played in the name of discipline, but that was not Ina's immediate design. Ina loved to see a child's face melt with fear. And if their bladder or bowels melted too, all the better, for that was two punishments all rolled up in one small transgression.

Ina's gift was to know what would terrorize a child the most, and for me it was the cupboard. A swirling rise of emotions choked my throat if I knew the cupboard was threatened. I can still taste each one: Bewilderment and wretchedness growing fast and hot to anger, and the hammering at the inside of the door that left my hands aching for days. Hate and disgust for the tiny space, the harmless piles of towels and sheets. The first blasts of fear; darkness, the feeling that I couldn't breathe. Then after a long time—for it was impossible to gauge the time spent, except by the growing hunger in my belly—the start of the terrors that shocked the heart rate, spasmed the brain, annihilated control of any part of my body. Eventually there was a swollen unconsciousness where my nightmares brought forth the beasts with curved teeth and the men with curved blades.

What do you think is in there, Ina?

Nothing compares. No other life experience has left me with such a sickening memory...

Until Linnet's knife sliced though my hair tight to my scalp. I'd been left out on a field of ice—I couldn't feel anything, not even my heart beating. Black patches were splattered over my vision. Pain built as Linnet removed more and more hair from my head. I could feel her working over me, as if I was the steak for her dinner.

I wanted to mourn for my hair. I'd taken almost ten years to grow it—and in a few more moments, Linnet would be holding all of it in her hand. But I didn't have time to mourn hair. It was my life that was in real danger.

Linnet had dragged me to the block with rope trailing behind me, but she was too absorbed with her new obsession to worry about the ropes that had bound me. I tried my hands, focusing my thoughts on them. When I forced them apart, I felt the coils around my wrists give.

I moved my hands in a circular motion, felt rawness as flesh rubbed over rope.

I gritted my teeth against the pain as the knife sawed through the final hank of hair and I fell, free from her hold, onto the floor.

Linnet's breathing was loud and ragged in her throat. She laid the heavy lengths of tangled, curling hair over the block and stroked it. I watched, mesmerized. Some sort of reaction had been set up in her with the cutting. Her shoulders shook. She leaned onto the butcher block as if unable to support her own weight. There was violent madness in her face. She raised the knife above the hair and roared. It was the roar of a wild beast—a monster—the evil witch who cooked children. She roared the knife above her head and roared it down. An inch of its point disappeared into the wood. I was hoping she'd never get it out again.

I didn't delay. I skittered across the kitchen like a wild animal seeking shelter. I bunched up in a corner by the sink. I must have looked done-in, helpless, lifeless. But my mind was whirling—fighting for my existence.

The trail of rope led from the block to my trembling form. She picked up the end of it. She was thinking again—constructing the perfect plan. I needed her to stay unfocused. I liked it when she talked; it made her forget to plan.

"Why didn't you go home, Linnet?"

"Home?" Her frame swayed. Maybe it was the whisky. The bottle was almost empty, but most of it had been poured over me, soaking my jumper. I prayed she wouldn't pour the alcohol on my scraped scalp. She looked desperate. Was she desperate enough to tell her story to someone who couldn't pass it on?

"Back to Arnie, and your mum."

She licked her tongue around the inside of her mouth. She was remembering. "Terry and Vron didn't believe in banks. They kept it all under the bed. I found an old sports bag and filled it with twenties. Their life savings. It wasn't all that much by today's standards, and you can bet your life it had all been nicked, but I felt as rich as a shipping magnate. I wasn't going to share that with my parents. I hated them almost as much as they hated me."

"But they didn't…" I trailed off. This was not the time to argue.

"I came back from burying the children. I had a bath in the grotty bathroom. I used up every scrap of hot water and bubble bath. I remember so clearly lying there… I knew they were dead—under the floorboards—but every time I heard the tiniest noise I almost jumped out the bath. I couldn't stay in that house another hour. I did my face with Kissie's makeup and got into some of her clothes. She had nice clothes; thought a lot of herself, she did. I packed the rest of them and everything of use. I washed the bread knife of blood and put it back in the kitchen drawer. Then I drove all night, north, north, careful not to draw attention to the van. When the traffic started building, I holed up in a cheap hotel. I didn't look much like a runaway—not driving that van and thick with makeup. They were happy enough to take my cash."

She was almost glowing with the story, the words spilling out like winnings from a slot. Meanwhile under cover of the shadows of my corner, I was easing my wrists apart from each other. The bonds held; they were looser, but I couldn't get my hands out. At least I could feel my hands now—pins and needles jabbing all over them.

"It's not just the name." I kept my voice low, not wanting to rile her but desperate to understand. "The Linnet I met in your office… had drinks with… that's not the same person as Patsy."

She shook her head several times, as if in disbelieving agreement. "I thought I'd spend that cash like it was the spit from my mouth. Party time at last! But I was too obsessed with what I'd done. Was I guilty? If I'd been caught, charged, taken to court, what would a judge say about my crime? Would he say that stabbing two murderers to death was an execution they deserved?"

She hadn't answered my question. Maybe she didn't know herself. She came towards my limp body, the rope in her hand. I looked away. I wasn't up to a fight. I had no strength left. She lifted my feet. She wound the rope round my ankles and finished it with a couple of half-hearted knots…half hitches, Girl Guides call them. I'd never even been a Brownie, and I regretted my lack of knot knowledge now.

"I was witness, arresting officer, jury…lawyer," she went on, as if tying my legs was something I'd requested. "I argued the case in my head—searched out books in the library."

I'd imagined an expensive school, prosperous parents to pave the way to a top law degree. I was way off on that one.

"Night school," said Linnet, as if she guessed my line of thinking. Her eyes burned red. "Remember the phoenix? Yes, it does work, that myth. You can combust into flame and be reborn. I never wanted to be Patsy Napper ever again. And I did want to help people, Sabbie. Because I hated Kissie and Pinchie. Those bastards never stopped being thirsty for pain, for blood, even after they died. Wanting to do it again. And for a while—quite a while really—I fought against it. I prosecuted the accused and got convictions. It was how I kept them at bay, Sabbie. Kept them at a whisper for a good number of years. I helped send the guilty to jail."

She gave herself a shake. For a moment, she'd forgotten her agenda, but she was back on course. "Stay there, won't you?" It was a rhetorical question, but I don't think Patsy had been a Girl Guide, either; she was overconfident about her knots and underestimated me, something I attempted to reinforce by swooning back against the sink.

Her clipping shoes took a swerving course to the back door. I heard the lock turn and the door slam. What was she doing? How long would she take to do it? If I'd had my walking boots on, it might have been difficult to get out of the half-hitched bindings though not impossible—without boots, I easily slid one foot free and then the other.

I got up. The knife winked at me. I went over to the block. Everything in reverse. It is hard, using your hands when they are bound behind you. Like doing something in a mirror. I turned away and leaned backwards over the block. Then I felt something—a pressure—but my hands were still coming back to life—I wasn't sure if the blade was pushing against the rope or my skin. I didn't know if I could cut the rope, even though I was stretching it taut, keeping my hands as far apart from each other as possible. I didn't know if the knife would stay in place, embedded though it was. I couldn't see what I was doing, or if it was working. But I did trust the sharpness of Linnet's blade as I sawed, up and down, pressing as hard as I dared.

I kept glancing towards the kitchen door as I worked. As life came into my fingers, I felt sweat drip onto them, warm and sticky. Not sweat. Blood. I worked faster. Something gave. A sort of *ping*. It was not enough, not quite. I sawed again. I felt the knife slide away from me. It was coming loose. My hands broke apart just as it clattered to the floor. I struggled out of the final lengths of rope.

At last I stood, holding my arms in front of me. It was wonderful to see them again. I'd cut the heel of my left hand, just a slice of flesh gone, no real harm done. I bent down and gripped the handle of the knife, moving it from fist to fist to get my hands working. I doubted it had as much as sliced a carrot since its arrival in this kitchen, and now it was smeared with my blood and my hair. It was both adversary and ally.

I knew I would not follow Linnet. I never wanted to see her again or hear Patsy's voice come out of her lips. I stumbled across the kitchen, into the hall. Opposite the office with the dreadful tunnel fireplace was the front door, leading to the porch. I wrenched the catch open. There lay my walking boots, a memory of ancient times. I reached for them, fumbling with the laces.

Darkness had fallen. On the other side of the glass porch door I could see nothing but night. Then the brilliance of a flashlight swung across the dark garden. I felt my blood curdle. Not that way. I turned and hurtled along the passageway towards what must have been one of the original cottage doors, low and with a latch, which stood at the very end of the passage. I was hoping it would let me out into a different part of the garden, closer to the car, but steep cottage stairs loomed up in front of me, confined by a wall on each side.

I took a quick glance behind me. The passageway, framed with insipid floral pictures, stretched the length of the house. There was no sign of Linnet. I closed the door behind me and scrabbled up the stairs, my legs trembling with terror, pain, and exhaustion, until I reached the next floor.

What was I doing here? In films, the victim always climbs, putting themselves in further peril as they inch along a window sill or up the skeleton of some suspension bridge. Now I knew the instinct is true—I had fled upwards. But I was also searching for Aidan. I opened each door as I moved along the upstairs landing. The first two were empty bedrooms, furnished for guests who had never arrived. The last was Linnet's bedroom. I stood on the threshold, taking in the sight.

The room was stuffed with toys, displayed on every surface and shelf. I took a cautious step closer. It was like being in Toys "R"

Us. An array of packaged goods—train sets and scooters, dolls and dollhouses, games and puzzles. But mostly, soft toys.

A hundred expensive teddy bears, shiny bows around their necks, and the squashy equivalent of every other animal that walked the face of the earth. Pastel shades and primary colours, fluffy fabrics, suede, leather, tartan, velvet, satin. The beady eyes stared at me as if I was an unwelcome stranger. This was a shrine to early childhood.

Linnet's lost childhood, perhaps? It was not her childhood that Linnet had lost, but rather her opportunity to be a mother. A purpose concealed even from her own full sight. When she'd found Josh, trying to hide from his brother on the Bristol Downs, it wasn't just Kissie and Pinchie who had whispered … *take him … take him.* Linnet had longed to own a child. I could see her leading each of them into this room—*choose anything, choose as many toys as you want*—and watching, perplexed, as their lips trembled. *I just want my mummy.* Maybe the boys really had been given an overdose that was accidental. She was a lawyer, after all, not a doctor.

Something was out of place. Between the toys and teddies, the lacy frills and silken pillows. I snapped out of my shock and hurtled towards the phone that lay on the dressing table. I punched the three nines. A man's voice came through, calm, reassuring. When he asked me which service I required, I almost screamed down the phone, remembering to drop my voice at the last moment "Police! Ambulance! Murder, Murder!"

"Is someone hurt?"

"She murdered them," I heard myself babbling, "the boy they found in the moors. Josh Sutton. She murdered him. She took Aidan Rodderick. It's her!"

"Is anyone hurt," the man persisted.

"Get DS Buckley, Bridgwater division. He's on the case. It's the solicitor—tell him it's Linnet!" I sobbed at the stupidity of it all. "I think he'll be dead. She's got a knife. She's mad. She cut off my hair"—I could hardly speak the word—"she *scalped* me."

I took a few moments to gather the other information in my head as I spit out the complexities of Linnet's address ... quaint sounding villages ... dark forests and gingerbread houses.

I watched the bedroom door like a hawk as I whispered, phone in one hand, knife in the other. But suddenly, I felt my gaze being pulled to the window. It was no longer pitch black outside. A powerful light beamed across on the clipped lawn, with its statues and mature trees, and in that light a slight movement caught my attention, so that the voice on the phone faded. For a moment, I was sure I had seen the wings of a large white bird, slowly rising from the ground. It had to be a vision, something in my own mind. Then I realized. It was neither bird nor vision. I dropped the phone and ran.

TWENTY-NINE

I CAME OUT FROM the front porch and pinned my body flat to the side of the house, moving slowly along the wall, keeping my footsteps silent. As I turned the corner, the grass below me turned from green to black as the security light switched off. It wasn't detecting me, at least.

From the upstairs window, I had seen a white door rise slowly, like a swan taking flight, illuminated by headlights. Now, I located the door. It was part of the double garage. But as I pressed into the wall, I realized the headlights were not coming out of the garage. Their beam was directed the opposite way. This car had come up the drive. I peered through the darkness. It was *my* car. It now stood by the open garage door, its engine running, doors open like flapping ears. For a long moment, I could only gawp. What was she doing with my car?

Then I saw her. She came out of the garage, struggling under the weight of a large, pale bundle. She dipped down, hefting the thing awkwardly into the back of my car. Apparently I wasn't the only one to regret that Mini Ha Ha only had two doors.

The interior car light was on. Its tiny yellow glow fell on the bundle as Linnet heaved it. I saw a pale oval, the face of a child, deathly still, eyes wide and unblinking. *The eyes of the dead*, I thought, and my mind turned red.

Linnet was taking Aidan's body away to dispose of it.

I sprinted towards the car, my newly exposed and raw scalp burning in the cold night air. She stood, staring, her mouth open. She'd left me in the kitchen, tied, bleeding, half dead. I might have come from my own spirit world.

"You!" she exclaimed.

"Yes. Me." I stood with my feet apart, the knife in both hands. "Me." I could hear my breath rasp through my throat. "Going to the moors, Patsy?"

She smiled. She seemed calm. She didn't believe I could use the knife. "Get in the car, Sabbie, you useless fucking female."

I thought about running. But she was good at turning common items into lethal weapons—a kitchen knife, a bottle of Calpol, a chopping board. My little car, gaily ticking over, had never looked so threatening. But I had the knife now, and I was not going to let Linnet get anywhere near the steering wheel. I stood my ground.

"I can see what you're scheming. You'll take Aidan's body to the burial site and soon as Cliff is released, you'll make him go there. How will you do that? Text from an unregistered phone? Do you really think he's that stupid?"

She laughed. The sound made me grip the knife harder. She was genuinely amused. "And where is Sabbie in that equation? Running to fetch darling detective Rey? Not quite. This is what we will do: We will drive to your house. *Your* phone will text Cliff when he's released. Summon him to you. He won't suspect a thing when I open the door to him. You...well, you're freshly dead, bleeding over your carpet, whisky oozing into the blood—what's not already oozing in your bloodstream anyway. Somewhere in the house, he'll find Aidan. And at that point, he'll do himself in, knife through the heart."

"They'll see through it!" I yelled. "Rey will see through it!"

"Ah, but Sabbie, they won't want to. Josh's death has only ever had one prime suspect: Cliff. When they find Aidan, they won't look any further. Except with Cliff dead—by his own hand and in your house—they'll be over your car like a rash. Forensics will be conclusive."

Her words fired out, staccato shots. I faced her, the knife directed at her. I had the power, the weapon, the red haze of anger upon me. Because I was suddenly sure. She'd kidnapped Aidan to set Cliff up. Not like Josh—not because she'd longed for a child, or even because the ghosts in her head screamed at her to do it—but because she needed Cliff to look the guilty party. She wanted retribution, and she'd taken a child's life to get it.

"Come on, Sabbie. Just drop the knife."

"Fuck off." I could do it. I could lunge forward with the knife. I could. I felt my muscles tense, ready.

The security light blazed on. I heard the roar of an engine. I sucked in the cold night air. The police! They had arrived! So soon! So magnificent!

I turned my head, just a glance. The car screeched to a halt, spraying gravel. A tall figure emerged. He was armed, legs splayed, gun primed. But this was no officer of the law.

Ivan.

"You bitch." He gestured at me with the gun. "I've caught you, you *whore*. It's taken me *all fucking night*, you perverted two-timing *dyke*."

"Point the gun at *her*, Ivan!" I yelled. "She's a killer!"

I turned my gaze on him for one second, imploring him to understand, but in that second, Linnet was upon me. A slash of new pain stung my cheek. She had put all her weight behind the blow. I landed against the wall of the house and slid down it. The knife flew through the air and she scooped it from the drive.

Ivan was watching us both, his face confused, the gun trained first on Linnet, then me. "I have driven round the whole of *fucking Somerset* looking for you. Looking for you and that damn detective." He took a step towards us, getting us both in his sights. "Took me a long time to work it out. They told me in the village. Hartley's Wood. A woman. Keeper's Cottage. Keeps herself to herself."

"Ivan—"

"What the fuck'd you do to your head? Bloody short-haired fanny lovers."

"She killed—Josh Sutton," I screamed. "And Aidan!"

"Who?" There was uncertainty in the line of his mouth. His face was less hostile. He seemed to finally grasp that the fantasy world he'd invented was being replaced by a horrific reality.

"Aidan Rodderick." Linnet's voice was unruffled. "Surely you watch the television news, you caveman."

Without a thought, she ran at him, driving her arm into him. I saw the knife sink deep. His arms and the rifle were across his chest and she went for the stomach ... *right into me belly, once, twice.*

Ivan was coughing, his mouth tight in shock and pain. He crumpled to his knees like a toy dropped by a child, his free hand over the wound, the blood running through his fingers.

Linnet turned and came towards me. Her face was manic with triumph.

"You see?" she said, examining the blood on her knife as if it were a piece of court evidence. "I can kill." She took another step.

She wouldn't wait any longer. She wanted me dead. But I was not watching Linnet. Ivan was still on his knees. He did not hesitate. He didn't even need to check the safety catch.

The blast of noise was deafening. Blood exploded over the house walls on either side of my head. I felt it splat against my cheek. Linnet did not make a sound. She lifted her hands and put them behind her, feeling for the wound on her shoulder. Her pupils disappeared behind her eyelids. She made a single, high-pitched moan, then there was a thud as her head made accelerated contact with the gravel. She did not move. As she lay there, Ivan finally succumbed to his own wound. He sank, rather than fell, onto his face, his air rifle trapped beneath him. I felt a wave of nausea gurgle into my throat.

Aidan was the only one I cared about. I ran to the car and opened the door. The small body was curled into a blanket like a foetus. I heard a high, hiccupping sob. Now I was close to him, I could see his lips, as pale as lily petals, were moving. His eyes were wide with fear, not with the shock of death.

"Aidan," I whispered. He was looking at me with intensity, as if I was a new menace he might have to deal with. "Aidan, can you hear me?"

As the blanket fell away, I saw that he had been bound in rope, just as I had. I lifted him from the back seat like a swaddled baby and carried him away from the car and the slumped figures. Lightly, I took him to the lawn and laid him on it. I wanted to wrap my arms around him, but it didn't seem right to hug someone so tightly bound. My throat constricted. Aidan lay quiet. Perhaps he was too scared to speak, or maybe too stunned.

"Aidan," I repeated. "It's okay now, it's okay … it's over." I trailed off. It didn't seem to me that my words were at all comforting. My shaking hands worked at the knots that bound him. "You're safe, now.

Mummy and Daddy will come and get you. They've been so worried. And your granny."

"Nanny Nora." It was the first thing he'd said. He was correcting me. I was startled at his composure.

"Aidan, try to tell me," I asked. "Did she make you drink something out of a bottle?"

He nodded at me, his huge eyes fixed on mine. I felt my stomach cramp. I had no idea how to ask what was needed—how long ago? How much?

"Nanny Nora makes me have it." His voice was piping, but strong. "It's 'orrible. I sicked it up."

In the bald light, I could see that his chin was covered with the sticky syrup. I felt like singing out with joy. "Clever boy," I whispered. "We're so lucky. So lucky."

"'Cause I rubbed his tum," said Aidan.

"That's right, darling." I thought he was half delirious. "Rub your tum to stop the nasty medicine."

"Not *my* tum," said Aidan. A smile flickered onto his face. "My Buddy. You rub his tummy for good luck."

"Oh, you gorgeous, gorgeous boy, no wonder everyone loves you. Everything will be all right soon. There'll be police and an ambulance." I glanced round. Ivan and Linnet still lay unmoving. I didn't care to check if they were alive or dead. Aidan was way up above them on my priorities.

"They're coming," he said.

"Who dear? Who's coming?"

"The p'lice." He struggled to sit up, the rope falling from him. "*Neeh-na, neeh-na!*"

As if he'd pulled a trick on my mind, I heard those sounds echoing in the distance.

His sharp little ears had been right. Into the cold, dark night came the sirens.

THIRTY

Four Weeks Later

"Thank you for doing this," I said to Gloria.

"Girl, I would never let you go to this place on your own. They'd have to put me in chains."

I gave my foster mother a pained look. "Let's not mention chains."

"You are one brave lady, doing this."

I laughed. "Oh no, Gloria. This doesn't count as brave. Surviving abduction is brave. And that goes for Cliff as well as Aidan."

Even so, my hand went involuntarily to the headscarf I wore round my head at all times. I had been so proud and fond of my heavy, dark locks. As soon as the wounds in my scalp had begun to heal, I'd gone to Debs, a friend of mine right back from our time at The Willows. She was now a hairdresser and beautician. She had actually wept as she'd shaved my remaining hair with a number one razor, but it had to be done. At least now it was an even length, and in the last two weeks had grown enough to almost conceal the scabs. But when I looked at myself in the mirror, the sight sickened me. I was reminded of the creature in my vision. I would never know—had she been Patsy's past, or my own future?

"That woman," said Gloria, shaking me out of my dream. "She should hang, in my view. I know I'm gonna invite your wrath with my small-minded attitude, but that's how I feel. Hanging's too good in fact."

"Precisely," I said. "Well, you know what they'll call it. Balance of her mind."

"Disturbed?" barked Gloria. "Ha!"

"You didn't see it," I said. "Her bedroom, stuffed full of toys ready for them to play with, and the place she'd held them. She used the word *cherished.*"

We had found the room she'd made for the kidnapped children while the paramedics were easing Aidan into the ambulance. The garage remote was on the seat of the BMW, and as the second door slowly lifted, the strangest sight was revealed. The garage had been turned into a nursery. There were toys and stuffed animals everywhere—at least as many as those still untouched and unloved in Linnet's bedroom. A rocking horse of solid, polished wood; a little pedal bike that had nowhere to go; a remote control car, bashed to pieces, all told their own story. Most horrifying was an entire collection of Slamblasters with the Slamblaster Fortress, which stood untouched. In the centre was a low divan bed. A Manchester United duvet had slid to the floor, showing a sheet stained with splashes of ketchup. Coke cans, Miss Millie cartons, and pizza boxes, only half empty, were scattered over the floor. An off-cut of thick carpeting covered the concrete base. Overhead strip lighting and high wall heaters had attempted to create a habitable room in this brick box, but that didn't detract from the chilling genius of the security. Linnet had converted her garage into a prison.

"Didn't Rudi want a Slamblaster Fortress for Christmas?" I asked Gloria.

"Yes, he did. But I talked Charlene out of it. It smothers creative play. We're making one out of junk, instead."

I turned my head away to smile but didn't quite make it. I was still there, standing outside the second garage, while paramedics dealt with Ivan and Linnet, dressing wounds, putting up tape and coping with Linnet's screams. As Ivan himself would've pointed out if anyone had cared to ask him, air rifles can make a mess, but they rarely do much damage. She was standing up in court to face a refusal of bail a week later. I felt a certain satisfaction that she would be well enough to stand trial.

One of my abiding images of that night was Rey's face as he had finally arrived with the third wave of police cars. The lights of his own car coloured the shocked whiteness of his skin as he found me, tucked into hospital blankets, ready to leave the scene. He had stood in front of me and put one hand onto my shoulder, but said nothing. And I was too shocked to say anything more coherent than, "I found the tunnel." I'd been trembling uncontrollably and had wanted to explain that it was due to the bitter coldness that comes before dawn, but I could find no further words.

It had been my intention to say nothing about the way Ivan had threatened me at my home, or the fact that he had brought his air rifle along for a rather different intention. But by the time I was in an interview room, a polystyrene cup of tea in my hand, I realized that it would be foolhardy to step around the plain truth. My first loyalty was to Cliff, and to Josh and Aidan; if I tried to protect Ivan as well, it would only distort matters.

I did enquire as to his well-being. Although he had lost a lot of blood that night and needed some corrective surgery, he was discharged soon after. I hoped our paths would never cross again. I hoped he had learnt his lesson and thrown his air rifle into the nearest river. There are enough of those to choose from in this corner of England. Maybe he'll have to undergo an anger management programme or even do community service. I have no idea and even less inclination to find out.

"We're here," said Gloria. She said it so softly, I hardly heard. She pulled on the handbrake and put her car into Neutral. "You okay for this?"

"Yeah. I'm fine." I got out of the car and breathed in Somerset air.

Brokeltuft Cottage loomed like a ghost above us, a shimmering white spectre. A youthful police constable stood by the broken gate. He watched as we moved forward.

"Sabbie Dare," I introduced myself. "And this is my mum."

"We appreciate you coming, Miss Dare," said the constable.

"It's no problem."

No problem? I could sense a trembling in me, not the sort that makes your fingers shake, but the kind that begins in the very core and chills you from the inside.

A few weeks after Linnet had been dragged away from the gingerbread house, I'd been contacted by a gruff-voiced Rey.

"I came round," he said. "But you weren't at home."

"I went up to North Wales for a while, and then I went to stay with my mum."

"Good," he said, a sudden surge of energy in his voice. "That's good. You should recuperate. So does that mean you're not available as a shaman at the moment?"

"I am working." I told him. "I'm seeing Cliff. Can't afford—"

"Not to work, I know. Actually, I wondered if you might consider a paid assignment."

"Sorry?"

"For us. The forensic team at Brokeltuft, I mean. They're finding it … well, there's this odd atmosphere."

"They're picking up sensations?"

"Don't ask me," Rey had barked. "Cops don't usually act like wusses."

"You want me to go over there?"

"Would that be hard?"

"Not at all." I hadn't wanted him to think I was a wuss as well. But I had hoped that he would have the decency to meet me here. It would've been nice if he'd said sorry … about constantly doubting me, about conning me with the phoney Slamblaster. But apologies didn't sit comfortable with Rey Buckley. I figured asking me to work for the team was the closest he'd get.

The constable took us around the side of Brokeltuft, to where they'd set up HQ in a caravan. A female officer helped me kit myself out in the protective gear of the forensic team. It felt as if I was getting ready to be blasted into space. We left Gloria sipping a cup of police tea and moved out of the van as if through an air lock that led onto an alien planet.

The back garden had been flattened and was pockmarked with holes. The lawn had disappeared, as if a bomb had fallen into its centre, except this was a smart bomb—the hole was tidy-edged and flat-bottomed.

"Did you find anything?"

"If it hasn't been on the news, I can't tell you," said the constable. He smiled, as if suggesting that made him sorry, and held open the back door for me.

I glanced round. I wanted to check the black poplar was still there. "You won't touch the tree, will you?" I said. "It's been very kind, over the years."

"We'll try, miss," he said. "If you think it will help."

It took me a second or two to realize he meant it. They'd asked me to come and were prepared to take my advice. But as I was thinking these things, I passed through the back door.

The cottage had become a shell. The walls were knocked through, and the ceilings, which had fallen in places when I was last here, had been taken down entirely. Looking up, I could see right into the rafters. Looking down, I saw the floorboards had been replaced by sufficient chipboard panels to get from room to room. They were pale and new but already layered with fine dust.

"You must have used some big skips to empty all this out," I said.

"You might say that, miss," said the constable. "Take care as you walk."

I followed the angular path of the chipboard, like a rat in a maze, until I reached what had been the front room. Everything was so changed that it should have been difficult to locate the place where the sofa had once stood, hiding two bodies, but it was not hard at all. Although the bodies had been the first things out of here, I had a clear impression that the fullness of their spirits remained.

As I came to a halt and put down the carrier bag I'd brought with me, the policeman said, "Er … yes, that's sort of the worst place. Martin lost the tip of his thumb there. When we opened …"

I turned back. His back was against the far wall. He was lit by one of the spotlights the forensic guys were working by, stock-still as if caught on stage without his lines. He was not going to accompany me into this vortex of energy.

I took another step. I could feel it on my body, a sensation of cold pressure. It made me light-headed and numb, sick in my stomach. I stopped. They were down beneath my feet, where they had dwelt for so many years.

I hadn't thought much about what I would do. I remembered all too clearly the way I had descended into a trance without even having to try, as if their presence under the boards had sucked me in to them. I stood watching and almost waiting. My heart was yammering in my chest. I had to fight to stop myself turning round to see if the policeman could hear it. All I knew was that I was standing near a concentrated core of power, so bleak and dark that the forensic team had been unable to work within it.

"C'mon," I whispered. "Show yourselves." Nothing stirred. "Okay you bastards. I'll get you up."

Inside my mind, I drew the shield of my cloak around me. I felt the folds of the hood brush my face. I dipped into my carrier bag and retrieved a bundle of herbs, tied round with unbleached cotton. Native Americans call this a smudge stick, I believe, but these were plants raised in Somerset soil . . . lavender, sage, rosemary, and the end of a yew branch. The flame from my lighter curve around the bundle, caressing it until the dried leaves crackled. Smoke trailed off, a clean scent that made me seize the first proper breath I'd dared to take in this putrid place.

I raised my arms above my head and called out the words I use every day. They keep my clients and me safe in my therapy room, and I was hoping they'd have the same affect here.

"I call upon spirits, seen and unseen, the spirits of the four corners of the earth and the spirits above and below the earth, to be present and work in peace. I call upon their power, benevolence, guidance, and protection to be with me in this place today."

I'd come woefully unprepared. It's not impossible to for me to work without the defence of my black dress with its totems, bells, rattle, and wand, but now that I'd begun, I heartily wished I'd brought more than a smudge stick from my garden and an imaginary cloak. There was no way I would be able to find true north or any quadrant—it was going to be hard enough to walk in a circle. But I had to try. I had to enclose these murderers with my own shamanic allies and guardians. I felt Trendle settle on my shoulder.

Just do it, he said. I stepped as lightly as I could, my herbs held aloft, leaping from one board to another.

I enclose these loathsome and damaging spirits in the purity of love and protecting strength … and … the justice of the natural world.

I was winging it now, letting the words come into my mind without a thought between them.

Pinchie! I called to him first. *Kissie! We bind you in this circle, not to punish or drive you out, but show you an endurance of love that has no beginning and no end. We wish for you to seek out such love and let yourself fuse with it.*

I had come full circle. I could see this because, in the garish beam from the spotlights, the smoke I'd trailed in the air had become a ring, end touching end. I lowered myself down, using the empty carrier bag to protect my rump. I crossed my legs and rested my arms on my knees. I kept hold of the smudge stick with both hands so that its smoke circled around my face. I felt it caress my closed eyes and seep into my nostrils. Sweet herbs perfumed the air. It was enough to tip me over.

Trendle stared at me with prettily lashed eyes. I fell into their depths, into the hole in the floor, into the den that these terrible spirits had made for themselves. The air was thick and dingy beneath the gaping boards. A mist, as yellow as the smogs of Avonmouth, oozed upwards. I could see it swirl within itself, as if two strands of smoke were twisting in a dance, or in a fight. I watched as the strands came apart and flew into one another, twisting, clutching, capturing, churning the air. There was no sound at all from the mists, but inside my head was the boom of my throbbing arteries, punctuated by the hiss of my breath, fast and shallow. This rhythm seemed to pull me further into the trance, until their forms separated in my sight, congealing until I could discern arms and legs, and finally, the expressions on their faces.

I could see Kissie's sallow features, her gleaming blade of a nose and her painted lips, stretched open in a silent cry of agony and desperation. Her eyes were staring straight at me. She could see me. She called to me with the vacuous dryness of her mouth. Around her neck was the gleaming yellow of a muscled forearm. It reminded me of the statues of Soviet Russia—the iron strength of working men's limbs. Pinchie was trying to pull her back into their grave. He was half hidden behind his wife, the shine on his hairless skull outlined against the black foundations of the cottage. His mouth was a grim line, his eyes half closed with the determination of his task.

The first time I was in this room, I had run away, gibbering with crazed fear, forgetting every magical protection. I had learned so much in the short time since then. I held the stick of smoking incense tight in both hands, and when I leaned my head on one side, Trendle's damp fur rubbed against my chin. With him on my shoulder, I could stand my ground.

Veronica Campion, I said. Her yellow frame shuddered and I saw her husband's other arm come up and grasp her shoulder. *Veronica—surely there must be a more fitting place than this one.*

I thought I heard a whimper. I was concentrating so hard that I missed the first seconds of Pinchie's sudden movement. He expanded out of the space below the joists and shot into my face. The yellow mist surrounded me. I was too shocked to shriek or even breathe. His gruesome presence enveloped me. The final days of the victims, every sensation they had experienced, permeated the aura around my body. My pulse stopped its thrusting beat for long seconds. I remembered what Cliff had spoken of: they didn't want tears. Or screams even.

Now I knew why I had run from Brokeltuft that first time. Their vile spirits could invade like a pestilence. Mentally, I swung the edges of my cloak so that not a chink of my body showed through.

I have drawn a circle around you, Terrance and Veronica Campion. No longer will you be able to move outside it. If you choose to remain here, you must stay inside your sorry grave, trapped forever. But there is no ceiling to this rim of spirit power. If you choose to go, you can rise up and leave this place forever. The spirit world is waiting to embrace your souls, help you pass to the next stage you should have reached twenty-three years ago.

I didn't speak aloud. I hadn't spoken except in my mind to the two dead murderers. They had heard me loud and clear.

I felt Terry Campion's ghostly arms wrap around my neck. The yellow flesh of his upper chest smelled of overripe fruit and chicken shit. It dried my mouth so conclusively I could not swallow. I was afraid that if I breathed in, the fog of Terry's spirit would enter my lungs. I could do nothing more than stare back at them and brandish my cleansing stick of smoke. Clearly my circle was holding them, and if I moved, I would break its power.

Then my gaze was lifted upwards. Something moved fast, rising and accelerating. It was Veronica Campion. Freed of her husband's grip, she had made her choice and taken her chance. I felt Terry loosen his hold on me as he realized something was wrong. But

Veronica had already gone; she'd swum into the spirit world as naturally as Trendle dives into his brook.

Pinchie was more tenacious. His spirit was expanding, filling the circle I had drawn in smoke, pushing at its boundaries. He was not easily daunted. In life he had found pleasure in the torture and murder of the most innocent and inoffensive; I certainly did not scare him. He was searching for a way through, determined to overrun the rest of the house.

You are not welcome here, I told him. *This is the world of atoms and molecules. You are spirit and you must find your spirit plane.*

He gathered up the last of his pitiful body and rounded on me again, so that all I could see was his roaring mouth. There was no tongue or teeth or palate. Just empty darkness.

Go! I launched the smudge stick, tossing it from my hands. It fell through the smog of Terry's body, leaving a line of black. It crashed into the dark hole where they had lain. The last of its dying smoke mingled with the vapoured spirit of the Wetland Murderer, and wherever it mingled, it took over. The smoke seeped into him, changing him. Large gaps were torn in Terry's yellow frame. His face became a wide, black hole. I didn't know if he was yelling at me or screaming in pain. I hoped it was the latter.

"Go!" I roared aloud. I was at least as angry as he. I was livid for all the lost children, for Aidan and Cliff and even Linnet. "GO!"

The swirls of gas struggled against my bidding for what seemed a long time. My ears felt as if they'd been plugged with wax, so that all sound came from inside me. His evil smell forced the contents of my stomach into my mouth. I compelled myself to stare into the streaks of yellow, watch their torturous movements until the very last smear of Terrance Campion had strayed upwards and followed his wife from their grave.

My head felt as if it had been blown up like a helium balloon. There was a trail of sick staining the front of the protective gear. My knees wouldn't straighten from my cross-legged position. I was locked into it. Strong hands were helping me up, my feet dangling uselessly. I focused on a familiar face.

"Well done, Sabbie," said Rey.

"Rey. I thought you hadn't come."

"I got held up. I really hoped to be here before you arrived. To say thanks for doing this. It can't have been easy." The tone of his voice, if not contrite, was grateful.

He took me out of the house and back to the van and placed me in a lightweight chair next to Gloria. She spat on a tissue and wiped my face. There was a glass of water in my hand. I couldn't remember taking hold of the glass, but I hadn't spilt it, for which I was grateful. I was even more grateful that I had not peed my pants during the ordeal, something that I'd been close to doing at several moments.

"How d'you feel?" asked Rey.

"Okay," I replied. "Bit like I've just woken up from an anaesthetic."

"I've got a message for you. Might cheer you up. Stella and Garth want to say thank you."

"Oh, gosh," I said. "How's Aidan doing?"

"Not bad, apparently. Pleased his mum and dad have got back together, I think."

"Stella's gone to live in the van without wheels?"

"Not at all. Garth Stanford has gone to live with them at Nora's."

"I don't believe it. Garth and Nora come from different planets." I remembered the yearning I'd detected when I'd held Aidan's

Buddha. "It was his deepest wish," I told Rey. "Before any of this happened. For his mum and dad to be together."

Rey looked away. "Seems a hell of a thing to have to endure to have such a simple wish come true."

"Aidan was amazingly brave."

"You were brave, too, Sabbie," said Rey. He lurched suddenly forward and captured my hand. His hands were warm and I could feel the roughness around their edges, but there was a softness in the heart of the palm that made me want to cry. "I—I didn't trust you enough, did I?"

"Couldn't blame you. You were right. I am a 'damn dumb civvie.'"

"No," said Rey, "no, that's not the case. You've come here as a professional and you've really helped—the team are so grateful."

"Have you seen Linnet, Rey? Are you still interrogating her?"

Cliff had already explained to me how Linnet had managed to infiltrated his life. She had never been the family lawyer, as the police had assumed, nor was she a duty solicitor. She'd turned up at the station and asked to see Cliff Houghton the morning after his initial arrest and, as a respected local lawyer, she'd been shown straight to an interview room. It was Cliff who had assumed she was on duty. He'd refused legal representation directly after his arrest, believing a request for legal aid was tantamount to a confession of guilt. By the time Miss Smith arrived in her full regalia of matching blue accessories—shoes, scarf, and fine quality leather gloves—he'd changed his mind.

"Only hours after Aidan had been snatched," Cliff had told me, "she turned up at my flat. I didn't think solicitors did that, but she was very kind. We sat down and she advised that I go about my usual business."

Then she'd asked if she could use his loo, taken Josh's Slamblaster from her document bag, and slipped it under his bed.

"Yes, that did come up in questioning," Rey was saying. "She has also confessed to planning to plant further evidence with Aidan's DNA on it at Caroline's house."

"She asked me to go with her. While I thought Caroline already knew Linnet, she knew that I already knew Caroline. She'd've dropped the stuff and initiated the search for the planted evidence. Masterful."

"Psychopaths often are," said Rey.

I didn't argue with that assessment, but I couldn't buy it. I had returned to Brokeltuft mostly because Rey had asked me, and partly because it was right that the Campions' spirits should be released. But I'd also done this for Linnet, although no one would want to hear that. The media was awash with the story, but while Cliff was being hailed as a misunderstood and dreadfully abused person, Linnet had been painted as Kissie and Pinchie's sidekick, the girl who'd enticed Cliff into the house of torture, rather than the one who had helped him escape.

I could not think of her in that way, even after she had hurt and abused me. I had met her tormentors, and all I could find in my heart for her was pity.

———

"Right, girl." Gloria revved her car up the lane, as if very glad to be away from the shrouded cottage. "I'm going to buy you a drink. You deserve it, for God's sake."

I raised my head, which I'd been leaning against the car seat. I'd been deep in an airbrushed memory, back in the police van tearoom, replaying the moments between Rey and me. I'd wiped out the reality—that Rey was on duty and I'd lost the power of speech. In my dream, our kiss was shy and tentative at first, deep with promise by its breathless end. In actual fact, we'd shaken hands like colleagues.

"You should get paid directly into your bank account. You do have one, don't you?" Ray had asked.

"Of course. Don't forget, it's not all scrape-a-carrot-from-the-soil." My cheeks went dusky. Would he remember he'd said that of me at the Sunday boot sale? And if so, would he think it odd that I'd remembered his exact words? Which meant I was obsessing about him. But he was a lager-and-crisps-supper bloke—would he work that one out? And did it matter anyway? Wasn't it better if he knew I was a bit keen?

A *bit keen*? I was as bitten as dog with fleas.

"Good," he'd said, oblivious. "Well, you're on the payroll, now. Any time we need a shaman…"

I couldn't tell if he was joking. But I did know one thing: we were still shaking hands. Just as we had on that first meeting. If Gloria hadn't handed me my coat, we might still be there now, idiotically pumping our hands up and down and staring into each other's eyes.

"There has to be a pub round here somewhere," said Gloria, pulling up at the junction ahead.

"Not a drink, Gloria." I had the feeling that if one unit of alcohol passed my lips that day, I wouldn't stop until I was senseless. Besides, Gloria hates pubs, unless they're serving Sunday lunch. She only ventures across their portals when someone has given her a push from behind.

We'd reached the triangle of green, the signpost that still read, Middlesprings Farm, and I remembered Sandy, and Trevor the dog, and the box of free vegetables with the flyer hidden at the bottom. Without that connection, I would never have found Brokeltuft Cottage.

"I can think of something much better," I told her. "I'm going to give you a treat you won't be able to resist."

She flashed what I think of as the Gloria Glance—a sort of old-fashioned disapproval—but followed the directions I gave her.

"What's happening with the lad who was released?" she asked.

I breathed in. "Pretty shattered. Now he has to recover from the recent traumas, wrongful arrest, and time in prison, as well as all the other stuff he'd blocked out for years." I turned towards her, like a plea. "I don't know where to begin. I've suggested he sees a counsellor, but he wants to carry on with me."

"Quite right," said Gloria. "He'd be in jail if it wasn't for you."

"I think I just have to trust to my former judgement. My plan had always been to rescue the parts of his shattered soul from where they've become hidden in his spirit world."

Cliff had arrived for our first session since his release looking drained of blood. We were gentle with each other—we drank a lot of tea and talked openly about what we'd both been through.

"Cliff is actually a very plucky person," I told Gloria. "Now he realizes what was holding him back, he's really dealing with it. He's been to the barbers for the first time in twenty-three years. He's back at work, and he's joined a local history group. I'm hoping he'll find friendship there. Oh Gloria, turn up here—slowly—it can be muddy."

Sandy recognised me as soon as I came into her shop. "How are you?" she asked.

"Ready to treat my mum to the best food you have in your shop."

We chose a lovely piece of venison. I wasn't going to enjoy a single morsel of it, but I knew that Gloria would cook loads of the veg we were piling up in the cardboard box on the counter, a Sunday lunch to beat them all, and she'd even make me that special gravy from caramelised onions to pour over everything.

Sandy totalled up on her calculator and told me the damage.

"Holy water, Sabbie, you can't spend all that!" said Gloria.

I grinned at her. "Just watch me. I haven't finished yet."

"A jar of pickles?" said Sandy "I've got some nice preserves."

"Have you still got any of your chicks?

She must have already sensed that something was up with us—something we were quietly congratulatory about—because she returned with half a dozen yellow cheeping balls of fluff. These were not day-olds, but half-grown chickens, possibly already part of her larger flock. "These are on the house," she said.

I didn't argue. It felt right and proper. If it hadn't been for Sandy, I would never have found Kissie and Pinchie. We were in this together, even though she knew nothing of her role.

Sandy helped us load the boot of the car. The wrapped venison sat snugly against the cornucopia of veg and fruit.

I nestled the box of chicks in my lap. They were packed in well, almost unable to move about, but it wouldn't be long before they'd taste the freedom of my back garden.

All the way towards Bridgwater, I sat with their warmth heating my thighs and the sound of their cheeps like a song in my ears. A sort of love for my new charges grew in me until it gurgled into my throat, tasting like warmed milk and honey.

The End

© Andy Chittock

ABOUT THE AUTHOR

Nina Milton holds an MA in creative writing, works as a tutor and writer for the Open College of the Arts, is a prize-winning short story writer, and has authored several children's books, including *Sweet'n' Sour, Tough Luck,* and *Intergalactic Holiday. In the Moors* marks her debut with Midnight Ink.

ACKNOWLEDGMENTS

I would like to thank all the shamans who opened a door into a magical but tangible world and allowed me to walk through.

I would also thank the Bristol Women Writers, especially Gail, for their unremitting support, and the cops in my life—James, Sharon, and John—for their advice.

Most importantly, I'd like to thank my agent, Lisa, the best writing buddy a girl can have; and my husband, Jim, for being the fulcrum of my life.

WWW.MIDNIGHTINKBOOKS.COM

From the gritty streets of New York City to sacred tombs in the Middle East, it's always midnight somewhere. Join us online at any hour for fresh new voices in mystery fiction.

At midnightinkbooks.com you'll also find our author blog, new and upcoming books, events, book club questions, excerpts, mystery resources, and more.

MIDNIGHT
INK ®

MIDNIGHT INK ORDERING INFORMATION

 Order Online:
- Visit our website www.midnightinkbooks.com, select your books, and order them on our secure server.

 Order by Phone:
- Call toll-free within the U.S. and Canada at
  1-888-NITE-INK (1-888-648-3465)
- We accept VISA, MasterCard, and American Express

 Order by Mail:
Send the full price of your order (MN residents add 6.5% sales tax) in U.S. funds, plus postage & handling to:

> Midnight Ink
> 2143 Wooddale Drive
> Woodbury, MN 55125-2989

Postage & Handling:

Standard (U.S. & Canada). If your order is:
   $24.99 and under, add $4.00
   $25.00 and over, FREE STANDARD SHIPPING

AK, HI, PR: $16.00 for one book plus $2.00 for each additional book.

International Orders (airmail only):
   $16.00 for one book plus $3.00 for each additional book

Orders are processed within 12 business days. Please allow for normal shipping time.
Postage and handling rates subject to change.